Also by Janet Elizabeth Henderson

Romantic Suspense Books

Reckless

Relentless

Rage

Ransom

Rich

Run

Reset

Invertary Romantic Comedy Books

Lingerie Wars

Goody Two Shoes

Magenta Mine

Calamity Jena

Bad Boy

Here Comes The Rainne Again

Caught

Invertary Too

Come Fly With Me

Sinclair Sisters Romantic Comedy Books

Can't Tie Me Down

Can't Stop The Feeling

Can't Buy Me Love

And more on my website
Janet Elizabeth Henderson

About Who's Afraid of the Big, Bad World?

Comic book artist Annabelle Simmons has walls. She put them up ten years earlier after she was kidnapped for ransom. They're big, strong brick walls, forming the literal warehouse that's been her entire world for years. But after she witnesses a murder in the street outside her home, her walls come under threat. The killer knows her location--and Annabelle's agoraphobia means she's a sitting duck. She can't run, she can't hide--even into her comic book world--so she hires Benson Security to protect her. Expecting the tcam to turn her home into a fortress, she's surprised when they move into the building instead--and into her life. Forcing her walls to expand to accommodate them.

Ex-cop Noah Merchant has walls. He started building them around his heart after he lost his wife to cancer five years earlier. He won't put himself, or his kids, through that kind of loss ever again. Now his job is to protect a woman who seems to know how to find all the cracks in his own defenses, while he's busy shoring up hers. Tasked with keeping her safe from attack, the former cop can't retreat emotionally the way he usually does. Especially not when the enemy is coming. An enemy who desperately wants the quirky artist dead.

Walls.
There to protect us.
There to imprison us.
There to keep the big, bad world at bay...

Dedication

This book is dedicated to the group of core readers who've stuck with me through some tough times these past few years. They make me laugh in my Facebook group and support me in my Insiders subscription group. I appreciate every email and message you've sent and hold your encouragement close to my heart. I really hope you enjoy Misfits 1, because it's especially for you.

Here's to better years going forward.

And to LOTS of new books!

Janet x

Who's Afraid of the Big, Bad World?

Benson Security - Misfits
Book 1

Janet Elizabeth Henderson

Chapter One

Noah Merchant had planned to spend the fifth anniversary of his wife's death getting drunk in the local Irish bar. Instead, he watched Violet Lee, one of his fellow security specialists, pound on the door of a red brick warehouse located on the edge of the Warehouse District in Central Houston.

"She isn't in there." Violet scowled at him. "This is pointless."

Noah checked his phone. "It's the right address, so she definitely lives here. The message says she has an apartment on the top floor." He glanced up at the old three-story building. The windows were dark.

"I'm telling you." Frustration thickened her Scottish accent. "She isn't in there. This is a waste of time."

Violet wasn't known for her patience—he'd learned that the hard way when they worked together in the London office of Benson Security. To say he'd been dismayed when she'd also joined the Houston team would be putting it mildly. As a former cop, he preferred his colleagues to remain calm under pressure, especially now they were working in a country where every second person was armed. Strike that—this was Texas. Most likely, *everybody* was armed.

"She *has* to be in there," he said with all the patience he could muster. "She's agoraphobic."

The diminutive ball of barely contained rage glared at the door. "Then she's just refusing to answer. I don't like it when they don't cooperate."

Yeah, he'd found *that* out the hard way in London too. Yet again, he tried to explain that not everyone they dealt with was the enemy: "This woman isn't a perp. She's an important witness in a high-profile case."

Noah pulled up the details their new boss had texted and called the witness' number. No reply. He stepped back into the dark, empty street and eyed the building. Long and narrow, it took up the corner position on a block of older industrial businesses. A narrow alleyway ran between the building and its neighbor. The alley had been fenced off with tall ironwork. The main entrance was on the narrow side of the warehouse, facing what would be the busiest street during office hours. A larger goods entrance sat at the rear of the building, although the old wooden doors had been replaced with heavy steel ones that looked rarely used.

The front entrance also had an abandoned air about it. The sign over the door was cracked and faded, but you could still make out the words *Bella's Antiques*. Noah peered through the dark and grimy storefront window. The interior was crammed with all sorts of junk, the kind of stuff you'd find in a garage sale, and most of it was covered in dust. He looked up and spotted a camera in the corner above the door. A shiny new security camera. At last, a sign of life.

He rang the bell again—the one Violet had abandoned

after declaring it didn't work. "Can you see an alarm system?" Maybe they could call the security company to find out if it'd been tripped.

"Aye, it's one of those cheap ones you can disarm by cutting the main wire." She pointed through the small window beside the hefty door. "I could knock out a pane of glass and access it from here."

"But it's still functioning?"

"Looks like it."

"Then nobody got here before us and disarmed it. She must still be inside."

Violet wasn't impressed. "She could have let an attacker in and then reset the alarm. Maybe a delivery guy or maintenance crew or someone from the DA's office. They're the ones with the leak, aren't they? She's probably already dead."

"You're a ray of sunshine, you know that? She could be sleeping. Or in the bath. Or wearing headphones. There are a million reasons why she might not hear the door. We're two floors beneath her, and she isn't expecting anyone to turn up. She's probably just busy."

Violet smirked knowingly. "You were one of those *nice* cops, weren't you? The ones who join the force to actually serve instead of hunting down bad guys." Her words dripped with disgust as she opened one of the many zippered pockets on her cargo pants and withdrew a set of lockpicks.

"You can't break in." Noah pinched the bridge of his nose, desperately wishing he was sitting in O'Loughlin's, nursing a single malt, instead of dealing with Scotland's most unhinged cop. Make that *ex*-cop—they'd fired her ass for being a health risk to everyone around her.

"Watch me." She set to work.

"Seriously," he said, "you can't go around picking locks."

"We sure as hell can't break down the door. It's solid wood and a good six inches thick. And we can't climb through the windows because of the bars." She cocked a thumb at the metal security shutters pulled across the inside of each window.

"We don't need to break in at all. We can call the local cops. Or the security company. Hell, the sheriff's department only a few blocks away. They'll get us in and walk us through the building."

"The Assistant District Attorney called Benson Security because she isn't sure who she can trust in local law enforcement—or in her own office. So, no calling the cops. Which reminds me, when we're done here, I need you to explain all these different police forces to me. In Scotland, there's the police. Full stop. Nothing else. Do Americans think competition will make their officers work harder? Because that's just dumb."

"The point is," Noah said with long-suffering, "picking locks is illegal."

"There's illegal, and then there's *illegal*," she said.

"What the hell's that supposed to mean?"

"In case you've forgotten, we aren't cops anymore. We don't need to follow the rules."

"Uh... yeah, we do. They're called *laws*. Everybody needs to follow them."

"Boy Scout," she muttered as she carried on breaking in.

Noah longed for the good old days when Violet barely spoke to her teammates. He stared up at the camera. "If you're watching, we're security specialists with Benson Security and former cops. We've been sent here by your contact in the Harris County district attorney's office, and our orders are to ensure your safety. Your location's been compromised. We are not breaking in to harm you, only to check on you."

"You about done?" Violet frowned at him. "Can we get this woman out of here now?" She swung the door wide.

Noah reluctantly followed her into the store, making sure to close and lock the door behind him. While he doubted there was anything in the shop to tempt a thief, this wasn't the greatest of areas, and junkies weren't known for being picky.

Violet gave the dust-covered stock a look of disgust. "I can't believe I'm missing *The Bachelor* for a babysitting job."

Okay, he did a double take at that little piece of info. "You watch *The Bachelor*?" For some reason, he'd assumed she only watched documentaries about serial killers or YouTube videos of preppers turning everyday objects into weapons.

"It's psychology in action." She glanced over her shoulder at him. "So many personality disorders in one place, all being examined under the camera."

"Ah, so you watch it for the romance," he teased.

She shot him her trademarked "look of death."

"So." Seeing as Violet's nickname on the Scottish force had been *Violent* Lee, Noah thought it best to change the subject. "According to the new boss, our *babysitting* gig lives on the top floor."

"Then we go up." She pushed the door to the stairwell open.

The stairwell was wide, and its walls inlaid with Art Deco tiles in various shades of blue. It was the kind of decorative touch you'd never see in a newer industrial building, where everything was concrete and metal. It made Noah wonder when exactly builders had decided that functional meant ugly.

"In a few years, when gentrification has made it this far into the Warehouse District, this building will probably sell for a fortune and be converted into trendy condos." He ran his fingertips over the tiles. "Then the place will be overrun with avocado-toast-eating, micro-brewery snobs who won't appreciate its history." He gestured to a plaque inlaid into the wall: *Watson & Co, Exotic Imports Ltd, est. 1905.* "Wonder what they imported."

"Avocados?" Violet suggested, her expression deadpan.

"And here I was thinking you didn't have a sense of humor," Noah said.

"I don't." Came the flat reply.

They pushed open the wide door to the second floor but found only a corridor filled with abandoned offices.

"Nobody's been in here in a long time." Violet pointed to the undisturbed layer of dust on the floor. "What a waste."

They carried on to the top floor. This time, there was no corridor, just a small lobby area and a reinforced steel door.

"This is more like it." Violet retrieved her picks and eyed the multiple locks.

"We knock first," Noah ordered, doing exactly that.

There was no reply. He dug out his phone and called the client's number again while Violet blithely set about breaking and entering. A faint ringing sounded inside the apartment, but no one answered.

"Phone's in there." *Now* he was worried. They had scant information, only that the woman was the key witness in a high-profile case and that some very dangerous people wanted to stop her from testifying. Unfortunately, there was a leak in the DA's office or law enforcement, so those dangerous people now knew where she lived—not to mention that she wasn't likely to run from them. Apparently, Annabelle Simmons hadn't left her apartment in years.

"We're probably too late," Violet said. "Do we still get paid if the client's dead?"

"She isn't the client. She's a witness. The client is the DA's office. And if they've killed her, why lock up on the way out?"

"Why do killers do anything? Because they want to, that's why." She pushed the door open. "Whoa, not what I was expecting. I thought this chick was a housebound senior, but this place is yuppie heaven."

"Nobody says yuppie anymore," Noah muttered as he looked around. He had to agree with Violet, though. This wasn't what he'd expected either—especially given the unkempt state of the other two floors.

Almost the entire top floor of the building had been turned into one vast open-plan space—aside from a couple of doors set in a plain white wall at the far end of the room, which Noah assumed led to a bathroom and storage. Over-sized windows lined three walls, although one set looked out onto the brick wall of the neighboring building. Three massive skylights set at equal intervals in the high ceiling allowed a pristine view of the night sky. Support columns broke up the space, with partitions separating sections according to their function.

To their right, in the area directly above the shop, sat three sofas, several low tables, stuffed bookcases, an array of green plants, and an impressively large TV. The middle section contained a kitchen area against a three-quarter-height brick wall, which created a wide corridor between the kitchen and the windows facing the building next door. Yet more plants topped this wall, and two enormous potted trees sat at either end. Appliances ran along the dividing wall while an island counter faced it, and an old wooden dining table sat on the other side of the island, close to the windows that overlooked the street.

Just beyond the kitchen was a workspace, partially shielded from view by two rolling wooden screens with intricate cutout designs. Behind the screens were two drawing tables, a multi-monitor computer setup, and easels holding memo boards covered in pinned images. Beyond the work area was a more permanent partition made of glass bricks, and through the glass, Noah could make out the outline of a bed. To the left of the bed area, in the corner near the doors, was a treadmill and an exercise ball. And right in the middle of the whole space, behind the partial wall that divided off the kitchen, an old-fashioned swing hung from the ceiling. Plants were dotted everywhere, and the walls held an array of framed artwork in bright colors.

"I could be agoraphobic if I got to live somewhere like this. Lots of light and space, nice high ceilings, and a place to work out. Apart from the fact she's trying to grow a jungle, it's pretty much perfect." Violet wandered through the office area. "Cartoonist? No, comic book artist. Must make a good living to afford this building. Think she owns the whole thing? Or just renting this space? But then, why wouldn't her landlord turn the second floor into apartments too? It's money down the drain to leave it empty."

"I think she owns the building and doesn't want anyone else in it." Noah paused at a noticeboard filled with photos —all taken from the windows of the apartment. On the table beside them sat a state-of-the-art camera with a telephoto lens.

A series of photos showed a woman holding a small child's hand. The little girl clutched a balloon, and the pair were laughing. There was something deeply sad about the images. As if longing were an invisible third person in the frame. It made Noah wonder what it must be like to watch life happening outside walls that were both a sanctuary and a prison. Had to be lonely, that's for sure.

"Does all her shopping online," Violet said from the open laptop. "Looks like she's in some Facebook groups, though, so she isn't just walking around her apartment, talking to herself."

The glow of the streetlamps seeped into the space, bathing it in warm, diffused light. Although all the windows had white shades, none were drawn, and beyond the living room area, you could see the built-up high rises of central Houston.

Noah rounded the glass partition to check out the bedroom and froze in place. "Uh, I've found our witness."

"Is she dead?" Violet sounded almost hopeful.

"Why is that always your first thought?" Noah said as his partner came to stand beside him.

"Experience."

They gazed down at the witness in silence. Annabelle Simmons was younger than Noah had expected, early thirties at the most. It was impossible not to notice her bronze skin was smooth and blemish-free, seeing as all she was wearing were French-cut panties and a camisole. She lay sprawled on her stomach across the massive bed. Her nose was red, her mouth hung open, and she was softly snoring. Her long, mahogany hair was a tangled mess about her face and shoulders, and crumpled tissues covered the bed. Beside her left hand rested an empty cough syrup bottle.

"Well, that explains a lot." Violet picked up the bottle. "Heavy-duty stuff. Probably drank the whole lot while washing down these." She held up a box of well-known decongestants. "There's a warning on the label about it making you sleepy. I think the witness may have medicated herself into a coma." She leaned over and prodded the woman's shoulder.

A loud snore erupted, but Annabelle didn't move.

Violet strode from the bedroom area. "I'll get some cold water."

"Coffee would be better."

"Not for her to drink." Her tone made it clear she thought he was the idiot. "To throw at her and wake her up."

"Let me try something a little less aggressive. Wouldn't want you to drown the witness." He crossed to the bed, put his hand on Annabelle's shoulder, and shook gently. "Miss Simmons, we need you to wake up now."

She just groaned.

Noah shook her a little harder. "Annabelle, you have to wake up. You're in danger."

"This is pointless," Violet said. "I'm getting the water."

"Give me a minute." He used a firmer touch. "Annabelle Simmons, you are in danger. Wake up!"

Annabelle shot upward so quickly that the back of her head caught Noah on the chin and sent him reeling against the wall. She knelt in the middle of the bed, her long, dark hair wild around her face. Her eyes, wide and unfocused, stared at them in dazed horror.

"We're the good guys," Violet said unhelpfully.

Noah rubbed his chin. "The assistant DA sent us. You're in danger, and we need to take you to a safe house."

Annabelle blinked several times as though working to clear her vision. As it registered that there were strangers in her home, her body tensed, and her breathing sped up. She inched toward the edge of the bed nearest the windowless wall—seemingly uncaring that it took her closer to him.

He held out his hands in a calming gesture. "Please don't be alarmed. You can check out our story with the district attorney, but you're in danger and need to come with us. Please put some clothes on. We have to hurry."

"No," Annabelle whispered. "Not again."

Before he realized what she was going to do, she launched herself off the bed, slammed her hand on the wall beside the huge mirror that sat between the two unaccounted-for doors, and shouted, "Stay away from me!"

The mirror slid aside, revealing a doorway.

"Panic room," Violet snapped. "Grab her before she gets inside."

But it was too late. Annabelle disappeared through the gap.

Noah didn't think. He just reacted. And threw himself through the door after her, narrowly making it into the room before the concealed entrance slammed shut behind them.

Chapter Two

Annabelle found it difficult to remain upright. The floor felt as though it were made of sponge, and the walls seemed to move in and out. She staggered to the corner beside the desk and sank into the narrow space. She drew her knees up to her chest and hugged them tight. Shapes were distorted, the air felt thick, and nothing was as it seemed. It was as though she was looking at the world from the bottom of a swimming pool.

And she wasn't alone.

Maybe?

A small part of her brain insisted she was hallucinating.

But he looked real to her. And she was sure she'd never met him before. She would have remembered. He reminded her of a bulldog in its fighting prime, all broad shoulders, compact muscle, and controlled strength. If he thought his sports blazer gave him a more civilized air, he was wrong. He wore faded jeans with a neatly pressed T-shirt and carried a gun—she'd caught a glimpse the holster at his waist when he rushed after her into the room.

"I'm not going to hurt you," he said softly. His voice was rich and warm. At odds with his rugged appearance.

"Wh-what do you w-want?" Unlike her captor, she sounded tight and terrified.

"To help you."

"By k-keeping me p-prisoner?" He stood in front of the door, blocking her escape. Controlling her... Her teeth chattered she was shaking so hard, and she couldn't seem to catch her breath.

Slow breathing, slow and deep. Inhale, one, two, three. Exhale, one, two, three.

"I'm not keeping you here," he murmured. "I only followed you in because I really need to talk to you. The district attorney's office sent me to help you."

The man headed to the wall farthest from the door, moving slowly. He lowered himself to the floor beside the unused camping toilet, stretched his legs out in front of him, and crossed his legs at the ankles.

Her gaze darted between him and the door.

"You can leave anytime you want," he said. His low, soothing voice, with its gentle rolling accent of one of the southern states, had a calming effect on her, even though she didn't want it to.

But then again, it could just be that she was zoning out. It took all of her energy to concentrate on what was happening around her when all she wanted was to sleep. Hesitantly, never taking her eyes off him, she got to her feet and, back to the wall, inched along the desk toward the door.

"My name's Noah Merchant." He seemed completely unbothered by her glacial attempt to escape. "I can show you my ID if you'd like?"

Annabelle licked her dry, cracked lips as the room swayed around her. "B-bad guys have ID too."

His lips curled. "True. But most of them are fake. Mine's real."

She frowned at him. Was he joking with her? She reached up to push her hair away from her face and felt her skin burn. *Fever. Flu.* It came back to her in a rush. She'd caught the flu from the woman who delivered her groceries and had taken some medicine. A vague recollection of emptying the bottle surfaced in her mind. Had she drunk too much? Was this all just a feverish dream?

"Are you real?" she asked the stranger.

Would a hallucination tell her the truth?

"Sometimes I wonder." He slowly reached into his jacket and pulled out a wallet. He flipped it open in a gesture she'd seen TV cops make a thousand times. "I work for Benson Security. We've been hired by the DA's office to get you to safety. Here's my ID. I don't have an official badge, but you can call the assistant DA for verification." He carefully tossed it toward her.

Without thinking, she reached for it. Fumbling before she caught it. Once she had it, she froze. Was this a trick? Would he lunge at her now and try to subdue her? Her heart pounding against her rib cage, she waited to see what he'd do. But he didn't move. He just watched her, quietly waiting.

Fingers trembling, she opened the leather wallet. His ID appeared behind a plastic window, the words blurring as she tried to read them. It took a while, but she eventually realized she was looking at an Atlantic City driver's license that'd expired two years earlier. The name on it was Noah Merchant.

The worn edge of a photo peeked out from behind the

license. Annabelle pried it free, aware that her movements were awkward. A studio portrait of a happy family stared up at her. Two parents and two kids, all of them smiling. One of the parents was Noah.

"Even criminals have families," she muttered.

"True." He nodded. "In my time as an Atlantic City cop, I met plenty."

"How do I know this is real?" She was talking to herself because a bad guy, or a hallucination, wouldn't give her an answer she'd believe.

"Call whoever you need to call. Check it out." He sounded reasonable and appeared completely relaxed.

In her experience, kidnappers didn't behave this way.

The last ones she'd encountered hadn't been calm at all.

She glanced around, searching for her phone before remembering it was still beside her bed. There was an old-fashioned wired landline on the wall near Noah's head, but she didn't dare go near it for fear he'd grab her.

"I don't have a phone," she said.

He took one out of his jacket pocket and tossed it to her. It slipped through her fingers and landed on the floor.

Annabelle winced. "Sorry." Then she realized she was apologizing to her captor and felt incredibly stupid.

Clutching the desk to steady herself, she retrieved the phone and stood back up. The screen displayed an image of the same two boys in the family photo. They looked older this time, and their eyes were sad—like their father's.

She tapped the screen. "It's password protected."

"Linebacker360, capital L and no spaces." There was no hesitation in his reply.

"You shouldn't give people your password," she said automatically.

His smile was wider this time, softening his bulldog appearance. "I think I can trust you."

A loud thump on the door made Annabelle jump. She dropped the phone again, and it slid across the floor toward Noah.

This time, she didn't apologize.

"Open the door," an angry female voice demanded. "Noah, open the bloody door."

"My partner." Noah sounded weary. "I apologize in advance for anything she does or says. May I?" He pointed at the phone. "She'll keep banging on the door unless I talk to her. I could shout, but you look like your head hurts, so it might be better to call."

Annabelle nodded slowly. "Put it on speaker," she managed to say.

"Of course." He leaned forward to grab his phone, tapped the screen, then placed it face upward on his thigh.

Another loud thump on the door. This time, it sounded like a kick.

The phone rang inside and outside the room, making the situation even more surreal.

"Open the door," the angry voice said when she answered the call.

Scottish? Annabelle blinked, trying to clear her head. "Your wife's Scottish?"

"Not wife. Work partner," Noah said.

There was another kick at the door. "Get her out of there, Merchant. We're running out of time."

"Stop banging the door, Violet," Noah said. "You're scaring Annabelle."

"She should be scared," Violet shouted. "Her life's in danger, and she's wasting time. We need to get her to a safe location. Fast."

"A safe location?" Annabelle pressed a hand to her stomach as a wave of nausea assaulted her.

They couldn't mean...

"Yes," Violet snapped. "We need to leave."

Leave?

"No. No, no, no." Annabelle shook her head. "I can't. I can't. You can't make me. I can't leave. I won't go. You can't take me from my home. You have to leave—"

"Nobody's taking you anywhere," Noah said evenly. "Violet's just throwing out suggestions."

She shook her head again, making herself dizzy. "That wasn't a suggestion."

"No," the angry Scottish woman said. "It wasn't."

"Violet," Noah snapped. "You aren't helping. Once we get Annabelle out of this room, we can discuss our options."

"Discuss options? To hell with that. Knock her out and throw her over your shoulder. We need to get out of here."

Annabelle sucked in a breath, preparing to scream.

Noah held up a hand, staring at her earnestly as he spoke quickly. "I'm hanging up, Violet. I need five minutes to talk to Annabelle." He cut the call and gave her a rueful smile. "I already apologized for her. There's no excusing or explaining that woman, but believe me when I say no one will knock you out or take you from here against your will."

She stared into his dark eyes for what felt like an eternity. "Promise?"

"I swear." His words were a solemn vow, and even though she shouldn't believe the stranger, she began to feel she did.

"Here." Noah gestured with the phone before tossing it to her again. "Call the assistant DA." He repeated his password once she'd caught it.

Her hands shaking, it took several attempts to enter the

password and more stabbing at the screen to get the DA's number. She put the phone on speaker while it rang.

"District attorney's office," a female voice said. "How may I help you?"

"Please put me through to Assistant District Attorney Grant," Annabelle said.

"I'm sorry, she's busy at the moment. Can I take a message?"

"Tell her it's Annabelle Simmons, and it's urgent." She was aware her words were slurred and hesitant, but she couldn't do anything to change that. The fog in her head wouldn't allow clarity.

"Oh," the woman exclaimed. "One second."

The phone fell silent, and then the crisp, no-nonsense voice of Margaret Grant came on the line. "Annabelle, are you safe?"

Relief at hearing Ms. Grant's voice made Annabelle weak at the knees. She grasped hold of the desk beside her. "Did you send someone called Noah Merchant to get me?"

"Yes, he's from Benson Security. Is he with you? Please tell me you aren't still in your house. You need to get out of there. Listen to me carefully, Annabelle. We have a leak. You aren't safe, and you need to do whatever Mr. Merchant tells you. You can trust him."

To his credit, Noah didn't look smug.

"I can't leave my house," Annabelle whispered, fighting to suppress her shame. "You know I can't."

"What I know," Ms. Grant said, "is that your life is in danger, and you need to let Benson Security protect you. There is no other option here, Annabelle. Do you understand me?"

"I can't," she whispered.

"You don't have a choice." The assistant DA was forceful. "I have sympathy for your condition, but your life is in danger here. You have to let the Benson Security team take you to a safe house. Just go with them. They'll take care of you."

Just go?

Annabelle almost laughed. If it were that easy, she'd have left her apartment long ago. She'd have joined clubs. Experienced dates in restaurants, instead of her living room. Had a family. Lived.

"Annabelle," the assistant DA snapped. "Are you there?"

"May I?" Noah asked from right in front of her.

He'd moved across the room, and she hadn't even noticed. *Way to stay safe, Bella.*

Carefully, he eased the phone from her shaking hand.

"Ms. Grant," he said, not taking it off speaker. "I'm here, and we're dealing with the situation. I need to hang up now."

"Just make sure you keep my witness in one piece, Merchant. Or I'll make sure this is Benson Security's last case in my district."

"Understood." He ended the call while looking at Annabelle. She didn't know what to do or say. She was barely able to remain upright. The room moved around her, picking up speed like a ride at a fair she remembered from her childhood, and all she wanted was to find a cool space to lay her head until the world stopped spinning.

"You're shivering." Noah picked up the handmade quilt from the narrow bed and wrapped it around her shoulders. Suddenly, she was enveloped in more than an heirloom comforter. His warm, masculine scent surrounded her. It felt reassuring. Almost heady. And for a second, she had a crazy urge to curl into him and fall asleep in his arms.

"I c-can't leave," she told him. "I have a-a condition." Her cheeks heated with shame. "I'm not normal."

"Who is?" His lips quirked. "How about we deal with one thing at a time?" He gently led her to the bed. "Sit down and rest while I try to find something for that fever."

The mattress was a cotton cloud beneath her, making her want to sink into it and float away. As she watched, Noah rummaged in the first aid box and fetched a glass of water.

He crouched in front of her. "Aspirin," he said, holding up the bottle to prove it. He emptied a couple into her palm and handed her the water.

As she swallowed the pills, she studied his face. There was something fascinating about him.

"You have soulful eyes," she said seriously. "You remind me of a sad bulldog."

He flashed her a lopsided smile. "Is it the drooling or the jowls that give it away?"

Annabelle frowned, confused by his question.

His phone rang, and he answered it, putting it on speaker. "I asked for some time, Violet," he said as he took the half empty glass from Annabelle.

She wasn't sure if it was the soft bed or the warm quilt, but her eyes began to close all on their own. If she could just rest for a moment, everything would make much more sense. Just a moment...

"There are eight men." His partner's voice came from far, far away. "Heavily armed and heading into the building. Time's up."

Her words made no sense. It was as though they bounced off Annabelle and faded to nothing in the surrounding air. Sleep had her in its hold, wrapping her up in its comforting embrace, soothing her with promises of relief and safety. Of peace. There was no fighting this temptation. All she could do was surrender.

Through barely open eyes, she watched as the room toppled onto its side. The blissful touch of cool cotton against her cheek, and then her eyes closed completely.

Chapter Three

Noah ran a hand down his face as he watched Annabelle lose the battle with sleep. She was out cold by the time her head hit the bed, her feet still on the floor. He took the phone off speaker and held it to his ear. This assignment had gone to hell. What should have been a simple protection job had turned into an armed siege. He wished he'd ignored the call from his new boss and gone to the Irish bar as planned. Or better yet, quit Benson Security when he left London.

"Where are you?" he asked Violet, keeping his voice low because he was aware that the room wasn't sound-proof. His partner had proven that not five minutes earlier.

"In the alley across the road, behind a dumpster. I was watching the street when the cars arrived. They split up, taking the back and front entrances to the building, so I headed down the fire escape between the buildings and scaled the fence."

"You called the team?"

"Of course I called the team. What did you think I'd

do? Go all Rambo on their backsides and take them out one at a time?"

That's exactly what he'd thought. "Okay, that's good," he said into the phone.

Behind him, Annabelle snored gently.

"What about the cops?" he asked Violet.

"On their way. I called it in as an armed robbery."

He thought for a second. "The alarm didn't go off."

"Told you it was a piece of crap."

Noah looked around the small panic room. There was a desk with two monitors attached to the wall above it. Beside it was a tiny kitchen area with a hot plate, toaster oven, sink, and cupboards he assumed were stocked with the basics. There was a single bed against the wall that faced the door, and the remaining wall held a set of shelves filled with bedding and clothing. A portable toilet sat beside the shelves. On a shelf, next to the door, was the first aid kit he'd just raided, a flashlight, a personal alarm, and an old pistol that had clearly never been maintained.

It would have to do.

"I'll try to barricade us in," he said, aware time was short and running out fast.

"Just don't make any noise," Violet said. "You can hear pretty much everything inside that room. Those walls won't stop any bullets, either. She'd have been better off hiding in the claw-foot tub in her bathroom."

"Yeah, I figured as much when you were going postal on the door."

"Should've carried her out when I told you to," Violet said. "I'll do what I can from out here. Don't get shot." The line went dead.

As Noah tucked the phone back into his pocket, he studied Annabelle, wrapped up like a burrito in the heirloom quilt. She was completely vulnerable, unable to defend herself or her home.

"*Good she has you then,*" said the voice only he could hear.

Noah wasn't surprised to see the ghostly image of his dead wife standing at the end of Annabelle's bed. Therese had been appearing in his imagination since the day they buried her. At one point, thinking he must be going crazy, he'd sought professional help. The therapist had reassured him he wasn't seeing ghosts; he was simply processing his grief the way he knew best—by creating an imaginary friend.

Yeah, that sounded perfectly sane.

"I don't have time right now, Therese," he muttered as he switched on the monitors above the desk.

"*If I'm not real, why do you talk to me?*" She rolled her eyes dramatically while tapping her bright red nails on the arm of her black leather biker's jacket.

As images from inside the building appeared on the screens, Noah turned his attention to them instead of the woman he'd fallen in love with before he'd been old enough to understand the word. Today, she wore her "*My Cousin Vinny*" outfit—lots of black leather and tight, tight leggings that showed off her shapely legs. It didn't take much effort for Therese to channel Marisa Tomei's ballsy Italian American character from the movie. It came to her naturally. Damn, but she'd been sexy as hell when she dressed like that...

He shook his head and focused on the building's security setup. One camera covered each floor, one the main door, another the back door, and one the stairwell.

It wasn't nearly enough.

There were far too many shadowed corners where

assailants could hide. A wireless keyboard and mouse sat on a shelf under the monitors. Noah set them on the desk and tried to bring up an audio feed. There wasn't one.

Violet was right. The security system was a piece of crap.

On the screens, he could see eight armed men: four in the stairwell, heading straight for Annabelle's apartment, and four sweeping the first floor. It was clear from watching them that this wasn't the first time they'd done this kind of thing. They were focused, organized, and worked well as a team. These guys wouldn't hesitate to shoot if they found a target. And plasterboard walls sure as hell wouldn't stop their bullets. The panic room was more of a death trap than a safe haven.

Glancing around, he established that the desk was the only solid piece of furniture in the room. He had to move fast. In mere seconds, any noise he made would give them away. He flipped the desk onto its side, forming a barrier between the door and the most protected corner of the room —the area beside the kitchen.

Therese nodded approvingly. *"Good idea. Barricades always work in Westerns."*

"This isn't a movie," he muttered as he gently lifted Annabelle and placed her on the floor behind the barrier. She didn't stir, which was a blessing. With any luck, she'd remain asleep and silent for the duration.

Next, he propped the mattress against the desk as an extra layer between them and any bullets that came their way. It was the best he could do. At least their position took them out of the direct line of fire if the men found the door and aimed at it.

Now all he could do was wait.

Therese gazed down at Annabelle with sympathy.

Her emotions had always been written all over her face. It had been one of the things he loved most about her. There was never any guessing where he stood with his wife.

"She must be so lonely," she said. *"My heart breaks for her."*

Noah took up position beside Annabelle and drew his weapon, keeping his eyes glued to the monitors. Four men sneaked into the loft, spreading out to sweep the vast space, their guns aimed and ready.

"You need to take good care of her, Noah," Therese said.

"I'm trying." It was barely a whisper. "You're distracting me."

"Well, excuse me!" She glared at him. *"If you die here, I will kick your ass in the afterlife."*

"Noted."

The vision of his wife faded, leaving only the woman sleeping on the hard floor beside him. She emitted a gentle little snore that seemed far too loud in the enclosed space. Noah froze, waiting to see if anyone had heard. A bead of sweat made its way down his spine as he watched the men draw closer to the panic room. One gun against four wasn't good odds, especially when one of the men carried a semi-automatic weapon.

Time stretched out in agony as Noah waited. Shouldn't there be sirens by now? The cops were only blocks away. Instead, all he heard was the muted movements of the armed men as they searched the loft.

Noah watched them open the two doors on either side of the panic room's entrance. They were so close that he could hear their every word through the paper-thin walls. Guess *now* he had audio to go with the cameras. If they made it out of this alive, the first thing he'd do was rip out her security system and replace it with something that actually did the job.

"Nothing," one of them said as he came back through the door Noah had assumed led to a closet. "Coupla empty rooms. No girl."

"Where the fuck is she?" a tall, thin man demanded as he turned his back on the camera.

The patch on the back of his sleeveless denim jacket came into focus, and Noah's stomach tightened when he read the insignia—Demon Brothers MC. He let out a slow, silent breath. What the hell had Annabelle witnessed that had the Demons after her? This wasn't good. This was as bad as it could get. The gang had been in its infancy when he'd been a cop in Atlantic City, but the tales he'd heard about them turned his stomach. They weren't the largest motorcycle club in the States, but they were one of the deadliest.

Noah clenched his teeth, fighting back the anger that could cause him to make a mistake. He needed a calm head. Needed to focus. He'd deal with the assistant DA later and ask why she'd failed to mention the Demons' involvement when hiring his team. Even a last-minute job required a briefing on the essentials. And knowing who they were up against was *definitely* essential.

"She gotta be hiding." A short, stocky guy with tattoos running up the back of his neck and onto his bald head gestured around the room with his gun. "She's too scared to leave the building. Stoop said she ain't been outta here in years. Gets sick if she tries."

"Then we search." The thin guy motioned to his fellow Demons. "Loco, Runner, rip the place apart. Bone, call the guys, fill them in."

The stocky guy nodded and pulled out his phone as the

other three spread out and started searching. They weren't delicate about it either. They overturned the bed and emptied the kitchen cupboards, and anything in their way was knocked down and trampled on.

Beside Noah, Annabelle stirred, disturbed by the noise. He watched her closely, ready to stop her from talking if she surfaced. How, he didn't know, but he'd figure it out. However, after a few seconds, she settled, and Noah could breathe again. He returned his attention to the monitors.

Just as Annabelle coughed.

Chapter Four

Where the hell were the cops?

Violet had called them a good five minutes ago and there was still no sign of them. Given that Noah was right and the main sheriff's office was only a few streets away, she'd expected someone to arrive almost immediately. Or maybe the sheriff's office wasn't who answered emergency calls. Maybe it was the other cops. The city police?

She growled in frustration. The American legal system was confusing, and she didn't like to be confused. She also didn't like hiding outside on the street while her partner was having all the fun inside the building. If anyone was going to shoot somebody, it ought to be her.

Violet eyed the two sedans parked across the road, their engines still running. Four men had climbed out of each, which she thought was overkill. They'd had three big guys squished into the back seats like sardines in a tin. How many men did it take to kill one housebound woman? Pathetic.

The drivers were cautious, constantly scanning the

roads around them, meaning it was impossible to sneak up on them. Pity. Because she would have enjoyed pistol-whipping them into a coma.

She tried to remember if it was illegal to shoot them. Noah would know. But Noah wasn't there. Surely she'd be justified in shooting them, seeing as they were bad guys waiting for their armed friends to kill an innocent woman. If that wasn't the definition of an accomplice, she didn't know what was. Violet wished she'd watched more American crime shows and less reality TV. If she had done, she might know whether she had the right to shoot the drivers.

There was nothing for it but to ask her boss, so she pulled her phone out of her pocket and called Rochelle Davis.

She answered straight away. "Talk to me."

"Eight armed guys in the building. Two waiting outside in cars. No gunshots so far. Noah's stuck in a panic room with our client, who's out cold from overmedicating her flu. No sign of the cops yet. What I want to know is, can I shoot the drivers?"

A second's silence, then, "No. You can't shoot the drivers."

"How else will I distract the guys inside and delay them from getting away? They're bad guys. Doing bad things. Surely that's justifiable cause or whatever the hell it's called."

"This isn't a Hollywood movie. We don't shoot first and ask questions later. We obey the law. Stand dow—"

Violet hung up. It was clear she wouldn't get any help from Ms. By-the-Book. Her phone vibrated as she put it back in her pocket. Ignoring what would no doubt be another pointless call with their team leader, she scanned the surrounding buildings, searching for a distraction. Something to flush the hit men back out into the open.

But nothing jumped out at her.

* * *

"Shut up!" the thin guy shouted. "I heard something."

The Demons stilled, listening.

Noah grabbed the glass of water from the counter and crouched beside Annabelle. He placed his gun on the floor and raised her head with his left hand while pressing the glass to her lips. It was a desperate and pointless effort. She was sick and needed to cough. There wasn't a whole lot he could do about that. Still, he had to try.

"Sip," Noah whispered to Annabelle.

Her eyes were unfocused, and her body was limp. She was barely awake, and the heat radiating from her was ferocious. With a feeble mew, she tried to do as he instructed.

"I don' hear nothing," one of the guys said.

"Just fucking listen," their leader ordered. "It came from behind me."

With a glance at the monitors, Noah saw the four men turn toward the back wall.

And the panic room.

Noah focused on Annabelle again. She was completely out of it and burning up. As her lips touched the glass, she coughed again. Only this time, much louder.

They were caught.

On the monitor, as one, the four men strode straight toward them.

"She's in the wall," the leader said.

"Secret room?" one of the men asked.

"Gotta be behind the mirror," another said.

Annabelle had stopped coughing and was sipping the water now. Her eyes were closed, and she was fast asleep again within seconds. But the damage had already been done. Noah lowered her to the floor and, still crouching behind the barrier, swiveled to face the door. His wrists resting on top of the wooden desk, he aimed his gun at the door.

Sweat pooled in the small of his back, but his breathing remained steady and his mind calm and focused. There was no point in thinking about the odds of getting out of the panic room alive. He had a job to do. That was all that mattered. An image of his boys flickered in his mind, but he ruthlessly pushed it aside. They knew he loved them, and thinking about them now was only a distraction. His heart clenched at the thought of never seeing them again, but he swiftly locked those feelings away. Feelings could get you killed.

As the men knocked on the wall surrounding the mirrored door, Noah glanced at the screen. All four men were frowning. One of them hooked his gun into his jeans and grabbed hold of the mirror. With some effort, he ripped it from the door.

"Look what we have here." The leader smiled maliciously. "Open it," he ordered the guy next to him.

The guy looked baffled. "How? There's no handle. There's nothing."

"Fucking idiot." The leader ran his hand down the wall beside the door, easily locating the thin seam that revealed the pressure panel that opened the door.

He pressed.

Nothing happened.

The door was locked from the inside.

"Bitch," he muttered. "Ram it." He gestured to the other Demons.

The biggest one took a few steps back and ran at the door.

It felt like the whole building shuddered. But the door held fast.

"Frame's gotta be reinforced," the big guy said.

The stocky guy tapped the wall again and slowly grinned at the others. "Doesn't sound like the walls are anything but plasterboard."

The leader did a chin lift, signaling for them to step back.

Noah's stomach tightened as he watched them line up in front of the panic room door.

As one, they raised their guns.

And fired.

As the world around him exploded in a barrage of bullets, Noah threw himself over Annabelle, praying the barrier would protect them. She coughed, but the noise was lost in the sound of battle and carnage. Dust filled the air. Debris flew. Noah jerked as a searing pain registered in his left calf muscle. He glanced back to see a rip in his jeans and blood on the denim, but there was no time to do anything about it. A stray bullet struck the toaster oven, propelling it off the counter and into his back. He grunted in pain, his ears ringing as shots boomed and echoed in the small room.

Then suddenly, silence.

With a grimace, Noah clambered to his heels and took aim at the entrance. Bullet holes peppered the wall and the door. He swallowed hard, trying to clear the dust from his mouth. The stench of gunpowder and destruction heavy in the air. Behind him, Annabelle coughed and gasped to breathe.

"Bitch is still alive."

There was a thud.

No point in checking the monitors. They were in pieces, along with everything else in the room. His attention shot to where one of the men was attempting to kick his way through the compromised wall. Noah took aim and fired. A squeal came from inside the apartment.

"She shot me. The bitch shot me!"

"Shut the fuck up. She only got your foot."

A figure passed in front of one of the larger holes but was gone before Noah could shoot.

"Hard to see through the dust, but looks like she's holed up in the corner. Loco, kick the wall in. We'll cover you."

Noah ducked behind the barrier as more gunshots rang out. In the midst of the gunfire, a heavy thud hit the wall close to the corner where they hid. With his eyes scrunched against the dust-thickened air, he aimed at the spot directly above where someone was kicking a hole.

His bullet passed straight through the flimsy plaster.

A grunt. A thud. And the shooting stopped.

"Fucking bitch shot Loco!"

There was a scuffle on the other side of the door. "He's dead! She fucking killed him."

"What the hell's going on up here?" a new voice shouted.

Great, the rest of the group had arrived.

Now there'd be seven men shooting at the panic room.

Noah reached up to wipe the sweat from his brow, and his hand came away bloody.

Damn.

He glanced back at Annabelle, who was now wide awake and huddled in the corner, staring at him in terror and confusion. Tears traced through the dust on her cheeks.

"She's in there," the leader shouted. "Get something to break through the wall. We'll cover you."

Noah took a breath and steadied his gun. A few more shots, and he was out of ammo.

Where the hell were the cops?

* * *

Violet was running on fury by the time the shooting stopped. From her position in the alley, she'd seen flashes of gunfire through the windows on the top floor of the building. Noah was in there. Trapped. With eight guys firing at him.

And she was stuck outside, her hands tied by their new boss. Her previous boss, Callum, would never have told her not to shoot the bad guys. He'd have told her *not* to get caught.

It wasn't like there was anyone to see her shoot anyway. The streets were empty, and the cops were nowhere in sight. For all she knew, any help she could offer her partner was useless now. He might already be dead.

The world was painted in a wash of red.

She was a doer, not a waiter.

Her eyes bore holes into the cars in front of her.

And then it hit her.

Her goody-two-shoes boss told her not to shoot the drivers. She hadn't said anything about their cars. Violet raised her gun. Aimed. Fired. If the drivers happened to get shot accidentally, well, that wasn't her fault.

Her first shot struck the engine of the lead car with cool precision. Steam rose from its hood, and the driver screamed like a baby. He stuck his arm out of the window and shot wildly. Aiming for nothing. Hitting everything.

Violet aimed again. This time, she took out his wing mirror. As a string of expletives filled the air, she turned her attention to the second car and fired. Jackpot. The car's alarm went off just as the first driver blasted his horn.

That should get some attention.

With a smile, Violet slipped back into the shadows.

Gunshots sounded from the street below. A car horn blared. Right on top of that, a car alarm went off.

Noah listened to the men inside the loft.

"Somebody's shooting up our vehicles!"

Noah silently gave thanks to God for *Violent* Lee.

Above the noise of the cars, he heard sirens, growing louder as they drew nearer.

Now he could have kissed his partner.

"Five-O's here. We gotta go," someone said.

"What about the girl?"

"We'll get her next time," their leader said. "Do you hear that, bitch?" he shouted. "You're dead. We're coming for you. We'll burn you out if we have to. Fucking bitch!"

There was the sound of running footsteps, slamming doors, and louder sirens.

Noah stayed in position, staring at the door, his gun ready. He couldn't take any chances that one of the gang would stick around to finish the job. Annabelle moved behind him, slipped her hand beneath his jacket, and curled it into his T-shirt at the small of his back.

The hand shook.

"Noah," she whispered, her words slow and filled with confusion. "I think somebody's shooting at us."

And even as the pain from his injuries began to register, Noah smiled.

Chapter Five

The paramedics insisted that Noah head to the hospital for stitches. He only agreed to go once his boss had arrived and promised not to let Violet take Annabelle from the premises by force. By the time he got back to the warehouse, the place was overrun with cops, forensic techs, and the medical examiner's team.

They'd cordoned off the apartment as a crime scene and moved Annabelle to one of the abandoned offices on the second floor. She was sound asleep in what looked like a walk-in storage closet off the large office area. Noah greeted his team before heading straight to her, limping some as he crossed the room.

Annabelle lay on a single mattress, which was obviously brand new, placed on the bare wooden floorboards. Someone had set up a small lamp beside her, and she was still wrapped up in the heirloom quilt. A paramedic knelt at her side on the floor, changing out the IV bag attached to her arm.

"Fluids," he said as Noah approached.

An older woman with a bob of steel gray hair stood at

the end of the makeshift bed, watching the paramedic's every move. She wore a simple black dress, and her back was ramrod straight.

"Noah Merchant." He offered his hand.

"Dr. Mallory." Her handshake was firm. "Annabelle's physician and psychiatrist."

"Dual duty, huh?"

"I was a family doctor before I trained in psychiatry, so I function as both for Annabelle because it's easier for her."

"I'm sure she appreciates it." He did a visual sweep of Annabelle, checking for injuries, and was relieved to find none evident. "It's unusual for a doctor to make house calls in this day and age."

Dr. Mallory was clearly amused. "Some of my patients can't make it in to see me."

Noah smiled sheepishly. "Of course. Sorry, I took some pain meds. My brain is a bit slower than usual. Is she gonna be okay?"

"It's purely a bad dose of the flu. Her fever had gotten a little out of hand, but the fluids will help, as will the medication we administered. All she needs now is to rest and let her body fight it off."

The paramedic finished up, nodded at the doctor, and left the room. Noah stepped out of his way, wincing as pain shot through his injured leg.

"Sit down, Mr. Merchant," the doctor said. "Before you topple over."

Someone had moved a couple of old wooden chairs into the room, and Noah gratefully sank onto one of them. It groaned under his weight.

"Bullet skimmed my leg," he told the doctor. "Took a chunk of skin."

"Looks like that's not the only injury you've sustained." Her attention was on his bandaged head.

"No, but it's the one that hurts the most. Does Annabelle have any injuries?"

"A few scrapes but nothing serious." She seemed to look right into him and see things he didn't want anyone to see. "You did a good job of protecting her."

"It was mostly luck." He nodded at the sleeping patient. "Have they filled you in on the situation?"

"Yes." Her lips thinned. "Annabelle saw a man being killed and is a key witness in his murderer's trial. Tonight, some of his gang members tried to stop that from happening."

"The ADA wants us to move her to a safe house. Is that even possible with her condition?"

The doctor sighed and took the chair beside his, sitting just as straight as she'd stood. "Agoraphobia's a crippling condition, and contrary to public perception, it doesn't always mean that the sufferer is housebound. It can mean they stick only to places where they feel safe and never leave that defined area. For Annabelle, that means this building."

Noah wished he'd had time to read up on the condition before being thrown in at the deep end. "What would happen if she's forced to leave?"

"Honestly, I suspect she'd experience a full psychotic break and have to be institutionalized."

"So, she can never leave this warehouse?" There went their plan to move her to a safe house.

"I'm not saying that. With time and work on her part, she could extend her comfort zone beyond this building. But forcing her out of it is something else entirely. She isn't mentally equipped to deal with such a violation. Do you know anything of her history?"

Noah shook his head and instantly regretted it because it made the wound on his scalp throb. "We got pulled onto this job just a couple of hours ago. Been kinda busy since then."

"So I see." The doctor smiled kindly. "I'm not betraying Annabelle's confidence by telling you what she experienced. It's public knowledge, and a basic internet search of her name would bring up news reports." Her gaze rested on the sleeping woman with fondness and sympathy. "Annabelle's mother died during childbirth, and her father raised her—with the help of his older sister. They were very wealthy—family money and wise investments. When she was in college, two men abducted her from the street on her way home from a date one evening. They held her ransom for three days." She shook her head. "It isn't like in the movies. It takes time to amass the kind of cash her kidnappers demanded."

"I've worked a kidnapping or two in my time," Noah said quietly.

"Then you understand," the doctor said. "By then, her father was in his seventies and had a severe heart condition. The stress of Annabelle's kidnapping proved too much for him, and he died of a heart attack before his daughter was returned."

Noah cursed under his breath.

"Exactly," Dr. Mallory said. "The ransom was paid, and Annabelle came to live with his sister, her aunt. She's been here ever since. Anxiety and fear made it hard for her to leave the building, and after a couple of years, she stopped trying."

Hell, no wonder she had issues. "So she hasn't left this building in what? Ten years?"

"About that," the doctor agreed as she brushed at a mark on her dress. "We made some progress while her aunt was alive, but her passing was a setback. There was no one left who was close enough to her, who she trusted enough to help her step out into the world."

"How did her aunt die?"

"Old age. She fell asleep and never woke up."

They watched Annabelle in silence for a moment.

"There's no way we can move her from this building, is there?" Noah said at last.

"Not unless you want to render her incapable of testifying for the prosecution."

That's what he figured. "What about having other people in the building? Will that freak her out?"

"No. Rose, her aunt, was very good in that respect. When she was alive, the shop was open every day, and this floor was rented out to various small businesses. She ensured that the world came to Annabelle, seeing as she couldn't enter the world. That socialization is why I have such high hopes that one day, she'll step outside this building."

"But the place has been empty and the shop closed for a while now?"

"Annabelle isn't great at the business side of things. She meant to get new tenants, but she gets wrapped up in her work and forgets."

Noah gestured toward the outer office, where his team was busy making themselves at home. "Well, she has new tenants now, albeit temporary, whether she wants them or not. No effort required on her part."

Dr. Mallory studied him and appeared to come to some

conclusion. "She'll be safe with you, won't she?"

"You have my word that I'll do everything within my power to keep her safe. I've been with Benson Security for years, and not only are these people good at what they do, they also care about doing it right."

"That's all I can ask." She stood and smoothed down her dress. "I've arranged for a nurse to check on her over the next couple of days. I suspect she'll be out of it for a little while yet, so don't be surprised if she's disorientated and frightened when she wakes. Someone should be with her at all times to help her and explain what's going on."

"I'll make sure that happens." Because he would do it himself.

"I was good friends with her aunt," Dr. Mallory said wistfully. "She would have liked you."

With that, she turned and strode from the tiny room.

Noah inched his chair closer to Annabelle, leaned over, and gently swept her hair back from her face. Whatever the doc had given her ensured she was sound asleep. "Looks like we're stuck with each other for now," he whispered. "Sleep well. We'll watch out for you."

Her eyelids fluttered open for a second, and she looked up at him with an unfocused gaze. "Bulldog," she mumbled with a smile before falling back to sleep.

At the sound of movement behind him, Noah turned to see one of the Scottish triplets, the youngest members of his new team, carrying in an old armchair. He settled it in the corner, near Annabelle's bed.

"Boss said you'd want to camp in here tonight," he said as Noah struggled to remember which one he was. Logan or Harris, he figured, because the other triplet, Evan, favored bad Hawaiian shirts. "I suggested another mattress, but she figured the girl would scream if she woke up to find somebody sleeping beside her—even if there was a space between the beds."

"I can sleep in a chair." Hell, the way Noah felt, he could sleep anywhere.

Noah had been around the brothers a week or so now and still found it disconcerting that they were basically indistinguishable from each other. They were all tall, lean-muscled, and topped with auburn hair. Their square jaws and mischievous blue eyes meant women stopped in their tracks wherever they went—individually or together. Although when they were together, it magnified the effect. Noah had witnessed women walking into walls as they stared at the brothers. As far as he knew, at least one of them had done some modeling in the past, which was no surprise.

Evan, dressed in a shirt that should have come with sunglasses for those around him, crowded into the room behind his brother. "I made signs," he said.

Noah frowned with confusion as he settled into the armchair but watched with interest as Evan stuck a large sheet of paper to the ceiling above Annabelle's bed and another to the wall above his chair. He grinned when he read the handwritten messages not to panic. It was the kind of thing his kids would do. Sometimes, it was hard to remember these guys were in their twenties.

"Logan thinks he was deprived of oxygen in the womb," his brother—Harris, Noah now knew—said drolly. "I reckon he got one too many elbows to the head from the rest of us."

"What?" Evan said. "This will help. I'd freak out if I woke in a different room with strangers all around me. Anyone would."

"Thanks, boys," Noah said before they could start arguing. "I'm going to get some sleep now, if that's okay."

Harris eyed him critically. "Have you had enough pain meds?"

"Plenty. I'm rattling from them."

"Okay then, sleep well, and shout out if you need anything. We're taking turns keeping watch tonight, although the place is still crawling with cops, so it's unlikely there'll be another attack anytime soon." Harris glanced back into the office space. "We're setting up beds out there, so we'll be close by."

"Appreciated," Noah said, meaning it.

"Team briefing at eight in the morning," Evan said.

"I'll be there." He stretched out his legs in front of him, feeling the wound smart where the bullet had grazed him. At least there was no throbbing pain.

"Night, then." Harris left the door ajar, enough to allow some light in and for Noah to hear danger approaching. He flicked off the light inside the closet before disappearing.

For a few moments, Noah watched Annabelle sleep while listening to the muted sounds of his teammates moving around in the room outside his door. Despite her being unwell, there was no denying their new mission was attractive. Based on her coloring, it seemed she was an American mutt—just like him: a mix of races and nationalities in her heritage. Although his leaned toward Irish and Eastern European, whereas hers seemed to lean closer to warmer climes. Even ashen with illness, her warm brown skin tone spoke of Caribbean beaches.

He closed his eyes and sighed at himself. The pain meds were making him think crazy thoughts, waxing lyrical about their charge's appearance. She was a job. Her looks didn't matter.

He opened his eyes again to study her. There was no denying she was pretty, though...

"You're doing it again," his dead wife's voice sounded in his head.

Noah wasn't surprised to see her standing beside Annabelle's bed. "Doing what?" he whispered.

"You've gone into white-knight mode. You want to save the girl." She studied Annabelle for a moment. *"She's a gorgeous woman and feisty too. I like her. But she isn't some puppy you can adopt, you know that, right?"*

"It never even occurred to me that she needed rescuing, let alone adopting. I'm just doing my job, which is to protect her."

"Yeah, right." Therese was unconvinced.

"Yeah, right," Noah whispered firmly.

"You know," she said speculatively, *"it's been five years since I died. Don't you think it's time you moved on?"*

"I'm sore and tired, and I need to rest. I don't have time to talk to a ghost right now," Noah told her, closing his eyes. Maybe if he couldn't see his delusion, he wouldn't hear her.

No such luck.

"I'll admit, if you'd walked into another relationship five years ago, when my body was barely cold, I'd have made your life hell. But now, I'm worried about you. Do you plan on being alone for the rest of your life?"

"I'm not alone," he muttered. "You're here. All. The. Time."

"But you can't touch me," she said with sadness. *"And the boys would be okay with it now—you moving on, starting again with someone new. Just think about it."*

"Therese, please." He opened his eyes only to find the room empty except for his charge, who was still sleeping deeply.

With a shake of his head at his own craziness, Noah closed his eyes again and let his battered body relax.

Chapter Six

"So, how's it going?" Noah asked Rochelle Davis the following morning.

It was half an hour before their team meeting, and Noah was showered and changed, thanks to someone having picked up some clean clothes from his new house. Sleep had done wonders for him, and apart from the odd ache, he felt fine. Well, if you didn't count his slight limp. He pulled up a chair at the borrowed desk their boss had set up in the large office and stretched out his sore leg in front of him. If he could have willed it to heal faster, he would have.

"Let me see." She folded her arms as she stood beside the desk, surveying the room. "Half the police force is upstairs, tramping over Annabelle's apartment while the crime scene techs pry bullets out of her walls. We've been on this case barely a day, and one of my team's already injured, another is aggravating the local cops, and our client can't be removed from the building for fear she'll have a complete psychotic break."

"So, it's going well then?" Noah fought a smile.

"Going great," she said wryly. "The ADA just chewed my ear off about moving her witness to a safe house, and I had to tell her that wasn't possible. Which was fun."

"You spoke to Annabelle's doctor, though, right?"

"Yes. And I agree with her diagnosis. Taking Ms. Simmons from here by force would cause irreparable psychological damage and be completely irresponsible."

Noah had known Rochelle for years, but it was still easy to forget that before becoming an FBI agent, she'd been a certified medical examiner and forensic pathologist. Dressed in a pristine gray pinstripe pantsuit, the statuesque African American woman screamed law enforcement rather than medicine.

"How are your injuries?" she asked him.

"I'll be fine in a couple of days," Noah assured her. "Worst was my leg, and it's barely a scratch. What's going on here?" He nodded toward the partition the triplets were removing.

"We're creating one large office space. I want this team where I can see them. Especially those three."

As they worked, the triplets were arguing with each other. Something about a girl they'd all liked and who she'd loved best. It made him feel old.

Rochelle perched against the desk, close to Noah, and lowered her voice. "I have no idea what Lake Benson was thinking, bringing those three on board. A hacker, a thief, and a conman? They're professional criminals, and this is a reputable security team."

"I prefer the term fixer to conman, Boss," Harris MacDonald, the most clean-cut triplet, said. "We also have great hearing."

"And criminal records," Rochelle said, apparently unfazed.

"Not me," was Harris' smug reply.

"And *our* records are based purely on misunderstandings," added the one with a beard and awful Hawaiian shirt, which made him Evan, their resident hacker.

"Aye." The last triplet, Logan, grinned. "We're reformed. I only steal for you now, Boss." He batted his lashes at her in a blatant attempt to appear innocent.

Rochelle looked skyward. Probably praying for patience.

Noah felt sorry for her. But not so much that he'd take the job off her hands. "Wish I'd been there when Violet found out they were on the team," he said.

Apparently, Violet had arrested the brothers a few times when they caused trouble as teens in Glasgow. She considered them the lowlight of her police career, and to say she wasn't their biggest fan was putting it mildly.

"It did take a while to talk her down," Rochelle said.

"And we thank you for that," Logan called out. "Officer Lee's a wee bit temperamental."

Evan elbowed him. "You don't need to call her officer. She isn't with Strathclyde Police anymore."

"Nope," Harris added. "She's in America. With us... and she's armed."

The brothers paled. Or perhaps it was a trick of the light.

"Concentrate on your task," Rochelle told them. "This is a private conversation."

There was much grumbling, but the triplets got back to work.

"Where's the rest of the team?" Noah asked Rochelle.

"Violet's in with the detectives, giving her statement. They're good guys, sound cops. But even they realize this situation is untenable. They've mentioned, more than once, that it would be better if Annabelle were moved. They're not wrong."

"Yeah, I met them last night, Johnson and McMillan, right? It's hard to argue with them. In any other circumstance, we'd have the client out of danger in a split second."

"They've got their hands full with this mess," Rochelle said. "I just spent half an hour with them, explaining that Violet was given clear instructions not to fire at the men in the cars downstairs. Who knows what she's telling them now. Nothing helpful, that's for sure."

"Obviously, you didn't order her not to shoot the cars," Noah said with amusement and a hefty dose of sympathy.

"Apparently, my orders have to be spelled out for some of my new team. You're up next for your statement. You gave them your weapon already?"

He nodded. "Handed it over to the local cops as soon as they arrived."

They'd need it, seeing as he'd used it to kill a man.

"You had no choice," Rochelle said as though reading his mind. "It was them or you."

"I know." It wasn't the first time he'd taken a life in the line of duty, although it never seemed to get any easier. But then, he wouldn't be too happy if it did.

"Rodrigo's upstairs," Rochelle said. "He's keeping an eye on the cops—seeing as we don't know who we can trust right now."

"Good. Nothing much gets past him."

"So I hear, though I'd be much more comfortable if I knew exactly what his skill set involved."

"Good luck getting that info," Noah said.

He'd first met Rodrigo De la Cruz in South America when they'd faced off against a cartel. Nobody knew who he'd worked for, exactly, only that his cover had been blown, and rather than taking a new assignment with his no-name agency, he'd signed on with Benson Security.

"Katrina's at the hotel, sorting out the last of our permits and paperwork," Rochelle continued. "And I have no idea where Abasi Otieno is."

Noah arched an eyebrow. "Is he still joining the team?"

A large part of him hoped that the former London mobster would change his mind about Benson Security. Why he wanted to join in the first place was a mystery to everyone who knew him, and why Lake Benson had offered him a position was even more confounding.

"That's anybody's guess." She lowered her voice further. "You knew him in London. Exactly how concerned should I be about having him on my team?"

"I didn't know him well. He's connected to the London office through their tech specialist, who treats him like a brother. Her actual brother was Abasi's best friend, and the two of them helped run a London mob for years. Marcus, the brother, was being groomed to take over before his father killed him. When he died, Abasi went into revenge mode and burned the organization to the ground. He's dangerous *and* connected. I wouldn't trust him as far as I could throw him."

Rochelle let out the faintest of groans. "Just what we need. I'm already dealing with three baby criminals who act like puppies that need training. Not to mention the ticking time bomb that is Violet Lee. I do not want to add a renegade with a serious criminal background to the mix."

"He *does* have skills and connections." Noah played devil's advocate.

"So did Al Capone."

He didn't want to make things worse by telling Rochelle

that he thought Abasi was a whole lot more dangerous than the famous Chicago gangster.

"Look," Noah said, "I was a cop. You're ex-FBI. Rodrigo was with some kind of law enforcement agency. Violet, for all her faults, was still a good police detective. Not everyone on your team has to be taught how to play with others. Half of us already know how to toe the line."

"And the other half don't even know where the line should be drawn," Rochelle added.

"Then there's Katrina Raast," Noah said. "Lucky number nine. Neither law enforcement nor a criminal."

"No, she brings a whole different set of problems to the table."

While it wasn't public knowledge, Noah was aware of Katrina's history—he'd worked alongside her brother in London. "Katrina's worked hard to put her experience behind her. She's smart and capable. She won't let you down."

Rochelle rubbed her temples. "This team's full of misfits and castoffs. How the hell are we going to make it work?"

"Don't look at me, *Boss*." Noah grinned. "That's why you get paid the big bucks."

"Asshole," she muttered.

"Yep." He laughed. "But a smart asshole who had the sense not to take responsibility for this team."

"You also skipped out on the task of fortifying this building. It's the only way we can keep Annabelle safe. I'd really like to not screw up our first job as the new Benson Security office."

Noah winced, and this time, it wasn't in pain. "Fortify the building? Who's footing that bill?"

Rochelle gave him a wry smile. "Questions like that are

the reason why they offered you the job of heading up this office before giving it to me."

"I don't want that kind of responsibility. That's why I gave them your name." He grinned at her. "You're welcome."

"Oh, I can't thank you enough for volunteering me," she said dryly as she studied him. "You sure you're okay?"

"I'll survive. Don't worry about me doing my job."

"You're the only one I don't worry about," she said grimly.

Noah hadn't lied. He was going to be fine. He wasn't even that badly injured. Although it was clear his pain meds were wearing off. His head had begun to throb, probably from the piece of monitor glass that had embedded itself in his scalp and had to be removed at the hospital. He now sported an attractive white bandage where a chunk of his hair used to be. On top of that, he had a bruise the size of a toaster oven on his back and stitches in his leg where a bullet ate a chunk of flesh.

Sure, he was lucky the bullet hadn't caused any real damage, but it still felt like he'd gone several rounds with his buddy Beast—a professional mixed martial arts fighter. There once was a time when Noah barely noticed an injury, but these days, he all but creaked when he walked. He sighed as he watched the triplets remove the old partition between the offices to make one large, open-plan space. Their youth and endless energy made him feel every one of his thirty-five years.

A door banged open behind Noah, and he turned as Violet stalked back into the room. One of the triplets opened his mouth to say something to her, but she held up a hand as she glared at him and barked, "No." He shut his mouth again.

"That was fast," Rochelle said.

"They're bringing in another officer to talk to me. Apparently, the one I spoke to wasn't capable of taking my statement." Violet glowered. "I have no idea why."

Noah had a good idea why. She'd either pissed them off or scared the crap out of them.

She cocked a thumb over her shoulder. "You're up. Good luck. American cops are dumb as dirt."

"I *was* an American cop," Noah reminded her as he levered himself out of the chair.

She simply stared at him as though he'd proven her point.

"Where are they?" he asked.

"First office beside the stairs." She looked at Rochelle. "And just a heads-up. From the behavior of the cops out there, I'd say police royalty has arrived. Guy's in uniform and doesn't look happy. Must be the big boss."

"Great." Rochelle fastened her suit jacket before following Noah to the door. "I'll head him off. You're on guard duty, Violet." She gestured to the room where Annabelle slept. "Nobody goes in or out."

"Got it." Violet sat at the desk, her back to the triplets and her eyes on the storage room door. "As long as I don't have to deal with Copy, Paste, Repeat over there, I'm fine."

"We heard that," one of the triplets said.

"The rest of you," Rochelle said, "carry on in here and monitoring the law enforcement personnel upstairs. We'll postpone our briefing to later today."

There were nods of agreement as Rochelle headed out of the room.

Noah followed her into the hallway. "Has it occurred to you," he said, "that the owner of the building may not like the fact we're moving in?"

Her expression hardened. "She doesn't have a choice."

As Rochelle went to introduce herself to an unhappy police chief, Noah let himself into the small office by the stairs and shook hands with the two detectives. One was around Noah's age, and the other a kick-in-the-ass off retirement. They had the sharp-eyed yet world-weary look of cops who'd seen pretty much everything.

"Take a seat." Detective Johnson, the younger of the two, gestured to the empty wooden chair across the desk from them.

McMillan studied Noah with open curiosity. "Atlantic City cop, huh?"

"Twelve years," Noah said with a smile. "Made it to detective."

Johnson smiled back. "We looked into you. You had a good track record before you left the department." He glanced at his partner. "Benson Security is an interesting choice."

McMillan shifted in his chair, his shirt straining over an ample belly. "Most cops wait until retirement before going the rent-a-cop route."

Noah wasn't offended. He understood their cynicism. When he'd been on the force, he'd encountered his fair share of security officers who thought they were full-fledged cops. Or worse, that they were better.

"I wanted a change of scenery," he said easily.

Johnson tapped his pen on the open folder in front of him. "I'm sorry about your wife."

Yeah, they'd done their homework on him. Made Noah wonder what they'd managed to dig up on the rest of his new team. From their position, the Benson Security Houston team must seem like a bunch of criminals and burned-out cops.

Noah nodded, acknowledging the detective's condolences. "Do we have a problem here?" He was tired, sore, and not in the mood to tiptoe around the issues.

Johnson's expression suggested he appreciated getting to the point. "Mac and I were discussing the new players in town. You've been here about five minutes, and already, bullets are flying."

"Hey." Noah spread his hands wide. "The Demons attacked us. It was shoot back or lay down and die."

Johnson's lanky frame was perfectly relaxed as he smiled. "We're not questioning the shooting. It was definitely justified."

Inside Noah, a wary tension uncoiled. Although he knew he was in the right, there was always a question mark over these things until they were thoroughly investigated.

"What we're questioning," McMillan said, "is the validity of your team." He ran his hand through thinning hair. "Some of your buddies have criminal records."

"And," Johnson added, "some have no records at all. We still haven't been able to verify that Rodrigo De la Cruz actually exists."

"I can introduce you to him if you want," Noah said helpfully.

"Smart-ass," McMillan muttered. "Just what I need. Six months off retirement, and I get to deal with a hot shot new group full of smart-asses and wild cards. My luck stinks."

Johnson grinned at his partner. "You have three ex-wives, a second mortgage, and a heart condition. Your luck's been nonexistent for years."

"Go screw yourself," McMillan said with an easygoing smile.

"So"—Johnson turned back to Noah—"you know you need to get the witness out of here, right? Forget all that agoraphobia bullshit. If you guys stay here, you're nothing more than a sitting target for the Demon Brothers."

"Rochelle's talked to you about this," Noah said. "Leaving isn't an option."

"Then you've got a death wish," McMillan said in disgust.

"Nope. I have a woman who'll lose her grip on reality if she's forced out of her home. And a vicious gang out to kill her before her court date. Oh, and a team who barely knows each other, let alone trust one another. Not to mention a bullet wound in my leg, a bruise that covers my back, and a patch of skin missing from my skull. That's what I've got." He leaned forward, staring the two men in the eyes. "Nothing about this job is easy, so I got to say, Detectives, if you can't help, I don't have a whole lot of time for you."

McMillan gave him a shrewd, assessing look while Johnson considered him with a tad more respect than he'd previously shown.

"What can we do to help?" McMillan said at last.

Noah sank back into his chair with a sigh. "Regular patrols past the building would be a good start."

The two detectives shared a look.

"We can do that," Johnson said.

And Noah felt like he'd made it over another hurdle. Only a million more to go.

Chapter Seven

The next couple of days were filled with cleaning up, fortifying the building, and gathering information on the gang who were after Annabelle. Thanks to his injuries, Noah hadn't been much use with the more physical jobs, so he'd focused on research and strategy —with the assistance of Evan, who'd fast revealed himself to be a certified computer genius.

Together, they'd not only managed to get the large open-plan space that used to be two decent-sized offices into shape but had also filled a whiteboard with information their team would need. Noah was pleased with their temporary office space. It took up about two-thirds of the second floor, with old desks arranged down the center of the room and a row of tables stretching around one corner, sporting a state-of-the-art computer setup. Above the monitors, a handwritten sign tacked to the shabby beige wall read: Evan's Domain. Don't Touch.

Sheer blinds covered all the windows, letting in a diffused light but keeping out prying eyes. The setup reminded Noah of a police station bullpen in Atlantic City, making him feel right at home. The conference room the London office used for briefings had always been a little too formal for his liking. And unlike their UK team leader, Rochelle didn't hide away in a private office. She wanted to be right in the center of things with everyone else.

New office, new team, new dynamics. It would take some getting used to. Although, unlike some of the other team members, Noah had worked this way before his time in London, so it was easier for him to adapt. Violet, on the other hand, kept muttering about how unnatural it was that Rochelle had a desk beside everyone else.

"How are the cameras looking?" Noah asked Evan as he came up behind his "control center"—his terminology, not Noah's.

"Great." Evan motioned to the bank of monitors in front of him. "They're all on separate systems, so if one's knocked out, we can still see the rest. Also"—he swiveled in his state-of-the-art gaming chair—"I took the liberty of installing a second system, using tiny hidden cameras. Their range is limited, but if something happens, we'll at least have eyes on all the main spaces."

"Good thinking," Noah said.

The triplets were growing on him. Their morality might be questionable, but there was no denying they were intelligent men who weren't afraid of hard work.

"We have sound everywhere too, right?" Noah asked. He didn't want a repeat of his experience in the panic room.

"Sound's sorted." Evan tapped some keys, and a blueprint of the building's layout appeared on one of the screens. "Harris and Logan are finishing up the wiring on those doors you wanted fitted with remote locking systems. I've installed the app to control the locks and access the surveillance feeds on everyone's phones—except for Officer

Lee's." He winced. "Sorry. Habit. She won't hand over her phone."

"I'll talk to her." Although there was a good chance several of them would have to hold her down and take the phone from her. Violet didn't play well with others. Noah pointed to another screen. "I see Rodrigo's done with the panic room."

Evan nodded. "Reinforced walls and door. As well as a mini security hub, just in case. He's a handy guy—I mean, handy man type guy, you know, with tools and stuff."

"I do know." Noah hid a smile.

"You still want a lockable weapons cabinet in there?"

"Absolutely. Has Katrina ordered one?"

"I don't know, but I'll check." Evan scribbled on the paper notepad beside him. Something his London counterpart would have considered sacrilege when there was a computer right in front of him.

Rochelle walked into the room, drawing their attention. She held her phone to her ear and had a frown on her face.

"No," she said. "She isn't awake yet. She's been drifting in and out of consciousness for the past two days. I told you I would call your office as soon as she's coherent." She paused, listening to what had to be the ADA. The woman had called several times a day for updates on her witness. "Yes, we have a nurse coming in each day to give her pain meds and fluids. She's improving, but she isn't well yet." Another pause, during which Rochelle's lips thinned. "I understand that you've hired us to do a job, and we're doing it. Your witness is safe. I'll call you when she wakes." She ended the call.

"The ADA wants you to wake Annabelle?" Noah asked as Rochelle wandered over to the whiteboard he'd filled with information on the Demon Brothers.

Rochelle scoffed. "She wants her to be medicated so she's aware enough to talk to the ADA. I keep telling her that Annabelle's illness needs to run its course. She isn't listening. The trial is in two weeks, and she wants to prep her witness. How is she today anyway?"

"Better." Noah joined her at the whiteboard. "She managed some chicken soup last night, and I think the fever's passed. She was more coherent the last time we helped her to the bathroom. I suspect it's just exhaustion that's making her sleep now."

"Good. That's good." She pointed to the photos of Eddie Hanson, the leader of the Demon Brothers motorcycle gang. "The ADA still has eyes on him. He isn't lying low, which makes it easy to keep tabs on his activities. Eddie's well aware there's a team following him, though. He laughs and waves in their direction."

"Mocking them."

"Yeah."

"I don't like that he's out on bail," Noah said. "But honestly, a guy like him could organize a hit from prison anyway. Weird that he didn't do the job himself last time."

"He's too smart for that." Rochelle sat at her desk, her attention still on the board. "He doesn't think like your usual gang leader. When he was in high school, they tested his IQ, and he scored in the MENSA range. I read his file. He was on track for a full scholarship to an Ivy League school if he wanted it. Instead, he joined the local branch of the Demons and rose straight to the top. There's a reason they haven't been able to take him down until now. Not only does he rule with violence and fear. He's also too smart to get caught red-handed."

"Except for the hit Annabelle witnessed," Noah reminded her.

Rochelle glanced into her empty coffee mug before getting up to refill it from the pot on the table behind her. "It's a miracle Annabelle saw anything. I had Violet and Rodrigo canvas the immediate area. This is the only residential building within a four-block radius. All the businesses on these two streets"—she gestured to the streets that made up the corner where the warehouse sat—"keep regular hours. A lot of them start work even earlier than that and close by midafternoon. This area's a graveyard by early evening. There's no reason for anyone to be here after that. The nearest evening activity is three blocks away, where that little nightclub and the bowling alley sit. The chances of anyone seeing the Demon Brothers execute a man around here must be about one in a billion." With her mug refilled, she returned to her desk.

"And Annabelle didn't just see it." Noah pulled up a chair near her. "She took photos. Bad luck for the Demon Brothers."

Rochelle sipped her coffee and grimaced. "Did we buy the cheapest beans possible? This tastes like coffee-flavored dirt."

Noah grinned. "You sent the Scots shopping. They're big tea drinkers in Scotland, not coffee. Last time I was in Glasgow, they were drinking instant coffee."

"That's just wrong." Rochelle put down her mug. "Next time, I send an American." She leaned forward, forearms resting on her knees as she considered what they'd learned about the gang. "Even if we get Annabelle through the trial, I'm not sure she'll be safe afterward. Eddie Hanson's an evil son of a bitch who delights in revenge. He'd take her out just for the pleasure of knowing she'd paid for putting him in prison."

Noah's stomach lurched as his gaze shot to the storage

room where Annabelle slept. The urge to jump up and stand over her, gun ready to deal with the threat, was almost too overwhelming to resist. He tore his eyes away and looked back at Rochelle.

"Witness protection program?" Even he knew it was a foolish suggestion. There was no way they'd convince Annabelle to move from her comfort zone to somewhere she wasn't familiar with, purely to be safe.

Rochelle shook her head. "All we can do is ensure this place is as secure as it can be. We can't watch over her forever."

It was on the tip of his tongue to protest. "Then we hope he loses interest in her. He'll have enough to deal with fighting for himself. This is a death penalty state. There's a good chance the ADA will request it."

"You could sit around hoping things go your way," an English-accented voice said from the doorway, making them spin toward the speaker. Noah had his gun drawn and pointed at the newcomer before he realized who stood there. Abasi Otieno, the final member of their team, looked amused to see Noah armed. "Just put a bullet in his head and be done with it," he said.

Rochelle got to her feet, frowning as Noah put away his weapon. "That's not how we do things around here, Mr. Otieno. Nice of you to join us. You're over a week late."

If Abasi was bothered by her reprimand, it didn't show. Dressed in a bespoke suit, the elegant black man sauntered into the room, his eyes scanning the space as though assessing every weak point and exit possibility. His every movement spoke of a man used to action. One who was fit, capable, and could take care of himself. From his shaven head to his thousand-dollar shoes, Abasi exuded danger.

Flashing a charming smile, he held out a hand to

Rochelle. "Ms. Davis," he said, "I'm afraid business delayed me."

"In a place where there were no phones?" Rochelle shook his hand, showing no sign of intimidation.

"None that I wanted to use." Abasi shrugged before nodding at Noah. "Good to see a familiar face. Not sure about the setup, though. I liked the London office better. Chelsea was a classier area, and the townhouse had charm."

"This is temporary," Rochelle said before Noah could reply. "We're protecting a witness."

"I know." Abasi unbuttoned his suit jacket and helped himself to a chair. He crossed his legs, appearing relaxed. Only a trained eye would make out the shoulder holster under his tailored jacket. "Annabelle Simmons, thirty-two. Witness to a Demon Brothers hit. Should have been taken into protective custody in a safe house somewhere, but her agoraphobia won't allow it. She's been in and out of it from a fever since the Brothers shot up her loft. Benson Security has moved in and turned the warehouse into a fort, hoping to keep her alive until the trial in two weeks. The police and prosecutor's office can't be trusted because someone is selling information. And Noah here got shot up in the last gun battle. Did I miss anything?"

There was a moment of stunned silence until Evan breathed an awe-filled "wow" and broke it.

Rochelle slammed her palms on the desk in front of her. "How the hell do you know all that?"

Abasi's eyes were cold and hard even though he smiled. "I just told you. There's a leak in Houston's law enforcement community. Word's spreading."

"To a London mobster?" Rochelle demanded.

"*Former* mobster." Abasi smiled again. "Although, I'll always be a Londoner. Here's the thing about the world's seedy underbelly, former FBI Agent Davis, it's a small community. If we don't know each other by name, we've heard of each other. News of the Demon Brothers and their business interests reached London years ago. They wanted to expand their network into Europe and sent out feelers. So, yes, people talk—even to a former mobster—and lately, they've been talking about the Houston gang who could be taken down by a housebound comic book artist. And, just so you know, nobody thinks Benson Security has a chance in hell of doing its job."

"Well, you'd better hope we do because you're a part of Benson Security now too, Mr. Otieno." Rochelle's words dripped with ice. "Aren't you?" It was a challenge.

"Please, call me Abasi. After all, we're on the same team." Abasi widened his hands in a gesture resembling surrender. "We're all part of Benson Security. Trust me when I say that Lake Benson has my loyalty."

The unspoken words *"for now"* hung in the air between them.

"You put any of your teammates in danger, and I will take you out myself." Rochelle's words were low, her tone a promise. "Do you understand?"

"I wouldn't have it any other way." Abasi stood. "So, I gather we can take assassination off the table as an option. What other ideas do you have for dealing with the Demon Brothers?" He glanced around the office space. "I'm hoping one of those options isn't just sitting around waiting for them to attack again."

"We're still gathering data and fortifying the building," Rochelle said, her voice tight. "The plan is not to deal with the Demon Brothers unless absolutely necessary. We're on protection duty, which means keeping the witness safe and alive until she can testify. Now that you're here, you can help patrol the perimeter and keep an eye out for trouble. Noah will fill you in on what you need to do. How did you get into the building anyway?"

"Violet let me in." Abasi strolled over to the whiteboard.

"Of course she did. I need to go have a word with her," Rochelle said as she headed for the door. "Nobody gets in or out of this building without me being informed first." She looked back at Noah. "Set him up with somewhere to sleep. It's getting late."

"No need," Abasi said. "I've taken a suite at the Four Seasons."

"Of course you have." Rochelle opened the door. "Wouldn't want any of your ill-gotten gains going to waste now, would we?" She disappeared into the hallway.

"I don't think the boss likes me," Abasi said as he watched her leave.

"Well," Noah said. "You have been a bit of an ass."

Evan sucked in a breath, reminding Noah he was still in the room. The young guy looked halfway between shocked by Noah's audacity and awestruck by Abasi.

Abasi ignored the triplet. "It comes with the territory," he told Noah. "Not a lot of social skills taught in the thug life."

Evan barked out a laugh, then looked stunned that he'd done so. Mumbling something about needing to talk to his brothers, he hurried from the room.

"I think you've impressed the youngster," Noah said dryly.

Abasi glanced around the room before speaking again. "I don't want to impress anyone," he said quietly. "I would have been here at the same time as everyone else, but I had to clear up some issues with what remained of the James Family."

Noah sobered. The James Family was the mob that had tried to kill their London computer expert and had succeeded in killing her brother. The same mob Abasi had systematically dismantled after dealing with its leader.

"Got it sorted now?"

Abasi nodded grimly. "The James Family is history."

Noah studied him for a moment. "Is joining Benson Security some kind of penance?" He decided that being straightforward was the best approach.

"No." Abasi stared into the distance for a second. "It's a new start."

He couldn't have said anything that Noah would understand more. "Then we work." He pointed at the board. "Let me fill you in on what you don't already know."

"Pretty sure that isn't possible." Abasi grinned.

"See, there you are, being an ass again." Noah tapped a photo and launched into what they'd learned about the person in the picture.

For the first time since meeting the man, Noah felt like Abasi might grow on him. Hell, he might even prove to be an asset to the team. If he was even capable of being part of a team. And if he managed to get Rochelle to trust him.

Seemed there were a whole lot of ifs when it came to the Houston office.

Chapter Eight

Annabelle woke slowly, feeling as though her muscles had forgotten how to work properly. She blinked several times, and as her brain began to clear, a sign on the ceiling above her came into focus. Written in purple marker pen on a large sheet of paper, it read: Don't panic. You're on the second floor of your building. You've been sick.

What the...?

Gingerly, she maneuvered herself onto her elbows and looked around. She was on a mattress on the floor of one of the second-floor office storage rooms, and a man was sitting near her. He was asleep in an old armchair that'd been down in the shop the last time she saw it, his legs stretched out in front of him—his feet almost touching her makeshift bed. He was dressed in worn-in jeans, an old T-shirt with a message too faded to read, and a scuffed pair of boots. A firearm sat on the little table beside him. Above his head, another notice was pinned to the wall: Noah. Protector. The DA's office hired him and our security team.

Noah?

As she stared at his face, trying to remember if she'd met him, a vague memory of a bulldog dressed as a man fighting in a war zone popped into her head.

Helpful...

But what really confused her was she'd woken in a room that wasn't her bedroom, with a stranger beside her, and yet she wasn't afraid.

She did a quick mental survey of her internal state—no racing heartbeat, no desire to run, no stark terror.

Huh?

Cautiously, because her muscles were so stiff, she sat and swiveled until her feet rested on the ground. She wore pajamas. Which was strange because she didn't own any. These had a Wonder Woman emblem printed on them and were at least a size too big.

"I must be dreaming," she muttered, because nothing made sense.

"Sorry to disappoint you," a deep voice said, making her eyes snap up to the man in the chair. "But this isn't a dream. It's great to see you awake, though. Good morning."

His smile could have melted ice cream in winter. It transformed his rugged face into something sensual and sexy as hell.

She swallowed hard, her mouth dry. "Noah?" She pointed at the sign.

He nodded as he sat up and then reached for the bottle of water at his side. After he'd unscrewed the cap, he handed it to her. "Doc says you need to keep your fluids up."

Grateful for the water, Annabelle sipped it as she studied him. "Have we met?" she asked once she'd drunk her fill.

His smile turned wry. "Oh yeah, we've met. You were a

little out of it with a fever and seemed convinced I was a hallucination. Before you passed out, that is."

Flickers of memories that made little sense danced before her eyes. "You have two sons," she said hesitantly, not really sure how she knew that.

"Yep."

Noah smiled some more. It was distracting and had a strange effect on her stomach—like someone had switched on a soda machine inside her, filling her up with bubbles. She glanced at the water bottle and wondered if it was just a bad case of gas.

Sounds began to register, and she noticed voices coming from the other side of the storage room door. She frowned at it, trying to make sense of her strange situation. "Are your sons here?"

"Nope, they're in Atlantic City, visiting their grand-parents."

The image of a photo surfaced in her head. The perfect American family, all smiling for the camera. "With your wife?" she asked.

A flash of soul-deep sadness appeared in his eyes before disappearing almost as fast. "My wife died five years ago. Cancer"

"Oh, I'm sorry." Her cheeks flushed with an embarrass-ment that made no sense.

"You didn't know." Noah rested his forearms on his knees and leaned toward her. "The voices you can hear belong to my team. We're with Benson Security. We specialize in keeping people safe and, well, some other stuff, but the main thing for you to know is that your assistant DA hired us to take care of you."

"I got that much." She pointed to the sign on the ceiling.

Now it was his turn to look embarrassed. "One of my

younger teammates was worried you'd wake up and start screaming. He figured a bit of information might head that off."

Annabelle shrugged. "I think the signs are cute. And they worked."

His soulful eyes captured hers, making it hard to look away. It was as though the surrounding air had become charged. If she'd drawn it, she would have made the room's background dark, then had threadlike lines of gold darting between them.

She blinked, and the moment was gone. "Why did the DA's office hire you?" she asked before drinking more water.

He ran a hand over his short, sandy hair and winced. There was a nasty-looking wound where some of his hair should have been.

"What happened to your head?" she asked, not waiting for his reply to her first question.

"First," he said, "either the DA's office or the cops has a leak, and the guys you're testifying against found out your location. Second, they came to stop you from testifying, shot out a monitor screen, and part of it embedded itself in my head."

A wave of memory almost knocked her back onto the mattress. "The panic room! Gunfire! My apartment!"

Annabelle shot to her feet, threw the door open, and ran out into a room full of people. She screeched to a halt as they all turned to smile at her.

"Nice jammies," a tall, redheaded man said with a grin.

Two exact copies of him stood at his side.

And that's when she knew what had happened. Her greatest fear had come true.

She'd completely lost her mind.

As Annabelle started to shake, Noah stepped in front of her. He gently grasped her shoulders, making her look up at him.

"Take a breath," he said calmly. "It's a lot to take in."

She took several breaths. "Tell me the truth," she whispered, "am I in an asylum and suffering from delusions? Am I hallucinating? Did I have a psychotic break?"

"No," he said firmly. "You had the flu, and you've been out of it for three days. But you aren't imagining anything."

She leaned closer to him. "I'm seeing three versions of the same man."

Noah fought to hide a smile. "They're triplets."

Her hazel eyes stared at him. "How do I know this is real and not some psychotic delusion? It's just like that Buffy episode where she's in a mental institute, dreaming about life in Sunnydale. That episode shattered my faith in the Buffyverse. After that, I wasn't sure if it was real or not."

Noah's lips twitched. "I'll help you out here. Buffy isn't real. The triplets are. They're part of my team."

He moved to her side. But it wasn't close enough to give Annabelle the reassurance she craved, so she closed the distance even further, almost plastering herself to his side.

"Annabelle," Noah said as he gestured to the people dotted around the room, "meet the Benson Security team tasked with keeping you alive and well. Introduce yourselves, guys."

"I'm Harris," the man who'd commented on her pajamas said, "and these are my brothers, Evan and Logan. You don't need your eyesight tested. We're identical triplets. We're also IVF babies. I'm pretty sure our mother ordered us up this way on purpose just so we'd have to spend our lives telling people they weren't seeing things. Her sense of humor's dodgy at best." His broad Scottish accent lent itself to the surrealness of her situation. "Evan is our computer geek, Logan's our procurement officer, and I'm public relations." His descriptions seemed to amuse his brothers.

"You're... from Scotland?" she asked.

"Aye, but we work here now." Harris' smile was dazzling, but it didn't have the same effect on her as Noah's.

"I'm Violet Lee." A petite Asian woman, looking to be in her early thirties, stepped forward as she spoke. She had the same accent as the triplets and looked angry. "I used to be a police detective, but now I work for Benson Security."

Annabelle looked up at Noah. "Is everyone on this team from Scotland?"

"Only the crazy ones."

A confident and polished African American woman in a gray business suit approached them. Her curly black hair sat neatly around her face, and the lines around her eyes testified to maturity and experience.

The woman held out her hand. "I'm Rochelle Davis, former FBI, and I head up this team. We're very pleased you're feeling better, Annabelle, and want you to know we'll do everything in our power to keep you safe and comfortable. You are very brave to testify, and we have a lot of respect for your courage."

Annabelle shook her hand. She felt solid. And real. It was reassuring and gave her the confidence to ask the question that terrified her: "You won't try to take me away from here, will you?"

"No." Rochelle smiled warmly. "We've turned this building into your safe house instead." She gestured behind her to the large open-plan space, which was double the size Annabelle remembered. "I'm afraid we took some liberties and set ourselves up in here. I promise we'll put everything back as we found it when it's time to leave."

"Oh, come on," Evan groaned. "It was a pain in the backside taking that partition wall down. Please tell me you don't intend for us to put it back up."

"Actually," Annabelle said before his boss could reply, "I like the space better this way."

"That's it," Logan said to his brothers. "She's perfect. I call dibs on her."

Annabelle's eyes went wide as Noah raised his voice. "Nobody's calling dibs on the client." He looked down at her. "They're idiots. Ignore them."

To Annabelle's surprise, a giggle escaped her.

As he gave her a rueful smile, a gorgeous, tall Latino man crossed the room.

"I'm Rodrigo De la Cruz." He held out his hand. "Noah's right," he said with a faint Spanish accent. "If one of the toddlers bothers you, talk to an adult in the room, and we'll deal with them."

"I get the feeling people are picking on us," Logan said to Harris.

"It's insulting," Harris agreed.

The door to the office space opened, and another woman walked in. She was graceful and painfully thin. Her chestnut hair was cropped to a feathered cap that set off her delicate bone structure. She wore a high-necked blouse, wide-legged pants, and designer running shoes. In her hand was a folder and an iPad.

When she saw Annabelle, she smiled. "You're awake. Has anyone given you something to eat or drink yet? Or shown you where your clothes are?"

"Uh, Noah gave me water." Annabelle glanced down at her pajamas. "Clothes would be good."

"Typical." The new woman turned to Rochelle. "Do

you need her for anything, or can I get her cleaned up and fed before you brief her?"

"She's all yours," Rochelle said. "Annabelle, meet Katrina Raast. Our resident project manager and reminder that we all need to learn some manners. We have another team member, Abasi, but he's patrolling right now. You can meet him later."

Katrina appeared to tense at the mention of her last teammate, but she quickly recovered and handed the folder to Rochelle before smiling at Annabelle. "Come on, we've stocked the kitchen on this floor, so I can cook you some breakfast while you get showered and changed. There are clothes for you in the bathroom down the hall. You must be desperate to get cleaned up after being in bed for days."

Annabelle sucked in a breath as she reached up to touch her hair. If it looked half as bad as it felt, she was sporting a greasy, knotted mess. How humiliating!

Noah squeezed her shoulder. "You're fine. You look exactly like someone should after they've been ill. Go with Katrina, and we'll talk soon."

Annabelle hesitated, suddenly anxious at the thought of having him out of her sight. A strange montage of memories flashed through her mind—Noah giving her medicine, feeding her soup, mopping her brow...

"You took care of me," she said, awed. It had been a long time since anyone had been there to care for her when she was ill. However, the awe was soon shattered by another thought that heated her cheeks. "Who changed my clothes?"

"That would be me," Katrina said. "I apologize for the Wonder Woman pj's, but I shopped in a hurry."

"Oh." Annabelle's shoulders relaxed. "Thank you."

"Come on," Katrina said. "Let's get something other than chicken soup inside of you."

Annabelle found herself looking up at Noah for reassurance.

The corner of his mouth quirked. "You're safe in this building, and Katrina might look delicate, but she can shoot circles around anyone in this room."

A little embarrassed, Annabelle reluctantly left the warmth of his side Katrina. "What do you mean, cook me something down here? I can get something from my kitchen upstairs after I've cleaned up."

Katrina's face was filled with sympathy as Annabelle walked with her out into the hallway. "Your apartment sustained some damage during the gunfight, but the cleanup crew's been in, and we're just finishing up in there. It'll be good as new by the end of the day. Better even. We've upgraded your security system and fortified your panic room—so bullets won't get through the walls in the future."

Annabelle tripped over her own feet. "Gunfight? Bullets in the future? Exactly what state is my home in?"

She was almost afraid to go see. The news was hard to believe. Everything was. There was a security team in her building. Workmen in her loft. And tales of near-death experiences she could recall only as a haze-filled dream.

"It's okay." Katrina patted her shoulder. "I promise you'll feel safe and secure in your home. We won't let anything happen to you. Don't try to process everything all at once. For now, just focus on getting cleaned up and having breakfast. You'll need your strength to deal with all the information that will come your way today." Her lashes lowered as she spoke. "I know how hard it is to get your head around all of this, but the best way to do that is to focus on one task at a time." She took a deep breath, looked up at Annabelle, and smiled. "And right now, your priority is definitely a shower."

"I smell, huh?" Annabelle tried to sniff herself, but she was too close to judge.

Katrina held up her index finger and thumb, her eyes sparkling. "Teeny bit."

"Shower it is, then. But afterward, I have questions. Lots of questions."

"And we'll answer them all. Now hurry up. Food will be ready when you're done."

"Thanks, Katrina," Annabelle called as she entered the old bathroom.

"It's my pleasure," came the reply.

After steeling herself against the grime of the unused room, Annabelle was pleasantly surprised. The bathroom had been thoroughly cleaned—in fact, it gleamed. A small stool held some of her clothes, folded neatly and freshly laundered. The spotless shower boasted a new showerhead, and there were plenty of products lined up on the shelf. Warm, fluffy towels hung on a heated towel rack that looked brand new.

Noah's team had taken liberties while she'd slept. Rearranging offices, tearing down partitions, and adding the things they needed. She stood for a moment, waiting for outrage at their behavior to hit, but it didn't. Instead, she found herself experiencing a sense of wonder.

It'd been a long time since the building was full of people, not since her aunt died and her curio shop closed, and Annabelle had gotten used to being alone. Sure, she chatted with the delivery people who came to her door and had online friends. Some of those friends visited and even stayed over, but not as frequently as she'd have liked. In truth, the corridors of the old warehouse often echoed around her.

But not today.

Today, the place was abuzz with people and activity.

It was a shame it'd taken a threat to her life for her world to expand. Annabelle shuddered at the memory of bullets flying but tamped down her fear. She was home. Surrounded by security specialists. Safe.

She hoped.

Chapter Nine

"This is *not* why I hired Benson Security."

The crisp, clipped tones of Harris County's assistant district attorney halted Annabelle as she approached the door to the office Benson Security had claimed. Although clean, fed, and watered, she still wasn't ready to deal with Ms. Grant. The woman was single-minded and intimidating.

"There's no time to waste," Margaret Grant said. "You have to get Annabelle out of here and into a safe house today."

"Ms. Grant," came the calm, soothing tones of the Benson Security boss, "as I told you on the phone, several times, Annabelle's physician strongly recommends that we don't remove her from this building. Her mental well-being is tied to remaining here. She's convinced that Annabelle may well have a full-blown psychotic break if forced to leave."

Out of sight on the other side of the door, Annabelle cringed. Great, now everyone knew exactly how crazy she was.

"That's a risk we have to take," Margaret said forcefully. "It's either her mental health or her actual life. Someone's feeding information to Eddie Hanson. We don't know who or whether they're in the police ranks or in my office. All we know for certain is that Eddie will use that information to ensure Annabelle doesn't testify. Hanson's a cold-blooded killer, the leader of the most depraved motorcycle gang in the country. This is our best chance to get him off the street and dismantle the Demon Brothers for good. Do you understand how important this is? It isn't only Annabelle's life or well-being that's at risk here. It's every single person the gang will torture, abuse, intimidate, and murder if we don't go to trial."

"I am well aware of the stakes," Rochelle said evenly.

A hand came to rest on Annabelle's shoulder, making her start. She turned to find Noah smiling at her and relaxed.

"Sorry," he said. "I thought you heard me."

Her cheeks heated. "I was eavesdropping," she confessed.

He squeezed her shoulder before dropping his hand, and Annabelle immediately missed the physical connection. "Try not to let it get to you. The ADA's focus is the goals of her job, which affects how she sees everything around her. Just remember that her goals are just that—*hers*. You need to think about what you're comfortable doing and do that. It might make other people unhappy, but that's their problem. Don't let them pressure you."

"If I don't testify, other people will suffer." Her stomach clenched at the thought. "I couldn't live with knowing I could have helped them and chose not to."

Noah's mouth quirked at the corner again. "I was

talking about you leaving the building or staying. Never once occurred to me that you'd renege on testifying."

That surprised her. "You don't even know me. What on earth gives you that much faith in my decision-making process?"

"Well, there was our life-and-death situation in the panic room. Which, by the way, wasn't much of a panic room. Those walls were like cardboard. But I digress." His dark eyes twinkled. "You've also been out for a few days. I got bored, so I read your comics. You can tell a lot about a person by what they write."

Now her cheeks burned so hot he must have felt the heat from where he stood. She shuffled uncomfortably, unsure where to look or what to do. Apart from her agent and editor, she wasn't used to meeting anyone who read her work—at least, not in the flesh.

"Uh, um." She cleared her throat. "You read my comics?"

"Most of us have. You've gained a few fans."

"Are you one? I mean, did you like them?"

"Hell yes," he said readily, and a wave of relief swept over her. "What's not to like? The heroine's smart, skilled, and sexy as hell. And the bad guys get the justice they deserve. That's my kind of story."

Annabelle was painfully aware that she was the antithesis of her comic book persona. Jade Justice was everything Noah described. And more. While Annabelle had no fighting skills, was terrified of stepping outside her front door, and wouldn't know how to be sexy if she tried. Thankfully, it'd been her experience that you could learn almost everything from the internet. Somebody out there had a site called "Seduction for Dummies," she was sure of it. What she wasn't sure about was why on earth she was thinking like this when her life was at risk. Being sexy should be the last thing on her mind.

"Come on." Noah placed his hand on the small of her back, making her shiver and yet again distracting her from the matter at hand—her life. "We'd better get in there before Violet shoots the assistant DA."

"Not Rochelle?" Annabelle asked curiously. The security team was a mystery, and she found she wanted to know everything about them. Or possibly just sit in a corner and watch them for hours on end. Maybe with popcorn.

"Rochelle has too much self-control to snap. Whereas Violet's trigger-happy and has the patience of a two-year-old."

"Should she be armed?" Annabelle lowered her voice as they entered the room and heads turned toward them.

"You try taking her gun from her and see what happens," Noah muttered.

Annabelle glanced at Violet's face and silently agreed that taking her weapon wouldn't be wise. The small Scot glared at the ADA and, as she did so, seemed to increase in size. It made Annabelle's fingers itch to draw her. She'd make her a morphing superhero. One who doubled in size and strength when triggered. She'd embody the qualities of fierceness and determination. And perhaps be a little too eager to shoot first and ask questions later.

"Annabelle." Margaret rushed over to her, breaking the spell of her imagination. She placed a hand on Annabelle's arm. "How are you? I asked Ms. Davis to call me the second you woke up. We've all been so worried about you."

Annabelle took a step back, the lawyer's intensity making her nervous. "Better now, thanks. Still a bit weak, but fine."

"Good, good." Margaret took the hint and removed her

hand before folding her arms over the jacket of her severe black skirt suit. "Then we should talk about getting you to a safe house." She waved a hand to indicate the building. "Obviously, you can't stay here now. Not after that attack in your apartment."

She delivered her words with such conviction that Annabelle began to shake again. Every instinct within her told her to run. To hide. To get away from the threat embodied in the smiling persona of the assistant district attorney. She stumbled back and stepped on Noah's foot.

He grunted.

"Sorry," she muttered, feeling foolish.

"It's fine," he murmured against her ear. "Just remember what I said, okay? You're in control here. It's your decision as to how we proceed."

His words gave her confidence as she addressed the ADA. "I-I can't leave. I need to stay here."

Margaret threw up her hands in exasperation, making Annabelle break out in a cold sweat. The ADA had all the power in this situation. At a snap of her fingers, a station full of police would do her bidding. They'd take her away.

Outside.

Where she wasn't safe.

Where anyone could snatch her from the street and...

A hand settled on her shoulder. "That was then," Noah said against her ear. "This is now. Be in the present. The ADA can talk, but she can't force you to do what she wants."

Annabelle took a deep breath and refocused on what Margaret was saying.

"There were so many bullet holes in your panic room wall that it was completely shredded," Margaret said. "This building isn't safe. Be reasonable about this, Annabelle.

Your life is in danger, and you must allow this team to take you somewhere safe."

Annabelle glanced at the faces of the security team as they watched her from around the room. She saw no judgment in any of their expressions. They were simply waiting to hear what she had to say.

"This is your decision, Annabelle," Rochelle said, earning a furious glare from the ADA.

Annabelle turned to Katrina. "Is my loft fixed? Can I move back in?"

"Are you insane?" Margaret demanded.

Annabelle bit her lip while keeping her attention on Katrina.

The woman consulted her iPad and answered as though the ADA hadn't spoken. "There's just some tidying left to do. We had to move some of your belongings to complete the work we needed to do. The last big thing was the mirrored glass shutters for the windows. We didn't have time to replace your window glass with bulletproof panes, and Noah thought you'd hate it if you had to keep the shades pulled all the time, so we came up with a temporary solution. The mirrored glass will ensure privacy while allowing you to look outside."

Annabelle blushed, oddly touched. "He's right. I'd have hated it if my view was blocked."

It worried her how easily she'd become dependent on a man she barely knew. Noah was a solid presence that seemed to anchor her in this scary new world.

"Mirrored glass won't stop bullets." Margaret sounded exasperated. "Or prevent another attack."

"No, but that's why she has us." Violet continued to glare at the lawyer.

Menace practically vibrated from her. Enough to make even the ADA notice and put more distance between them.

"I realize we're in Texas." Margaret's tone dripped with sarcasm. "But I don't want a replay of the Alamo on my hands. If you recall, *that* siege didn't end well for the good guys."

Evan's hand shot up as though he were still in school. Annabelle appreciated that he was easy to identify by his quirky, some might say bad, taste in clothing. Otherwise, she would never have known which triplet was talking.

"I know this," he said, looking pleased with himself. "William Travis and the Bowie knife guy—not to be confused with David Bowie, the singer died defending an old church from an attack by the Mexican army. They were outnumbered and hadn't bothered to stockpile supplies beforehand. There's also something about a cannon firing horseshoes and nails. And then a general called Houston— gonna go out on a limb here and say this city's named after him—fought the Mexicans by rallying his troops with the battle cry: '*Remember the Alamo.*' I think it's a song too."

"Well done." Harris patted his brother on the head. "You get a gold star."

Evan beamed.

Margaret Grant clearly wasn't amused. "I can see I made a mistake by hiring Benson Security to keep my witness safe." She turned to face Rochelle. "Please pack up your belongings. You're no longer needed. My office will take over from here."

Noah stepped up beside Annabelle, standing close enough for her to be aware of just how tense he'd become. "You mean the office with the leak that puts your client in danger?"

The ADA glared at him. "My office has been protecting witnesses for a very long time, Mr. Merchant. We know what we're doing." She focused on Annabelle. "I'm afraid you no longer have a choice in the matter. I'll have a detail sent over to take you into protective custody while we await trial."

Could she do that? Annabelle's mouth went dry. And then Noah moved closer to her, offering his support and strength. The eyes of the room were on her. Waiting for her to say something. Clearly, they believed the next move was hers, not theirs.

Taking what little courage she had in hand, Annabelle wet her dry lips before speaking. "If you do that, I'll refuse to testify," she bluffed.

She held her breath, waiting to see if Margaret could tell she was lying.

The lawyer's eyes were hard as she studied Annabelle. "All it would take is a subpoena to compel you to testify. And with a warrant, I can have you taken into protective custody until you do so."

Annabelle sucked in a breath as Rochelle stepped forward, holding out her hands as if to break up a fight. "It would be better for everyone if we didn't let our tempers get the best of us," she said evenly before looking at Annabelle. "You want to testify, don't you?"

"Yes," she said in a rush, unable to look at the determined ADA.

Rochelle turned her attention to Margaret. "And you'd like to have a credible witness on the stand rather than one who's medically unfit to testify, right?"

Margaret sniffed and nodded.

"Then it's clear that the best plan of action is for Annabelle to stay in the place that ensures her mental well-being and makes it possible for you to get the result you need. If you force her out of here, you won't get what you want. We *all* have to compromise so everyone gets what they need in this situation. Wouldn't you agree?"

She sounded so reasonable that Annabelle found herself nodding.

Margaret, however, wasn't as easily swayed. "I refuse to use my budget to finance a bunch of cowboys who've already put my witness in danger."

"First," Rochelle said, "we didn't put her in danger. Your office did. Second, we kept her safe—"

"And third," Logan said, "thanks for calling us cowboys. Now I feel like a real Texan." His grin was wide, but his eyes were sharp.

His humor did just enough to defuse the tension in the room to the point where it wasn't about to explode.

"I'll pay them," Annabelle blurted out, literally making the decision as the words left her mouth.

Evan looked outraged. "Please tell me you don't plan on mortgaging this fine building to do it. You'd be putting your home at risk, and you don't want to miss out on living here. This area's great. A few streets over, there's a goth nightclub squished between an artist's studio and a retro bowling alley. You can buy Day of the Dead masks from the Mexican deli, and there's a cinema that shows only black-and-white movies—they even have a pianist for the silent ones. Everywhere you turn, there's something crazy going on. You can't jeopardize being a part of this community. It's totally cool."

His brothers groaned.

"What?" Evan demanded.

"She's a-gor-a-pho-bic." Logan stretched out the word. "So, carry on telling her about all the things she *can't* go outside to do, you numpty."

"Oh!" Evan's head turned beetroot as he grinned sheepishly at her. "Ah, well, there's also the swing upstairs. You should keep the building for that alone."

"Great save, bro." Harris shook his head in disgust.

Even though the topic was serious—the threat to her life —Annabelle couldn't help but be amused by the brothers. "The building isn't at risk. I have some money in the bank. I'm sure there's enough to pay for your services. If you're willing to stay on with me, that is."

"I vote yes." Evan's hand shot up again.

Rochelle smiled as she faced the ADA. "It seems we've found a solution. We will act as bodyguards until the trial. Answering to Annabelle, as she'll pay the bill."

Margaret pursed her lips in disgust. "Do you honestly think you're capable of keeping her safe?"

"Yes," Rochelle answered simply.

"I'll be talking to my boss about this." The ADA snatched up her purse and strode toward the doorway on her power heels. She stopped level with Annabelle on the way. "This decision's completely against my professional advice. You're putting your life in the hands of a team that I do not consider capable of protecting you."

"You know," Noah drawled, "you might want to do some background research on Lake Benson and his teams before you go jumping to any conclusions. We're the guys they call in when other security companies can't get the job done."

Margaret wasn't impressed. "I'll return to prep you for your testimony. Court is set for two weeks from today." With that, she sailed from the room.

Annabelle watched her go, wondering if her decision to hire Benson Security had been too hasty. What did she know about them—other than they'd kept her alive through an attack on her life and fed her chicken soup until she was well? These people were total strangers. They were also her only option to stay in her home.

"Don't worry," Rochelle said with a smile. "We actually do know what we're doing."

Noah bumped her shoulder again. "We'll keep you safe." It was a vow.

"Or die trying," Evan said cheerily.

The rest of the team turned on him with groans and orders to shut up.

And Annabelle found herself laughing.

Chapter Ten

The triplets had gone to fetch lunch—Tex-Mex from a food truck in Market Square Evan had been raving about—so Annabelle told Noah she wanted to check out her apartment. He said he'd go with her, telling her that the builders had gone, but there were some changes he needed to explain. And that, as her main bodyguard, he had no intention of leaving her side.

Honestly, that was okay with her. Noah was like a rock: steady and unmovable. He reminded her of the Thing from Marvel's Fantastic Four, ready to stand between his friends and their enemies as a wall of protection. As they climbed the stairs to her loft, he wondered what character he could embody in her graphic novels, her fingers itching to get to her drawing board.

"You look nervous," Noah said as they reached the door to her apartment.

"I don't have any clear memories of the place being destroyed, and I'm worried it won't look like home now."

"We kept it just the way you intended it to be... mostly." He smiled and pushed the door open.

Her stomach clenched tight, Annabelle entered her home—and took a deep breath. "It's okay," she said, relieved.

"Told you." Noah bumped against her.

"They're ugly, though." She pointed to one-way mirrored shutters on her windows. "Not that I don't appreciate them."

"It's cool, I understand. Just remember, they're only temporary. Once this situation's over, you can have them taken down."

"I am glad you came up with a way for me to see outside. Thanks for that."

"Team effort," he mumbled as he gestured to her work area. "Your phone was smashed, and your computers didn't survive their gunshot wounds. Although we managed to save the hard drive from one of them. I'm afraid there was nothing we could salvage from the rest of it."

Annabelle tried not to get emotional about the loss. They were machines and could be replaced. Still... her tech was her connection to the outside world, and now it was gone. "I back up everything to the cloud," she said, reaching desperately for that silver lining.

"Thought you might," Noah said. "You'll need to talk to your insurance company about replacing everything, but I don't see why you couldn't order new stuff in the meantime."

"Does insurance cover damage caused by a gun-toting gang?"

He shrugged. "Seeing as this is Texas, I'm gonna guess yes."

"I suppose I'll find out soon enough." She wandered further into the loft.

"Some of your drawings got trampled in the attack,"

Noah said. "But we didn't throw any away. We just piled them up on your desk."

Annabelle's heart ached as she ran her fingers over the comic book panel she'd been working on before her life went to hell. It was torn, crumpled, and dirty. Her artwork was her baby, and it hurt to see it damaged.

She became aware that Noah was watching her intently and cleared her throat. "This whole situation seems so surreal. I remember the attack only in weird flashes, like a movie trying to depict a drug high or something. There are random bits and pieces, but mostly it's distorted and out of focus and like it happened to someone else." She paused, her hand resting on the ruined drawing. "Now I'm here, seeing the aftermath of the assault, and I feel..."

"Vulnerable? Victimized? Unsafe?" Noah offered.

"Not unsafe, not with you and your team here. But definitely the other two." She gestured around the room. "This is meant to be my safe space, but it doesn't feel like that anymore."

"It will again," he said solemnly. "I promise you."

Annabelle nodded, although she wasn't sure she shared his confidence. How safe would she feel once the Benson Security team was gone and she was all alone in the building? She shuddered to think.

Noah touched her shoulder. "Are you okay?"

It was on the tip of her tongue to say yes because that's what you do when people ask, right? Instead, she gazed into his dark eyes and said, "I could really use a hug."

Noah smiled. "We're a full-service security agency. Hugs are included in the package," he said, and she stepped straight into his arms.

Annabelle was sure she should have felt ashamed for asking him to hold her, but she couldn't muster the energy.

She needed comfort, and she wanted it from the man who'd protected her when she was completely incapable of doing it herself. He'd been injured because of her. And even though she knew she was suffering from a touch of hero worship, she didn't care. Noah was a real-life hero, and she was grateful.

His arms felt good around her—firm and solid and real. She pressed her cheek to his chest and breathed deeply, letting his warmth seep into her. She could have stayed there forever.

"You know, if this is included in the service, and I'm paying your bill..." She grinned up at him. "Does that make you a gigolo?"

Noah's laughter vibrated throughout her body before he gave her one last squeeze and stepped away. "Come on," he said. "I need to explain where you're sleeping."

"In my bed, I hope."

"Sorry, your bed's gone. It was bullet-ridden. And a few of your plants didn't make it either. Everything in the panic room was shredded and had to be replaced. We fortified the walls and door while we fixed it up. Now that it's steel reinforced, it's much less likely to let bullets through than plasterboard," he said with disgust.

"You really weren't impressed with my panic room, were you?"

"Considering I nearly died in it, no."

"Fair point."

Annabelle tried not to let the big damage to her apartment get to her. The security team, along with the builders they'd vetted before hiring, had done a good job of cleaning up the place and getting it ready for her. The broken and missing items were, at the end of the day, only things. Most of them could be replaced or repaired. However, she wasn't sure it would be possible to fix the tear in her sense of security.

"Did my camera survive?" There was no sign of it.

"No, unfortunately. Some of your mementos, pictures, and books were damaged too." He pointed to the living area. "The TV's fine, though."

"As long as I can still watch Marvel movies, we're good." Annabelle tried to smile bravely but suspected she didn't quite pull it off.

She stepped around the glass brick wall into her empty sleeping area. "I'm going to need a bed. It was time to buy a new mattress anyway. So that's convenient." Putting a positive spin on the situation was proving harder than expected. "Where will I sleep until my new bed arrives?"

"Actually." Noah strode toward the panel entrance to the panic room. The mirror that'd once hung in front of it was gone, but the new door blended seamlessly into the wall. "I want you to sleep in here until this is over. It's the safest room in the building—now we've upgraded it. Your usual bedroom's a bit too exposed for my liking."

Curious, Annabelle followed him into the small room. It had been transformed since the last time she'd been in it. The larger space to her left now held a large bright yellow sofa bed made up with new navy blue bedding. To her right, where her desk used to stand, was a small kitchen area and a large built-in cabinet in the corner where they'd hidden from the bullets.

Noah pointed to the narrow space beside the sofa. "Folding stool and table for you to work at if needed." He gestured to the wall next to the door. "TV and security monitors." Lastly, he indicated to the large closet. "Toilet."

"Really?" Annabelle opened the closet door to find a compact bathroom, the kind you'd find in a motorhome.

There was a tiny sink, and a showerhead on the wall above the toilet turned the whole cubicle into a shower if needed. "Why are tiny things so fascinating?" she asked. "I love this."

He gestured to a button on the wall facing the open door. There was a small display panel above it, with a miniature keypad. "Press the button," he said.

She did so, and another sliding door silently opened into one of the guest bedrooms behind her loft area.

Noah came to stand beside her. "Imagine my surprise when we discovered two bedrooms and a bathroom behind the end wall of your loft. If I'd known we could have escaped that way and snuck down the fire escape stairs, things would have gone a little differently. I thought the doors beside your bed led to a bathroom and a closet, but nope—one led to a walk-through closet and bathroom, the other to the rest of your apartment."

"It is a big building." Annabelle stepped into the bedroom in the corner facing the street, with windows in two of its walls.

Noah indicated another small panel, identical to the one inside the panic room, on the wall of the guestroom. "That's the lockdown panel. You can use it inside the room to lock it tight. You can also lock it from the outside, if needed."

"In case you want to imprison me?" She cocked an eyebrow at him.

"In case you're incapacitated, and we need to secure you inside while we deal with a situation. We'll put an app on your new phone, when it arrives, that will let you override any locks in the building. You won't ever feel trapped."

She grinned at him. "You mean, more than I usually do?"

He had the grace to smile sheepishly.

Annabelle took pity on him and gestured around the guestroom. "This was my aunt's room." She pointed through the open door to a small hallway beyond. "My room faced this one, and I had full use of the bathroom between us." She gestured to the wall that backed onto the bathroom and closet accessed from the loft. "This used to be a door to her ensuite. When I renovated the living space and added a bedroom area to the loft, I moved the entrance to suit my new bedroom."

"I think I'd prefer to sleep in here rather than in the loft," Noah said. "I like walls in my bedroom—especially with two young boys in the house."

"Privacy isn't an issue when there's only you in the apartment." She cringed. That made her sound like Suzy No Friends. "When my friends stay over, they sleep in these guest rooms, and I have all the privacy I need out in the loft."

"What if they get up in the middle of the night to get a drink or a snack?"

"Usually, they're very respectful and quiet. Plus, it's not like I sleep naked or anything."

His smile was teasing. "Now *that* would definitely make for an interesting guest experience."

Annabelle's cheeks heated as she changed the subject. "Aunt Rose had a thing for pink chintz. This room looked like a Barbie bordello when she was alive."

Noah barked out a laugh. "Well, I'm glad the pink's gone now because this is where I'll be sleeping for the duration."

"Here?" The word came out as a squeak. "I mean, don't you have to go home to your sons at night?"

"Not right now. They're on an extended visit with their

grandparents. And I need to stick close to you at all times. Which means I'll sleep in here, and we'll keep the panic room door open between us, just in case."

Annabelle glanced back at the panic room. You could clearly see the sofa bed through the open door. If lying in it, she'd be able to see Noah in the guest room bed, and that felt a little too intimate. "I'm not sure I can sleep with someone staring at me."

"That's fine then because I'll be asleep too. No staring involved. Promise."

"Then why do you need the door open?"

"Because if anything happens, I need to get to your side as quickly as possible."

"It takes barely seconds to open the door," she pointed out.

"Yes, but if the door's closed, I can't tell if someone's in the panic room with you. We added soundproofing after that debacle with the gang attack. They could hear every sound coming from inside the room."

"Okay, I get that you hated my panic room, but why on earth would anybody be in there with me now?" Her eyebrows shot up. "Are you worried I plan to jump one of your teammates?"

Noah seemed stunned, but she carried on regardless.

"I know everybody thinks that because I've not left this warehouse for years, I don't see anyone. But I do. I socialize. My friends visit, and I've had relationships. I'm not desperate. I wouldn't seduce one of your team members just because they were convenient. Proximity isn't one of the qualities I'm looking for in a life partner."

His smile was sensually wicked as his eyes twinkled with amusement. "I was talking about making sure the

Demon Brothers don't sneak in to finish the job rather than any seduction you might have planned."

"Oh." Her whole face was on fire now. "Well, that's mortifying."

"Good to know you aren't lacking for company, though," he teased.

Great. Now it sounded like there was a revolving door on her bedroom. "I don't just call up a date for the night, if that's what you mean. I'm picky. Not that I haven't been dating. I date. I date all the time."

"Understood." He nodded solemnly. "You're just used to sleeping alone."

"Yes. No! I've had sleepovers. With men." She waved a hand, trying to look casual and worldly and knowing she'd failed miserably. "Not a lot of men. Enough. Not enough as in I've had my fill. Just a normal amount of men." She paused. This wasn't going well. "Okay, the number is two… plus one in college. So three in total. But two men have come to my loft and spent the night." Argh, that made it sound like she hired male escorts. "I mean, while I was in a relationship with them. Each of them separately and consecutively. Not together. It wasn't a threesome or anything like that. And it wasn't every night."

It was as though he'd handed her a shovel and told her to dig a hole under herself. The words kept coming, and the hole just grew bigger. Annabelle glanced longingly at the door to the panic room, the urge to lock herself inside and never come out again was strong.

"Why are we talking about this?" she asked with a touch of desperation.

To his credit, Noah was clearly fighting the urge to laugh. "I think you're trying to tell me that you don't want to sleep with the panic room door open."

"Yes! I like privacy when I sleep." Why hadn't she just said that right at the start?

"You've slept in the same room as me for the past few nights. It didn't seem to bother you."

"I was unconscious!"

"More like sound asleep," he said, ignoring her protest. "And happy to have me nearby. You kept waking up, smiling at me, and saying 'my bulldog' before falling back to sleep. Definitely no sign of a problem sleeping around me."

My bulldog??????

Annabelle's mouth opened and closed a few times, although nothing came out. Mainly because she had no idea what to say other than *kill me now*. She was tempted to call the Demon gang and ask them to come back and finish the job. It would be a whole lot better than dying a slow death from humiliation.

"Don't worry," Noah said as he strode past her, through the panic room, and into the loft. "*Your bulldog* has your back."

Fortunately, a man she hadn't met strode into the room, saving her from saying anything else she'd instantly regret.

"Lunch is ready," he announced in a crisp English accent.

Annabelle wasn't sure if it was the suit or the way he moved, but the man reminded her of James Bond.

"Annabelle," Noah said. "Meet the final member of our team, Abasi Otieno."

"Pleasure." Abasi nodded.

They headed downstairs to the office area, where the triplets were dividing food onto paper plates. As Annabelle watched Abasi join his team, an old *Sesame Street* song entered her head: *One of these things is not like the others...*

"Predator," she whispered, used to talking to herself.

Only this time, there was somebody else to listen and reply. "Everyone in this room can be deadly when necessary," Noah said.

Annabelle believed him, but she suspected Abasi was the only one without the "when necessary" modifier. The man was just plain deadly. She shivered as she accepted a plate of food from Harris.

As she ate, she observed how Abasi fit in with the rest of the team. Rochelle seemed tense, her gaze returning to him frequently, making it clear she was keeping an eye on him. Violet didn't pay any attention to him at all, while Rodrigo looked both relaxed and amused by his presence. The triplets appeared torn between being awestruck and intimidated. And as soon as Abasi entered the room, Katrina got up to refill her coffee, but instead of returning to her seat, she moved to the opposite side of the room from him without once glancing his way.

Interesting...

It was like watching the Nature Channel in real life. And Annabelle had never been more fascinated.

Chapter Eleven

With the help of the triplets, and under Noah's supervision, Annabelle organized her home the way she liked it—or as close as possible. It would be a couple of days before her new computer and phone arrived, and there were gaps around the loft where her broken belongings had been broken and had yet to be replaced. But overall, it felt more like home than when Noah first took her around it.

As a thank-you for the team, she'd decided to make spaghetti for dinner. It felt good to be back in her kitchen, doing something she enjoyed. Something that didn't involve thinking about a murder or the men out to get her.

"I love this swing," Evan declared as he kicked higher. "What we need now is a slide. We could get one of those spiral tube slides and insert it between floors. That would be cool. Oh! Or a fireman's pole."

"How old are you?" Noah asked from the living room sofa, where he was keeping an eye on the road outside as well as on Annabelle. "Twelve?"

"Twenty-four," Evan replied in all seriousness.

"Weird," Logan said. "So am I."

Noah shook his head as Annabelle grinned at the brothers. She'd asked Logan to repot a couple of plants she'd managed to save while Harris was rehanging some pictures that had come off the wall and been sent out for reframing. Evan was... playing.

"You know what else we could do?" Evan said. "We could set up a basketball area on the roof."

"We're Scottish." Harris stood back to examine his handiwork before stepping forward again to straighten the picture. "We don't play basketball. We play football." He cast Annabelle a pitying glance. "That would be soccer to you."

"Aye, but a football pitch would take up the whole roof," Evan said. "And we could learn how to play basketball." His head poked out from behind the kitchen wall as he swung forward again. "Why haven't you turned the roof into a garden? It's perfect for it, and you love plants."

Annabelle shrugged as she stirred the spaghetti sauce. "I've never been up there."

It took her a moment to realize that all four men were silently staring at her.

"Never?" Logan sounded incredulous.

"Nope. It's outside. I don't do outside. The closest I come is opening the door to collect the mail."

"But the roof is part of the building, so you should feel safe there." Logan was obviously confused.

"Maybe, but like I said, I've never been up there to find out."

"It's totally flat," Evan called. "There's a little wall around the edge, and the view's fantastic. You could have a vegetable garden, and a patio, and a basketball court. You should go up and take a look."

"Maybe."

Annabelle's stomach tensed at the thought, even though she knew that there was little chance of being snatched from her own roof. Still, there were fire escape stairs that led up there, so it wasn't completely safe. People could still get to her. And if they did, she might end up...

No.

She couldn't think about that. There was enough to deal with in the present without raking up the past.

"Do you know what else would be cool?" Evan called out to them. "You know that alleyway between this building and the one next door? The warehouse wall in there would make a perfect climbing wall."

"Let me get this straight," Noah said. "So far, you want a slide running through the building, a basketball court on the roof, and a climbing wall outside. It's like working with my kids."

Annabelle grinned at him. "How old are your kids?"

"Jacob turns fourteen soon, and Sammy's nine. And they're both more mature than the triplets."

"Hey!" Logan complained. "I'm not the one who wants to turn this building into a jungle gym."

"You know," Evan said, "there's that big pit in the loading area behind the shop. One side of it slopes down from the rolling door. If we tiled it and fitted it out, it'd make a perfect swimming pool."

The men groaned while Annabelle smiled. "I used to love to swim."

"Then you should think about it," Evan said seriously. "What was that pit used for anyway?"

"I'm not sure. I think it had something to do with horses and carts. To make it easier to lead them down into that area, so that loading the carts would be faster. But I wouldn't testify to that in court." She swallowed hard, the words a stark reminder about what was to come.

It seemed the guys hadn't missed what she'd said either, as they all turned somber.

"I've been thinking about that," Logan said. "If you can't leave the building, how will you testify?"

"Video link."

"Makes sense."

"What did you see anyway?" Evan asked as he swung past.

Annabelle stilled while stirring the rich and meaty tomato sauce as memories of that night rushed back to her. Apart from when she was kidnapped, she'd never been so scared as when she witnessed that man's death.

"You don't have to answer that." Noah glared at Evan, who was oblivious.

She tucked her hair behind her ears. "It's okay. I need to get used to talking about it."

Annabelle turned off the burner under the pasta pot and reached for the strainer.

"Let me." Noah had appeared at her side, and she hadn't even noticed he'd moved from the sofa.

"Thanks." Leaving him to drain the pasta, she took a seat at the island. "I have a weird sleeping schedule sometimes, like when I'm on a deadline or there's a lot of stuff fighting for space in my head. It means I'm often up at strange hours, but since I'm the only person in the building and there's no one to disturb, I don't really give it too much thought."

Annabelle watched Noah stir the thick ragù sauce before turning off the burner under that pan too. He faced her, leaning back against the counter, his arms folded over another faded T-shirt. Evan, who'd stopped swinging and come into the kitchen, pulled out a stool and sat beside her. Harris and Logan also gave her their full attention.

She should have felt self-conscious, but instead, she felt protected. It was a good feeling, one she held close and cherished.

"So," she continued, "one night, I was pacing the loft, trying to figure out a plot point in my latest graphic novel, when I heard shouting outside. My lights were off because there was plenty of light coming in from the streetlamps, and I like it that way. Also, it makes my building appear empty. Not that anyone would expect someone to be living here." She shrugged. "My mailman tells me there aren't many people living in these few blocks. It's mostly businesses with set hours. And, to be honest, with the state of the shop downstairs, most people would think the warehouse is abandoned anyway."

"Which means someone up to no good might think this was a quiet, out-of-the-way place to do what they liked," Harris said. "Conveniently witness-free."

"Exactly." Annabelle nodded. "I noticed the noise first. They were shouting, and it was scary. I mean, it wasn't like rowdy drunk people or something; it was fighting. So I went to the window to see what was going on, but I kinda stood to one side because I didn't want anyone to see me."

"Smart move," Noah murmured.

"There were five men in the alley between the buildings across the street," Annabelle continued.

"The one where Violet hid behind the dumpster?" Noah asked.

"No, on that street." She pointed to the long side of the building. "One of the men was backed up against the wall and clearly terrified. Another man stood in front of him, quite close. The other three men were fanned out behind him. They kept looking around, like they were ensuring they were alone."

Annabelle took a deep breath and clasped her hands in front of her on the counter. They were shaking, and she hoped no one noticed. To her surprise, Noah moved away from the counter, leaned over the island, and covered her hands with his.

"It's a normal reaction," he said softly. "Nothing to be embarrassed about."

"Thanks," she whispered before continuing. "The guy intimidating the man against the wall wore a black muscle shirt. His head was shaven, and tattoos ran up the side of his neck and down his arms. He was too far away for me to make them out, but he was still very distinctive.

"As I watched, he shouted some more, then spat at the man against the wall. By this time, the cornered man was begging, holding up his hands as if surrendering." She licked her dry lips, and Harris filled a glass with water and placed it in front of her.

"Thanks," she said, but she didn't want to move her hands from Noah's to pick it up. "It all happened so fast after that. The guy in the muscle shirt—"

"Eddie Hanson," Noah said.

"Yes, Eddie. He reached around to the small of his back and pulled out a gun. The v-victim was pleading, but it made no difference. Eddie held his arm out straight and shot him in the chest."

Annabelle kept her gaze fixed on Noah, as though he were a lifeline. He squeezed her hands, offering reassurance and strength.

She took a deep breath before continuing. "The victim slid down the wall and toppled to his side. Eddie stepped forward and shot him in the head. I freaked out and jerked backward, tripping over my own feet and landing on the floor. I scrambled to my work area, grabbed my camera, and ran back to the window. Eddie was crouched in front of the victim, his gun in one hand as he took something from the man's pocket with the other. His three friends now had their guns out too and were very alert, watching every shadow around them.

"I made sure to stay out of sight while taking as many photos as I could, but I was shaking so badly that they were all out of focus when I looked at them later. They were taken with the wrong settings too because I forgot to adjust for the low-light conditions."

"That's why your testimony is important to the DA," Noah said with understanding. "The photos aren't enough on their own."

"No, they aren't. Each of the men kicked the victim before they sauntered out of the alley as though nothing had happened. They were laughing when they got into their car. I-I couldn't take any more photos after that." She swallowed down a wave of shame. "I was too busy vomiting. When I was done, I called the police, but I, uh, didn't let them in until my therapist got here." She paused, feeling all kinds of pathetic. "I didn't know who else to call."

"You made the right decisions," Noah said. "Calling the doc was perfect. You needed someone in your corner while you dealt with the cops. As for throwing up, don't sweat it. We've all been there. Right?" He glanced at the triplets.

To her surprise, it wasn't the guys who replied but Violet, who now stood at the entrance to the loft. Annabelle had been so focused on her story that she hadn't heard her come in.

"I vomited the first time I attended a murder scene,"

Violet said. "Totally screwed up the evidence. It's a natural reaction."

Evan looked at his brothers. "I didn't know she had those."

As Violet gave him a death glare, Annabelle smiled tremulously at Noah. "Have you ever thrown up at a crime scene?"

"More than once." And he didn't look the slightest bit bothered by it either.

For a moment, it was as if they were the only two people in the room, whispering to each other and sharing secrets. She was aware of his hand covering hers, the heat of his skin warming her. Memories of him holding her were foremost in her mind, and she feared that her hero-worshiping might be getting out of hand.

"Must be his age," Harris said, shattering the moment. "I hear the older you get, the more sensitive your stomach becomes."

"I swear," Noah said, stepping away from the island and taking his warmth with him. "It's like dealing with my kids. So, you saw the leader of the Demon Brothers Houston Chapter kill a man while three of his gang backed him up. No wonder the ADA salivates every time she sees you. You're about to hand her one of the biggest cases of her career on a platter."

"If I survive long enough to do it," Annabelle said.

"That's the spirit." Evan patted her on the shoulder.

"I hate to break up this party," Violet said. "But the boss wants you downstairs, Noah."

"Don't worry," Harris said. "We'll look after her. You know, Annabelle, it occurs to me that without a computer, you don't have access to your 3D modeling software—which means no ability to pose figures for your drawings. I just wanted you to know that I'm willing to step in until you get your new computer. You may not know this, but I used to be a professional model—"

His brothers groaned loudly, making Annabelle laugh. She glanced over at Noah and found he was checking on her too. He smiled, cocked an eyebrow, then shrugged. She could almost hear his apology for leaving her alone with the triplets.

Annabelle beamed at him and shooed him out of the room. She'd be fine until he returned.

Chapter Twelve

Dinner went well. Everyone, except those on guard duty, sat around her huge dining table, enjoying spaghetti Bolognese and homemade garlic bread. And Annabelle loved every minute of it. She'd wanted to take plates to Abasi and Logan, who were on duty, but Rochelle had insisted they needed to focus and would eat later. So Annabelle had contented herself with fussing over everyone else. It was as though she had family around for dinner, albeit a large, dysfunctional family, still sizing each other up.

It'd been a long time since she'd had a proper family dinner; even then, it'd just been the three of them—her father, her aunt, and her. Dinner parties had expanded after she'd moved in with her aunt, although the table hadn't been filled with family—it had been filled with an eclectic mix of friends belonging to both. Her aunt had been notorious for adopting people. She readily made friends and loved inviting them over to eat. Meals could be boisterous. Sometimes, there were musicians and artists; other times, politicians and lawyers. You never knew who you'd be eating with when Aunt Rose hosted a dinner.

Annabelle hadn't realized how much she'd missed those dinners until her apartment was filled with people again: talking, laughing, arguing people. It would be hard when they left and the building reverted to its usual empty state. In the meantime, she planned to make family dinners a regular thing while the team was there. There weren't many upsides to witnessing a murder, being shot at for testifying, and fearing for your life. But it had brought the Benson Security team into her life, and Annabelle planned to make the most of having them there while it lasted.

Fresh from her shower and dressed in one of the three identical pairs of Wonder Woman pajamas Katrina had bought her, Annabelle walked into her new bedroom. She refused to call it the panic room while sleeping there. Panic wasn't exactly conducive to sleep.

The door between her room and the guest room stood partially open, and she could see Noah sitting on the edge of the bed. Still fully dressed, he held up his phone, obviously on a video call. He lifted a hand to her in greeting, and she nodded in return. She was a little self-conscious in her new night clothes but grateful that they covered a whole lot more than her usual nightwear. Although Noah had already seen her in that.

Annabelle hadn't intended to eavesdrop, but considering the door was open and he was facing her, it was impossible to avoid.

"I scored two goals!" The excited voice of one of his sons came through the doorway.

"That's fantastic, Sammy," Noah said with enthusiasm. "I wish I'd been there to see them."

Annabelle winced, aware she was the reason he'd missed his son playing.

"We have the advantage," said a different voice, which must have belonged to his other son, Jacob. "All that soccer we had to do in England means we're way ahead of how they play here."

"I'm the best player on my team," Sammy piped up.

"By far," Jacob agreed solemnly, making Annabelle smile as she grabbed a bottle of water from the mini fridge in her new kitchen area. "It's so cool that they let us play, even though we're only here for a few weeks."

"Yep," Sammy said. "They're going to miss us when we're gone. They won't win any games without us."

Noah's laughter was deep and rich, like molasses. "Sounds like we need to find you two permanent teams when you get back to Houston."

"Totally," Jacob said.

"Do you think they have rubbish players in Houston too?" Sammy sounded hopeful.

"Course they do," Jacob said. "Uncle Callum says Americans don't know how to play a real sport like soccer. That's why they wear all that protective gear to kick a ball."

"It might be time to remind *Uncle Callum* we *are* Americans," Noah said drolly.

"Not me!" Sammy piped up. "Uncle Callum says that seeing as I spent half my life in England, I'm half English."

"Yeah," Jacob said. "But he said we have a long ways to go to be Scottish like him."

"I'm going to try real hard to be Scottish," Sammy said.

"Bet we'd be good at that too," Jacob added.

Annabelle smothered a giggle as she listened to the boys. Noah was right. They did sound like the triplets.

"Right, you two, time for bed. Tell Gran to stop keeping you up so late and spoiling you." Noah's love for his sons was clear in his voice, and it made Annabelle's chest ache to hear it.

"We can't tell her not to spoil us," Sammy said in a stage whisper—clearly, their grandmother was listening in. "Grandpa said old folk should be allowed to do what they want before they die."

Annabelle couldn't help the laugh that burst out. She caught Noah's eye through the open doorway and saw he shared her amusement.

"Yeah?" he said. "Well, tell Grandpa to stop filling your head with garbage too."

"Let an old guy have his fun," a male voice shouted in the background, making the boys giggle.

Noah rolled his eyes. "Get to bed. I'll talk to you tomorrow."

"Love you, Dad," the boys chimed in unison.

Noah's face softened. "Love you right back." He ended the call, still smiling as his eyes met Annabelle's. "They're going to finish this visit addicted to sugar, and I'll have to check them into rehab."

Annabelle moved to the doorway. "Sounds like you have awesome parents."

"I do, but these are my in-laws." He grinned. "Seriously though, they're pretty awesome too. Just a tad overindulgent."

"Must have been hard for them," Annabelle said, "losing their daughter. It's no wonder they spoil their grandkids."

"Yeah, I know. They're good people. I'm lucky." For a moment, he seemed lost in thought, and Annabelle wondered if he was thinking about his wife.

"What was she like?" she blurted out, then blushed. "Sorry. It's none of my business. Forget I asked."

Noah didn't seem bothered by her asking such a personal question. "You mean my wife? I don't mind talking about her."

"No, it's okay. I overstepped the line. I mean, you're here to do a job, not spill your guts about your personal life to your client."

"Honestly," he said, "I can tell you about Therese, if you really want to hear."

"I'd like that," she said, wandering into the room to sit beside him.

* * *

"Don't hold back on telling her how fantastic I am," Therese said from where she stood near the window. *"Feel free to wax lyrical. You can't share too much."*

Noah stifled a groan as he fought to keep his eyes off his deceased wife. He smiled ruefully at Annabelle. "Therese was... a pain in my ass."

That surprised laughter out of Annabelle, while Therese stamped her foot. *"If I could move things, that lamp would be flying at your head right now."*

Noah couldn't help but smile. "She was fiery," he told Annabelle. "Some would say mouthy. She had an opinion on everything and stuck her nose into everyone's business, but she had a heart of pure gold."

"That's more like it." Therese sniffed. *"Carry on."*

"She sounds formidable." Annabelle toyed with a button on her ugly pajamas.

"Oh, she was a presence, alright. If Therese was in a room, you knew it. She had a way of making people open up

114

to her, and then she'd step in and meddle with their lives. Funny thing was nobody ever got upset about it."

"Probably because they realized she meant well."

"Probably." Amusement bubbled inside him as he remembered what life had been like with Therese. "She was always on the go, always busy with something. I never knew what she'd do next. She lived life to the full, you know? Almost as if she knew what was coming."

"I didn't," Therese said. *"I just had a lot I wanted to do. How people can be bored, I have no idea."*

"I remember you saying it was cancer?" Annabelle said softly.

"Yeah, it came on fast, and there was nothing anybody could do. She was a fighter and a planner right to the end, though. She made loads of videos for the boys to watch on their birthdays. Every year, there's a message from her to them, along with some piece of wisdom she felt they should know."

"What a wonderful thing to do." Annabelle's eyes teared up, and she blinked them away.

"See?" Therese said. *"She totally gets me."*

"She made one for me too," Noah said. "I've never watched it, though."

Therese threw up her hands in disgust. *"Which annoys me no end. I put a lot of effort into that video."*

"Too hard?" Annabelle nodded with understanding.

"It's more that the title freaks me out." He smiled wryly. "She called it 'advice for your next relationship—so you don't screw up.'"

Annabelle's laughter felt like bubbles against his skin. "I bet I would've enjoyed knowing your wife."

"Damn straight," Therese said. *"For a start, I'd have*

gotten her out of this building. It's not healthy for a young woman to live like this. You need to fix her, Noah."

Yeah, he'd get right on that. An ex-cop could totally do what a trained psychiatrist couldn't. He shot his wife a disbelieving look before speaking to Annabelle. "We grew up together, were high school sweethearts, and got married straight after graduation. There was a group of us, five guys and Therese, and we'd all hang out together. Therese had a group of female friends too, but that didn't stop her from interfering in the lives of my friends. Not that they ever complained about her always being around—or any of the stuff she talked them into doing. We all miss her."

Annabelle seemed surprised. "You're all still friends? I don't have any school friends left, just a couple from college."

"I couldn't shake those guys even if I tried." Noah grimaced. "And trust me, there have been times when I've tried. We all went our separate ways for a while but kept in touch. Now, we all work for Benson Security in some capacity or another. Two of the guys have full-time jobs and freelance with the team when they can."

"They're all in Houston?" Annabelle frowned, obviously wondering why she hadn't met them yet.

"No, one's in Scotland, two are in London, and the other travels a lot. I was with the London team before they started up this new crew. Thought it would be good to get back home for a while."

"But Houston isn't your home, right?"

"Atlantic City born and raised."

"Why have we stopped talking about me?" Therese interrupted. *"You haven't told her about my great impersonations of our friends or how I was an awesome mother, not to mention that I baked the best damn chocolate cake in the*

world. You can give her the recipe. It'd go great with her spaghetti." She'd become food-obsessed in her ghostly form.

"Funny how you all work for the same company now," Annabelle said. "I wish I was that close to my friends."

He shrugged. "It worked out pretty good for all of them. They met their wives through Benson Security. And that's more of a miracle than you'd guess because I was sure at least two of those guys would die alone."

"Amen to that," Therese said.

"I'm glad you had someone like Therese," Annabelle said. "And I'm sorry you lost her."

"I'm not lost; I'm right here. Wondering why you haven't given her my chocolate cake recipe yet. You could eat it tomorrow."

He wouldn't get any peace until he gave in, so Noah listened to the figment of his imagination and said, "She was an amazing cook, just like you."

Annabelle flushed and tucked her thick hair behind her ear. "I'm not sure about amazing, but I enjoy it."

"Therese made a fantastic chocolate cake that would've gone great with your spaghetti. You want the recipe?"

"About time," Therese said.

"If that isn't too weird," he added because it sure as hell felt weird.

"No, not at all." Annabelle smiled at him. "I'd love to try making it."

"Okay then." He glanced at Therese to see her looking smug.

"It sounds like you were really lucky to have her in your life," Annabelle said softly.

"Hey," he said, "I think she was pretty damn lucky to have me!"

"Of course she was." Annabelle rolled her eyes as she patted his arm.

But her words caused something within Noah to shift. She was right. He was the luckiest man alive to have had Therese, even for a little while.

Annabelle stood and headed for the panic room. "I'd better get to sleep. I'm still kinda wiped out from that virus. Door partially or fully open?"

"Partially is fine." Noah stood. "I have some work to do on my laptop, then I'll call it a night. Make sure the other door to the panic room's locked. If you need me, shout. And if I'm not here for some reason—" He noticed her eyes widen and clarified: "Like I'm in the bathroom or talking to a teammate, just go to your old bedroom. Rochelle and Katrina are sharing that room. There'll be team members on guard during the night too, and someone will always have their eyes on the cameras. You're safe here."

"I believe that." And she sounded sincere. Annabelle hesitated at the door. "Thanks for telling me about Therese. I feel like I know her now." And with that, she disappeared into the room, and seconds later, her light went off.

Noah sat staring at her open door for a few minutes, unsure of what he was feeling or thinking. He just knew that something was happening. Something had changed inside of him. For the first time in years, he'd been able to talk about his wife and focus only on the good times instead of feeling like he was drowning in a sea of sorrow. It felt... right to focus on the many ways his life had been blessed rather than on what he'd lost. And that rightness somehow freed the weight he'd carried around for so many years.

"You know," Therese said, shattering his epiphany. *"I think it's time you watched that video I made you."*

"Seriously?" Of course she'd take this opportunity to press the point.

"Did you say something?" Annabelle called.

Noah frowned at his dead wife. "Just talking to myself."

"Oh, okay. Good night then."

"Night," he called back, his eyes still on Therese.

"*My bad,*" she whispered, even though only he could hear her. "*Think about the video. I'm going to check on the triplets.*" She waggled her eyebrows. "*Those boys are built!*"

"I did not hear that," Noah muttered.

"*There's nothing wrong with looking. After all, I'm dead, so it's not like I can cheat on you.*" She paused, suddenly serious. "*You do realize that my death ended our marriage, right? 'Till death do us part'? Finding love again wouldn't mean you were cheating on me. You understand that, right?*"

"Don't you have some voyeurism to get to?" Noah whispered.

"*Fine, don't discuss it, then.*" She grinned. "*If I'm lucky, I'll hit shower time.*" Then she disappeared.

Noah sat on the edge of the bed, looking between the spot where he'd seen his wife and the door to the room where Annabelle slept.

It was definitely time he made an appointment with a psychologist.

Chapter Thirteen

It'd been a quiet few days. Their only visitors were ADA Grant, to prep Annabelle for her testimony, and the court's audiovisual people, who'd set up the remote link for her to testify when the time came. The team was on edge, stretched thin from being constantly on alert. Nerves were beginning to fray, and the younger team members showed signs of cabin fever. Noah almost wished the Demons would attack again and get it over with. He'd rather shoot at them than die from waiting.

Annabelle seemed to be the only person in the building who wasn't going stir-crazy. Probably because she was used to not leaving the warehouse. She'd stopped worrying about the Demon Brothers, trusting that the team would do their job protecting her. Instead, she seemed determined to live life as usual and enjoy the company. She'd insisted on cooking for them every evening and sent the triplets out to do her grocery shopping. There was even a chocolate cake one day, much to Therese's delight. Annabelle's living room had become an unofficial break room for anyone wanting a few moments of downtime, and she was happy with it that way.

But it was her interactions with the triplets that Noah found particularly entertaining. The little group had already formed a strange dynamic. It was as though the brothers had adopted Annabelle while she treated them like the younger siblings she'd never had.

Today, Evan had picked up empanadas for lunch from the local Mexican deli he raved about, and they were eating in the second-floor office rather than the loft. While they did so, Annabelle teased the triplets like she'd known them for years.

"So, have you three ever fallen for the same girl?" she asked, a wicked gleam in her eye.

"Logan and I dated twins once," Harris said. "Does that count?"

"No, but what happened?"

The two brothers pointed at Evan.

"Don't blame me," he said, reaching for another empanada. "I got lumbered with the younger sister because she felt left out. The girl was a psycho. She had Beanie Babies that she pretended were our children. They had names and everything. I had to get out of there before I woke up married and chained to the bed."

"How old was she?" Annabelle asked.

"Sixteen, two years younger than we were at the time." Evan looked disturbed by the memory. "She scared me."

"She also wouldn't take no for an answer," Harris continued the story. "So he broke up with her on social media. Her sisters were livid."

"Evan ruins everything," Logan said.

"Desperate times call for desperate measures," Evan said. "I'd break up with her in person, and she'd carry on as though nothing had happened. It was weird as hell. I had to go public. I had no other choice. At least she couldn't ignore a TikTok video."

"You broke up with her on TikTok?" Annabelle almost choked on her food.

"She wasn't on Facebook," Evan explained.

Noah caught Rodrigo's eye, and they grinned at each other. If nothing else, the triplets were entertaining.

"Lunchtime's over, kiddies," Rochelle said, clearing away her empty plate. "We have work to do. Harris, why don't you take Annabelle upstairs? Now her new computer's here, I'm sure she's eager to get back into it."

"Okey dokey," he said, getting to his feet.

Annabelle glanced at Noah, as if checking to see if it was okay for her to go.

"Harris will keep you safe," he said. "It's Logan's turn to patrol, and Evan will keep an eye on the camera feed while we have our meeting. I'm only a shout away if needed."

"Okay." She prodded Harris in the back. "It would be good to upload some work to my editor, so don't go distracting me."

"You'll barely know I'm there. And if you need a model for any new drawings, I'm happy to help. After all, I've done some professional modeling in my time."

"I know." She grinned. "You told me."

"He's told all of us," Rodrigo said.

"Repeatedly," Noah added.

"Well, it bears repeating," Harris said before cocking his head toward the door. "After you, pretty lady. By the way, is there any chocolate cake left?"

"Not if you annoy me." Annabelle sparkled with delight, and Noah's chest tightened.

As her main bodyguard, he should be going with her.

Not Harris. Damn it, he was behaving like a toddler who had to share his favorite toy. He mentally smacked himself on the back of the head.

"Evan," Rochelle said, "you and your brothers need to sort your gun permits. See Katrina about what you have to do."

"I looked it up," Evan said. "We're in Texas, we don't need permits."

"Texas might not require them," Rochelle said icily, "but I do. And tell them I want all of you at the range. Nobody gets a weapon until I'm satisfied you can fire it without hitting one of the team. Got it?"

"What do we do in the meantime?" Evan said. "I mean, if somebody attacks again."

"I suggest you get properly trained as quickly as possible," Rochelle said. "Until then, use your brains and your fists, and let the rest of us take the frontline on this."

"I'm going to die," Evan muttered.

"Right," Rochelle addressed everyone else. "Let's go over everything we know."

She spun the whiteboard so the blank side faced the room and wrote the words Demon Brothers and Eddie Hanson in the top left-hand corner.

"In the London office, we had a data projector and PowerPoint presentations." Violet clearly disapproved of the new, low-tech format. "There were handouts."

"You're not in London anymore, Ms. Lee." Rochelle continued to write on the board while Violet tried to burn a hole in her back with the power of her glare.

Once finished, Rochelle faced her team, all business. "The trial is in ten days, and Eddie Hanson's still out on bail, thanks to his very expensive lawyer. According to the ADA, he's keeping a low profile but isn't hiding. Apparently, he likes to smile and wave at the police detail following him."

"Polite guy," Rodrigo muttered.

Rochelle removed her suit jacket, beige this time, and hung it on the back of her chair. "What have we learned about him? If we can get a decent picture of his past behavior and motivation, we can, hopefully, predict what he'll do next and be more prepared."

Abasi slowly shook his head but said nothing.

"I read through the police files." Rodrigo sat forward. "He doesn't have any family—so no weak points to squeeze, and there's no close love interest that I can find. With his looks, money, and rep, he attracts a lot of beautiful rich women who want to dance with the darker side of life. None of them hang around for long, and he tends to keep them on the periphery of his operation. When it comes to his personal life, he's untouchable. There are no vulnerable areas."

"What's his usual MO for dealing with threats?" Violet tapped the board marker on the desk in front of her.

Rodrigo spread his hands. "What you'd expect. He gives the order, and the threat dies bloody. As far as I can tell, he doesn't do second chances. You cross him once, and you're gone. He doesn't play games either. Death is usually swift. He does, however, make a point with each execution—if you steal from him, you lose your fingers. If you snitch, you lose your tongue. If you spy, it's your eyes. One guy lost something a whole lot more personal after sleeping with Eddie's woman of the moment."

The men in the room all flinched as one.

"Does he mutilate before or after death?" Rochelle was still very much focused on Eddie's psychology rather than his penchant for lopping off body parts.

"He doesn't care what order it happens in," Rodrigo said. "That's up to whoever's carrying out the order. Like I said, Eddie doesn't play around. If anyone crosses him, he wants them dead. The rest of it's done as a warning to everyone else, and if his men want to torture before they carry out the kill, that's okay with him. Just so long as they do what he told them to do."

"Does he deal with men and women differently? Does he spare children?" Rochelle frowned, her FBI-trained mind paying close attention.

"No," Rodrigo said solemnly. *"Eddie es un hombre peligroso. Y loco también."*

"Yeah," Noah said. "But crazy like a fox. The guy's still walking free."

"I don't get it," Violet said. "His gang just blindly carries out whatever order he issues? Nobody has that sort of control. I dealt with some serious gangs in Glasgow, but there were always a few members who thought they knew better than their leaders. Or were just too stoned to care."

"Not in the Demon Brothers. The gang's full of psychos and cowards," Rodrigo told her. "They either enjoy following kill orders or are too scared not to. Word is, he kills anyone who doesn't follow his order to the letter. One thing's for sure, he doesn't like people questioning or arguing with him."

"What does he cut off if you disobey an order?" Violet said.

"Your head."

"That's just overkill." Violet seemed unimpressed.

Noah ran a hand down his face, his stomach knotting at the thought of what this gang wanted to do to Annabelle. "Eddie's been running the Demons for years. It's hard to believe Annabelle's the first chance the DA's had to nail the guy."

Rodrigo sat back in his chair. "He keeps it tight. The gang isn't big, and the members are obsessively loyal. Law enforcement can't get anyone in undercover, as each member is hand-picked and monitored twenty-four seven. If a member's arrested while committing a crime, he'll take the fall completely, refusing to say a word about the gang. There have been some serious attempts to turn a member against the group, but they've all come to nothing. On top of that, any witnesses to gang activity are dealt with swiftly and violently. Annabelle's the only witness to last this long."

"Obviously," Rochelle said, "they also cultivate sources inside law enforcement. Otherwise, Annabelle would still be safe."

"They use a combination of money and intimidation," Rodrigo agreed. "A couple of moles have been weeded out, but they chose prison rather than turning on the Demons. They were that scared."

"Even with the promise of witness protection?" Katrina, who'd been taking notes, spoke for the first time.

"So far, nobody's believed that the WITSEC program can keep them safe."

A wave of tension rippled through the room, the gravity of the situation written on everyone's face.

"They're just people," Abasi said, breaking the tension. "Every organization, every criminal, has a weakness. Don't go thinking these guys are unstoppable."

"Uh-huh," Violet smirked at him. "And what would you do to stop them, oh wise one?"

"I already voiced my opinion. A bullet in Eddie Hanson's brain would put an end to this situation fast."

Rochelle shook her head. "Somebody else would just

step up to fill Eddie's shoes, and the Demons will carry on. Eddie has to be convicted so that the authorities can make his gang believe he's sold them out. That way, they have a chance of convincing some of the weaker members to testify. And with that information, they dismantle the Demons for good."

"Our job isn't to take down the Demon Brothers. It's to protect the witness." Abasi showed no emotion as he spoke, even though he knew Annabelle just as well as most of the team. "That makes it simple. If you want to protect the girl, you take out the threat. You want to bring down the organization too, well, that's something else."

"FBI, DEA, all the alphabet agencies want this group," Rodrigo said to Abasi. "We can't screw that up for them. You were in the life, so you'd have a good idea of what the Demons are into. That shit *has* to be stopped."

Abasi's cold eyes were unflinching as he stared at Rodrigo. "You remove one gang, and another one steps in to take its place. There's no stopping any of this shit. Trust me. I know. You can't make that sort of a difference. You can't wipe out gang life or stop all organized crime. It just isn't possible. All you can do is what you're being paid to do— protect the girl."

Katrina cleared her throat, drawing everyone's attention. Her eyes were on Abasi, but her face remained carefully blank. "Are you suggesting we do nothing about the Demon gang, or any gang for that matter? That it's all hopeless anyway? What about all the other people involved with the gang and at risk? The family members whom the Demons make examples out of, the women and children they traffic, or the innocent bystanders whose lives are destroyed because they got in the way? Don't they deserve to be protected too?"

Abasi was unmoved. "Our job is to protect the witness. That's what we're being paid for."

"Don't you care about the rest?" Katrina asked, sounding incredulous.

"I ain't no crusader," Abasi said evenly.

"No." Katrina stood. "You aren't. If you'll excuse me, I have calls to make. Rochelle, I'll catch up with you later."

She strode from the room without sparing Abasi so much as a glance, but he didn't take his eyes off her until she was out of sight.

"Okay," Noah said once she was gone. "Let me see if I have this right. What you're saying is that the Demon Brothers are untouchable, and all we can do is sit here and wait for the next attack. That about it?"

Rochelle headed for the coffee pot. "Unfortunately, waiting seems our only option. We can't take the fight to them, not without ruining the ADA's case and law enforcement's chance of taking down the entire Demon Brothers operation. It certainly looks like we're stuck playing defense."

Evan raised his hand and cleared his throat to attract attention.

Rochelle's expression made it clear she was fast losing patience with him. "Evan, this isn't a class, and I'm not your teacher. If you have something to say, speak up."

The young Scot was unfazed. "Okay, so I was digging through the Benson Security records and saw that the London office helped take down the James Family." He visibly gulped under the sudden intense scrutiny of Abasi Otieno. "Th-they played them off against other gangs and started a turf war. Can't we do something like that? Can't we get other bad guys to take out our bad guys for us?"

Attention turned to Abasi, who, as everyone knew, had

been high up in the James Family leadership. "It won't work. The Demons are too insular, whereas the James Family was structured like a classic Italian mob. Plus, from what I've heard, no one will fight with the Demons, not for turf, or business, or pretty much anything. But... we could destabilize them another way, depending on how skilled our hacker is."

"What other way?" Noah demanded.

Abasi shrugged. "We take away their money."

Chapter Fourteen

"I don't like it," Rochelle said as she helped herself to more coffee. One day, Noah was going to force her to get a blood test, just to see how much caffeine ran through her veins. "Us going after their money could interfere with the prosecution's investigation into the Demon Brothers, and the last thing we want is to jeopardize their case."

"Plus," Evan said, looking dejected, "technically, I'm not allowed to hack anymore. I got into a bit of trouble with the government, and Mum, who's a big-time human rights lawyer, stepped in to cut a deal. She's friends with Lake Benson and talked him into helping. Next thing we knew, the government made us an offer: join Benson Security or go to jail. Do not pass 'Go.' Do not collect two hundred dollars. Worse, never see a computer again. I chose to accept Lake's kind offer."

"Which government did you piss off?" Violet asked, seeming not the slightest surprised by Evan's disclosure.

He scratched his beard. "Take your pick. I was in my activist phase and wanted to prove a point to the overlords who rule us. Next thing I knew, the FBI, SIS, and Interpol were knocking on my door." He shrugged. "I blame Mum. When we were kids, she dragged us to every protest march she could find. You can't feed three young boys a steady diet of 'we must monitor our leaders and hold them to account' and expect them not to do exactly that. Just sayin'."

"If you can't hack"—Violet narrowed her eyes at him—" what the hell is the point of having you around?"

"Damned if I know." Evan shrugged. "Like I said, the choice was this or prison. It was a no-brainer."

Violet opened her mouth to say something else, but Rochelle spoke first. "Violet, why don't you go help Harris?"

She didn't need to be asked twice. She was out the door in seconds. Back in London, Violet had made it clear that she saw meetings as a waste of time. Obviously, nothing had changed.

Noah considered his team. "Is it *really* hacking if he's investigating a criminal's money trail?"

Rochelle glared at him. "You're supposed to be a good influence around here."

Noah was offended. He was definitely one of the adults in the room. "It's not like we're asking him to break into the Pentagon. We're talking about accounts set up by gang members who traffic human beings. I'd say that's a gray area when it comes to hacking."

Their boss plopped down in her seat and stared at Evan for a moment. She heaved a sigh. "Could you track their money? Is that something you can do?"

Evan stretched out his arms in front of him, linked his fingers, and cracked his knuckles. "In my sleep." He flashed a cocky grin.

Rodrigo spoke up. "Their accounts are probably already

being monitored by several agencies. It's not exactly rocket science to figure out that you have to trace their money."

"First thing they do," Abasi agreed. "Thing is, the money ain't so easy to trace. If the Metropolitan Police could have cracked where the James Family hid theirs, they'd have taken them down years ago." He lifted his chin in Evan's direction. "What makes you think you can do what governments and law enforcement can't?"

"Ah." Evan settled back in his chair. "You want my CV. Okay, I was first arrested when I was ten and hacked into MI6—I wanted to find out if James Bond was real."

Noah couldn't stop the laugh that escaped him. It was exactly the kind of thing his kids would have done—if they'd had Evan's ability.

"Sorry," he muttered when Rochelle glared at him again.

"After that," Evan said, "Mum encouraged me to use my skills for the greater good. She had me mess with various politicians' computers, depending on what she was protesting at the time. Nothing malicious, you understand, mainly stupid stuff to annoy them. I hacked the education minister and made maths problems pop up every time he tried to log in. Unless he solved the problem, he couldn't access his data. Guy was an idiot and shouldn't have been in charge of the country's schools. He couldn't even solve the most basic equations."

"Yes, Evan, we get it. You can hack." Rochelle rubbed her temples. "And you started young."

"I'll skip to the good stuff. Every now and then, I'll do some work for a government agency. Different agencies. Different governments. If it's something that wouldn't annoy my mum, I take on the job. It's one of the reasons I got the option to stay out of prison. The FBI tried to recruit me, but I have standards. If a job doesn't pass Mum's morality test, I won't do it."

"To sum up, you're saying you *can* hack into the Demon Brother's finances?" Noah wanted to be clear.

"Is Iron Man a rich narcissist?"

"A simple yes or no answer, please." Noah had begun to regret bringing up the topic.

"Yes. I just need a place to start." Even cocked his head at Abasi. "You might be able to help me with that."

"I know nothing about the Demons' money," Abasi said.

"But you might know who they'd get to launder it or which offshore bank they'd use to hide it. I only need a small thread, and then I can pull it until the whole thing unravels."

Abasi looked intrigued. "I might have a thread or two you can try."

Evan grinned. "Gr—"

An alarm sounded, and everyone was on their feet and running. A red light flashed above Evan's control center, and he spun toward it.

"Front door," he shouted after them.

They ran down the stairs, guns drawn. Above them, Noah heard voices and knew Harris was ushering Annabelle into the panic room.

As they turned the corner to take the last flight of stairs down to the entrance, Noah saw Violet had beaten them to it. The front door was open, and she was outside.

Her gun trained on a woman who stood with her hands in the air.

"Check the street," Rochelle ordered as they rushed through the door.

Rodrigo went left, Abasi right.

Noah backed up Rochelle and Violet, eyes scanning the

street and the surrounding buildings. Nothing jumped out at him, so he turned his attention to the woman caught in Violet's cross hairs.

It took a second for the situation to register.

The woman's tanned skin tone had turned ashen as she stared down the barrel of the gun. She was about the same height as Violet but a little rounder. Her dark eyes were wide behind her purple-framed glasses, and her mouth was open—as though she wanted to scream but didn't dare. She wore a hot pink shirt over black shorts, white socks, and running shoes. At her side was a large pink roller bag. And on its side was printed: *Get your mind out of the gutter.*

Noah lowered his gun. "Put down your weapons. She isn't with the gang."

"G-gang?" the woman sputtered.

"How do you know?" Violet's voice was ice.

"The bowling ball bag's a dead giveaway. So's the bowling shirt. Hell, she has her team's name embroidered on the pocket."

Violet leaned in to read the text. "Betty's Brigade?" She straightened. "Could be a cover. If I wanted to scout the place, I'd send in a middle-aged woman with a bowling bag. How do we even know there are balls in that bag? It's big enough to store a shotgun."

"May I?" Noah indicated to the pink bag, and the woman nodded her head furiously.

He rounded Violet and unzipped the bag. There were three balls inside.

"Are they real?" Violet didn't take her eyes off her target. "Or cleverly disguised bombs?"

"Want me to throw one at you to find out?" Noah asked.

Rochelle put away her gun. "Do you have any ID on you, ma'am?"

Slowly, her eyes still on Violet and her gun, the woman lowered her hands and unzipped her small cross-body bag. She handed her wallet to Rochelle, who flipped it open.

"Janice Mason, from Alabama." She frowned at the woman. "Why are you in Houston?"

"B-b-bowling," the woman said.

"Violet, put down the gun," Rochelle ordered as Abasi and Rodrigo came back around the building.

"Clear," Abasi said.

"And this side," Rodrigo added.

"This is obviously a false alarm," Rochelle said to the woman as Violet reluctantly holstered her weapon. "I apologize for my security team's reaction. We're working as a protection detail in this building and on alert for threats. Is there a reason you came to our door?"

Janice visibly swallowed, her eyes darting between them all. "The Uber driver dropped me off at the wrong address. I'm looking for the bowling alley and just wanted directions."

"I know where it is," Evan said as he came through the door. He too wore hot pink and could easily have been a member of the woman's bowling team. The only difference was that his Hawaiian shirt and shorts had colorful parrots printed all over them. "It's beside my favorite Mexican deli. Remember that retro bowling alley I told you about? It's pretty cool. I can take her there."

"Count me in," Janice muttered.

Evan reached for her bag and offered her an arm. "Come on, Janice. Let's get you to your game."

When she turned, the back of her shirt came into view. Embroidered on it was a large blue bowling ball with a cute yellow bird perched on top of it. Underneath, it said: *Bowling, Alabama's Other National Sport.*

"That might have been a clue too," Noah muttered to Violet.

"What kind of security team is this?" the woman asked Evan in a shaky voice as they walked away.

"The jumpy kind," he replied.

As they made their way down the street, Rochelle caught Noah's eye. She was all business. "When he gets back, start tracking the money. You're right. If we don't do something about the Demon Brothers, there's a good chance we'll shoot the next stranger who comes to our door."

As Noah nodded, a window opened above them, and Logan stuck out his head. "Where's Evan going?"

"Bowling alley," Noah said.

"The one beside the Mexican deli?"

Noah nodded.

Logan whistled loudly, and when Evan turned, he shouted, "Get churros!"

Rochelle pinched the bridge of her nose, her eyes closed.

Noah patted her on the shoulder. "I'm sure it'll get better, Boss," he said in an attempt to reassure her.

"I struggle to see how it could get any worse," Rochelle said as she headed for the entrance.

Chapter Fifteen

nnabelle and Noah had fallen into a comfortable bedtime routine. She'd get ready first, sticking to her Wonder Woman pajamas, seeing as the building was full of people. Once she was secure in the panic room, Noah would get ready. He dressed for bed in a T-shirt and sweatpants so he could be up and running instantly if needed. And he kept a worn pair of boots by his bed, ready to slam his feet into and run. His gun sat on the nightstand, next to an iPad showing the security cameras' video feeds.

Every night, he checked the windows in her apartment, making sure they were well covered and locked before ensuring the other door to the panic room was secured too. After that, he'd call whoever was on guard duty for a security update on the rest of the building. When satisfied that everyone was doing their job and the warehouse was locked up tight, he'd ask her if she needed anything.

It was becoming increasingly difficult not to reply, "*You.*"

Yeah, her hero worship had morphed into a full-blown

crush. Her therapist would probably tell her she was mistaking feelings of gratitude for attraction. Or that she'd developed an unhealthy bond with the man because he was her protector. Annabelle had been through enough therapy to know the routine, and she didn't require a professional to help analyze her feelings. For that, she had the internet, and according to the many search engines she'd consulted, Noah was suffering from "White Knight Syndrome" while she was craving a "Rescue Romance."

The internet sucked.

The truth was, Noah Merchant fascinated her. There was nothing else to it. He wasn't the best-looking guy in the building, or the tallest, or the youngest, but he was... solid, confident, capable, and caring. She loved the way he interacted with his kids and the bittersweet look in his eyes whenever he talked about his wife. There were even moments when Annabelle experienced a pang of jealousy over the love and loyalty he'd given Therese. A horrible thing to have to admit. Maybe she did need to talk to her therapist after all.

"You need anything?" Noah asked from the open doorway between their rooms.

Annabelle swallowed the answer on the tip of her tongue. "No, thanks. I'm good."

She closed the sketchpad, balanced against her legs as she sat with her back to the sofa headboard and the bedding tucked up around her.

"What're you drawing?" He folded his arms over the faded T-shirt he wore to bed. His sweatpants hung low on his hips, and his feet were bare.

He took her breath away.

"Just sketching," she said. "Nothing important."

"Can I see?" His eyes sparkled, and she knew he suspected she'd been drawing his team.

He wasn't wrong.

"Okay," she said somewhat reluctantly.

Noah came to sit on the edge of the sofa bed beside her and held out a hand for the sketchpad. Like she'd just hand it over. Uh, no. There were drawings in there that *nobody* should see. Instead, Annabelle opened it and turned to the first drawing, then angled the sketchpad so he could see the image on the paper.

As soon as it registered, he threw back his head and laughed deeply. "I love it," he said at last.

"Don't tell the triplets," Annabelle pleaded.

His eyes sparkled. "That'll cost you."

Annabelle tore her eyes from his and considered her drawing. She'd portrayed the triplets as a set of three identical superheroes in tights and flowing capes. They stood in the classic superhero position—hands on hips, chins high, staring into the distance. Written across their chests in bold letters were their hero names: Copy. Paste. Repeat.

"Violet's gonna love this. So cool how you've put Harris and Logan in Scottish blue, but Evan's in a bright pink and orange suit. Show me more."

With a mixture of relief, pride, and vulnerability, Annabelle turned the page. This one showed Violet morphing from a tiny cop into an oversized warrior who dwarfed the triplets. Godzilla Violet lifted a foot as though to stomp them out of existence."

"Perfect." Noah shook his head in delighted amusement.

She turned another page to reveal Abasi seated in a glass box of a prison while Rochelle stood outside, saying, *"You can help us fine from in there."*

Abasi looked relaxed and amused in his signature tailored suit, while Rochelle was clad in full RoboCop armor.

"Hilarious." Noah grinned at her. "But he needs more guards."

Annabelle laughed. "I can sort that."

He pointed at the pad. "Where am I? You've drawn the whole team, right?"

She bit her bottom lip while debating whether or not to show him.

"Come on," he coaxed. "I won't be offended. Hell, I'm flattered that someone with your skill wants to draw any of us. Show me. Pretty please."

"You're pathetic." She sighed and turned to the page where she'd drawn him.

His face blank, Noah studied it intently. It was impossible to tell what he thought of her drawing. She'd put him in a series of comic book panels, showing him transforming from a ferocious bulldog into a pumped-up avenger, dressed in jeans and a T-shirt and toting a gun. Fearless, he confronted a faceless gang while a small family cowered behind him in the background. He was larger than life. Immovable. Their defender. And all his character said to the gang was, "*No.*"

"That's..." He seemed at a loss for words. "Amazing," he finished at last, looking up at Annabelle. There was an intensity in his gaze that she couldn't decipher. And suddenly, the room seemed a whole lot smaller and way more intimate than when he first walked in.

Swallowing hard, she quickly shut her sketchbook, her cheeks burning as if they were on fire. She shouldn't have shown him the drawing. It gave away far too much. Hell, it was practically an ode to hero worship.

"Can I have it?" Noah's question surprised her, making her eyes snap back to his. He shrugged, holding her gaze. "I mean, if you don't plan on doing anything with it."

"I don't have any plans. I was just sketching for fun."

"Well, if you don't need it, can I have it?"

Annabelle searched his face. "Are you sure you want it?"

His lips quirked into a smile that felt like a caress. "Just give me the drawing, Bella."

She sucked in a breath. Her aunt was the only one who'd ever called her Bella.

"Sorry," he said. "I meant Annabelle... but I still want the drawing."

"Bella's fine," she whispered as she carefully ripped the page from the sketchbook and held it out to him.

His fingers brushed against hers, and it felt like an electric current running through her body. She froze, the drawing suspended between them. For a moment, it was as though the air had transformed into fog, making it difficult to breathe and shutting out the world around them. The walls of the room seemed to move closer, the space forming an intimate cocoon.

"Noah?" she whispered.

He wet his lips, his eyes darting between her eyes and her mouth, and for a second, he appeared to move closer. She held her breath as time suspended. And then... he shot to his feet, taking the drawing with him.

"Thank you." His voice was low and rough. "I can't wait to show my kids. Good night, Annabelle."

Without looking back, he strode from the room, leaving Annabelle alone to wonder if the previous few moments had taken place only in her imagination.

* * *

"*Coward*," Therese said in disgust as Noah strode into the room.

She stood by the window, arms folded over her form-fitting red minidress and balancing on four-inch heels in matching blood red.

"Don't start," he muttered to her as he carefully put the drawing on the top shelf of his closet, where it would be safe from damage until he could get it home. He closed the door a little more forcefully than intended before getting into bed.

Therese paced beside the window, a scowl on her face.

"*I can't believe you bailed on her like that.*" She jabbed her hand in the direction of the panic room. "*You were this close*"—she held up her index finger and thumb to show him —"*to a Hollywood movie first kiss,*" she finished dramatically. "*And don't tell me you didn't want to kiss her. I've seen that look in your eyes often enough to know what it means.*"

Noah turned away from her, pulled the covers up around him, and punched his pillow—a little too enthusiastically—to make it comfortable.

Unfortunately, that left him facing the panic room, and as he watched, the light went off, plunging it into darkness. Annabelle would be curling up to sleep now, her thick hair spread out around her face on the pillow. Her eyes would close slowly, those dark lashes settling like crescents on satin smooth cheeks. And as she fell into a deep sleep, her full lips would open slightly.

He squeezed his eyes shut against the images inside his head.

"*What's wrong with you?*"

Unfortunately, he couldn't close himself off from the voice in his head.

Noah reopened his eyes to find Therese crouched beside the bed, her anger replaced with compassion. A ghostly hand reached out to stroke his cheek, and he almost believed he felt her caress.

"*Noah,*" she whispered. "*You've lived like a saint for five years. You need to move on.*"

"I don't know how," he whispered back. "I don't know how to let go of you."

"*Silly man.*" She smiled sadly. "*You can't let go of me. I'm a huge part of your life, and our boys are a walking, talking reminder of everything we had. I'll always be here. But you don't need to let me go to create space in your life for someone else. There's room enough for both of us.*"

Noah's throat tightened around the words he couldn't get out. Words about fear. About loss. But he didn't need to express them; Therese knew what he was thinking.

"*My poor darling,*" she said. "*You can't control who stays and who leaves, and no matter how many barricades you build, you can't protect yourself against the future. But if you keep trying to do that, you'll never really live. You have to be brave, Noah.*"

Only Therese and possibly his childhood friends could get away with calling him a coward.

"I love you so much," he whispered, aching deep to his bones.

"*Of course you do.*" There were tears in her eyes. "*But here's what I've learned: people who love deeply are more likely to love again. You can't help it. There's too much of it bottled up inside of you, and it has to go somewhere. Plus, you need to think of our boys, Noah. If you're afraid to let go, afraid to love again, they'll grow up thinking that's normal.*"

And you don't want them to miss out on what we had. What you could have again. Do you?"

"I don't miss that you were always smarter than me," Noah said.

"And always right," she said. *"Don't forget that part."*

"How can I when you're always here to remind me?"

"Go to sleep." Therese leaned in to press a whisper-faint kiss to his brow.

Before he could reply, she'd faded away. Leaving him alone, staring at the door to the panic room. The door that led to the most fascinating woman he'd met since Therese's death. It was only a few short steps from his bed, yet it felt like a chasm.

Do your job, he told himself. Worry about everything else later.

With those thoughts foremost in his mind, Noah fell into a fitful sleep.

Chapter Sixteen

Annabelle woke with a scream, but it was lost in the wailing siren that echoed through the panic room. She threw back the covers, jumped out of bed, and ran for the open door and Noah. They collided halfway.

Noah grabbed her arms to steady her as he leaned in to be heard over the screeching alarm. "We're under attack. The ground floor's on fire."

"Fire?" The word stuck in her throat as her sleep-addled brain struggled to make sense of it.

"Shoes," he ordered.

"Shoes?" Another word that seemed alien. "I don't have any. I have slippers. Somewhere." She looked around as though they might magically appear.

"Noah," a man's voice barked from the hallway. "You got her?"

"We're heading upstairs now." Noah took her hand. "We'll worry about shoes later," he told her while hauling her out of the room.

Abasi stood in the narrow hallway. His suit jacket was

gone, the sleeves of his crisp white shirt were rolled up, and he held a gun in his hand.

"I've got your six." He gestured to the doorway at the end of the hall. The one leading up to the roof. Not the one that opened into the other bedroom. Surely they didn't mean to go upstairs? To go outside?

Annabelle shook her head. No. They couldn't mean that.

"How many in the building?" Noah asked as he slid past Abasi, taking her with him.

"No clue. Comms are down, and phones are dead. The arseholes have a signal jammer."

"Sprinklers?"

"Somebody shut off the mains water supply."

"Fire extinguishers?"

"We're doing what we can with them."

They rushed past the doorway leading into the loft area. Rochelle stood in the darkness, wearing pajama shorts with a T-shirt and her hair tied up in a messy topknot. She had her firearm trained on the living area.

"We need to get away from the building to call the fire brigade," she said brusquely.

"I'm taking Annabelle to the roof," Noah answered. "I'll see if there's a signal up there."

Roof?

No. Just no.

She'd already dismissed that option. But only inside her head. She needed to speak it out loud. They'd made a mistake. They knew she couldn't go to the roof.

"You're heading the wrong way." Annabelle dug in her heels. "I can't go to the roof. I can't go outside. You know that. This is a mistake."

Noah spun toward her, invading her space. "Listen to

me. This is our only option. We're going to the roof. And you will be safe because I'll be there." His tone was implacable.

"So will I," Abasi said.

Annabelle shook her head. "You don't understand. The panic room. We'll go there. It's safe now. We don't need to go to the roof."

"Not from fire," Noah said.

He wasn't listening to her. He didn't realize how serious this was. Her stomach lurched, and she fought the urge to vomit. The room spun as her hands shook. Inside her head, a voice screamed: *Run! Hide! Don't get taken!*

"We're running out of time here," Rochelle said.

"We'll keep you safe, Annabelle," Noah said. "We won't let anyone take you from the roof. You'll still be *on* the building. We just need to get somewhere safe where you won't breathe in smoke. Okay?"

Annabelle pressed a hand to her stomach. It was already hard to breathe, even without the smoke coming their way. She tried to back away from Noah. To go... somewhere. Anywhere that didn't involve stepping outside her sanctuary.

Glass smashed inside the loft, and Annabelle started. She clung to Noah as a whooshing sound registered.

"Firebomb," Rochelle snapped. "They're on the fire escape. Go. Now!"

She fired her gun as she moved into the loft, out of Annabelle's sight.

"You heard the boss. We need to get going. We'll talk at the top of the stairs," Noah said as he wrapped an arm around her.

He half carried her, half led her up the stairs.

Her brain couldn't process what was happening fast

enough. But her body was already in a tailspin. Tears streamed down her cheeks as it became increasingly difficult to control her breathing. By the time they reached the door to the roof, she was gasping for air in short, shallow breaths.

Annabelle stared at Abasi as he slid open the steel bar that secured the door. She'd never been through this door. Never opened it. In fact, it had been years since she'd been this close to the roof door. There'd been no need to get this close. Because she'd never seen herself stepping outside into the wide-open space that made up the roof.

Somewhere in the back of her mind, she registered that she was hyperventilating now. Dizziness made her disorientated, and the urge to run, or fight, or hide was overwhelming. Only Noah's firm hold grounded her. And even then, it wasn't enough to stop the panic from pulling her into the abyss.

More gunshots rang out below.

"R-Rochelle," she managed to say.

Noah replied, "The team's down there. She has backup. Our job is to take care of you."

He turned to face her and put his hands on her shoulders again as he stared into her eyes. "Let me protect you. Trust me to take care of you. I can be your wall." He motioned to the warehouse. "Brick and mortar. I can be a different kind of wall. All you have to do is stay close, and I'll shelter you. I promise."

There was a sharp pain inside of her where she was desperate to believe him. To believe *in* him.

"No more time," Abasi barked. "Take her out to the roof before it's too late."

As if punctuating the urgency, an explosion rocked the building, sending Annabelle into Noah's arms. She clung to him and stared into his eyes, searching his face for reassurance, desperate to believe his promise as she felt cast adrift. Terrified. Lost.

"P-please," she forced through chattering teeth. "D-don't leave me."

"Never." He wrapped his arm around her waist and held her tight against him. His back pressed against the door, swinging it open, and without hesitation, he rushed into the night.

Into the outside world.

Into the fear that'd controlled her for more than a decade.

The glow from the streetlamps illuminated the flat landscape of the warehouse roof. It might as well have been the surface of the moon as far as Annabelle was concerned. It felt just as alien as if she'd been propelled into space. Clouds reflected the yellow lights of the city, and the downtown skyline sparkled in the distance.

For a split second, she saw everything clearly and individually before the colors and lights blurred and swirled, blending together in one vast, overwhelming kaleidoscope of information.

"C-can't b-breathe." The words were strangled and lost in the rush to get to safety.

She *knew* it was Noah who held her, who carried her away from danger. Logically, she *knew* that this time, she was being taken to safety and not being stolen by men who intended her harm. But her emotions, her overwhelmed nervous system, couldn't perceive a difference in the circumstances. All she *felt* was someone big, strong, and scary lifting her and taking her away. Stealing her from the security she'd come to depend upon. Changing her life forever.

Suddenly, she was back there.

It was late afternoon. The sun was sat low in the sky but still felt warm on her face. She smiled, amused by something her friend Sherie said during class. She was happy. Optimistic. Excited about life.

Then, a van stopped beside her on the road.

Annabelle didn't think much of it until the side door slid open and two men in ski masks jumped out. For a moment, it didn't seem real. And then they grabbed her. Her heavy bag, full of books, fell to the sidewalk with a thud. Arms wrapped around her. She drew in a deep breath and screamed. She kicked out, hitting nothing. A hand covered her mouth, silencing her. She breathed in leather and sweat. Faces stared at her. Other students. Frozen in horror as the van door slammed shut. Tires screeched, and a nauseating stench of oil and blood filled the air. She tried to reach the door, but the world tilted and spun around her. And then she slid to the metal floor of the van as everything faded to darkness.

Again.

* * *

Annabelle slumped against Noah, and he tightened his hold on her as he rushed to find cover. There weren't many options—the stairwell housing, a large water tank, and an old chimney. He dodged around the loft skylights, heading for the chimney. When he got there, he sank down behind it, holding Annabelle close.

Seconds later, Abasi joined them just as Annabelle started to come around. She let out a moan as Abasi said, "There are too many ways they can get onto this roof." His voice was low as he crouched, ready to shoot at anybody who came close. "They're on the fire escape, but the building next door looks clear so far."

"Too far to jump to the neighbor's roof," Noah said, watching Annabelle.

Her eyelids fluttered open. "Noah?"

"Hey," he said soothingly. "It's okay; you're safe. You're with me and Abasi. Breathe slowly and stay calm. You're fine."

She blinked several times before her eyes sprang fully open. She sucked in air, filling her lungs, preparing to scream.

Noah stroked her cheek, stopping her. "Look at me," he ordered. "Only me. Don't take your eyes off me. We need you to stay quiet. You're safe with me. Don't stop looking at me. Got it?"

She nodded furiously, staring into his face, her fingers curled into the front of his shirt, nails scraping his chest. He didn't care. He just needed her to remain quiet and calm.

"Got a signal?" he asked Abasi while maintaining eye contact with Annabelle.

"No." Abasi tucked his phone back into his pocket. "Who knew these dickheads were smart enough to bring a signal jammer?"

Annabelle was stiff as a board beside Noah. Every now and then, she shivered, but she didn't scream. She didn't panic. She didn't run. These were all good things.

"Focus on your breathing and my face," he told her. "Count it in and out. That's all you have to do. Concentrate on me and on counting through your breathing. Nod if you understand."

She gave a sharp nod.

"Good, you're doing good." He didn't ease his hold on her, wanting her to feel the solidity of his presence and stay focused on the now. "I'm looking away briefly, but I'm not going anywhere. Keep your eyes on me. Okay?"

Another terse nod.

"You're doing great," he soothed her before glancing across the rooftop. "Can you try to get to the building next door or find a way down to the street? We need to see if we can get a signal," he said to Abasi.

"Not a good idea. Who'll watch your backside?"

"Getting help is more important."

Dark eyes met his. They were unflinching. "You have your job. I have mine."

"You are a pain in my ass," Noah said, looking for another option.

There weren't any.

Gunfire rang out below them. The fire alarm suddenly cut out, and there was a weird moment of silence in which he could hear Annabelle's breathing. It was broken by a grunt, then a distant thud. Another grunt. Another thud. They came from the space between the two buildings.

Something slammed against the stairwell door, making it shudder, and Annabelle's nails dug into his chest. He whispered reassurance to her as smoke rose in the air.

"You see anything?" Noah whispered to Abasi.

Abasi shook his head, aiming past the edge of the old brick chimney.

A screeching whistle rent the air, followed by tapping on a megaphone. "Attention, all Demon Brothers," a male Scottish accent bellowed into the night. "We have you surrounded. Lay down your arms and surrender. Otherwise, you will feel the wrath of Benson Security."

Abasi and Noah shared a surprised look.

"Evan," they said at the same time.

"Shouldn't he be watching the camera feed?" Abasi said.

There was the sound of breaking glass followed by a scream, then a sickening thud.

"Looks like our resident miniature psychopath's taken out yet another member of your gang," Evan shouted cheerily. "Better give up before she ninjas her way through the rest of you."

"I think he's multi-tasking," Noah said.

Annabelle made a strange hiccupping sound that could have been due to shock or a strangled laugh. Noah glanced at her face. Definitely shock.

There were another two grunts and thuds in rapid succession.

"And we have two more down!" Evan announced. "This time, taken out by a canny Scot armed with a beanbag gun. Logan, your aim is spot-on as usual. Bit of an embarrassment for the away team, who think they're such badasses with their automatic weapons and amateur tattoos."

There was another loud bang at the stairwell door, followed by the sound of gunfire.

"Never get caught in a confined space with a pissed-off former FBI agent," Evan called. "Score another one for Benson Security. That takes us to seven-nil to the home team. Will the away team concede the game? Or are they dumb enough to keep playing?"

Automatic weapon fire sounded like a series of ill-timed fireworks.

"Seems the answer's yes," Evan said when the gunfire stopped. "The away team *is* dumb enough to keep playing."

There was a loud explosion a couple of blocks away,

and a fireball lit up the night sky. Annabelle gasped, but she didn't stop looking at Noah.

"Sorry, boys," Evan said. "Looks like you've lost your ride home. Please put your hands together in appreciation for my brother Harris, who is not only a charming bastard but can also blow up pretty much anything he wants. I hope you weren't too attached to those motorbikes."

Annabelle started to shake in Noah's arms. She tore her gaze from his and buried her face in his chest.

"It's okay," he reassured her. "You're safe."

It took a moment, but she looked back up at him. Tears streamed down her cheeks, but a tremulous smile curved her lips. "Th-they're insane," she managed to say.

It took him a beat to register what she meant. "The triplets? Yeah. I'm getting that."

"Th-they make me look normal." She hiccupped again in what seemed to be a weird little hysterical laugh.

"They make all of us look normal," Noah assured her.

He'd never been more grateful for the brothers than in that moment. To see Annabelle smile through her terror made every crazy stunt they pulled worth it.

At a scraping noise behind them, Abasi spun around, aiming in that direction.

"Don't shoot," Logan said as he hurried toward them, keeping low. "I scaled the wall to let you know we managed to get a call out. Help's on its way." He grinned, looking like he was having a blast. "Although I don't think we'll need it. Harris just took out their motorbikes. They parked a few streets over, so we didn't hear them arrive. Violet's been picking off the gang one by one." His eyes danced. "She's tiny, and they don't see her coming. Rodrigo has the fire under control on the ground floor; rest of it's mainly smoke damage. He can also do this cool thing where he puts the bad guys in a headlock and knocks them out in seconds. I need to learn how to do that. But I was the one who tied them up." He looked so proud of himself that Noah had to resist the urge to pat him on the head.

In the distance, sirens wailed. Yet again, the cavalry was running late.

"Oh!" Logan reached into his back pocket and produced a Hershey bar. He offered it to Annabelle, who appeared bewildered by his gift. "Sugar," he said. "I hear it's good for shock, and you must be shocked out of your mind now that you're outside the building. Eat it. Feel better."

Annabelle's eyes were so wide that Noah thought they might pop out of her head. Slowly, she smiled, and then she began to shake. As the sirens grew louder, a slightly hysterical giggle escaped her. And by the time the fire crew arrived, she was laughing hard.

"Should we worry about that?" Logan asked Noah, pointing at Annabelle.

Noah hugged his charge and shook his head. "Laughter beats passing out or panicking and running off the roof."

That made Annabelle laugh even louder.

"True." Logan placed a gentle hand on Annabelle's arm. "So, what do you think of the roof?"

She collapsed against Noah in hysterical laughter. "St-stop being funny. My stomach hurts. I can't take any more."

"What'd I say?" Logan asked, looking confused.

"The cops are on the pitch," Evan announced through his loudspeaker. "They think it's all over. It is now."

"Soccer references," Abasi muttered, shaking his head. He glanced back at Noah. "Didn't have to deal with this in my last job."

"No," Noah said. "You had to deal with sociopathic criminals."

Abasi shrugged like it was no big deal. "She good?" He lifted his chin toward Annabelle, who'd calmed down somewhat.

"I don't know." Noah gently nudged Annabelle. "You okay?"

She'd been staring up at the stars and slowly turned her attention to him, her expression one of pure awe. "I'm outside," she whispered.

"Yes, you are." He smiled down at her as he held her tight.

Chapter Seventeen

Detectives Johnson and McMillan stood beside Noah and Rochelle on the sidewalk outside the warehouse. Together, grim-faced, they stared at the building in the early morning light. It didn't look good. Windows were smashed, soot clung to the brick on the ground floor, and the shop was completely burned out. The stench of smoke and fire extinguisher chemicals hung in the air.

The fire crew were packing up and the chief walked over to join them. "Most of the damage was contained to the shop area." She brushed back the hair that'd worked loose from her ponytail, smearing soot across her cheek. "The damage is cosmetic, with the worst of it contained to the store—mainly because that had the most to burn. Aside from some isolated patches of fire damage on the other two floors, from the Molotov cocktails before they were doused with fire retardant, it's mostly smoke damage." She glanced back at the building. "Helluva clean up, though."

"But it's safe to remain in the building?" Rochelle asked.

"I'm not sure why you'd want to stay in there, but yeah, it's safe."

"Thanks," Rochelle said with sincerity.

The fire chief nodded at them before striding off to join her team.

"I'll get the team to board up the shop windows," Noah said once she was gone. "No point in replacing the glass right now. We need to look into protecting the sprinkler system too."

"You reckon they'll try this again?" Johnson asked, making no effort to hide his skepticism.

"Who knows what they'll do next?" Noah said. "It's clear this isn't the end of it, though. How many Demons do you have in custody?"

"Eleven," Johnson said. "That includes the ones taken out by beanbags while climbing the fire escape. Of course, we have another three in the hospital with gunshot wounds. No dead. This time." He shook his head, a grin on his face. "I gotta ask—beanbags?"

Noah inclined his head toward Rochelle. "The boss made the mistake of telling the triplets to use their brains to defend the place, seeing as she won't let them near a gun until they've had some training. They took that to mean they should improvise—hence the megaphone and beanbags."

McMillan frowned. "Would have been good if they'd stopped at that. Your boy blew up some bikes, taking out a streetlight and windows in the process. You might want to tell Ms. Simmons that she's pissing off the neighbors."

"I'll get right on that," Noah said drolly.

"What I'd like to know,' Rochelle said. "Is where was the patrol car that should have been keeping an eye on the place?"

The two detectives exchanged a look, their expressions dark.

"We don't know," Johnson said at last. "Somebody gave the order to stop patrols. They pretended to be Mac to do it."

"Trust me," McMillan growled. "We're just as pissed as you are about this."

"I doubt it." Rochelle's eyes were ablaze. "You didn't spend half the night fighting off people intent on barbequing you."

McMillan glared at her. "They used *my* name to put you in danger."

Rochelle was unmoved. "Again. We were the ones dodging flames."

"Hey." Johnson held out his hands, asking for peace. "Nobody's saying you guys haven't been through it. Mac's just angry at being used. We're all on the same side here, remember?"

"Are we?" Rochelle's eyes narrowed at them.

McMillan exploded, his head turning purple, which couldn't have been good for his heart condition. "What the hell is that supposed to mean?"

Unintimidated, Rochelle took a step closer to the man. "There's a leak, and I'm wondering if it's in the DA's office or your department. Where do you think it is, Detective?"

"Okay, enough." Noah stepped between them. "This isn't helping." He looked at Johnson. "You're investigating that order, right?"

"You bet your life we are." Johnson swept back his navy suit jacket and planted his hands on his hips. He had a good few inches on them all, but his frame was mainly skin and bone. Didn't mean there wasn't muscle in there somewhere. He just hid it well.

"This can't go on," Johnson said. "You know that." He glanced at the warehouse. "Your safe house is falling apart. The smart move is to get Ms. Simmons out of there before things get worse."

"Worse how?" Rochelle demanded. "So far, they've broken in to shoot at her, and now they've tried to burn her out. They're running out of options—and gang members. Plus, you know we can't move her. As much as I'd like to get her out of here."

"Maybe you can get one of the guys you picked up last night to turn on their boss," Noah said, knowing it was a long shot.

McMillan scoffed. "I'd say the chances of that are about the same as you getting your client to leave the warehouse."

"Surely there's something you can use for leverage," Rochelle said. "Some way you can put the pressure on. There must be somebody inside the Demon Brothers who wants out and is happy to snitch on Eddie Hanson to do it."

"We know how to do our job," McMillan barked.

Johnson pinched the bridge of his nose. "Do you two need a time-out? We're all on the same side here, remember?"

"Yet someone inside the police department called off our support." Rochelle was clearly angrier than Noah had realized.

McMillan bristled again, closing the distance between him and Rochelle. "Are you calling us crooked?"

He'd picked the wrong woman to try to intimidate. "No. I'm asking you outright. Are you in Eddie Hanson's pocket?"

At this point, Noah and Johnson wedged themselves between the pair, breaking them apart. Noah stood in front of Rochelle. Not to protect her, more to stop her from punching the older cop.

"This isn't achieving anything," he said to Johnson.

"No kidding." Johnson had a hand on his partner's arm. "I get why you might think we're dirty in this situation, but we aren't. All I can tell you is that we'll find out what happened last night, and in the meantime, we'll double the patrols. This time, we'll make it clear that the only order they follow to stop driving by here comes from us in person. Does that help?"

"Yeah," Noah said quickly, before Rochelle could lose her cool again.

"Come on." Johnson clapped his partner on the shoulder and turned him toward their car. "Let's go interview some of those Demon Brothers."

"You think we can be trusted with that?" McMillan called over his shoulder to Rochelle.

Thankfully, she didn't reply.

They watched as the two men got into their sedan and drove away.

Noah turned to face his boss. "Okay, why were you prodding those guys?"

"I needed to see how they reacted," she said, looking weary.

"And did it tell you anything?"

"Yeah. I don't think either of them is in on this."

"Then perhaps they can help."

"Maybe." She didn't look convinced.

"I'll get this place secured," Noah said.

Rochelle nodded. "I need to have a word with the triplets. There's using your brain and improvising, and then there's making a laughingstock of Benson Security. I mean, the beanbags I can buy. But a megaphone? Not to mention, we're facing a bill for the damage Harris caused when he blew up the bikes."

"It helped, though. All of it did."

"This time. Who knows what they'll do next time."

She had a point.

"Can you leave it until later? I need them to board up the windows first," he said.

"Sure." She glanced down at her ruined nightwear. "I could use a shower and change anyway."

Noah watched her walk into the building while making a mental list of everything they needed to shore up the place. He hoped Annabelle hadn't been too emotionally attached to the contents of her aunt's old shop because they were gone. At this rate, they wouldn't have to worry about moving Annabelle—the building would disintegrate around her, and she'd be forced to leave by default.

He sent a quick text to the triplets, who appeared almost instantly. Once they were set up, he went upstairs to find Annabelle and Katrina clearing up the latest mess in her apartment.

Annabelle smiled at him. "Abasi and Rodrigo were looking for you. I think they're down in the office now."

"You okay?" he asked, searching her face for the truth.

"I don't know," she said with a tight laugh. "Ask me again later?"

"You've got it." After one last glance at Katrina, who nodded that she had everything under control, he went back downstairs.

The damage on the second floor was minimal. The Demons had focused on setting fire to the first floor, blocking exits, and attacking the top floor. Although their use of fire, supplemented with smoke bombs, meant the whole building reeked. They'd intended to smoke

Annabelle out, literally. Almost succeeded too. But he couldn't think about that.

He found Rodrigo and Abasi sitting at Evan's computer station, while he was downstairs helping his brothers board up windows. They looked to be deep in conversation, which stopped abruptly as soon as he entered the room. When they saw it was him, they looked relieved.

Curious.

"Is Violet on patrol?" he asked as he pulled a chair up beside them.

"She's stationed herself on the roof for now," Rodrigo said, "and she's armed to the teeth."

Noah wasn't sure if that was a good or bad thing. "What's up? Annabelle said you were looking for me."

Rodrigo got up, crossed to the door, and shut it.

Curiouser still.

"We have a plan," Rodrigo said when he sat back down, keeping his voice low.

"Is it a plan Rochelle wouldn't approve of?" Noah asked.

Rodrigo smiled with amusement. "Oh yeah."

"Is somebody gonna tell me this plan, or do I have to guess?"

"Abasi and I have been talking," Rodrigo said. "We don't like the current situation. We're living on borrowed time just sitting here, waiting to be attacked, and we reckon it's time to change the game."

Noah frowned at Abasi. "You can't shoot anybody in the head."

"This is a new plan," he drawled, perfectly relaxed.

"You see." Rodrigo sat forward and rested his forearms on his knees. "We can't start a war with any of the other gangs because nobody's dumb enough to take on the

Demons. But there's nothing to stop us from disrupting their day-to-day activities."

"I thought we were doing that." Noah rubbed his chin, suddenly aware that he smelled like a smokehouse too. "Aren't we chasing their money?"

"We're talking about something a little more immediate," Rodrigo said. "They have supply chains going through Texas. If we found out the where and when of what they've got going, we could sneak in and mess things up for them."

"No business. No money. No power," Abasi said. "And a whole lot of pissed-off customers."

"They'll have plenty to worry about other than Annabelle's testimony."

Noah considered their proposal for a moment. They were right that Rochelle would never go for it—especially if it meant interfering with ongoing official investigations. "I assume you mean for this to be a three man operation."

"Violet isn't good at stealth," Rodrigo said, which was a massive understatement.

"Or at not killing people," Abasi added.

"The triplets are too young and inexperienced," Rodrigo continued. "Katrina doesn't have the training, and Rochelle would stop us. Which leaves us three."

"How do we find out what they have going on?" Noah didn't challenge their assessment of the team. "We'd have to bring Evan in on this. If we do it," he added hastily.

Rodrigo shook his head. "Evan will tell his brothers. Or freak out over whether his mom would approve of whatever he's hacking."

"Then where do we get our info?"

"I still have contacts," Abasi said. "I didn't burn all my bridges when I took apart the James Family."

"And," Rodrigo said with a smile, "we have Elle."

Noah's eyebrows shot up at that. "You want to leave our own tech specialist in the dark but call in the one in the London office? Let me count the ways *that* could backfire."

"Abasi's practically her brother," Rodrigo said. "She'd do anything for him."

Abasi didn't contradict him. "At least this time, she's half a world away from any physical danger."

"Elle can find trouble wherever she is." Noah wasn't joking. Sometimes, he suspected the young, blue-haired hacker went searching for it.

"I'll make sure she knows the parameters of her involvement," Abasi said.

"So, what? We dig up whatever info we can get on the Demons' operations and then sabotage them?"

Abasi and Rodrigo shared a look.

"That sums it up," Rodrigo said.

"And we do this without the rest of the team knowing? Or even noticing we're missing?"

"Yeah." Rodrigo grinned.

"I don't like it," Noah said. "I don't like going behind Rochelle's back. It doesn't feel right. Plus, I don't like the idea of leaving Annabelle alone."

Abasi was unimpressed. "Told you he'd go all Boy Scout on us."

"He's just thinking it through," Rodrigo said before turning back to Noah. "You won't be leaving Annabelle alone. We'll get Violet to watch her."

Noah cocked an eyebrow at him. "Can't tell you how reassuring that is."

"Look." Rodrigo was earnest. "You don't know a whole lot about my past, but believe me when I tell you that I have extensive experience dealing with organized crime."

"And I used to *be* organized crime," Abasi added.

Rodrigo shot him a look that said he wasn't helping. "Noah, it's nine days until the trial. Last night was only the beginning. We can't just fortify the place and sit around waiting for someone to shoot at us. We need to take the fight to them. You know I'm right about this. Benson Security isn't a passive organization. You've been on plenty of missions where the job was to undermine the enemy. That's all we're asking you to do here. This op's covert. Disruption only. It will buy us the time we need to keep Annabelle safe, I promise."

Noah rubbed his sore leg. It was healing nicely, but he still experienced a twinge of pain now and then. They were right. Things would only get worse if they didn't do something proactive. But he didn't have to like it.

"No killing," he said firmly.

"Stealth operation," Rodrigo said with a nod. "We're in and out without them even catching a glimpse of us."

Noah stared Abasi down. "No. Killing."

He smiled. "I heard you the first time. Scout's honor. No killing."

"And if there's even a hint that Annabelle won't be safe while we're gone, we call it off."

"Agreed," Rodrigo said readily.

Abasi nodded.

"And you call Elle." Noah pointed at Abasi. "I need some deniability here."

"So, you're in?" Rodrigo asked as the two men held him with their gaze.

"I'm in." Noah stood. "Don't make me regret this."

With that, he left the office. Already second-guessing his decision.

Chapter Eighteen

Noah didn't make it to the loft. Watching over Annabelle would have to wait for the time being because the assistant district attorney had arrived with her boss in tow.

From the second-floor landing, Noah watched the district attorney sweep into the building like it was just another stop on his campaign trail. All bleached teeth and expensive hair plugs, the man oozed synthetic charm as he held out his hand to Rochelle in the foyer below. At least she'd had time to shower and dress in one of her many suits.

"There's more people coming through here than Grand Central Station," Noah muttered to Abasi, who'd come up beside him.

"The man has expensive taste in suits." From his expression, Abasi was busy tallying up the cost of making the DA look perpetually camera ready.

"So do you." Noah cocked his head at Abasi's Italian suit.

"Yep, and I know how *I* can afford to look this good. Got

to wonder where a public lawyer gets the money for that sort of wardrobe."

"District attorneys make decent money. I'm sure he can afford a bespoke suit."

"From Italy? Or Sackville Row? Maybe he could afford one or two. But I did some digging and this guy has a wardrobe full of them. No DA on the planet makes enough to finance that."

"I'll take your word for it, seeing as I buy my clothes at the mall. We should probably dig into his background and finances. The leak could be anyone."

Abasi's expression made it clear he thought Noah had said something as obvious as the sun is hot.

"Ms. Davis." The DA's voice echoed through the tiled stairwell. "It's a pleasure to meet you. I'm sure you already know, but please allow me to introduce myself. I'm District Attorney Dwight Carpenter. Margaret has kept me up to date on the job you're doing to protect our star witness. Isn't that right, Margaret?"

ADA Grant gave a non-committal grunt.

The DA ignored her. "Benson Security has quite the reputation." His smile was wide, and his gaze cunning. "Although, it seems you may have bitten off more than you can chew this time. I heard there was some trouble last night. How's our witness?"

Oh yeah, the DA had an agenda.

"Election year," Noah muttered.

"Duh," Abasi said.

"Thank you, DA Carpenter." Rochelle smiled serenely, her expression giving nothing away. "Ms. Simmons is perfectly fine. My team did everything within their power to ensure she remained safe and secure throughout the attack."

The DA gestured up at Noah and Abasi. "That's good to hear. Margaret tells me your team is quite experienced."

"In many different areas," Rochelle said evenly.

Noah leaned into Abasi and muttered, "Here's hoping he doesn't ask for specifics."

Abasi didn't reply.

"I gather," the DA said, as though speculating, "that most of your team is immigrants. They might not be used to the way we do things here in the States."

"They're fast learners," Rochelle said sweetly.

"Yes, but a steep learning curve is no substitute for local knowledge and experience. I have to agree with ADA Grant in this matter: it would be best if Ms. Simmons left her protection to the professionals." He smiled benignly at everyone around him. "We have a lovely safe house ready for her. She'll be quite comfortable there."

"As much as we appreciate the offer," Rochelle said, standing her ground, "Ms. Simmons is unable to leave this building, and to take her from it would render her incapable of testifying for your office."

His eyes narrowed. "That sounds suspiciously like a threat, Ms. Davis."

Rochelle smiled. "Of course not. It's just fact. If you want to discuss it with her psychiatrist, I'd be happy to call her."

"I don't believe that's necessary. I would, however, like to speak with our witness." The DA pointed to the stairs. "May I? I'm eager to meet Ms. Simmons. That's one courageous little lady."

"Little lady?" Noah whispered. "Are we in an episode of *The Dukes of Hazzard?*"

"More like Monty Python," Abasi grumbled. "I'm outta

here. I don't shake hands with snakes." He turned on his heel and headed for the office door.

"Of course." Rochelle stepped aside, no longer blocking the stairs and gestured for the DA to proceed. "Please, follow me. Annabelle's up in her apartment right now." She shot Noah a look, but he already had his phone out, texting Katrina to give her a heads-up while the DA and his police escort climbed the stairs.

"I heard you'd moved in," Dwight said, holding out a hand to Noah as he reached the second floor.

It was a firm shake. No clammy palm or attempt to assert his dominance.

"Only place to be when you can't move the client out," Noah said.

"True, so true." Dwight grimaced. "This can't be the job you expected when you answered Margaret's call for help."

"We know how to pivot at Benson Security," Noah assured him.

The DA sauntered into their office, his gaze taking in everything. The man might come across as a "good old boy," but he was shrewd and didn't miss a thing—qualities that probably made him excel at his job.

"Looks like a police station," the DA said with a grin.

"Well, half our team is former law enforcement." Rochelle joined him in the room.

"And the other half?" the DA asked.

"They have different skills." Rochelle gestured to the stairs up to the third floor. "Shall we?"

"Of course." Dwight's attention lingered on the whiteboard, full of information about the Demon Brothers, before he followed Rochelle up to Annabelle's apartment.

Behind them, Noah kept a close eye on the DA's

entourage while ADA Grant did nothing to hide her irritation at her boss's interference in her case.

"Polls down?" Noah asked as he fell into step beside her.

Her lip curled. "Nothing like a major case to bring the voters out in an election year." She glanced at her wristwatch with clear frustration.

"In a hurry?" Noah asked.

"This isn't my only case," Margaret said. "Although it will seem like it until it's over." She glanced around before lowering her voice. "How's Annabelle doing, really?"

"Good. She'll make an excellent witness."

"If we make it to trial," Margaret said darkly. "The Demon Brothers certainly stepped up their game last night. The shop looks like a bomb hit it."

"No, the bomb took out their motorcycles. The first floor just suffered a fire. I know things are worrying right now, and the Demons are certainly unpredictable, but no matter what happens, we'll keep her safe," Noah promised.

"I sure hope so," Margaret said grimly. "Because if you don't, we'll all go down for losing our witness, not to mention our only chance of putting Eddie Hanson away for a very long time. My job is hard, Mr. Merchant, but I'd still like to keep it."

"Interesting." Noah held the door to the apartment open for her. "I've been wondering if losing mine might be the best thing that could happen to me. There are only so many years a man can get shot at before he starts questioning what the hell he's doing with his life."

Margaret blinked at him, appearing surprised by his candor. "Have you ever considered that you might be in the wrong line of work?"

"Every damn day," Noah said as he followed her into Annabelle's home.

* * *

One minute, Annabelle was trying to figure out how to get rid of the burn marks on her wooden floor, and the next, Katrina was telling her to put on her game face because the district attorney had arrived. Seemed like everyone in Houston wanted to be in her old warehouse—invited or not.

"Ms. Simmons." The DA made a beeline for her, his hand outstretched. "May I call you Annabelle?"

"Sure." She shook his hand, all the while wondering why he was there. "Are you taking over from ADA Grant?" she blurted, unintentionally causing Margaret to bristle and glare at her boss.

"No, no, no. Nothing like that." The DA beamed at her and the ADA. "I just wanted to meet our star witness and ensure you're fine after last night's drama."

Annabelle was bewildered. She caught Noah's eye, and he smiled his encouragement. "Well, I'm a bit rattled, and my aunt's shop is ash and debris, but other than that, I'm fine. The team did a great job of making sure the gang didn't get near me. I feel very safe with them."

"Is that right?" The DA walked over to the window where she'd witnessed the murder. "This is where you were standing that night, isn't it?" He smiled back at her. "I've reviewed the case file, which contains several photos of your apartment." He glanced around. "Although I see some things have changed since then."

Annabelle wasn't quite sure which of his questions to answer first and was grateful when Rochelle spoke up.

"We spent some time fortifying this floor of the building

after the first attack," she told the DA. "Unfortunately, some of Annabelle's belongings got damaged during the shooting."

"Yes," the DA said, opening a mirrored glass screen. "It's clear Ms. Simmons was most fortunate to have you here that night." He gave her another smile. One that didn't make it to his eyes. "It was down there. The murder, I mean. Am I right?"

Annabelle was about to go over to him to point out what she saw, but Noah had crossed the room to stand beside her. He placed a hand on her back in a silent reminder to stay out of sight from the street.

"That's right," she said, staying where she was.

It seemed like the DA stared out of the window for far too long. At last, he closed the screen and turned back to the people inside the room. "I can't tell you how lucky it is that you were here that night. We very much appreciate that you came forward to report what you saw. I'm sure I don't have to tell you that this gang is serious business, and we owe it to the citizens of this fine city to get them off the streets. Isn't that right, Margaret?"

"That's what we're trying to do," she said through gritted teeth.

It didn't take a genius to figure out that Ms. Grant just wanted to get on with her job, while her boss wanted to insert himself into the trial for the publicity. Annabelle, who watched the news like everyone else, knew full well it was an election year. The DA hadn't hidden his desire to be reelected, and the media attention around the Demons case would go a long way toward making that happen.

DA Carpenter wandered through her loft, taking in everything with eyes that missed very little. "Great place you have here. A fantastic amount of space and a fine view of the downtown skyline. I can see why you want to stay at home rather than move to a safe house."

Annabelle frowned. Surely someone had told him that it wasn't a matter of choice. She literally couldn't leave.

"Leaving my home isn't an option," she said. "I have a condition which means I have to stay here."

"Is that right?" He spun to pin her with his intense gaze. "When was the last time you tested your theory that you can't leave this building?"

His question caught her off guard, and she was about to blurt out that, actually, she'd tested the theory just last night, but again, Noah patted her back in warning.

"Sorry, but that isn't how agoraphobia works," she said instead. "You don't test it by stepping out of your safe zone. That's why we have therapists."

"Yes, of course. You are such a brave young woman to live with such a debilitating condition."

Annabelle didn't know what to say to that, although the urge to order him out of her home was pretty darn strong.

Fortunately, she didn't have to say anything. The DA had moved on to her work area and was studying some of the photos she'd pinned to a board on her easel. "ADA Grant tells me you're quite the photographer. She says you've been taking photos of these streets for years. I imagine you've taken some fine shots. What with you being an artist and all."

"It's a hobby," Annabelle said, feeling awkward. Politeness made her want to offer her visitors coffee, but the signals coming from her security team made it clear they didn't want the DA and his police officers lingering.

The whole team were now in her loft, spread throughout, standing quietly, watching everything. She wasn't sure whether to feel reassured by their diligence or anxious about what their presence might mean. It wasn't often they all felt the need to watch over her. Did they really think someone in the room was the leak who'd sold out her location?

More to the point, did she trust everyone in the DA's office enough to believe they wouldn't do that to her?

Now that she thought about it, she was glad the team was paranoid on her behalf.

"You don't show your photographs in galleries?" the DA asked.

"No, I'm a comic book artist. I don't exhibit my work."

"Pity." He shook his head while indicating a few of the photos she'd framed and hung. "You've quite the talent."

Margaret cleared her throat pointedly.

The DA frowned at her before smiling at Rochelle. "I'm afraid I've run out of time. Meetings to attend. I'm sure you understand. I just wanted to come over and thank you personally. But..." He stepped into her personal space and held out a hand. Annabelle took it because it would be rude not to, and he closed his other hand over the top of hers, trapping her. "I want you to think long and hard about moving to a safe house. Last night's events have made it clear that your security team has a limited ability to protect you here. This building is falling apart now. You can't possibly be as safe here as you would be with us. And I know you think you can't leave this building, but there are options we could utilize to minimize the stress on you should you decide to take us up on our offer."

Her heart raced, and her throat grew tight. He couldn't mean what she thought he meant. Could he?

Noah stepped even closer. "You mean drugs." His words dripped with ice. "You want to sedate her until the trial."

"I spoke with the best physicians in Houston just before coming here," the DA said with a cold smile. "They assure me that no harm will come to Annabelle if this is the route we choose to take." He patted her hand and released it. "I would never suggest an option that endangered your health. Think about it. Talk to your own doctor and see what she thinks." He gestured around the loft. "While you're in a safe place, we could get this building back up to scratch for your return. Sometimes, Annabelle, the best options are the simplest."

With a parting nod, he strode toward the door, the two police officers falling in behind him. Rochelle and Rodrigo accompanied them. As she watched them go, Annabelle leaned into Noah, letting him take some of her weight.

"Sedate me?" she whispered. "He wants to keep me asleep until I can testify?"

It was too terrifying to contemplate.

Noah made a low growling sound before speaking. "If that's what you choose to do, we'll still protect you."

She was already shaking her head. "I'd never. No. I couldn't. You don't think—"

"No. I don't think you should let them knock you out and keep you sedated until the trial starts. It's barbaric. Plus, I don't trust anybody in the DA's office to keep you safe. It's still your decision, though, Bella."

"No." She shuddered. "Just no."

The ADA walked over to Annabelle, looking embarrassed. "I'm sorry, I honestly didn't know he was going to suggest that. If he'd made his intentions known, I would have protested beforehand."

"It's okay," Annabelle said, even though it wasn't. She cleared her throat. "He can't force me to..." She couldn't even say the words.

"No." The ADA frowned. "No. He can't. Now, let's go over your testimony again." She crossed to the dining table and set her briefcase on it.

"I'll make coffee." Noah headed for the kitchen.

The rest of the team kept to the shadows, watching intently, none of them happy with what they'd just heard.

Chapter Nineteen

Annabelle felt strangely numb when she eventually gained access to the first floor of her building and saw the extent of the damage for herself. She knew that one day, when all of this was over and she'd had time to process what happened, she'd grieve the loss of her aunt's shop. But for the moment, she couldn't think about that—or the fire itself... or the gang trying to kill her... or the hazy memory of people shooting up her panic room...

Nope.

She couldn't think about any of that.

Otherwise, she'd end up rocking back and forth in a corner, muttering about nothing being real. Because crazy stuff like this didn't happen to a housebound comic book artist. Instead, she'd pushed all her panicked thoughts and hysterical feelings into the vault at the back of her mind, which she liked to think of as a Gringotts vault from Harry Potter. She visualized it deep in the ground, sealed by magic and protected by a ferocious dragon. In other words, those thoughts weren't getting out anytime soon.

"I'm sorry about your aunt's shop." Noah came to stand beside her.

"There wasn't anything valuable in there anyway."

Except for memories.

"Still." He bumped against her, doing that weird, friendly nudge thing he liked to do. "It was a reminder of her, and I'm sorry. She named it after you, didn't she?"

Annabelle tore her eyes from the blackened mess to glance up at Noah. "She opened the shop not long after I was born. This was a family building, passed down through the generations, and she liked that its location put her smack in the middle of the arty zone. I suspect she was a bohemian at heart." She leaned over to retrieve part of a cheap, burn-damaged toy. "One with absolutely no taste or creative ability. She would've loved to have been a great artist, but she wielded a paintbrush like it was a two-by-four and she didn't have thumbs. Plus, she couldn't resist adding sparkles to everything she touched. Glitter was her friend. Dad said she inherited her drive for business from their father but lacked the direction or sense needed to take it anywhere. I honestly believe that if there hadn't been family money behind her, she'd have ended up a bag lady." She smiled sadly. "A very sparkly bag lady."

"She sounds like my kind of people," Noah said, smiling.

Annabelle's heart ached at the memories of her aunt. "Collecting other people's junk and selling it was as arty as she could get. Plus, she loved going to garage sales. According to Dad, her shop started out as an art gallery, but her bad taste meant most of the works she'd acquired were unsellable. So she repriced everything and started collecting what she called 'quirky castoffs' to supplement the store. She told me she called it Bella's Antiques to sound classy." She grinned. "There was nothing even remotely antique about the things she brought home from her buying trips."

"Did she ever sell anything?" Noah looked skeptical, and Annabelle didn't blame him.

"Not much. She mainly 'acquired' things. Every now and then, when the shop got too crowded with junk, I'd come down and box up stuff for donation—or the trash. I don't think she ever noticed." Annabelle felt quite wicked confessing her sins to Noah and also a little smug that she'd pulled off the mini heists.

He laughed before turning serious. "How are you holding up? Really."

The Gringotts vault buckled against the mass of stuff crammed inside. Its door groaned, and the dragon snarled, but the spell held.

"Are hugs still part of the service?" she asked hopefully.

A small, intimate smile tugged at the corners of his mouth. "C'mere."

Annabelle didn't have to be told twice. As his arms enfolded her, a familiar bone-deep sense of security wrapped her up tight. *Safe.* She felt safe. He clasped the back of her head, pressing her cheek to his chest, and the strong, steady drumbeat of his heart chased away the chaotic thoughts bouncing around her mind. In that moment, there was only stillness and peace. She knew Noah would protect her and that she could enjoy a brief respite from being constantly on alert.

"Are we hugging now?" Violet's disgusted and outraged tone shattered her peace. "If that's part of the job, I'm resigning. Where's the boss? I need to talk to the boss."

She watched as Violet turned on her heel and stormed back out of the burned-out shop. As Noah chuckled, it occurred to Annabelle that Violet would have made an excellent guard goblin for her vault.

* * *

By the time lunch came around, the first-floor windows and shopfront had been boarded up, and the warehouse was secure again. Proximity sensors were suggested, but Noah ruled them out. The building sat flush with the sidewalk so any passersby could trip the alarm. He did, however, have the sprinkler system secured and more fire extinguishers placed throughout the building. Although he doubted that they'd need them again after the failed attempt to smoke out Annabelle. Noah figured the gang would take a different route to get to their prey next time—if Benson Security didn't stop them first.

Lunch was another food-truck find by the triplets. As far as Noah could tell, all the brothers did during their downtime was scour Houston's streets for new places to eat. Today, it was a selection of pulled-meat sandwiches that melted in the mouth.

As the team, plus Annabelle but excluding Rodrigo, who was on patrol, sat around the desks in the office eating the lunch the triplets had fetched for them, Rochelle raised her voice, "Assignment updates, everybody. Evan, you first."

The brightly colored triplet wolfed down his sandwich before replying. "I've done some digging into the Demon Brothers' finances and think I have a promising lead. It's not on the Demons' money. I'm still chasing that. It's Eddie Hanson's personal accounts."

"I thought we were going after the gang money." Noah helped himself to another party-size sandwich from the massive share box.

"We are," Evan said. "For a while there, I assumed Eddie's money *was* gang money, seeing as he controls the finances, but his personal stuff is a whole different account. I'm not even sure the gang knows what he's squirreling away."

"You got into his accounts?" Noah was impressed.

"Nearly." Evan took two more sandwiches, put them on his plate, and then formed a barricade with his arms to stop his brothers from getting to them. He gave them the evil eye while still talking. "I managed to get into one before a fail-safe kicked me out. He had 1.8 million in it, and that's only one of several offshore accounts I've stumbled across." He growled low in his throat when Harris tried to pilfer one of his sandwiches.

"That's a lot of money." Noah marveled again at the unfairness of a world in which the bad guys grew richer while the good guys got deeper into debt. "Explains the fancy house and car."

"It's peanuts," Abasi scoffed. "And the house and car might look impressive, but I'll bet he's living well below his means. Eddie isn't about flashing the cash. He's about power."

Unlike the other members of the team, Abasi had brought his own lunch, and from the looks of it, he was eating some froufrou salad from a high-end restaurant. Just the sight of it made Noah shudder and reach for another sandwich.

"Peanuts?" Logan said, his eyes wide. "If that's peanuts, then you must have made a ton with the James Family. How much are we talking?"

Evan choked on his food, and Harris thumped him on the back.

"Dude," Harris said, "you don't ask a mobster about his personal wealth."

"*Former* mobster," Abasi corrected. "And I'm not talking about *my* money. I'm talking about the money the head of the James Family amassed over the years. It makes 1.8 million seem like peanuts."

Ignoring his brother's warning, Logan leaned forward, eyes fixed on Abasi. "What happened to all that money when the James Gang went belly-up?"

Everyone watched Abasi, who casually shrugged. "I took it."

There was a moment of stunned silence before Logan spoke again. "Gonna risk repeating myself here and ask, just how much money are we talking about?"

"All of it."

"No, seriously," Logan said. "Give me a figure."

Abasi just stared at him.

"So, Abasi," Noah said into the heavy silence, "you reckon there's a lot more money kicking around in Eddie's and the gang's accounts?"

"Definitely."

Katrina put her unfinished sandwich back down on her plate. "Money made from human trafficking, drugs, and arms dealing. That's what we're talking about here, isn't it?" Her comment was directed at Abasi, and it wasn't friendly.

"That's how you make the big bucks." He appeared unaffected by the judgment in her tone.

"Was the James Family involved in human trafficking?" Katrina asked, her focus on Abasi.

He stopped eating to stare straight at her. "No. Marcus and I shut that shit down. We ran some brothels, though. I'd be happy to supply numbers."

The tension in the room had become so thick that no one was eating anymore.

Noah cleared his throat and tried to steer the conversation into less personal territory. "Human trafficking's a huge problem here. Houston's a hub. Would be good if we could take that particular income stream away from the Demons."

Evan glanced nervously between Katrina and Abasi before answering. "I don't think we should be too fussy. I say we take away all their money from all their income streams."

"You reckon you're any closer to doing that?" Noah sipped his coffee.

Again, Evan shot Abasi a nervous glance. "With Abasi's help, yeah."

"And what will you do with their money once you take it away?" Katrina asked softly. "Do we keep it, like Abasi chose to do with the James Family's money? Or do we hand it over to the cops?"

Another strange, unspoken communication zapped between Katrina and Abasi, making the hair on the back of Noah's neck stand on end.

"I say we let Katrina decide what to do with it," Abasi said in a low, even tone. "She's the one with a vested interest in how they made their fortune."

Katrina paled but held his gaze as she raised her chin. "Then we donate it to charities working with victims of human trafficking." It was a challenge.

"Fine with me," Abasi said.

Rochelle frowned at them both. "I don't think that choice is one either of you gets to make. Let's find the money first before deciding where we move it. How much longer do you need, Evan?"

"I don't have a clue," he said cheerily. "It isn't an exact

science, but I'm working as fast as I can. Would be good to get some more help. Is it okay if I ask Elle in the London office to lend a hand?"

Noah kept his attention on his food, not wanting his expression to give anything away. He suspected Elle was already up to her ears in research for Abasi and wouldn't have time to help Evan.

"Sure, give her a call," Rochelle said before turning her attention to Noah. "Where do things stand on building security?"

"We're as secure as we'll ever be. The boys," he said, gesturing to the triplets, "still have to run some cables for the new cameras—the fire took out the last lot—but that's about it. The main thing is that the sprinkler system is now secure. Wish we'd thought of that before last night's attack." He shook his head. "Can honestly say it never occurred to me that it was possible to shut it off from outside the building. Hard lesson to learn."

"For all of us," Rochelle said. "Violet, what about weapons?"

"I've restocked the armory cabinets on each floor and bought more ammo."

Rochelle nodded. "Evan, is our video still backing up to the cloud?"

"Yep. I'm picking up a new satellite link later, just in case things go boom around here again. We don't want anyone interfering with the feed that goes to the secure server. Once there, nobody can mess with the recordings. Although the fire did a good job of taking out the ground-floor cameras. Hadn't figured that into my planning. I was anticipating a more sophisticated attack. Guess the Demons are more brawn than brain."

"And not to be underestimated." Rochelle looked back at Noah. "You still okay with being primary protection?"

"Yes!" Annabelle turned a delightful shade of pink. "He is. Aren't you?" Wide eyes pleaded with him to agree.

"I'm good," he told Rochelle, feeling amused.

"Any other business?" she asked the group.

"I have a question." Violet frowned. "Are we required to physically comfort clients now?"

All heads snapped toward Noah and Annabelle.

"That did *not* come out the way she intended," Noah said quickly. "Violet walked in on me hugging Annabelle and, well, reacted like *her*."

"You were cuddling?" Harris leaned forward and rested his elbows on the desk in front of him. "What kind of cuddling are we talking here?"

Noah's cheeks heated. "It was a comforting hug. Nothing more."

"Were you fully clothed at the time?" Harris asked.

"Harris!" Rochelle barked.

"What?" He held up his hands. "It's a reasonable question. Violet makes it sound like she walked in on them doing the special cuddle grown-ups do."

"That's it. I'm outta here." Abasi stood and strode from the room.

Noah wished he could follow him.

"Enough of this." Rochelle looked weary. "No, Violet, it isn't part of your job description to touch anyone else except in self-defense."

"Or to disable them," Violet clarified.

"Fine, that too." Rochelle rubbed her temples. "This meeting is over."

"About time," Noah muttered as he got to his feet. He

glared at Harris, but it was lost on him. "Come on," he said to Annabelle. "Let's get you upstairs."

The triplets all sat up straight, eyes like saucers as they stared at him and Annabelle. They looked like a bunch of meerkats searching for a threat.

"To work!" Noah snapped at them. "We're going upstairs to work. No hugging of any kind." He took Annabelle's arm and led her from the office.

"They know you're nothing but professional, so don't let them get to you," she said once they were in the corridor. "They enjoy it too much."

"No kidding," Noah grumbled.

"After all, it was only a hug. It's not like there was anything else going on." She fluttered her dark lashes at him. "Was there?"

Noah swallowed hard. "No, no, of course not. It was purely a professional hug."

"I thought so." She nodded solemnly.

Chapter Twenty

Annabelle couldn't concentrate on her work. Not while Noah was in the room with her. She was meant to be drawing new scenes for her latest Jade Justice graphic novel, but all she wanted to do was sketch the brooding man who sat sipping coffee at her kitchen island.

To be fair, it wasn't entirely Noah's fault she couldn't concentrate. Every time she dragged her attention away from him, she'd start thinking about the night before. It felt as though her Gringotts vault had sprung open, and no matter how hard she tried, she couldn't get it shut.

The memories were so clear in her mind that it was as if she were reliving them—the screeching alarm, the acrid smell of smoke, the darkness, and the gunfire. And the pure, unadulterated terror of going outside. Even thinking about it made her heart race and her hands shake. But more than that, it felt like it was happening now, not in the past. It was so real that she found herself scanning the loft to ensure there were no smoldering embers just waiting to reignite. As the urge to run and hide grew almost overwhelming, her breathing became shallow, and she rocked in her seat, unable to stay still.

"It's called hypervigilance." Noah's calm voice was a lifeline, saving her from drowning in her memories. "It's common with people who've suffered trauma, like cops." He smiled ruefully. "Focus on what's real around you. The feel of your desk, the pencil in your hand, the sound of cars passing by. Remind yourself that this is now. The present. And you're here. Not there. Then concentrate on your breathing, counting it in and out, pausing briefly between breaths. That's it," he said encouragingly.

Annabelle hadn't been consciously aware she was following his instructions as he spoke. For a few minutes, he talked her through breathing and reminded her where she was and that she was safe—all in that low, soothing voice of his.

"Better?" he said at last.

She did an internal audit and noted that she was calm, focused, and present.

"Much. Dr. Mallory taught me something similar but sometimes it's hard to remember what to do."

He shrugged. "We've all been there."

She smiled. "You truly are the full-service, close-contact, security specialist, aren't you?"

Whatever he was going to say was lost in the ringing of this phone. Noah glanced at the screen, and his expression softened. "My boys." He gestured with his phone.

"I'm good," she told him. "I can get back to my drawing now."

He nodded once and answered the video call, resting his elbows on the counter while he faced the screen.

"Dad!" The excited voice made Annabelle grin. "Can we stay another thirteen days? I've been picked by the first team to play in the semifinals, even though I'm not really part of the official team, and the game's in thirteen days."

"Twelve days," his older brother, Jacob, interrupted in his slightly deeper voice. "The game's on the thirteenth. Really, we need to stay another two weeks. Is that okay, Dad? Gran says your job might be done before then, but we can stay anyway, can't we? I mean, we miss you and all, but this is the semis."

"I might even get through to the finals," Sam said excitedly. "We have to stay, Dad. The team needs me. They'll lose without me."

"He's right," Jacob said. "He's their only hope."

Noah grinned at his kids. "Well, the client I'm protecting doesn't go to court for another week or so—"

"So we can stay?" Sammy shouted. "Dad says we can stay!"

"I didn't say that," Noah corrected patiently. "But I don't see why you can't hang around and play in the game."

"He definitely says we can stay," Sammy shouted, even louder this time. "I need to tell Coach."

"How about we finish talking first before you do that?" There was laughter in Noah's voice.

"Oh yeah, right." There was a beat of silence while Sammy thought of something else to say. "Is work okay, Dad?"

"Why, thank you for asking. Yes, it is." Noah's eyes sparkled.

It was clear to Annabelle that Sam just wanted to end the call so he could tell his team he'd be there for the game.

"Who's that?" Jacob asked. "The lady behind you."

Noah glanced in her direction. "That's Annabelle. She's the client I told you about."

"The artist?" There was definite interest in Jacob's voice. "Is she drawing a comic book right now?"

Noah cocked a questioning eyebrow at Annabelle.

"Yes, I am," she told him.

"Can we see?" Jacob asked excitedly before Noah could relay Annabelle's answer.

He looked at her. She shrugged. "Sure."

"You don't have to," Noah said to her, earning groans and complaints from his kids.

It was her turn to laugh. "No, it's fine."

"Be polite," he told his boys as he wandered over to her drawing table.

"Oh, Dad," Jacob grumbled. "We're always polite. What do you think we are? Delicates?"

"Delinquents," Noah corrected absently.

"That's what I said," Jacob said, in that long-suffering tone only kids can pull off.

"Boys, this is Annabelle Simmons, a famous comic book artist. Annabelle, these are my sons, Jacob and Sam."

"Hey, guys." Annabelle waved at the phone screen, feeling comfortable meeting them this way, as most of her social interactions happened online.

"You're famous?" Sam said in awe. "Did you draw Spiderman?"

"No." They were hilarious. "But when I was just starting out, I worked on a Fantastic Four book. Does that count?"

"Which one?" Jacob asked. "We've got some Fantastic Four comics back in Houston. I bet we have yours."

"I don't know. It's a pretty old one now. I have a copy, though, downstairs in my storeroom. You can come read it when you're back in Houston if you'd like?"

Jacob's eyes went wide, but he was thirteen and far too cool to express his excitement. "Can we, Dad?"

"Sure, as long as it's okay with Annabelle."

She nodded. "Anytime. I'm always here," she joked. "There's a whole filing cabinet full of comic books downstairs. You're welcome to read any of them."

"Wow," Sammy said, his eyes wide. At nine, he was unafraid of showing his awe.

"Are you drawing something now?" Jacob asked, angling his head as if to better position himself to see her board.

"I'm working on my new graphic novel about Jade Justice. She's a heroine I came up with on my own."

"Without Marvel?" Jacob looked intrigued.

"There are lots of comic book artists who don't work for Marvel or DC."

He nodded sagely, like he already knew that. "What're you drawing?"

"Well..." She turned toward her board but realized where Noah stood wouldn't provide them with the best angle. "May I?" She gestured to his phone.

"Sure." He handed it over.

Annabelle flipped to the rear camera so the boys could see her board. They let out excited exclamations.

"Is that guy turning into a werewolf?" Jacob asked.

"Is he the bad guy?" Sammy added.

"Are you drawing in pen?" Jacob rushed on. "How do you erase your mistakes?

"I wish I could draw like that," Sammy said in admiration.

"Okay." Annabelle shifted in her seat, turning more fully toward her board. "If you have some time, I can answer all of your questions and show you how I draw a panel. But it will take more than a few minutes. Do your grandparents need you for anything?"

"Gran?" Jacob shouted. "Do you need us, or can we watch Annabelle draw?"

There was a muffled response in the background before Jacob stared into the phone. "She says she's grateful for a break."

Annabelle swallowed a giggle. "Well, if it's okay with them and your dad..."

She looked up at Noah, who spread his hands in a helpless gesture. "Who am I to stand in the way of a comic book tutorial?"

"That's a yes," Sammy clarified for her.

Amused, Noah returned to sit at the kitchen island while Annabelle fitted the phone into a moveable mount attached to her drawing table. When it came to online lessons, she was a pro.

"Right." She reached for her pen and held it up under the phone's camera. "Let's start with what you use to draw. It's important that an artist has the right tools. Now, although I sketch things out in pencil first, I always use these pens to go over the lines and refine the drawing."

A minute later, she'd forgotten all about the attack on her building. She'd even forgotten that Noah was in the room. Her full attention was on taking the boys through the step-by-step process of drawing a comic book panel.

* * *

It wasn't lost on Noah that Annabelle, Sammy, and Jacob had forgotten he existed. Even from a distance, he could tell she was completely absorbed in explaining her work to the boys, and they were equally enthralled by everything she told them.

"Good luck getting their attention after this," Therese said from beside him. *"You're lost to them now. Nothing you do will ever be as cool as being a comic book artist."*

She wasn't wrong.

Annabelle was clearly in her element. Her enthusiasm and delight were contagious, and her skill was evident to anyone. And judging by his sons' excited questions, they were just as thrilled as she was.

"The kids like her," Therese said. *"And I like her. When are you going to admit that you like her too?"*

Noah scowled at her, noticing for the first time that she wore her wedding dress. "What the hell?" he muttered.

Her grin was smug. *"After giving birth—twice—I could never get back into this, but now I'm dead, it fits perfectly."* She smoothed her hands over the white lace minidress that clung to her curves like a second skin. *"Only a teenage bride would think this was classy. Still, I always thought it was a shame that wedding dresses are worn only once. I mean, they cost a fortune, and you should be able to get your money's worth out of them."* She gave him a mischievous grin. *"When you marry Annabelle, tell her to buy something she can wear again. She won't regret it."*

"Marry?" Noah blurted before he froze, waiting for Annabelle's reaction to his outburst.

But she was far too involved in her impromptu lesson to pay him any attention, which was a relief.

He glared at his dead wife. "That's not funny," he whispered. "And I keep telling you—she's just a client."

"No," Therese said. *"You keep telling yourself she's just a client."*

Noah got up from the bar stool and strolled toward the

living room windows on the pretext of checking security. All the while, he mumbled to the ghost haunting him.

"Don't you have something better to do than harass me? Isn't there a light you can walk into? Look hard. I'm sure you'll see it."

"*See?*" Therese said, sounding pleased. "*This grumpy attitude is a sure sign you're ready to move on. You never would have suggested I 'go into the light' a year ago. Back then, it was all: 'I miss you so much. I'm lonely without you. How can I raise our kids alone?' Admit it, Noah, you're at the stage where you want to let go; you're just too stubborn to do it.*"

"You may not have noticed, being dead and all, but I'm in the middle of a dangerous op here. Now isn't the time to be thinking about romance." He peeked out from behind the shutters to find quiet, empty streets.

"*Uh, please.*" Therese waved a dismissive hand as she dramatically rolled her eyes. "*Nothing has ever distracted you from 'romance.'*" She made air quotes around the last word.

"What's that supposed to mean?" he growled.

"*I lived with you through lots of ops, cases, missions, whatever, and you always had time for sex.*" She shrugged. "*You're good at compartmentalizing.*"

"I'm not talking to you about sex," he hissed, aware Annabelle wasn't that far away.

"*Why not? We always talked about it. After we turned thirteen and suddenly noticed each other's bits, it was all we could talk about. You've never had a problem talking about sex.*"

"With you. I mean, talking to you about having sex with you." He glared at her, wondering if she was being deliberately obtuse. "I'm not talking to you about sex with other women."

"Uh," Rodrigo said from behind him. "That's good to know."

Noah ran a hand down his face while Therese laughed her head off.

"Sorry, man," Noah said. He probably should have felt embarrassed but he didn't. At this point, he was beyond humiliation. He was in a whole other zone. "I never heard you come up."

"Who were you talking to?" Rodrigo said. "I don't see a phone."

Oh, what the hell, Noah thought. He'd made an ass of himself anyway. Being honest couldn't possibly make it worse. "My dead wife, that's who."

He expected Rodrigo to back away slowly before running to Rochelle with the information that Noah had lost *all* of his marbles and shouldn't be on the streets, let alone on the team. They'd recommend a nice padded cell. One with soothing piped music. Not to mention wall-to-wall appointments with a whole team of psychologists.

Instead, Rodrigo nodded sagely. "Is she giving you dietary advice? *Mi abuela* doesn't shut up about healthy eating." He shrugged. "Hey, where I'm from, we see all kinds of stuff other people don't."

"And where would that be, exactly?"

"South of here," Rodrigo said with a grin, covering a lot of territory with his reply. "So, you're arguing with your dead wife about sex. You do know you can't do that with a ghost, don't you? I mean, *hermano*, that's just not right."

Noah hung his head for a second before trying again. "Why are you here?" he asked Rodrigo.

His teammate's demeanor changed, and suddenly, he

was all business. "Elle got back to us on the Demons' business dealings. She has a lead on some business going down tonight. You got a minute to go over the plan?"

"I like him," Therese said before sauntering over to join Annabelle's art lesson.

"Sure," Noah said. "When you say tonight, exactly what time do you mean? There's no way I can skip out on Annabelle while she's awake, not without the entire building knowing about it."

"We're talking standard crime o'clock. Dark and very late. Or early, depending on your perspective. Abasi has the details."

"That could work." At least he'd be able to ensure she was sound asleep when he slipped out. He raised his voice. "Bella, I need to go talk to Rodrigo for a minute. Somebody's monitoring the cameras, and Violet's keeping an eye on the roof and the fire escape. You okay with that?"

Annabelle blinked at him several times. As though it took effort to focus on what he was saying.

"Sure, go." She waved him off and, a second later, was deep in art mode again.

"Don't worry," Therese said unhelpfully. *"I'll watch over her."*

With a sigh, Noah followed Rodrigo out into the stairwell.

"Bella?" Rodrigo said with a grin as they closed the door behind them.

"Shut up," Noah grumbled.

Chapter Twenty-One

It was closing in on midnight, and Annabelle couldn't fall asleep. Every time she closed her eyes, she swore she smelled smoke. She lay there, tense in the dark, imagining flames sneaking through the building. The fear only abated once she'd tiptoed over to the door between the panic room and her apartment, opened it wide, and checked for any sign of fire. Then, feeling reassured and a little foolish, she climbed back into bed. She had about five minutes of peace before the cycle started all over again.

Quietly, so as not to wake Noah, she eased back the covers and crept toward the door. Again. Telling herself that she'd check just one more time, and then everything would be fine.

"You okay?" a deep voice asked from the doorway she shared with Noah.

Annabelle spun around to see him leaning against the doorjamb, softly silhouetted by the light of the streetlamps that filtered through the sheer blinds behind him.

"I'm just..." She hesitated, unable to explain her

constant need to check the building and feeling foolish for having it.

"Scared?" He stepped into the room. "I get that. But there are extra smoke alarms all over the place, and the triplets are standing guard. We've checked the warehouse from top to bottom, and there are no smoldering embers anywhere. You're safe."

"I don't *feel* safe," she whispered as she twisted her hands in the bottom of her Wonder Woman pajama top. "Worse, I don't *feel* like you and your team are safe either."

"You spoke to your psychiatrist earlier, didn't you? What did she say?"

Annabelle had made the call not long before turning in for the night. "That I'm still in alert mode. That I have to remind myself that the danger's passed and we're all fine now." She stared up at him, silently pleading for him to understand. "I know all of that logically, but as soon as I lie down, all I can think about is that I need to check the building and make sure we're all safe. I get more and more wound up until I have to get out of bed and see for myself that we're okay. Then I feel relieved until I get back into bed, and it starts all over again. I'm going crazy here."

"Would it help if I sat with you until you fell asleep?"

His voice was a low tease across her skin, and Annabelle answered before pausing to think about it. "It'd help if you were in bed beside me."

Noah jerked slightly and then froze.

She rushed to reassure him. "Just to sleep, I mean."

Although...

No.

The last thing she needed was for her brain to go *there* tonight. She was tired and terrified, and now she was worried that she'd pushed Noah a step too far. She held her breath, waiting for his reply. Praying he'd understand that she needed him.

"I'm taking the side nearest the open door," he said at last, ripping his gaze from hers.

"We could close both doors," she offered, knowing she was pushing her luck.

"Get into bed, Bella," he rumbled as he ducked back into the spare room.

She didn't have to be told twice.

Annabelle climbed into bed on the side furthest from the guest room, careful not to take up too much space. Once she'd settled, Noah appeared again and got into the other side of the bed. The mattress dipped and the covers moved as he made himself comfortable. At last, they were both in bed—with a chasm between them.

Which was fine.

She'd just wanted him closer so she'd feel safe. So she could sleep. It wasn't like she'd expected him to snuggle. Still, the situation was a whole lot more awkward than she'd expected.

"You don't need to stay here," she said softly, because it was night, and they were in bed, and you were supposed to speak softly. Somewhere, she was sure, there were rules about proper bed etiquette, and whispering in the dark would definitely be one of them. "I'm worried I forced you to do this, and now it's awkward. You can go back to your room. I promise I'll stop getting up to check for smoke."

He let out a sigh. "No, you won't, and we both need to sleep. This is fine."

"It's not fine. I can't relax. It's weird. I'm afraid to move in case I touch you, which means I can't sleep because this bed isn't big enough to ensure I won't accidentally roll into you while I'm out cold. Maybe we should get some cushions and build a little wall down the middle of the bed?"

Noah muttered something under his breath that sounded suspiciously like a prayer for patience. Next thing she knew, he reached out, wrapped an arm around her shoulders, and rolled her into his side. There was nothing she could do but put her arm around his waist and rest her cheek on his chest. Honestly, it would have been rude to do otherwise.

"Better?" he demanded.

She considered her answer before giving it. "You're still tense, and it's contagious. Are you sure you can relax lying like this? There's always the cushion-wall idea. We could try that."

"The tension will pass. It's just ..." Noah paused for a beat before shaking his head. "I haven't slept beside a woman since my wife died."

"Oh no!" Annabelle tried to push away from him, but he held her tight. "I'm *so* sorry. I shouldn't have forced you into this just because I'm a walking, talking ball of anxiety. This is awful. I feel awful."

"Stop talking, Bella." He tugged her back down to his side. "If I didn't want to be here, I wouldn't. It's just... another first."

He didn't have to explain. There had to have been many firsts in the years since his wife died—first birthdays without her, first Christmas, first vacation, first everything.

They lay in silence for a few minutes, and even though Annabelle's mind raced with a myriad of different concerns, she soon relaxed against him. He was so warm. So solid. So safe. Being close to him chased away the fears that plagued her. All she wanted was to sink into him and be at peace forever. His heartbeat was a steady rhythm in her ear, better than any white noise machine she'd ever used. Cocooned and protected, she lay there in the darkness, breathing him in.

"I'm glad I'm your first," she whispered.

"Go to sleep, Bella." His voice sounded gruff, but she thought she detected a hint of a smile.

And then she did exactly as he'd ordered and fell asleep.

* * *

Noah was instantly awake the second he heard movement at the panic room door. He reached down to the floor beside the bed, where he'd stashed his gun.

"Don't shoot," Abasi whispered. "It's go time."

"I get it now," Rodrigo whispered. "This must be another one of those 'professional cuddles' Violet was worried about."

Noah was too busy extricating himself from the bed without waking Annabelle to flip the smart-ass off. Instead, he shooed them into the guest room and tucked Annabelle in.

Violet was sitting on the end of his bed. "Don't ask. Don't tell," she said solemnly. "I'm just here to guard her. I don't care about anything else."

"She was too scared to fall asleep," Noah explained, unable to stop himself.

Rodrigo nodded. "Me? I'd have given her a sleeping pill. But, hey, you do you. I'm sure climbing into bed with her worked too."

Noah glared at him and gestured toward the panic room and the sleeping woman they didn't want to disturb. Rodrigo prodded Abasi, and they both headed out of the guest room and into the loft. Noah grabbed a change of clothes, his boots, wallet, phone, and weapon before leaning down to whisper to Violet, "Don't let anything happen to her."

She just stared at him as though he'd said something incredibly dumb.

Noah took that as an agreement and went out to meet Abasi and Rodrigo—after getting changed in the small bathroom between the guest rooms.

"Who's monitoring the security feed tonight?" Noah asked as they made their way down the stairs to the front door.

"Violet. She's doubling up with watching Annabelle." Rodrigo grabbed a duffel from the bottom step on his way past. "Harris is taking the first shift on building patrol. We waited until he hit the roof before we got you. We've got a couple of minutes before he heads this way. By then, we'll be long gone."

Noah reset the alarm and locked the front door behind them. Together, they jogged across the road and down the alley to the parallel street, where they'd left the SUV they'd need for the night's mission. Abasi tossed the keys to Noah, who got into the driver's seat. Abasi called shotgun, and Rodrigo sat in the back.

"I have everything we need," Rodrigo said as Noah started the car and headed toward South Houston. "We're going old school on this. No tech backup. Elle's on a job, and it would have raised too many questions if she'd siphoned off time to act as our online eyes and ears."

Even at three in the morning, there were still cars on the road. Granted, nowhere near as many as during the day, but enough to notice if the SUV did something out of the ordinary, so Noah made sure to obey every sign and never exceed the speed limit.

"First up," Abasi said as they drove into the night, "Elle stumbled on a drug house. She hacked some texts saying it was full, and the residents needed to check out soon."

"In other words"—Noah stopped for a red light—"they have too much product and need to ship some of it out."

"*Si*," Rodrigo said as he unzipped the duffel and started taking out weapons.

"Do we know what they're dealing?" Noah asked. "I don't want to walk into a meth lab."

"It's high-grade coke." Rodrigo checked a weapon before handing it to Abasi. "Well, it was. Who knows what it is now, they could have cut it with anything. They've got a pipeline straight from Colombia and an exclusive deal with the Alvarez cartel, one of the smaller but smarter drug producers in the country. The Demons and the Alvarez cartel are known by reputation as being deadly and unstoppable. It's a very profitable partnership for both parties."

"Hopefully, not so much after tonight." Noah kept his eyes on the road. "If we can sow the seed of doubt about the Demons being trustworthy, we might be able to disrupt their supply chain. That should give Eddie something else to worry about."

"It's not enough, though." Abasi drummed his fingers against the passenger door. "One drug house is small potatoes for this gang."

"But that's not the only thing we're hitting tonight, is it?" Rodrigo said.

"Nope," Abasi said. "There's a long-haul vehicle we need to intercept before dawn."

"Just remember, no killing," Noah said firmly. "We're going to gift wrap what we can for the local cops, disrupt the Demons as much as possible, and then disappear. Got it?"

"Which reminds me." Rodrigo rummaged in his bag of magic tricks and pulled out two bundles of zip ties. "Don't worry about circulation when you cuff these guys," he said cheerily.

"We need to keep this operation tight and fast." Noah drove over one of the wide, multilane motorways that wound around Houston. He glanced at the other two men. Both were skilled and deadly and, like him, were dressed for the night in black. But there were only three of them against an army of Demons. "Maybe we should have included the rest of the team in this," he said worriedly.

"We've been over this. The boss would have grounded us, and the triplets would have got us killed." Abasi eyed Noah, his gaze cold and assessing. "Right now, I'm more worried about you than anything we'll face. You sure you're up for this? It isn't some by-the-book police raid with plenty of department backup. Things will get dirty."

"I can handle myself," Noah said evenly.

"I'd settle for you not getting me shot." Abasi stared out the window, watching the lights of Houston's skyline flicker as they passed.

Chapter Twenty-Two

"I thought you said this gang was smart," Abasi said as they sat in the SUV, watching one of the houses the Demons used for their drug operation. "If you'd shown me a satellite image of this neighborhood, I'd have pointed at this place and said, 'That's it; there's the gang house.' Amateurs." He shook his head in disgust.

He had a point. With its boarded-up windows, smashed glass, and overgrown yard—the parts that weren't filled with abandoned vehicles—the old wooden house looked derelict. The only thing in good repair was the wire fence, which had several signs attached saying: *Private property, trespassers will be shot.*

To Noah, the area didn't feel inner city, which meant he'd spent far too long in the UK. The road was wide and straight, stretching into the distance. It was also in desperate need of repair. Houses were spread far apart, and there wasn't any sidewalk, only unkempt grass verge. All the buildings they'd passed had been small, wooden, and in disrepair, many of them shielded from view of the road by trees and overgrown bushes. This wasn't a neighborhood where folks got together for street barbeques. No, these people were big on minding their own business, and Noah doubted any of them had the Houston PD on speed dial.

Which, considering their situation, was a plus for the three of them.

"I've got the front," Abasi said as he climbed out of the car.

"I'll take the back." Rodrigo followed him just as silently.

"Guess that leaves me as backup." Noah joined them in the darkness. "Rodrigo, I'll follow you. Abasi can take care of himself."

"And I can't?" Rodrigo adjusted the strap of his black backpack.

"Yeah, yeah, you're a badass too." Noah rolled his eyes. "Remember, this is a bag-and-tag operation. No fatalities."

Both men just looked at him, making no promises.

They kept low, moving fast and sticking to the shadows as they approached the property's fence. There was no sign of any dogs, so they jumped over the wire barrier and into the yard. As the three of them spread out, Rodrigo held up a signal jammer and indicated that he was blocking all communication for the next ten minutes. The last thing they wanted was for the gang to call for reinforcements. He slipped the jammer into the side pocket of his backpack once he was done.

The small group split up, Abasi heading for the front of the house and Noah and Rodrigo for the back. They moved slowly and cautiously, keeping an eye out for any sign of movement. Or any attempts at booby-trapping the place. They found nothing. Either the Demons had become lax in protecting the house or Elle's information was wrong.

Noah peered around the corner to the back of the

building and held up a fist to signal Rodrigo to stop. Two men sat on the remains of an old porch. Both wore vests with Demon Brothers patches sewn onto them. One was vaping, and the other was scrolling on his phone. From their relaxed postures, neither was too concerned about security.

Looked like Elle wasn't wrong after all.

Rodrigo gestured toward the guy vaping, and Noah headed for the other one. The gang members didn't even see them coming. Before they knew what was happening, Noah and Rodrigo came up behind them and had them in matching choke holds. They were out cold within seconds. It took another minute to hog-tie them with the zip ties and slap duct tape over their mouths.

Noah stepped back and eyed the unconscious men, lying sprawled on their bellies, hands and feet bound. They weren't going anywhere. He signaled to Rodrigo to cover the door with his weapon while Noah eased it open. There was no one in the kitchen.

As they stepped into the disused and filthy room, Abasi appeared in the doorway leading to the front of the house.

"One down in there," he barely whispered before gesturing to a door that stood ajar. "Basement."

The sound of a radio drifted up from below the house.

"Only one way in and out," Noah said, just as quietly. "No way of knowing how many are down there. If we go down those stairs, it will be a bloodbath."

"Are we sure we got all the guards up here?" Rodrigo asked.

Abasi curled his lip in disgust. "If you can call watching porn on a crud-encrusted couch guarding the place."

Noah rubbed his jaw. "Rodrigo? Got any flash-bangs in that bag of tricks of yours?"

His smile blinding in the darkness, he took off the pack,

dug inside, and withdrew four canisters. "How many do you want?"

"All of them."

Rodrigo handed out the stun grenades. "This is gonna make a helluva noise. Here's hoping we're right about having disabled all the guys on guard duty." He looked rueful. "Also, we probably should've done some recon on the nearby properties to see if any of them were gang-owned before we barreled in here."

"Elle did a search," Abasi said. "Do you think I would have walked in here without covering all the bases? What kind of agent were you?"

"The fly-by the-seat-of-your-pants kind." Rodrigo grinned. "Ready?"

They pulled the pins, fully opened the door to the basement, lobbed the stun grenades down the stairs, and closed the door hard behind them.

The noise was phenomenal. Even upstairs, Noah's ears were ringing when it was over. But they weren't the ones incapacitated. As soon as the noise died down, the small team didn't hesitate. They threw open the door and rushed down into the basement. Six men lay writhing on the floor, a couple with blood running from their ears. None of them were in any condition to fight back. The noise and bright lights of the stun grenades had rendered their senses useless. One guy in the corner was vomiting.

Needless to say, the group was easy to subdue.

Once they had them restrained, Noah looked around the large basement room. It was in much better condition than the house above. Someone had made sure the place was spotless and given a fresh coat of paint. Although their hard work was ruined now. A couple of tables had been overturned, but there was no mistaking the residue of cocaine and materials needed to cut it for sale. In the corner nearest the stairs sat heavy-duty metal shelves loaded with white bricks.

"They have this much coke lying around, and their security is beyond shit." Abasi nudged one of the bound and gagged men with the toe of his boot. The man groaned and blinked up at him, trying to focus while still partially blinded by the flash-bang. "Pay attention," he said to the gang member. "This is what happens when you get lazy and rely on your reputation to protect you."

"Uh, they might not be as dumb as we thought," Rodrigo said from the top of the stairs. "I hear motorcycles. Lots of them. Do we have a plan?"

One of the hog-tied Demons started to laugh and shout, all of it unintelligible behind the duct tape covering his mouth.

"Yeah." Noah stepped over the laughing gang member. "Get the hell out of here."

He and Abasi jogged up the stairs.

"Well, this was a complete waste of energy," Abasi said as they ran through the kitchen and into the yard. "The rest of the gang will have them untied and back to work in no time."

As they sprinted for their car, the distant motorcycle engines were suddenly drowned out by the wail of sirens. Before they'd even shut the doors properly, Noah had the car in gear, and they sped off in the opposite direction of the noise.

In the back, Rodrigo twisted in his seat to stare out the rear window. "Got a lot of lights coming this way."

"That would be because I texted our friendly police detectives before we got out of the car and told them to get their asses here as fast as possible." Noah grasped the steering wheel as they slid around a bend. "And before you panic, thinking I don't know what I'm doing, I used a program Elle set up for the London office that disguises your cell number."

"How did you know we'd be out of there before the cops arrived?" Rodrigo said.

"I didn't." Noah turned into a darkened street, heading back toward the city center.

"You didn't?" Rodrigo sounded outraged.

In the passenger seat, Abasi chuckled. "Looks like we'll be in plenty of time to meet that big rig after all."

* * *

For the second night in a row, Annabelle woke with a scream.

Only this time, Noah wasn't there to calm her.

Beside her, the bed was cold and empty.

A figure rushed into the room, and Annabelle screamed again. The lights came on, and Violet stood there, her gun sweeping the room.

"It was just a dream," Annabelle managed to tell her. "Unless... can you smell smoke?"

"The building isn't on fire." Violet seemed disappointed to have to holster her weapon.

Running footsteps preceded Rochelle and Katrina, who rushed into the panic room with weapons drawn.

"Dream," Violet said with disgust. "She's fine."

Annabelle brushed her hair away from her face, still disorientated from a nightmare in which they were all burning. She reached for the water bottle on the little shelf beside the sofa bed and gratefully drank while willing her heartbeat to slow the hell down.

"Where's Noah?" Rochelle asked Violet the question on the tip of Annabelle's tongue.

The ex-cop shrugged. "He had stuff to do."

Or, Annabelle thought, he'd been so freaked out by sharing a bed with a woman who wasn't his wife that he'd run away. She blinked several times, willing the panic residue from her dream to clear. Surely, she was wrong about Noah.

"What stuff?" Rochelle demanded, giving Violet a look that would have had Annabelle in tears if she'd been the recipient.

"How should I know?" Violet held up her hands. "Rodrigo said Noah needed someone to cover for him, so I agreed to watch the video feed from up here instead of in the office. No big deal."

The sound of heavy running feet made all three Benson Security women raise their guns toward the guest room door.

"Don't shoot." One of the triplets—Annabelle was too tired to tell which one—appeared in the doorway, also armed.

It was like having an NRA convention in her bedroom. With two of the attendees dressed in pajamas.

"Where's Noah?" Rochelle snapped at the triplet.

He shrugged. "I thought he was in here."

"Maybe he's going over some leads with Abasi in his hotel room," Katrina said. "Abasi wasn't scheduled for a watch rotation tonight, so he went back to his suite."

"Call them for me," Rochelle ordered, and Katrina nodded while leaving the room, presumably to get her phone. "Violet, neither Noah nor Rodrigo mentioned where he was going or what he was doing? You sure about that?"

"I didn't ask." Violet seemed irritated that Rochelle was still demanding answers.

Katrina returned to the panic room, phone in hand. "No reply from either Abasi or Noah."

"Try Rodrigo," Rochelle said grimly.

Katrina was already tapping on her screen. "It's going straight to voicemail."

Rochelle turned to the triplet. "Wake Evan; get him to trace their cell phones."

"On it, Boss." He rushed back out through the guest room.

"What's going on?" Annabelle asked the women. "Noah didn't tell me he was leaving. Has something happened to him?" She wanted to ask if the Demons had taken him but couldn't bring herself to voice her fear.

"It's possible he's holed up somewhere in the building, talking with Rodrigo and Abasi," Katrina said hopefully.

"Unlikely." Rochelle wasn't happy. "I'm going downstairs to see what Evan finds. Go back to sleep, Annabelle. Violet will watch over you."

"I can't sleep now." Annabelle threw back the covers. "I have nightmares. Noah was helping with them, and now I'm worried."

"We're all going downstairs," Violet said. "I'm not equipped to help her the way Noah can."

Rochelle turned back to Violet. "What way is that?"

"Cuddling." Violet shuddered. "That isn't in my job description."

Rochelle turned to study Annabelle and her bed. As her perceptive gaze took in everything—including signs that someone had slept on both sides of the sofa bed—her lips thinned and her jaw tightened.

"Noah was purely keeping me company while I slept,"

Annabelle rushed to explain, feeling like a teenager caught sneaking a boy into her bedroom. Something she'd tried only once because her dad's disappointment in her had ruined ever attempting it again.

Katrina's phone rang, and she answered it before talking to Rochelle. "Evan says he can't get a location on any of their phones. The GPS is off."

"Then get him to turn it back on. He can do that remotely."

"Um, no, he can't. He says they're using an app Elle designed, which blocks people from remotely accessing their GPS."

Annabelle wasn't sure she followed the conversation and had no idea who Elle was, but it didn't take a genius to figure out this wasn't good news. She pressed a hand to her stomach as it roiled wildly.

"Do you think someone kidnapped them from Abasi's hotel?" she asked, unable to hide the terror in her voice. The Demon Brothers could have been watching. They could have followed the two men. What if they'd hurt them? What if they were dead?

Annabelle gave a little squeak of alarm as her knees gave out. With a thump, she sat back down on the edge of her bed. Noah was in danger—and it was all because of her.

She became aware that Rochelle had crouched in front of her. "Try not to panic. I don't think the Demons have Noah or anyone else on our team, for that matter."

"Then what's happened to them?" Noah wouldn't leave her by choice. He'd promised to stay by her side and protect her. Something must have happened.

"I think"—Rochelle's eyes flashed fire—"that the boys have taken matters into their own hands."

"I don't understand." And she didn't. Noah was her main bodyguard. Just a few hours earlier, he'd lain alongside her in bed, protecting her from attack—both mental and physical.

"The boys have gone rogue," Rochelle said. "And I plan to skin them alive for doing it."

Annabelle's brain wasn't firing on all cylinders. She looked over at Katrina and Violet, who both appeared angry.

"I can't believe they left me babysitting while they went off to have fun without me," Violet raged.

Annabelle felt faint as the words sank in. "They've gone after the Demons?"

Rochelle nodded tersely before standing. "Looks like it. Let's get some coffee. None of us will sleep now anyway."

They headed downstairs to the office, where Evan sat in front of his computers, his hair standing on end.

"I think I've found a way of tracking them," he said excitedly. "I can hack the GPS in the vehicle they took."

"Do it," Rochelle ordered as she glanced at Katrina. "I'll take Harris and go fetch them. You, Logan, Violet, and Evan, look after Annabelle."

Katrina nodded as Rochelle hurried back upstairs.

Annabelle made her way over to Evan. "Where are they?"

"Gimme a sec." He tapped away at his keyboard, his fingers flying. "Got it! They're... in the middle of nowhere." He looked confused.

"Send the coordinates to Rochelle's cell," Katrina said. "Violet, make sure the building's secure. We're down half the team while she's gone."

Violet turned on her heel and went off to do as she was

told. In the meantime, Annabelle stared at the point on the map where Noah's vehicle sat, wondering what they were doing out there in the middle of the night.

Chapter Twenty-Three

According to their intel, a big rig was due to meet with Demon members under one of the many motorway junctions dotted around the city. There was no sign of it yet, but a brand-new pickup sat on the hard shoulder with three men inside.

"Gotta be the gang," Rodrigo muttered as they watched the pickup from where they sat—behind a bush big enough to hide their SUV.

A train track cut across the road nearby, and there was nothing but grass, overgrown bushes, and the odd abandoned building for miles. It was as isolated as you could get while still considering yourself in Houston.

"Our intel says they change drivers and license plates here before heading on to San Antonio." Abasi cast them a glance. "I say we take their place and meet the rig ourselves."

In silent agreement, the men left their vehicle and crept along the grass verge beside the road. It took them no time at all to deal with the gang members. Within minutes, they were hog-tied, gagged, and stashed on the ground beside the pickup, out of sight of the road.

"Truck coming," Noah said as headlights appeared in the distance.

They casually leaned against the pickup to wait for it.

The massive truck rolled to a stop behind them, and two men jumped down from the cab. They approached Noah, a swagger in their step. It was only when they drew close enough to see their faces clearly that the driver hesitated.

"I don't know you," he said.

The gang members still had their weapons tucked into the waistband of their pants. Without saying a word, Noah and Rodrigo were on the men. Noah tightened his arm around the driver's neck and felt him struggle before losing consciousness. Once he went limp, Noah let him fall to the ground instead of carefully lowering him. He retrieved the vehicle keys from the man and tossed them to Abasi, who strode for the back of the rig.

"Better disable their phones." Noah removed the battery from the one belonging to the driver.

"Already on it," Rodrigo said. "I'll go check we got all of them from the other guys too."

Noah gave a nod and then dragged the unconscious man over to join his friends. The gravel was rough under his captive, and Noah hoped the asshole got road burn. The rattle of the truck's roller door opening was loud in the night. Noah heard a scuffle followed by a thud and knew Abasi had found and dealt with another gang member. Made sense there'd be three to match the number waiting in the pickup.

By the time Noah and Rodrigo rounded the back of the truck, Abasi was securing the final gang member's feet.

Noah investigated the open trailer. It was full of boxes packed into the top of the rig.

"Think Elle got her info wrong?" Rodrigo eyed the boxes.

"Elle doesn't make mistakes." Abasi grabbed the back of the gang member's shirt and dragged him to the grass verge, where he dumped him unceremoniously.

Rodrigo, who'd already climbed into the truck, was busy opening a box with his pocketknife.

"What've we got?" Noah eyed the cargo.

"Paper towels." Rodrigo held up a two pack for them to see.

"Anything else?"

"Nope. Gotta be a cover for the drugs they're hauling. We'll need to pull all the boxes out to see what else is in there. Unless..." He ripped open the plastic packaging and licked the paper towel.

"Dude, gross." Noah winced.

"Came across a smuggler once who infused paper with drugs. This is just paper." He lobbed it onto the road before grabbing another box. "We need to get this baby emptied. Catch." He tossed the box to Noah.

At least it wasn't heavy. Noah threw it onto the grass verge.

They worked like that for over an hour until the trailer was empty and there was a massive pile of boxes on the side of the road. The gang members were all awake now, and the team had moved them to one spot beside the truck, where they could keep an eye on them. The men were furious, shouting incoherent threats from behind their duct tape gags while wriggling around, trying to break free of their bonds.

Noah ignored them as he climbed into the emptied trailer; they weren't going anywhere.

"Got anything?" he asked Rodrigo, who was busy tapping the walls in search of hidden compartments.

"Nothing yet."

Noah and Rodrigo continued searching, even checking the truck's cab to see if there was anything there, but they came up empty. On the ground, the gang members laughed at them.

"Cocky assholes," Rodrigo muttered.

"Watch them," Abasi said as he slid under the truck to check out its undercarriage with his phone's flashlight.

"See anything?" Noah asked.

This was beginning to look like a waste of time. The sun would be up soon, and they had to get out of there and back to the warehouse before the roads became busier. Or someone noticed they were gone.

"Nothing yet," Abasi called.

"Looks like Elle makes mistakes after all." Rodrigo ran a hand through his hair, his eyes on the gang members. "I say we just call the cops and let them rip the truck apart."

There was movement beneath the truck before Abasi appeared. His face was a cold, expressionless mask as he rushed past his teammates and into the trailer. As Noah watched, he fell to his knees and groped around on the floor. There was a click, and then a panel popped loose. Abasi ripped it away and stared into the space beneath it for a beat before springing to his feet. He stalked to the edge of the platform, drew his gun, and shot one of the gang members in the leg.

"What the hell?" Noah climbed into the trailer.

Abasi aimed again, but Noah was already moving. He threw himself at his teammate and tackled him to the floor.

"Shit!" Rodrigo joined them inside the trailer but didn't rush to help Noah subdue Abasi, who had clearly lost his mind.

No, Rodrigo fell to his knees and began pressing the floor as Abasi had done, moving frantically along the wooden boards. There was a now familiar popping sound, and another panel came loose.

"There's more of them," he said. "Stop fighting and help me."

Abasi tossed his gun aside, shoved Noah off him, and scrambled to the back of the trailer, where he pressed on the floor. Noah got to his feet and stumbled the few steps to Rodrigo. When he saw what was in the hidden compartment, he, too, fell to his knees.

It was a woman. Young. Partially dressed. Her blonde hair matted and her pale skin bruised.

"Is she alive?" Noah slid forward and reached into the shallow space to feel for a pulse.

He held his breath, waiting, hoping. "I have a pulse!"

"Me too," Rodrigo snapped.

"And here," Abasi said.

"Must've been sedated." Noah joined his teammates in searching for other compartments.

They worked in silence. Unearthing space after space. All narrow, shallow compartments, like cheap wooden coffins, each one containing an unconscious woman. Twenty-one in total. All of the women were young, damaged, and sedated—and stored like cattle. *No.* Noah grimaced. Cattle were treated better.

"We can't just phone this in and walk away." Noah vibrated with rage. Abasi and Rodrigo didn't look much better. "These women need medical attention, and we've no idea how long it will take to arrive. Do we take them out of the truck?"

Rodrigo shook his head. "Let the paramedics do that. We might cause more damage. At least now they have plenty of air." He cast a grim look at Abasi. "How did you know?"

"Holes drilled into the underside of the vehicle."

Abasi was the last to climb out of the truck. His gun was back in its holster, but Noah kept a close eye on him. The gang member he'd shot would live—probably. The team had done nothing to stem the bleeding from the gunshot wound to his leg, uncaring if he bled out. And yet, that was still better than they'd treated the women in the truck.

"Call it in." Rodrigo ran a hand through his thick black hair. "We'll wait for the cops and paramedics and deal with the consequences when they come."

Abasi's dark eyes never strayed from the captured men. "They need to die," he said simply.

Noah moved to stand in front of him, blocking his access to the captives while hoping Abasi wouldn't shoot him instead.

"You're right; they deserve to die," Rodrigo said. "But if we kill them, the investigation will focus on us instead of where it needs to be. Right now, we need them alive to talk to the cops. And we need to take care of the women."

Abasi didn't seem to hear him. He stood tense and focused, his face unreadable but his intent clear—he planned to put the men down like animals.

And Noah couldn't blame him for wanting to.

"Get out of my way," Abasi ordered, his voice low and cold as ice.

"You're with Benson Security now." Noah tried to

reason with him. "We don't just kill whoever we want. You're part of the team, which means you play by the rules."

There was nothing but cool determination in Abasi's eyes. "Whose rules? Rochelle's? Because we didn't give a damn about her rules when we started this." He slowly withdrew his weapon from its holster, making Noah wish he'd confiscated it earlier.

"We don't have time to deal with you right now, *hermano*." Rodrigo joined Noah to form a barrier in front of the gang members. "We need to get help for those women." He lifted his chin at Noah. "Call it in. I've got this."

Noah wasn't so sure, but he pulled out his phone as Abasi raised his gun to point it directly at Rodrigo's face.

"You've got this?" he said.

"Noah, make the damn call," Rodrigo said, refusing to take his eyes off Abasi. "If you're going to shoot me, aim to kill. You won't get a second chance if you miss."

"I don't miss." Abasi sounded detached. As though he'd disconnected from what was really happening.

Noah stayed alert while hitting his speed dial, ready to jump in if needed. Abasi teetered on the edge of a precipice. He could as easily pull the trigger on Rodrigo as on the men on the ground.

"Johnson," Noah said when he answered. "We intercepted a Demons shipment. Thought it was drugs. Instead, we have twenty-one women, all sedated and in bad condition. We need medical attention here fast." He rattled off their location.

"What the f—" Johnson snapped.

"Argue later. I have a situation here. Send help and get your ass here now." He hung up and rejoined Rodrigo. "Don't make us take you down," he told Abasi. "The cops are on their way. These guys are going to prison. The women will be looked after. You need to take a step back and calm the hell down."

"They need to die." Abasi was undeterred. "Move, or I shoot."

A car approached, speeding along the highway, and screeched to a halt behind Abasi. Noah and Rodrigo had their weapons out and trained on it before it stopped. Abasi still aimed at Rodrigo's head, unconcerned about the new arrivals—if he even noticed them.

"Great," Noah muttered as Rochelle climbed out of the driver's seat.

"Put down your weapons," she commanded.

Noah and Rodrigo did as they were ordered; Abasi didn't seem to hear her.

"Abasi," she shouted. "Put down your weapon."

He didn't respond. Instead, he moved like lightning, hitting Rodrigo with a left hook to the jaw that made him crumple to the ground. He strode past the fallen man toward the gang members, arm outstretched and gun unwavering. Noah rushed to stand in front of him, but Abasi froze in place, shook violently, and then collapsed in a heap beside Rodrigo—out cold.

Noah quickly disarmed him while eyeing the wires attached to his back. Wires that led to Rochelle and the Taser in her hand.

She glared at Rodrigo, who was awake and rubbing his face, then at Noah. "Do I have to Tase you too?"

"No, ma'am," he said, taking a step back.

Just as sirens announced that the police and ambulances had arrived.

Chapter Twenty-Four

The new Benson Security team was a fractured mess that was unprofessional at best and recklessly dangerous at worst. Noah didn't need to read Rochelle's mind to know that's exactly what she thought, because he thought it too. Lake Benson's American experiment was an unmitigated failure.

And Noah was part of the problem.

It wasn't a position he was used to being in. Even in high school, he'd been the good kid. The one the principal never called into his office. Somewhere along the line, he'd lost his way.

It'd been a very long day. There had been endless questions—from the police, the DA's office, and Rochelle. Dinner had consisted of a stale sandwich from the police station vending machine, and he had indigestion from all the lousy coffee he'd drunk while there. He'd had three hours' sleep, max. Had managed to piss off pretty much everyone he knew. And the day wasn't over yet.

Rochelle had assembled the team in their open-plan office and was currently pacing at the front of the silent room. Annabelle sat quietly in the corner near the computers. She hadn't once looked at Noah since he'd returned a few minutes earlier, and his chest was tight and aching from the need to go talk to her. But there wasn't time. And even if there were, he wasn't sure she wanted to talk to him.

"You totally stuffed up." Channeling Marisa Tomei again, Therese folded her arms over her black leather jacket and glared at him. *"You broke that girl's trust. How could you do that? You know how much she depends on you to get her through this, and you left her with Violet. Violet?"* She threw up her hands in disgust. *"You might as well have left her with The Terminator. All Violet cares about is shooting people."*

Noah couldn't reply to his ghostly wife, but he hung his head as she shouted at him. He deserved every word.

"You are so damned stubborn," she raged. *"So intent on clinging to a relationship that literally died five years ago that you're screwing up any future you might have. Are you hoping for a medal for being a martyr to our marriage? A sainthood from the Pope?"*

She stood directly in front of him, forcing him to watch Rochelle pace through her translucent form. *"You knew she was developing feelings for you, and you were too damn hardheaded to admit you were developing feelings for her too. Now you've thrown it all away. Do you even understand how hard it is for her to trust anyone? Yet she trusted you. And what did you do? You told yourself that you were eliminating the threat to her. That you were doing your job. When, really, you were screwing over Annabelle and your boss."*

Therese bent over until she stared him in the eye. *"What happened to you? Because this"*—she gestured toward him—"isn't the man I married. Hell, he isn't even the *teen I fell in love with. You're a coward, Noah Merchant, and I'm ashamed of you."*

She disappeared, leaving her words to resonate within him.

Noah glanced over at Annabelle, who was very deliberately staring at her hands. Therese was right. He hadn't rushed out with Rodrigo and Abasi to end the threat to Annabelle—although that was definitely part of it. No, he'd gone because deep down he was scared of how fast things were moving with Bella, and he wanted the mission to end before he got in even deeper. He'd destroyed her trust in him and done it because he was a coward. So afraid of being hurt again that he was too terrified to try. He was a sad example for his sons. They would never learn how to live and cope with loss by watching him. He'd let them down.

Let himself down.

At the front of the room, Rochelle stopped pacing and sat on one of the old wooden chairs. She put her hands on her thighs and looked at each of them, her expression inscrutable. Noah had expected anger, disappointment even, but there was no trace of either on her face. His stomach knotted as he watched her.

"I had a long chat with Lake," she said in a clear, even voice. "And I've decided that after this operation, I'm disbanding the Houston branch of Benson Security."

There was a moment of stunned silence before Evan shot to his feet. "You can't! I need this. If there's no Houston office, I go to prison."

"I'm sorry," Rochelle said without compassion. "The decision has been made. This is the first and last case for Benson Security USA."

"Why are you doing this?" Evan wailed as Harris put a hand on his shoulder.

"She's doing it because we can't work together," his brother said softly.

"I can work together," Evan protested. "I take orders and do my job. Don't I?"

He suddenly sounded as young as his age, and it made Noah hurt to listen to him.

"Weirdly," Rochelle said with a humorless smile, "you aren't the problem."

"Then why?" Evan demanded. "Is it because Noah, Abasi, and Rodrigo went off on their own last night?" As he stared at the three of them, it was clear he was silently pleading with them to say or do something to change Rochelle's mind.

There was nothing they could say, and Noah found he could no longer look Evan in the eye. He hung his head in shame.

"It's about respect," Katrina murmured. "In a team like this, we need strong leadership. Someone who makes the hard decisions and does what's best for the rest of us. But to do that, you need the team to allow it. Rochelle doesn't have that. You can't work together if you don't respect the person in charge or have each other's backs."

"I get it," Violet said. "I don't believe for one second that Abasi, or the triplets, or even Rodrigo would have my back in a crisis. I'm with you, Rochelle. This won't work. Plus, America is weird and I miss Scotland. I'm only here because the triplets' mother begged me to keep an eye on them."

"I'd watch your back," Evan protested.

"Only if you weren't distracted at the time," Violet said. "Or if you and your brothers hadn't come up with something better to do." She lifted her chin toward Abasi. "Or if you agreed with the decision in the first place, right?"

"Like you did when Rochelle told you not to shoot at those men in the cars that night?" Abasi said.

"I saved Noah and Annabelle by disobeying that order."

Abasi shrugged. "Guess the end does justify the means, then."

"And that's why this team is over," Katrina told him.

"It doesn't matter the why, where, or how of it all," Rochelle said, sounding weary. "Most of you are used to working alone and making your own decisions. I get why that would make it hard for you to trust the rest of us. But I can't work like this, and I definitely can't deliver a job to the standard Lake Benson expects with a team of renegades. We put our lives on the line daily with a job like this. You're all aware that Benson Security attracts the cases other agencies won't touch. Any mission we take could be the one that blows up in our faces. And I can't sit here and swear that when I needed you, each and every one of you would be there."

She stood and picked up her jacket from the chair beside her. "Eddie Hanson's trial starts a week from tomorrow. Until then, I ask that you prioritize keeping Annabelle safe to testify—assuming she still wants to employ us?"

"I-I need to think a-about it," Annabelle said, turning red.

"I understand." Rochelle shrugged on her jacket and turned toward the door. "I'll be in my room if anyone needs me. It's been a long day."

Noah pushed back his chair and stood. "Rochelle, I'm sorry."

Defeated eyes met his for a heartbeat. "So am I, my friend. So am I." And then, she was gone.

The room fell into a heavy silence before Annabelle

spoke. "Katrina, would you mind coming upstairs with me? I'd like to talk things over with you."

"Of course," Katrina said.

Without so much as a glance at anyone else, the two women left the room.

"What happens now?" Evan asked, looking a little lost.

"Now, we take some time to figure out if we really want to be part of a team or if we're only here because we don't know where else to go or what else to do. That's what I plan to do." Noah walked toward the exit, more disgusted with himself than anyone else in the room. "I'll see you guys in the morning."

Abasi stood and followed him out. He didn't say a word. As Noah turned to go upstairs, Abasi headed down to the front door. The door closed quietly behind him, leaving the building to echo with silence, the weight of their actions heavy on all of them.

* * *

When he got upstairs, Noah found Annabelle and Katrina sitting on the living room sofas, chatting quietly. From their expressions, they wished he'd gone elsewhere.

"Annabelle, can I have a minute?" He glanced at Katrina. "If you don't mind?"

The women shared a somber look, and when Annabelle nodded tersely, Katrina gave her hand a reassuring pat and got to her feet. "It's late, and I could use some rest," she said.

As she passed Noah on her way to the guest rooms at the back of the loft, she paused.

"Besides Rochelle, there was only one other person on this team that I didn't expect to go rogue, and that was you, Noah. I *know* you. You're a good man. One of the few I trust. We all make poor decisions, I get that, but please don't prove me wrong about you."

Noah wanted to give her some small reassuring touch, but he knew she wouldn't welcome it. Katrina was always careful to keep her distance from any of the men in the group. The fact she stood so close to him, even without touching, reinforced her every word.

"I'm sorry," he murmured.

She studied his face before nodding. "You need to fix this."

"I'll do my best," he promised solemnly.

Katrina glanced over her shoulder at Annabelle and raised her voice. "I'll be in my room if you need me." And then she walked deeper into the darkened apartment.

Noah waited for the door to the guest room area to close behind her before making his way over to Annabelle. Even though the sofas were massive, he didn't dare take a seat on one of them. Instead, he perched on the edge of the wooden coffee table. Annabelle had drawn her feet up under her and was curled into a ball in the corner of the sofa. She didn't look him in the eye.

Behind Annabelle, near the window, Therese shimmered into view. Unlike Annabelle, she had no problem meeting his eye, and judging by her pursed lips and tense shoulders, she was still angry with him.

He couldn't blame her.

Noah took a deep breath. "I screwed up," he said. "I made promises to you and to Rochelle, and I broke both. I'm sorry, Annabelle."

"It's okay." She picked at a loose thread on the cushion beside her. "These things happen."

He wasn't sure if Therese had been correct in saying he'd lost Annabelle's trust, but there was definitely a wall between them now. One where she said all the right things but meant none of them. Yeah, he'd hurt her, without a doubt. And he hated himself for it.

"No, Bella, I mean it. I'm sorry for leaving you last night, and I'm sorry for being such a coward."

Even though his words were spoken softly, it was as if they echoed off the warehouse walls. His heart raced at his confession, and his palms became damp. It took him a second to realize that what he felt was fear. Fear of being vulnerable. Fear of rejection. Fear of screwing up.

Noah cleared his throat and spoke again—this time, looking at his dead wife. "I've been making choices out of fear, and I don't want to do that anymore."

Therese nodded, and with a small smile curving her lips, she faded from sight, leaving him alone with Annabelle.

The real-life woman sitting in front of him frowned. "I don't understand. You're one of the bravest people I know."

"Bella." He rubbed at his chest—where his admissions hurt the most. "I told myself that by disrupting the Demons' network, we'd buy you safety. We both know that isn't true. Their network is too big, and all we did last night was prod the bear." He smiled ruefully. "More than one, actually, because now the DA's office is mad too."

"But you had the right intentions..." She sounded unsure.

Noah didn't blame her. "I didn't go out last night to somehow eliminate the threat against you, although that's what I told myself. I thought I was being professional, that I was getting the job done for the client, and that I had your best interests at heart." He rubbed a hand down his face, disgusted with himself. "It's all lies, Bella. There was no noble intent, and there sure as hell wasn't a wise decision involved. I promised to stay by your side and be your main protector, and I didn't do that. If you'll give me another chance, I won't make the same mistake again."

"I don't expect you to be perfect," she said. "Nobody is. And I realize you can't be with me twenty-four seven. I was just freaked when I woke up and found out you'd sneaked off after..."

"After we'd been close in bed?"

Annabelle nodded. "It felt like you'd run out on me, which is stupid because nothing happened. Between us, I mean. But I was scared for you too. I didn't know where you were or if you were in danger."

"I'm really sorry." Noah was happy to tell her that as often as it took to make her believe him. "And something did happen between us. We both know that. Getting into bed with you isn't part of the job description."

"Then why did you sneak out to do something you clearly didn't think you should be doing?"

"I was scared."

"Of me?"

She scooted closer to perch on the edge of the sofa in front of him. Her expression was easy to read and filled with confusion and perhaps a little hope. Either that or it was just wishful thinking on his part.

"Of the things you make me feel," he confessed softly.

"*For* me?" From her adorable little frown, he wasn't making himself any clearer.

"Yeah, *for* you. I shared a bed with you. I slept beside you." His face heated with embarrassment, and he tried to shrug it off. "I've been holding on to Therese for five years, telling myself that getting close to another woman would betray her memory. Betray the love and commitment we shared. When, really, I was just terrified of getting close to another person who could be taken away from me. No, ripped away."

"She was the love of your life," Annabelle said with compassion and understanding.

Noah shook his head. "No, she was the love of my youth, and I need to let go. I get that now. We met in kindergarten and loved each other as friends before recognizing it as more. We grew up together, made a family together. She was always there. Always a part of my life. And I believed she was my whole life." He hesitated, his heart beating so loudly he could barely hear himself think above it. "Until you."

"Noah," she whispered.

"You got under my skin, Bella. More than that, it was as though you just sauntered through the defenses I'd built after Therese died. You made me feel again, want again, need again. You terrified me."

Wide, stunned eyes blinked at him. "Past tense," she whispered. "You aren't terrified of me anymore?"

"Oh, believe me, I'm scared out of my mind." He chuckled mirthlessly.

"I know you think you're making sense," she said. "But I'm kinda lost here. What are you saying? What do you want?"

"Right now"—an unusual calm settled over him—"I very much want to kiss you."

Chapter Twenty-Five

And she wanted to kiss him too. She had done from the moment he'd crashed into her life like a loyal —but fierce—bulldog to protect her.

Still, she needed to be clear. "So, you're attracted to me but felt guilty because you were worried it was betraying your dead wife? Or is it that you were afraid of letting yourself get close to anyone again in case you got hurt?"

"All of the above," he said, his eyes sparkling.

"And you were too afraid to touch me, but now you aren't?"

"Nope. Still terrified." He smiled. It was slow and sensual, making her shiver with longing. "I don't know what's going to happen."

"You mean in the future, right? Not like with kissing and touching and stuff. I mean, you haven't forgotten how to do all of that, have you?"

Noah grinned widely. "They say it comes back to you, no matter how rusty you are. I think we'll be fine. And yeah, I'm scared of what will happen in the future."

"Oh, Noah, you idiot. We're all scared of that."

"Yeah, but I've decided to feel the fear and do it anyway."

Her eyebrows shot up her forehead. "Do it anyway? As in *it* with *me*? Your romance skills are seriously rusty."

"Hey, you just called me an idiot; that isn't exactly seductive." He fought to suppress a smile, and the last of Annabelle's weak resistance crumbled.

"You *are* an idiot," she said softly.

"How do you feel about kissing idiots?" he asked, gazing into her eyes.

"Fortunately for you, my standards are low." She leaned into him.

"That *is* fortunate for me." His hand cupped the back of her head, his fingers threading through her hair.

Their mouths were only a whisper apart now.

"Still scared?" she teased.

"Terrified," he whispered before his lips met hers.

They were warm and smooth and firm. Deliciously confident as they teased her to deepen their kiss. Annabelle's arms wound around his neck as he gently urged her closer.

For a moment, suspended in time, there was no threat hanging over her. No court date pressing ever closer. No anxiety about what she should and shouldn't be doing. There was just Noah, skillfully teasing her lips with his.

Suddenly, the scant distance between them seemed unbearably vast. Before she knew it, Annabelle climbed into his lap and straddled him without ever breaking their kiss.

That same sense of rightness she experienced whenever she hugged him enveloped her again. Only this time, it was even better. His hand flattened on the small of her back, holding her tight, and she reveled in the sensation of his strong, muscled body against hers. He felt solid. Powerful, yet tender. Holding her reverently, tempering his strength with control and care. His other hand tightened in her hair as they devoured one another. Her breathing became panting, and a small moan of need escaped her throat.

The room spun around them, and she never wanted it to stop. No, she wanted it to go faster and faster until they flew completely out of control. Lost in each other. Oblivious to anything else.

"Okay," a female voice said, bringing her back down to earth with a thud. "I know *this* isn't part of the job."

Annabelle whined in complaint when Noah's mouth left hers.

"Go away, Violet," he said, sounding breathless and needy.

"You go away," came the annoyed reply. "I'm on watch duty, and I sure as hell don't want to watch this."

"There is no such thing as peace around here," Noah muttered, making Annabelle bark out a short, startled laugh.

Carefully, hands on her waist, he lifted her and placed her on her feet in front of him. She swayed slightly, overly aware of his hands on her body, her mind desperately chasing that sense of wonder she'd experienced only moments earlier.

"Come on." He stood and held out a hand. "It's late, and Violet, although rude, is right. We need to let her do her job."

As Annabelle took his hand, her mind began to clear, and the ache in her body eased somewhat.

"I need a shower," he said as they made their way toward the back of the loft. "Long day rolling in the dirt with criminals." His smile was private, just for her.

"I'd better get ready for bed too. It's late." Even saying

the word bed made her shiver with awareness. Would Noah sleep with her again tonight? Would there be more?

Heavens above, let there be more!

He stopped at the door between the guest room and the panic room. "See you soon?"

"Yes," she said, perhaps a little too firmly.

With a grin, he gathered his things and headed for the shower.

* * *

Noah didn't want to leave Annabelle, but he hadn't been joking about needing a shower. He hurried down the hall to the bathroom he shared with the other guest room. There was no sound coming from Rochelle and Katrina's room, so he could only assume they were fast asleep. Part of him wanted to wake Rochelle and explain himself before telling her how much he regretted going behind her back. But she needed her sleep, and his apology would keep until morning.

Besides, he couldn't wait to get back to Annabelle.

He made fast work of showering and was in the middle of shaving when Therese appeared again. She looked ecstatic.

"Well done!" She did a speedy little finger clap in front of her face as she grinned at him in the mirror.

Noah set the razor on the edge of the sink for fear of accidentally slitting his own throat.

"Please tell me you weren't watching," he groaned.

"Just a little bit." Her ghostly form patted him on the back. He felt nothing. *"You did great."*

"Therese," he said with long-suffering, "if you want me to move on, you can't hang around watching me with other women. It's creepy. Plus, I don't need my dead wife grading my work."

"*Who said anything about women?*" She glared at him. "*What? You're going to go wild on me now? I gave my approval for Annabelle. Nobody else.*"

"Listen to yourself." He picked up the razor and made quick work of finishing his jawline before splashing water on his face. "I don't need you interfering in my fledgling love life."

"*Sure, you do. Without my interference, you'd still be crying alone at night, wondering if your libido died along with me.*"

"Not funny." He patted his face dry.

"*But true.*" She twirled her hair. "*You're going to bed with her now, right?*"

Noah cringed. "This is so wrong. I'm not discussing this with you." He spun toward her, pointing a finger. "And don't dare hang around to critique anything that may or may not happen."

She looked sympathetic. "*I get it. Performance anxiety. It's been a long time for you.*"

Noah pinched the bridge of his nose. "Therese, please, I'm begging you. Go harass the triplets or something. This whole situation is hard enough without worrying about my wife's ghost watching me."

"*Like I'd do such a thing!*" She sniffed indignantly, fooling no one. "*I don't want to watch you with another woman. That's just icky.*" She batted her eyelashes with feigned innocence. "*But I do believe you'd benefit from a few pointers beforehand. I mean, we don't want nerves getting in the way of you sealing the deal. I've put a lot of energy into this for you, and now that I'm invested, it would be great if you didn't screw it up.*"

"Do not say another word." Noah grabbed his gear and stalked out into the guest room.

The door between his room and the panic room was ajar—as usual.

"I just thought I'd remind you about the stuff you do that really works," Therese said.

It was official: Noah was completely insane. And there was no switching it off; otherwise, he'd have pressed the silence button on his wife long before now. He pulled on some sweatpants and stalked over to Annabelle's door. She was already in bed, Wonder Woman pajamas on and covers tucked around her waist.

"I need to pop downstairs to tell Rodrigo something. I'll only be a couple of minutes. Are you okay with that?"

Her smile was sweet. "You don't need to update me on every second of your day, Noah. Of course I'm okay. Rochelle and Katrina are just down the hall, and Violet's pacing out in the loft."

"Okay." He nodded, still uncertain yet also very aware that he was behaving weirdly. The last thing he wanted was to take a detour before going to bed with her. But there was no way in hell he'd go anywhere near Annabelle with his ghostly shadow in tow.

He left Annabelle and stalked through the loft to the stairwell. Violet barely acknowledged him as he passed.

"Where are you going?" Therese demanded. *"Get back upstairs and finish what you started with that woman!"*

Noah didn't reply. Instead, he went straight to the small office Rodrigo used for a bedroom. He didn't bother knocking, just threw the door open to find his teammate sitting at a small desk near his bed. He was still fully clothed and, from a glance at the screen, was working the case.

"Why aren't you in bed with Annabelle?" he asked as he swiveled his chair to face Noah.

"How did you...? Never mind. You were on the surveillance feed, weren't you?"

Rodrigo grinned. "Better me than one of the triplets. Next time, head for the panic room. There aren't any cameras in there."

"*Yes!*" Therese glared at him. "*The panic room, where you should be now.*"

"I need help." Noah sat on the edge of Rodrigo's bed.

Rodrigo's eyes almost popped out of his head. "And you came to me for advice? Has it been that long for you, *amigo?*"

"What?" Noah let out an exasperated sigh. "Not sex advice." He pointed at nothing because only he could see his wife. "Ghost advice."

"Ah." Rodrigo visibly relaxed, obviously far more comfortable with this topic of conversation. "What's the problem?" He reached for his mug and took a drink of coffee.

"Therese feels the need to coach me on my physical relationship with Annabelle."

Rodrigo spat his coffee all over the desk beside him. "What?"

"See?" Noah glared at his wife. "It isn't normal."

"Hell no, it isn't normal. Nothing about this is normal. Is she here now?"

"She's standing beside me."

"*I can't believe you've come to him for advice. He doesn't know you as well as I do. He's practically a stranger.*"

"And the only person on the planet who won't have me

committed for talking to you," Noah pointed out. A thought occurred to him. "Is your *abuela* here?"

"No, dude." Rodrigo looked offended. "She haunts my parents. She doesn't follow me around like…"

"Like Therese does me." He folded his arms and glared at his wife. "See? Other ghosts don't do this."

"We believe him?" Therese was annoyed now. *"How do we know his ghost is real, not just in his head?"*

Noah hung his head. "Rodrigo, please, I'm dying here. She's arguing about whether or not your *abuela* is a figment of your imagination. In other words, my delusion is questioning yours. I need serious help."

"No." Rodrigo sat forward, staring at the space where Therese stood. "You don't. I told you—this is common in my culture. Therese, you need to leave our boy alone so he can work out what he's doing with Annabelle."

"But he'll screw it up!"

Noah sighed. "She says I'll screw it up."

Rodrigo ran a hand through his hair. "We're gonna need a priest. As far as I can see, the only way out of this is to exorcise her."

"I'm not a demonic possession." Therese stamped her foot. *"I'm a ghost."* She threw up her hands. *"Your friend is a moron."*

"Not going to work," Noah said.

"Okay." Rodrigo nodded. "Therese, look around you. Can you see a light? A bright pathway that you need to follow?"

"I'm embarrassed for him," Therese said.

"No light," Noah said.

"Well, the only other option I can think of is that she stays here with me while you go do your thing." Rodrigo sat back in his chair.

Therese perked up. *"Stay with him?"*

"Stay with you?" Noah said.

"Sure." Rodrigo picked up his coffee again. "I need someone to bounce ideas off, and if Therese comes up with anything, she can tell you later. Plus"—he shrugged—"I'm lonely. It would be nice to have a woman to talk to."

"Only if you could hear her talk back," Noah pointed out.

"We can work on that." Rodrigo was unfazed.

"I take it back," Therese said. *"I like him. I can stay here and talk to him."*

"You're sure?" Noah asked. "No pretending to stay here then sneaking after me?"

"No," Therese said. *"You heard him. He's lonely, and he wants to talk about his problems. I'm good at fixing problems. I always helped our friends."*

"Fine." Noah stood. "She's all yours," he said to Rodrigo.

"My pleasure," Rodrigo said, a glint in his eye. "Us crazy people have to stick together."

With a shake of his head, Noah left the room, closing the door quietly behind him as Rodrigo updated the figment of Noah's imagination on the state of the Demon case.

Whether it was the power of suggestion or Therese's ghost really was in that room, listening to his teammate, Noah didn't know. All he knew for sure was that he was all alone when he climbed back up the stairs to the loft.

After nodding goodnight to Violet, who was monitoring the streets around the building, Noah made his way to the guest room and closed the door behind him. The connecting door to the panic room still stood ajar, and he eased it open.

"Annabelle?" he whispered into the darkness.

The only reply was an adorable little snore. She was sound asleep, in exactly the same position he'd left her in.

Of course she was asleep.

His luck wouldn't have it any other way. Just when he'd finally managed to get his head out of his ass, his dead wife cockblocked him, and the woman he cared about was out for the count. Life was cruel.

Noah walked back across the guest room and climbed into his cold, empty bed.

Chapter Twenty-Six

"What the hell were you thinking?" District Attorney Dwight Carpenter had dropped his good-old-boy persona and was just plain furious.

Noah didn't blame him, but he was tired of being chewed out for his mistakes. A man could apologize only so many times before he realized nobody was listening. He glanced at his partners in crime, Rodrigo and Abasi. Rodrigo looked resigned, while Abasi looked like he was eyeing the DA up for a casket.

"Well?" the DA demanded, singling Noah out. "You were a cop. You know this isn't how we do things. Do you understand the damage you've done here? Your actions last night have cast a shadow of doubt over the evidence we've gathered on the case going to trial next week. The defense has already filed a motion to dismiss. Not that they'll get it, but they're making it look like the DA's office obtains evidence illegally." He threw up his hands in disgust. "But it isn't my office that's at fault here, is it? And it sure as hell isn't the local cops. No, it's you." He pointed at all of them.

"Benson Security. I rue the day I ever heard your name." He glared at the assistant DA, who lowered her eyes.

Dwight returned his attention to the rest of them. "You were supposed to be the answer to our prayers. A professional security company with no ties to the Houston gang community. A group that couldn't possibly be in the pocket of Eddie Hanson. A team that could protect our witness, and our case. But no. It was too good to be true. Because this isn't a professional team of anything. You're a bunch of cowboys who think you have the right to take matters into your own hands." He glared at them. "You've been in this country five minutes, and you think you know better than the rest of us. Fucking amateurs!"

Standing beside her desk, Rochelle shifted slightly, drawing his attention. She looked him straight in the eye. "You have every right to be upset, but we aren't amateurs, and some of us were born here. In fact, some of us have worked in law enforcement in this country for a very long time. Let's stick to the facts, Mr. DA."

"The facts?" His eyebrows shot up his forehead. "Fine. We can stick to the facts. Fact one"—he counted them off on his fingers—"despite having no authority, you took it upon yourselves to cuff and detain members of a local gang. Fact two, you performed an illegal search of their vehicle. Fact three, you broke into a house and tied up more gang members before running from law enforcement. And fact four, you fucking shot someone while they were cuffed!"

He put his hands on his hips and hung his head, breathing deeply. Nobody moved. The silence was oppressive as they waited for the district attorney to continue.

Noah glanced around the room. Everyone sat stoically, aware that the local authorities had every right to blast them for their actions. The only people missing were Katrina and

Annabelle, who were upstairs while Bella gave his sons an online art lesson. It was a small blessing she wasn't there to hear exactly how bad things were.

The DA looked up at them. "I should bring charges against each and every one of you. God knows you've broken enough laws. I should lock you up and throw away the damn key. But I can't." He let out a stream of curses under his breath. "Because if I let it be known that you were working independently, that you weren't under my authority, then I can't use anything you've uncovered. Worse, I'd have to justify every piece of evidence you've touched since you became involved in our case against the Demons—including any influence you've had over our star witness.

"So, I have to suck it up. I have to tell the defense that you were working as investigators for my department. I have to back your behavior or make myself look like an even bigger idiot than I already do." He glared at Rochelle, vibrating fury. "I don't like being backed into a corner."

She folded her arms over her black suit jacket. "I've already apologized for my office regarding this matter. As I explained, Benson Security was hasty in assembling a new team. We went into the field before we were able to function as a cohesive unit. It won't happen again." She hesitated and then lifted her chin. "The team is being disbanded. This is the last case for the Houston office of Benson Security."

"Well, thank fuck for that!" Dwight adjusted his tie and straightened his shoulders. "The trial is a week today. How about you focus on keeping our witness safe? Although why she hasn't fired your asses yet, I have no idea."

Now Noah was pissed. They'd apologized, explained their reasoning, and accepted the consequences of their actions—after all, the team was being disbanded—but they sure as hell hadn't been unsuccessful.

He stood slowly, his attention on the DA. "If we're your investigators, then we just handed you enough evidence to shut down the Demons for good. Evidence you can use in court. In an election year. Not to mention twenty-one young women who wouldn't be here without us. Our team may have acted a little too independently for your liking, but we got a result that you're happy to run with. I'd say it's time to stop berating us, wouldn't you?"

As the DA's head turned an interesting shade of purple, Noah sensed Rodrigo stand beside him. "We handed you evidence of a human trafficking operation when your police department couldn't find any. I've been an undercover agent for most of my adult life. I know *all* agencies bend the rules when it comes to getting the information they need to prosecute criminals. We didn't cross the line as far as you want us to believe."

Abasi stood and slipped his hands into the pockets of his designer suit pants. "We didn't kill anyone. And, trust me, I wanted to. You're a smart man with political savvy, and you know we did you a favor. We don't want any credit. You can stand in front of voters come election day and explain how you—and your invisible team—cleaned up the city, making it a whole lot safer for women everywhere. We handed you the election."

Violet pushed back her chair. "If we're working for you in an official capacity as investigators, then there isn't an issue here." She turned and left the room.

"You know," Harris said, "I think that rather than ranting, you should be thanking us. Without Benson Security, you wouldn't have a witness *or* a slew of new cases against the Demons. A little respect wouldn't go amiss here."

"What he said," Logan agreed. "And Rochelle might be our boss for only a wee while longer, but she's done a damn good job with us and for you."

Evan stood with them. "You should also know that I'm this close"—he held up his index finger and thumb with barely any space between them—"to tracking payments made to the mole who sold out Annabelle's location. If we're *your* investigators, then I guess our boss would expect me to hand over that information to you as well. Isn't that right, Rochelle?"

Rochelle nodded slowly.

Noah took a step closer to the DA. "We didn't do things the right way. But we did the right things. This discussion is over." He turned to Rochelle, dismissing the DA. "Is there anything else you need from us?"

Something softened in her eyes. "No. Go do your job."

"Yes, Boss," he said before heading for the door, followed by the rest of the team.

"This is preposterous!" the DA exploded, making Noah and everyone else turn to him.

"No," Noah said to the DA. "We're done here." He turned to speak to Rochelle. "If you don't have anything else to discuss with the DA, would you like us to escort him from the building?"

ADA Margaret Grant lowered her head, desperately trying to hide her grin from her boss.

"That's okay, Noah," Rochelle said, taking a seat at her desk. "I'm sure Dwight can find his own way out." She smiled at the DA. "Thank you for dropping by with an update." Then she pulled her laptop toward her and focused on the screen, dismissing him.

The DA looked like his head might explode, but he cast

one more censuring look at them all before signaling to the officers accompanying him that it was time to leave.

"I'll expect a detailed report on your investigation into the mole," he snapped at Rochelle.

"Of course," she said not looking up from her laptop.

The team stepped aside as the DA, ADA, and the two officers with them headed down the stairs and through the front door. When Noah glanced back at Rochelle, she was smiling.

* * *

Noah had barely seen Annabelle all morning. Between apologizing to Rochelle and dealing with the DA, there hadn't been much time to catch up with her. So he went upstairs to relieve Katrina of guard duty, smiling when he saw Annabelle so deep in concentration at her drawing board that she didn't notice he'd entered the loft.

"How's it going?" he whispered to Katrina, who was working on her laptop at the dining table.

She smiled up at him. "She's a natural teacher. The boys are loving their lesson. So much so that they'll probably want to grow up to be artists themselves, or worse, become so addicted to comic books that you go broke buying them."

"I guess there are worse obsessions for them to develop," he said, sitting beside her. "You can go if you want. I've got this now."

Her smile was teasing. "I *bet* you do."

"Not you too," he groaned. Half the team had hassled him about getting caught on camera, kissing Annabelle. The other half, led by Violet, had no interest at all.

Katrina gathered up her laptop and indicated the

cameras with a twirling motion of her hand. "Remember, Big Brother is watching." She checked her watch. "Or in this case, Evan."

The last thing he wanted was the triplets perving over any unintentional on-camera antics. "I'll behave," he vowed.

"How did the meeting with the DA go?" she asked.

"About how you'd expect." Noah ran a hand down his face. "But there'll be no charges filed against us. Apparently, we're now paid investigators for the district attorney's office."

"Really?" She didn't bother to hide her skepticism. "This would be for a nominal payment, I gather?"

"You're in charge of the books, you tell me. But I'm going to go out on a limb here and predict he's given us a dollar at best."

Katrina's expression transformed into one of disgust. "I *really* don't like the district attorney. He may be angry about our work, but he sure is happy to take the credit for it."

"That's what you get when jobs turn into roles that require an election to fill."

She gave him a sympathetic smile before leaving the apartment. Noah heaved a weary sigh, but as he watched Annabelle walk his sons through the process of drawing a fight scene, his tense muscles began to relax.

Katrina was right—she had a gift. And she'd also enthralled his boys. She sat at her drawing board, the computer monitor on the desk beside her displaying his sons as they drew along with her. Above the drawing board, she'd rigged up a couple of cameras to show different angles of her work. She also had a camera trained on her face so the boys could see her when she talked to them.

He smiled. She'd done this before. It amazed him just how connected Annabelle was to the world she couldn't set foot in. She was part of a massive online community, chatted with people all the time, and had built up a base of local artist friends who visited frequently. Well, when she wasn't on lockdown as a key witness in the trial of the decade.

"You see?" she said. "The line tapers, creating a sense of movement. It's important that your lines follow the angle and shape of the body. That way, you can suggest form and movement with the minimal number of strokes."

"And leave lots of space for color," Sammy said eagerly. He was all about the coloring.

"This is so cool," Jacob said. "I can't wait to show the guys at soccer how to do this." He smiled shyly at her. "I've got them all reading your comics. They think you're amazing." He blushed, the adoration of youth in his eyes.

No doubt about it, she'd won his boys over.

"That's wonderful," Annabelle said enthusiastically. "I'm so glad they like them."

Of course, Sammy wasn't to be outdone. "I told everybody that you have a whole room full of comics. Can I bring my team over to see it?"

She laughed. "That might be kinda hard, seeing as I'm in Houston and all your friends are in Atlantic City."

"Oh, yeah." He nodded, unbothered by his mistake, and carried on coloring.

"Annabelle?" Jacob said. "One of the guys was telling me about Comic-Con. It's like a big... market, or fair, right? Only with comic book artists and people dressed up as characters. I looked it up online, but it was kinda confusing."

She nodded. "Probably too many videos about specific parts of it rather than a clear overview."

"Yeah, that." Jacob nodded.

"You're right, though. It's usually held in a massive hall

with lots of stands and booths. People sell stuff to do with comics or fantasy stories and art. There are actors from Marvel movies—"

"Spiderman!" Sammy shouted with a grin.

"Absolutely." She grinned back. "They do talks too and promote new movies and stuff. And there are definitely lots of people in costumes."

"It sounds cool. Do you think Dad would take us?" Jacob looked hopeful.

"I don't see why not. You should ask him."

"Will you go with us?" Jacob blushed. "Sorry, you're probably already there, giving talks and stuff or meeting your fans. Maybe we could see you there?"

Annabelle stilled before smiling softly into the camera. "I don't go to Comic-Con, Jacob."

"Why not?" Typical kid—no boundaries or tact.

Noah waited to see if he needed to intervene with his nosy kids, but Annabelle had it in hand.

"I don't go out," she said simply.

The boys stopped drawing and stared at her through the screen.

"You mean, like, at all?" Jacob frowned, trying to understand.

"Yep. I have this... condition. It means going outside is really hard for me. I get scared and have to run back inside before I faint. It isn't pretty. So I stay in my house and talk to people online, like you guys." She smiled at them.

Sammy's eyes widened. "I was scared when we moved to London. I didn't want to go."

"Because it was different from Atlantic City?" she asked with compassion.

Sammy nodded. "Yeah, and my friends weren't there."

"I didn't want to go either," Jacob confessed. "But Dad needed to go away, I think."

"So you went for him?" Annabelle said.

Jacob grinned. "And to see our uncles. They're all living in England and Scotland now. They're Dad's four best friends that he grew up with, and they're all really cool. One of them used to be a martial arts fighter."

"That's Uncle Beast. He's got loads of tattoos," Sammy enthused. "Lots of different pictures all over him. I bet he'd get one of your comic heroes on his back. He's got space there."

Her eyes sparkled with delight. "That would be cool."

"Aunty Belinda's married to Beast," Sammy said eagerly. "She acts in movies. She could be Jade Justice!"

"That's a thought," Annabelle said.

"He's not just being a dumb kid," Jacob said. "She's famous. So's her brother. We only met him once, but he was a superhero in a movie." He stopped talking, frowning. "I can't remember which one, but Dad knows. You should go meet them."

"She can't." Sammy elbowed his brother. "She has a condiment."

Annabelle laughed. "A condition," she corrected.

"You know," Sammy said, "you could go outside if you went with my dad. When I was scared of London, he held my hand, and I kept close to him. It really helped." He glanced at Jacob out of the corner of his eye before sitting up straight. "I was a little kid. It's okay for little kids to hold their dad's hands."

Noah placed his palm over his heart. It ached from missing his boys. Suddenly, they seemed too far away for comfort.

Jacob elbowed Sammy. "She can't hold his hand.

Grown-ups don't do that unless..." He turned beetroot and couldn't look into the camera. "You know."

"Know what?" Sammy asked innocently.

"Like if they're dating and stuff," Jacob mumbled.

"Oh." Sammy looked at Annabelle. "You need to date our dad so you can hold his hand and go outside. That way, we can all go to Comic-Corn and meet Spiderman."

"It's Comic-*CON*," Jacob said with long-suffering. "Not corn. And she can't just date Dad. That isn't how it works. You can't just tell people to date. They have to like each other first."

"Do you like our dad?" Sammy asked, determined not to be derailed.

"Yes, I do." Annabelle smiled. "I like him a lot."

Noah felt a warm sensation in his chest, in the spot where his hand rested.

"Then just hold his hand, and you'll be okay." As far as Sammy was concerned, the matter had been resolved. He returned his attention to his drawing.

Jacob rolled his eyes. "Don't listen to him. He doesn't have a clue. But seriously, Dad's almost as good at fighting as Uncle Beast. They all used to fight together, all the uncles. I'm sure he could protect you if you went outside. And maybe you could, like, only look at things close to you or something. When I was scared in London, Aunt Julia, who's scared of *loads* of stuff and really likes whiteboards, told me that she has a trick for not feeling scared. She doesn't look at everything. She just concentrates on the small things near her. Then the world isn't so big. Maybe you could try doing that."

"Thanks." Annabelle seemed genuinely touched. "Now, let's get this drawing finished before your grandparents fetch you for dinner."

"They eat too early," Jacob said.

"Old people," Sammy said wisely, making Noah chuckle.

On hearing a noise behind him, Noah turned to see a somber Rodrigo heading toward him.

"Hey." Rodrigo leaned over the table, keeping his voice low. "You gotta see this."

"What?"

"Come on." He jerked his head toward the door. "Not here."

"But I need to keep an eye on Annabelle."

"Got it covered." He nodded toward Logan as he walked into the loft, looking equally grim.

"I've got it," Logan said as he sat on a stool at the breakfast bar.

Worried, Noah followed Rodrigo downstairs to the office.

Chapter Twenty-Seven

"How long's he been down there?" Noah stood, arms folded, staring through the window at the street below.

"Coupla minutes," Rodrigo said. "I came to get you as soon as we spotted him on the cameras."

A large, brand-new SUV was parked illegally on the opposite corner of the intersection, facing the warehouse. Leaning against its hood—ankles crossed and sipping coffee from a to-go cup—was Eddie Hanson. His aviator sunglasses made it difficult to see exactly where he was looking, but the angle of his head suggested his attention was firmly on Annabelle's building.

"What's he doing?" Evan jostled his way through the rest of the team for a better view.

"Trying to intimidate us," Rodrigo said.

"No." Noah wasn't convinced. "I think he's taunting us. He's telling us that last night's events had no impact on him or his business."

"The guy has balls the size of boulders," Harris muttered.

"Psychopath," Abasi said. "I know the type."

Rochelle hurried into the room. "I was on a call with Lake. What's going on?"

"Take a look." Noah stepped to one side to make room for her.

Her lips pursed. "Katrina? Call the detectives, please."

"On it." Katrina turned from the group, her phone already at her ear.

"You don't want to handle this yourself?" Noah asked his boss.

She shook her head. "The cops can handle this one. I'm surprised you aren't arguing the decision."

He held up his hands. "I got the message. You're the boss."

"For now," she muttered before looking past him to Violet, who was glaring at the Demons' leader—even though he couldn't see her. "And no shooting him either."

"Hey," Violet said. "I'll be a good team player from now on. Even I can keep it together until we disband in a week or so."

"Somebody *should* shoot him." Abasi's tone was low as he studied Eddie. "He won't stop." His dark eyes met Rochelle's. "Ever. The trial, a conviction, none of it will stop him. I've seen this before; he's got us in his sights, and he won't let go until he's dealt with us."

"You mean kill us, right?" Evan asked, swallowing hard.

Abasi just stared at him.

"Aye." Evan nodded. "You mean kill us."

To Noah's surprise, Rochelle didn't immediately shut down Abasi's view. "I agree that Eddie's much more dangerous than I initially thought him to be. He seems very... driven."

"Psychotic almost?" Noah offered.

"Yes." Rochelle stared down at the murderer, looking thoughtful.

Sirens wailed in the distance. Again. It was a good job that Annabelle didn't have any close residential neighbors; recent events would have had them running for the hills.

"The detectives were already on their way here," Katrina said as she joined them at the window.

"I wondered at the fast response," Noah said.

Only the sheer blind stopped Eddie from seeing them all, although Noah was certain he knew they were there.

"Does Annabelle know he's down there?" Rochelle asked.

"No." Noah watched as the two detectives climbed out of their vehicle. "She's in the middle of an online art class."

"Good," Rochelle said. "That's good."

In the street below, the detectives approached Eddie, who remained relaxed. There was a lot of gesturing, and at one point, Johnson got out his phone—no doubt a threat to take Eddie in. At last, with a chilling smile, the Demons' leader pushed away from the hood of his car and sauntered to the driver's door. Before he got in, he grinned up at the warehouse and saluted.

The team, along with the two cops, watched him drive away.

As the detectives got back into their car to park it outside the warehouse, Rochelle turned to Evan. "Where are we on the Demons' money?"

"We're still doing that?" He looked surprised. "I thought because we're quitting the team, you didn't want anything else happening. I mean, stuff the cops won't know about."

"No, I never said to stop hunting for their money."

"Good." Excited, Evan sat at his desk. "Because I have something."

"5-O are at the door," Rodrigo said. "I'll let them in." He left the room.

Evan carried on. "I need to check a few things, but I think we've found the banks the gang, and their leader, use to stash their funds."

"How long until you're sure?" Rochelle studied the screen, her eyes sharp.

"End of the day? Tomorrow morning at the latest. I think."

"Good."

The main door opened and closed. The cops were on their way up.

"What do you want me to do once I find their money?" Evan said. "Just come tell you?"

"No." As Rochelle straightened, she caught Abasi's eye. "Take it all. Abasi will help you with where to put it." The former mobster inclined his head in approval. "Make sure there's no trail back to us," she ordered Evan.

The rest of the team stared at their boss, open-mouthed.

"I thought we didn't do this kind of stuff anymore," Violet said.

"That isn't what I said," Rochelle told her. "I said there's a hierarchy here. I'm the boss, and I get to approve or veto any plans we come up with. It's the only way to keep us all safe." She plastered a sudden smile on her face. "Gentlemen," she said as she walked toward the cops. "Thanks for the assist outside. Have a seat. Can we get you a coffee?"

"I don't think we gave the boss enough of a chance before we blew it," Violet muttered to Noah, her attention on Rochelle.

"Speak for yourself," he said before walking over to join her.

Detective Johnson sat with a sigh. "Mr. Hanson sends his regards."

"I bet he does." Noah pulled out a chair opposite them. "Doesn't his visit contravene the conditions of his bail?"

Johnson gave Harris a grateful smile as he took the offered mug of coffee. "It would, only, technically, he doesn't know where the witness lives or anything about her. As far as he's concerned, he has no information on her whereabouts and just stopped over the road for a coffee."

"Yeah, and he has no idea why his gang members keep turning up here either," Noah said, disgusted.

"He reckons he's stepped back from the gang to concentrate on his defense for next week's trial."

McMillan waved off the offered coffee. "Thing is, we can't prove either way that the gang was here with his blessing or that he knows for sure that Annabelle lives here. Although we can say he knows it now, because we just officially ordered him to stay away from the witness."

Johnson sat back in his chair. "Don't expect him to listen to us. The guy's a complete psycho."

"We figured," Noah said. "How are the women?"

"As well as can be expected." McMillan reached for the donut box in the middle of the table and opened it to check if there were any left. His eyes lit up when he found two to choose from. "They're all awake now. We've put guards at the hospital in case the Demons come looking for them, but they aren't talking yet."

"Mostly, they're crying," Johnson said.

Katrina came up beside Noah, standing much closer than usual. "Do you have female officers talking to them? Counselors?"

"Yep." McMillan frowned. "This isn't the first time we've dealt with this kinda crap. Sick bastards." He took a big bite of donut, making powdered sugar billow over the desk.

"They're malnourished and dehydrated," Johnson said. "Most of them were drugged at some point and are going through withdrawal. Don't worry, Ms. Raast, we're well aware these women are victims, and we aren't pushing any of them."

"Good." She nodded stiffly before mumbling about having work to do and leaving the room.

"We were on our way over to talk to Mr. Otieno about shooting one of the Demons," McMillan said around a mouthful of donut. "But Johnson here got a text from the DA saying we don't have to bother."

Johnson gave Abasi a wry look. "Apparently, it was self-defense. Still not sure how a guy who's hog-tied and lying face down in the dirt could attack you, but whatever. We have our orders, and there won't be any more inquiries into the shooting."

"For future reference," Violet said, "would it have still been self-defense if the wound was a little more life-threatening?"

"It's self-defense because the DA's in a hole and doesn't want to be buried under the dirt your team's generated," McMillan said. "But to answer your question, you can't call shooting an unarmed and restrained man self-defense under any circumstances. If the injury had been more 'life-threat-ening,' it would be considered murder. Something Mr. Otieno is very familiar with, isn't that right?" He cocked an eyebrow at Abasi.

"I don't know what you're talking about," Abasi said.

"Yeah, right." McMillan helped himself to another

donut, seemingly unbothered by the sugar coating he'd given his cheap suit.

Johnson set his empty mug on the table and stood, making McMillan follow him—donut in hand. "You got lucky this time," he said to the team. "Not just Otieno over there; all of you. If the DA wasn't desperate to use what you found, you'd all be under investigation. And trust me when I tell you, the charges would stick. I suggest you change how you operate from here on in. Unless you want to end up in adjoining cells with Eddie and his gang."

He nodded his goodbyes and strode from the room, followed by McMillan, who was too busy eating to acknowledge anyone.

Chapter Twenty-Eight

Night fell like a heavy velvet curtain, ending an act of a play. But unlike a theater, the lights didn't go up; instead, they remained low with nightfall as the audience waited for the final act.

Dinner was pizza, delivered by a teenager who'd been scared out of his mind when three heavily armed men opened the door to him. To make up for terrorizing the poor kid, Noah made sure his tip was on the hefty side.

It was a working meal while the team went over building security, ensuring the place was locked down tight. Once that was done, they moved on to helping Evan unravel the complicated systems the Demons used to hide their money. The reports were correct: Eddie Hanson was smart. Every contact they talked to, every clue they unearthed, led back to him. The man was a genius at hiding his money.

"It's unbelievable." Abasi slowly shook his head. "We would have killed to have a guy with these skills in the James Family."

"Pity he's a violent psychopath," Noah pointed out. "Hard to control those."

"Tell me about it." Abasi wandered over to help Evan decipher some info he'd uncovered in the Caymans.

While Abasi, Rodrigo, Evan, and Rochelle followed the money trail, Noah strolled to the corner of the room, where Annabelle sat curled up in the old armchair that he'd slept in, her sketchpad open beside her. She smiled up at him as he approached.

"Whatcha drawing?" he asked, crouching down beside her.

She turned the pad toward him. On the page was a picture of the two of them in the panic room on the day they'd met. Annabelle huddled in the corner, her hands covering her ears, while Noah stood behind a barrier, gun aimed at the wall in front of him. Bullets flew all around them, destroying everything in the room.

"It's amazing," he said. "But I thought you didn't remember much about that day?"

"It comes back to me in psychedelic flashes. I see everything through a cough-syrup haze."

"Pretty accurate for a hazy memory."

"Well, I have you to thank for that. Mainly, I've relied on what you've told me."

Noah rested his hand on her knee. "Why are you drawing this? Please tell me it isn't part of the boys' next lesson because, as far as they're concerned, their father shoots with a water pistol."

She grinned, as he'd known she would. "Nope, it's for my doctor. She suggested drawing my anxieties or the memories to get them out of my head. She thinks it might help me process things."

"And is it helping?"

Annabelle shrugged. "I'm calmer, but I think that's mainly because I just love drawing."

Unable to resist, Noah reached out to sweep her hair away from her face. It ran through his fingers like silk. "Can I get you anything?" he asked a little gruffly.

"No, thanks, I'm good." Her smile was intimate, just for him.

"We've barely had a minute alone since... last night."

Her eyes crinkled at the corners. "You mean when I fell asleep waiting for you?"

"I'm sorry about that. Talking to Rodrigo took longer than I expected. When I got back upstairs, you were out cold."

She reached down to link her fingers through his, and in that moment, it seemed as if everyone else in the room disappeared. "You know, you could have just crawled into bed beside me instead of sleeping in the guest room."

"You needed your sleep." He caressed the inside of her wrist with his thumb and watched as she wet her lips.

"I could have slept with you beside me," she said softly, her eyes darkening.

"I'm not sure I could have, not after that kiss." Blood pooled low in his body at the memory.

"That kiss seems like such a long time ago," she whispered. "I can barely remember it."

He shifted uncomfortably as his jeans became tighter. "I could refresh your memory."

Annabelle bit her bottom lip, gazing at him through thick, dark lashes. Her eyes flickered to the room behind him before she gave him a tiny smile. "Perhaps when we don't have an audience."

At her words, the room rushed back into focus, and

once again, he could hear the low chatter of his teammates and the hum of computers.

"No," he said wryly. "This isn't the best location."

"Noah?" Rochelle called. "Can you take a look at this? I think we may have hit the jackpot."

Reluctantly, he released Annabelle's hand and straightened. Turning his back on her proved much more difficult than it should have.

"What is it?" he asked as he approached Evan's control center.

Rodrigo and Abasi smiled knowingly at him and cast pointed looks Annabelle's way. He frowned at them. They were both worse than the triplets.

"This." Rochelle indicated the screen, which was filled with financial transactions. "It appears to be some kind of trust account."

"Like lawyers set up to hold money until a deal goes through?"

She nodded. "Exactly."

Noah leaned in to get a better look. "Do we know what the money's for?"

"Horses." Evan scratched his head, looking bewildered.

Beside him, Abasi pulled out his phone and wandered off.

"What do you mean, horses?" Noah asked their tech.

"That's what it says." He pointed at the screen. "This payment was held back in January. The notation beside it says it's for twelve unbroken Arabians to be delivered by the end of the month. Then here"—he ran his fingertip down the screen—"the funds were released at the end of January. Which means the horses must have been delivered."

Noah frowned. "Six million for twelve horses? What's the going rate for an Arabian?"

Evan brought up a search engine and typed in the question. "Says here that a rare, highly sought-after Arabian can go for as much as 150k. But they usually sell for about the fifteen to thirty thousand mark."

"So, these ones are selling way over market value, if they're paying six million for twelve. Are there more entries for other sales?"

Again, Evan tapped on his keyboard. "Last October, there was an order for fifteen horses, a mix of European breeds. They wanted these ones trained. And then in November, the money goes out for delivery of the horses."

"Anything more recent?" A nasty tingling sensation grew in the back of Noah's mind.

"Aye, this month, somebody wanted twenty-one American Quarter Horses, trained and of breeding age."

A chill ran up Noah's spine.

"How much was in the account for this purchase?"

"Two point one million."

Noah felt sick to his stomach. "They aren't buying horses."

"No." Abasi came up to stand beside him. "They aren't. I just got off the phone with one of my contacts. They're buying women."

Katrina leaped up from where she'd been working close to Annabelle and ran from the room. Noah heard the bathroom door slam behind her. Harris followed, and when he returned, he looked worried.

"I think she ate something bad," he said.

"Oh no," Annabelle said. "I'll go see if she's okay." She got up and rushed out of the room.

Noah nodded at Harris.

"I'll keep an eye on her," he said, following their client.

Noah looked at Abasi and saw that he, too, realized

exactly why Katrina had run. And it had nothing to do with the pizza.

"What else did your contact say?" Noah asked.

"That you can make a shit ton in human trafficking if you have the right product and the right clientele."

"People, not products," Rochelle corrected evenly. "Women, in this case."

Abasi nodded somberly. "He also said that there isn't a whole lot of trust in the business. Used to be it was money on delivery, but the guys picking up the women were being stiffed on payment and wanted some security. Hence, accounts like this. They aren't common, but they're out there."

"Administered by a third party?" Noah said.

"A broker," Abasi agreed.

"Who deposited the money into that account?" Noah asked Evan.

He jerked a thumb at Rodrigo, who was on a computer beside him. "He's working on it. All we know right now is that the account was set up for the Demon Brothers. All funds are released into their normal accounts." He swallowed hard. "You really think they're talking about people and not horses?"

"I'm afraid so." Noah clasped his shoulder.

Sometimes, it was easy to forget just how young the triplets were and how relatively sheltered their lives had been in Scotland.

He turned to Rochelle. "If we take the money out of that account, it will piss off whoever's paying for the women the Demons pick up. Could turn ugly for them."

"Or they could join forces to find whoever took the money." She frowned in thought. "Evan? Can we move the money out of there and into a Demon account before taking it from them?"

"Sure."

Noah liked how she was thinking. "Make it look like the Demons stole it." He nodded with approval.

There was motion behind them, and the two women walked back into the office space, followed by Harris.

Katrina was pale, but she smiled weakly at them. "Something must have disagreed with me," she said, her head held high and a hand pressed to her stomach.

Annabelle fussed around her. "How about I make you a nice cup of tea to calm your digestion?"

"Thanks, that would be great." Katrina sat back at her desk, keeping her gaze averted from her teammates.

"I'll help," Harris said when Noah gestured for him to follow. "We'll make a new pot of coffee too."

"Not you!" Rochelle's head snapped around. "Annabelle, have mercy on my coffee addiction, and don't let the Scot make it."

With a grin, she shoved Harris out of the room. "I'll make sure he sticks to tea."

"There's nothing wrong with how we make coffee," Evan grumbled and was ignored by everyone.

"So," Noah said to his boss, "we're taking their money, then?"

Her jaw clenched as her eyes darkened. "All of it. Every last cent we can get our hands on."

"Do we hand it over to the cops?" They were both aware that was standard procedure.

Katrina cleared her throat. "What happens to criminal profits when they're confiscated by law enforcement?"

Noah pulled out a chair, glancing at the clock on the wall above Evan's control center. It was getting late. Again.

"Usually, it's added to state funds or split between the departments involved in the investigation. Sometimes, you'll see cars drive past with 'bought by drug money' written on their sides. That's what it means."

"So, it goes to the state?" She frowned.

"Mostly. They can dish it out as they see fit."

"Does any of the money make its way to the victims?" she asked evenly.

"Sometimes they donate to charities that work with victims."

There was silence for a moment as everyone contemplated that, and then, as though functioning as one, they turned to Rochelle.

She nodded as though she'd made a decision. "Abasi, are you able to set up an account for the money to go into? We don't want the transfers to be traced to this account, and we don't want anyone to find out who's behind it."

"With Evan's help, sure, we can do that."

"Even though we were able to trace the Demons' accounts?" she asked him and Evan.

"They were good," Evan said. "But we've learned from their mistakes. Plus, Abasi knows a trick or two of his own, right?" He gazed at the former mobster with awe in his eyes.

"One or two," Abasi agreed.

Rodrigo swiveled his wheeled office chair. "I think I know who's paying for..." He cast a glance at Katrina. "Who's paying the Demons."

"Are you gonna make us guess?" Noah said.

Rodrigo rolled his eyes. "It's the Alvarez cartel."

"But I thought they were all about being a boutique drug mob," Evan said, looking confused. "Didn't you say they were specialists? Scary dudes who deal in cocaine?"

"They are." Rodrigo ran a hand through his hair. "Word

is, they started trafficking a few years ago when the international market for cocaine dipped—not so many drug deals during a pandemic. To reduce their costs, they started using slave labor. From there, they diversified. Human trafficking is a low-risk, high-reward crime. People tend to think of it as all being sex related, but there are unscrupulous assholes out there who just don't want to pay their workforce. It's modern-day slavery."

"And the Alvarez cartel is profiting from it." Noah rubbed his chin, feeling the rough growth of a day's worth of stubble. "Rodrigo, you're familiar with this cartel. How pissed will they be if the Demons take their money but can't produce the goods?"

"Let's put it this way, they might be one of the smaller cartels, but nobody touches them. Ever."

Rochelle stood, nodding. "Then we take it all."

She looked at Noah, and something passed between them. An understanding of sorts. As though she realized that even though the men had been out of line to go off without telling her, things were done a little differently in Benson Security than in regular law enforcement. Sometimes, justice and the law didn't run hand in hand.

"We take it all," he agreed.

Chapter Twenty-Nine

It was late by the time the team finished moving every cent they could find out of Eddie Hanson's accounts. Noah stood and stretched, his gaze straying to Annabelle, curled up in the old armchair. She'd been sound asleep for an hour or so, with his old denim jacket tucked around her and a fluffy pink cushion under her head. She was so beautiful—all soft curves and a mass of unruly dark hair. Just looking at her made him feel... blessed. Great, he could almost hear Jacob mocking him: "Do you mean *hashtag* blessed, Dad?" Man, he missed his kids. Lately, they'd spent more time with Annabelle than with him.

With a rueful smile, he addressed the remaining members of his, albeit temporary, team. "I'm turning in for the night."

Rochelle tore her eyes from the screens. "It is late. Think I'll call it a night too." She stood and grabbed her jacket from the back of her chair. "We should all get some sleep. Who knows what tomorrow will bring once Eddie wakes up to find his money's gone. You checked security again, didn't you? The building's locked up tight?"

"Yep. And we're doubling up on guard duty tonight. Just in case." Noah glanced at Annabelle again. "I need to get her to bed."

Rochelle cocked an eyebrow, amusement crinkling her eyes at the corners.

"To sleep," Noah corrected quickly, his cheeks burning.

"Is that what you old people call it?" Evan drawled, his attention still on the screen in front of him.

Noah absently reached out and smacked him on the back of the head. Rochelle laughed. It was good to hear.

"Go to bed," she ordered. "All of you."

"Yes, Boss," Evan said, rubbing his head.

Abasi slowly got to his feet and inclined his head toward Annabelle. "Need a hand getting her upstairs?"

"Seriously? You're suggesting I'm old too? We're the same damn age. I can carry her just fine on my own."

Abasi held up his hands in surrender. "I was just being helpful."

"Yeah, right." Noah scowled at them all. Bunch of comedians.

He crossed the room to Annabelle, scooped her up, and cradled her against his chest. She fit perfectly and snuggled into him like a little cat.

"Noah?" she mumbled.

"Time for bed, Bella," he murmured.

"I can walk," she made a token protest as she continued to settle in, wrapping an arm around his neck.

Yeah, she totally wanted to walk. "Carrying you is faster."

His team grinned as he left for the apartment upstairs. He was working with children. Easily amused children.

The loft was in darkness when he pushed through the door, although dim light seeped in from the streets outside, making it easy to see where he was going. Other than the low hum of distant traffic, the warehouse was peaceful. An oasis in the middle of the busy city—a well-fortified oasis with a team of armed security specialists stationed throughout the building.

Yeah, there was nothing normal about their situation. In fact, everything felt a little surreal, except for the woman in his arms. She felt real. Solid... soft, warm... precious. Noah wanted to wrap himself around her and protect her from every bad thing that came her way. He wanted to do everything within his power to ensure Annabelle Simmons had a beautiful life.

Damn it. He stumbled but quickly steadied himself.

He was falling in love with the client.

This wasn't just the first bloom of attraction growing in the fallow field of grief. It was the beginning of something far more. The feeling was hard to mistake, and despite having experienced it only once before, he knew what it meant. He was invested. All in. There was no going back— not without ripping his heart in two.

Noah cast his eyes around the apartment, half expecting Therese to turn up with a smug smile and a flippant *"I told you so."* But there was no sign of her. Noah wasn't sure if he felt relief at her absence or sadness that she wasn't there to share his epiphany. One of these days, he needed to let go of his imaginary friend and move on—just as she'd been telling him to do.

He elbowed the pressure panel on the wall that opened the door to the panic room and carried Annabelle inside. The door slid shut behind them as he gently placed her on the bed. She stirred, looking around, then relaxing when she realized where she was.

"I'd better get ready for bed." Lazily, she swung her legs

around under her and knelt up to look at him, suddenly far more awake than she'd led him to believe. "Are you sleeping here tonight?"

Damn, but she was pure temptation, all soft and sleepy, eyes heavy and cheeks flushed. It was impossible not to touch her. He ran his fingertips down her cheek. "I don't think that's a good idea."

Her frown was adorable. "Why not?"

"Because we're both exhausted, and if we lie down together, I'm not sure we'll get any sleep." Her eyes darkened as the tip of her tongue peeked out to wet her lips. "Plus, I don't think you're ready for what will happen if we get into bed together."

Her hands came up to cup his cheeks. "Noah," she murmured, "don't you think it's a little arrogant to tell me what I think and feel? Wouldn't it be better if you just asked me?" She cocked her head to one side. "Or perhaps you're projecting your fears onto me. Maybe it's you who isn't ready for what will happen."

Delight bubbled inside of Noah. "Oh, I don't know, I feel pretty ready. But I'm also fighting the urge to mansplain why you aren't."

Laughter danced in her dark eyes. "How about we just skip the part where we believe we can read each other's minds and ask instead? Noah"—she held his gaze—"I would very much like for you to come to bed with me. Naked would be best, don't you think?"

It felt like there was an explosion inside of him. Blood rushed to the surface of his body, making his skin tingle and burn with the need to be touched.

He cupped the back of her head. "You're sure?"

"You know, this good-guy thing only goes so far before it becomes annoying. Take off your clothes, Noah. I'm sure."

Chuckling, he leaned in to press his lips to hers. He burned with wanting her. But it was more than that; he needed to be close to her. To connect. To know her in a way only he could know her.

Oh yeah, he was definitely falling fast.

Their kiss felt right. Like coming home. They teased each other slowly, in no rush to take things faster. He liked that about her. He liked that the journey was just as important as the destination, because he wanted to enjoy every step of the way.

"You are so beautiful," he whispered against her lips.

"You look like a bruiser, but I'll take you," Annabelle said with a smile in her voice.

He was chuckling when her fingers found the hem of his T-shirt and her hands slid under it. They caressed their way up his abs to his chest.

"Lemme see," she demanded tugging at his shirt.

"No patience," he teased and whipped the shirt off over his head.

Annabelle sat back on her heels, her mouth hanging open. "Oh my, those abs... You look like Batman's suit," she said in wonder.

Noah burst out laughing as he reached for her. They tumbled onto the bed together, a tangle of limbs and laughter as they kissed, their hands exploring.

Annabelle tore her mouth from his, and he took a certain male satisfaction in seeing her swollen lips.

"What's this?" She prodded his side, straining to see what she'd discovered.

Noah pushed up and held himself above her with locked arms. He glanced down his body to the spot just above the waistband of his jeans on his left side. "Knife wound."

"Oh." Her brow puckered with concern. "Poor baby."

Adorable.

He angled his head to capture her mouth but sucked in a breath when he felt her hands on the fastening of his jeans. He backed off to kneel beside her.

"Too fast," he said, feeling lightheaded. "We need to slow down. I don't want to miss any stops on this journey."

"Okay." She knelt up to face him. "What's the next step?"

"Well, I'd say that shirt of yours needs to come off." He reached out and unfastened a button on her faded plaid shirt. Then another. And another. His eyes met hers. "You're not wearing a bra." His awe felt like that of a teenager. It would have been embarrassing if anyone had been there to witness his reaction.

Annabelle gasped. "I'm not?" She finished unbuttoning the shirt and stared down at her perfect breasts. "How did that happen?" Wicked, amused eyes met his. "I apologize for the oversight."

"Just don't let it happen again," Noah said solemnly, cupping her breasts and flicking his thumbs over taut nipples.

"I'll try not to." She groaned as she leaned into him, seeking his mouth with hers. He gave it willingly.

His hands slid down her rounded stomach to the button on her jeans. He fumbled. "Sorry," he muttered. "I'm out of practice. I'll get better."

"Noah." She reached down to help him. "I've slept with two men. I don't exactly have a lot of experience, but I remember the fundamentals. We'll be fine."

"Two is one more than my total," he confessed.

"Men?" she grinned widely. "Noah Merchant, you dark horse."

His cheeks heated. "You know what I mean. I've only ever slept with Therese." He shook his head and admitted, "I'm kinda nervous."

"Would it help if I gave instructions as we went?" She batted her lashes at him. "Maybe sketched some diagrams?"

"Smart-ass." He leaned forward and nipped her bottom lip.

Her laughter made him feel as if he were floating. "Stop worrying. We know what we're doing, and it will be fine."

"I was aiming for a little better than fine," he grumbled.

"Too much talk, not enough action." She unzipped his jeans and slid her hand inside.

The ability to speak immediately left Noah as her small hand wrapped around him. All he could do was groan.

"That's more like it," she said, leaning in to nibble at his throat.

* * *

Annabelle was giddy. She'd wanted Noah almost from the first moment she'd seen him, even though it'd been through a haze of self-medication. He had the rough, weary look of a battle-worn warrior. One who'd keep on fighting despite desperately needing to rest. Not physical rest, but emotional. Noah Merchant had carried far too much for far too long.

And all it'd taken to get his full attention was for her to shove her hand down his pants. Good to know. She smiled against the thick, muscled column of his neck. He was built to fight. There was nothing soft or pretty or choreographed about him. He wasn't some self-obsessed actor playing the part of a defender. Noah's instinct to use his body as a protective wall was hardwired into his DNA. You could sense it in every taut muscle and every ugly scar that marked him.

Annabelle toppled him onto his back and then scampered down his body, taking his clothes with her. Noah helped by kicking off his boots so she could slip his jeans over his feet. Now that she had him naked, she sat back on her heels and looked her fill. She was right. His character was written on his skin.

"So many scars." She ran her fingertips over a recent one—a line where a bullet had cut a channel on the outside of his thigh.

He shrugged. "Never intended to take up modeling, anyway. You're still wearing too many clothes. I don't think that's fair."

"You're right. And we're all about the fairness." Annabelle stood on the bed and stripped off her clothes without any fanfare. This wasn't a seductive performance; she just wanted the damn things gone. At last, she stood naked, straddling his ankles, the cool air caressing her exposed skin.

His hungry and appreciative gaze ran the length of her body, lingering here and there with heady appreciation. "You'd really suit a belly button ring," he said, surprising her. "Something in rose gold to bring out the warm tones in your satin skin."

"Noah," she breathed as his words wove images in her mind.

He flexed and sat up in one smooth motion, making his abs ripple and her mouth water. His hands clasped her hips as he nuzzled her rounded belly. Annabelle loved her curves; she'd never wanted a flat stomach—unless it came with a six-pack and a man attached.

"Right here." Noah nibbled the spot just below her belly button. "Something I could tease with my tongue."

Annabelle clasped his head, wishing his hair was much longer so she could anchor herself with fistfuls of it. "Go a bit lower," she said huskily. "You might find something else you can tease with your tongue."

"My thoughts exactly." He kissed his way down her stomach until his wicked mouth found juicier prey.

Annabelle gasped and threw back her head as her whole world centered on the tiny motions he made with his tongue. Her knees would have given way, making her crash to the bed, but Noah's hands tightened on her hips, keeping her in place.

"You could get a piercing here," he said gruffly before his mouth had better things to do than talk.

"Don't. Even. Think. About. *Oh!*" Sweet, agonizing tension coiled inside her as her thoughts became dancing sparkles she couldn't quite grasp.

Noah pressed in closer. Devouring her.

She tried to say something, anything, but the words were unintelligible. Her body shook, her muscles clenched. Everything teetered on the brink of a precipice. Waiting. Ready. Eager to fall. To jump. To...

A loud, guttural gasp rent the air as primed nerves exploded in a cascade of sensation. She toppled. Weak. Delirious. Panting and desperate for more. Strong arms lowered her to the mattress before Noah angled himself over her limp, sated body.

"I think we're okay," he said, satisfaction in his voice. "It's all coming back to me."

Oh. My.

She wasn't going to survive.

Chapter Thirty

Noah woke, instantly alert, with Annabelle sprawled across him. It was still dark, and as much as he strained to hear what had woken him, the building remained silent. Carefully, so as not to wake her, he eased Annabelle off him and got out of bed. He pulled on a pair of sweatpants and grabbed his gun—just in case.

He found the source of the disturbance in the loft. Therese's ghostly form stood by Annabelle's work desk, studying her artwork. She smiled at Noah as he approached.

"She draws beautifully."

Noah didn't want to discuss Annabelle's art. "I'm sorry, Therese," he said softly.

Her smile didn't waver, but there was a tender sadness in her eyes. *"For what? For sleeping with Annabelle?"*

He grimaced. "Please tell me you weren't watching?"

"Ew! No!" She silently glided over to the window. *"I just know you. And you've nothing to be sorry about."*

Noah joined her by the window and looked out toward

the ever-present lights of the downtown skyline. "I'm falling in love with her," he confessed to the woman who'd always owned his heart. "But I still love you."

"*I know.*" Therese bumped her hip against him, but he didn't even feel the air move.

"It feels wrong somehow," he admitted in a whisper. "But I can't stop it."

"*It isn't wrong, Noah. It's how life should be. You can't spend the rest of yours talking to a ghost; you need to live again. Really live. That's what I want for you.*" Her smile was bittersweet. "*And you always gave me what I wanted, didn't you?*"

His heart clenched. "Unless it was insane."

Her laughter was tinged with sadness and acceptance. "*You have a big heart, honey. There's plenty of space in it to love both of us. It doesn't have to be one or the other. I don't mind sharing with Annabelle.*"

Noah's throat tightened, making it difficult to swallow. "Will you still hang around?"

She turned to face him, so much love in her expression that it hurt to see it there. He blinked furiously, studying her face, drinking in the woman he'd loved for as long as he could remember.

"*I think I'm going to head to Atlantic City and pester the boys for a while.*"

"You don't have to go." He wanted to wrap an arm around her, to keep her close, but there was nothing left to hold.

"*No, I get that, but I think I should. You're in good hands now. You don't need me.*"

He fought to swallow again. Damn annoying throat. "I do, you know. I always will."

Therese looked wistful. "*We'll always have Paris.*"

Noah barked out a laugh before rubbing his eyes. "You hated that movie."

"*It was Bergman. She was always so stoic. I just wanted to slap her.*" She reached up to cup his cheek, and he told himself he felt the warmth of her hand against his skin. "*If you ask me, Sam was the best character. He was dependable, creative, a great piano player.*" She flashed him a mischievous grin. "*So good with his fingers.*"

He focused on breathing as he waited to be able to talk again. "Will I see you again?"

"*You can see me whenever you want. All you have to do is close your eyes. After all*"—Therese smiled widely—"*I'm a figment of your imagination, right?*"

"I-I hate letting you go." His words came out as a growl. "I *hate* it."

"*Would it help if I told you I was going to a better place?*"

"I don't know. Maybe."

"*I am. Atlantic City is far superior to Houston.*"

His chuckle was weak and his vision had blurred. "No goodbyes," he said fiercely.

"*No.*" Therese dropped her hand from his cheek. "*I'd say, see you in Heaven, but it's a bit trite.*" She cocked her head to one side. "*What happens when you love two people, and you all end up in Heaven? Do we have to share you? Is it a ménage à trois situation? Because I don't roll that way.*"

"When you find out, let me know." He let out a breath. "This isn't how I wanted life to go."

"*Me neither.*" Therese glided toward the loft's exit, as though she had to physically walk out of his life. As though seeing the last of her leave would somehow make it easier. "*Have Annabelle put me in a book,*" she called back to him. "*In a sexy catsuit.*"

He sniffed, nodding. "Will do."

"*I love you, Noah. Be happy,*" she said, and then, she was gone.

Noah doubled over, the sight of her leaving for good a physical blow to his gut. He rubbed his hands over his face as he stumbled toward a stool at the breakfast bar. Once there, tears like razor blades sliced his cheeks as they fell. He wasn't sure how long he sat with the raw, wrenching agony of their final goodbye, but eventually, he registered the loft door open.

He sat up straight, sniffing as he blinked away the last of his tears. Rodrigo appeared on the other side of the kitchen island and set a bottle of Scotch and two glasses on the counter between them.

"I was watching the cameras," he said as he poured them each a drink.

Noah didn't reply, and they silently drank together.

Chapter Thirty-One

Noah spent his morning watching over Annabelle while she ran another online art session with his sons. Hearing their joy as he paced the loft made him feel more complete than he had in years. The hushed murmur of their voices, their laughter, all wove together to make him feel *home*. It was a sense of rightness and belonging that'd been missing since Therese died, and he hoped she was there with their sons, enjoying the lesson too.

If ghosts even existed outside of his head.

After lunch, yet another street-food find by the triplets, Noah left Annabelle safely ensconced in the small office on the second floor, going over her testimony with the assistant district attorney. Today's visit was a little different in that the ADA had brought along a technician with a boatload of specialist audiovisual equipment to trial.

The new setup had made their resident geek giddy at the sight of it. Designed to take highly sensitive court testimony at a distance, it was supposedly impervious to hacking and physical tampering. Of course, telling a hacker something was hack-proof was like waving a red flag to a bull, and it'd taken Evan exactly ten minutes to get the ADA to officially invite him to test the system. He hadn't stopped grinning since.

But before Evan could run off to his happy place, Rochelle asked for a debrief on their progress with Eddie Hanson's money.

"We think we've found all of Eddie's personal money and most of the Demons' accounts too." Impatience rendered Evan unable to sit still. "And, with Abasi's help, we finished taking it this morning. Go us!" He held up his hand for a high five. Abasi just stared at it until Evan dropped it again.

"How much are we looking at?" Rochelle asked, her elbows resting on the desk in front of her.

Evan bounced in his chair. "Close to forty million."

There was a stunned silence while the team processed that information.

"I know. It isn't much," Abasi said at last. "But you need to remember they're still a relatively small and new operation. Plus, that amount doesn't take into account their assets."

Noah almost laughed at his blasé attitude. "Forty million sure sounds like a lot of money to me."

"And that's why you aren't a criminal."

"Yeah," Noah drawled. "*That's* the only reason."

Abasi cocked an eyebrow. "Escobar's fortune was around thirty billion when he died. The Gambino family was worth about five hundred million during Gotti's reign. Makes forty million seem like small change."

Rochelle sat back in her seat. "So, we have forty million worth of *small change* in a hidden, secure account, right?"

"Yep." Evan grinned. "But it doesn't need to stay there. If we split it, we could all retire on our share. It'd be roughly four and a half million each."

"When you think about it," Harris said morosely, "that wouldn't go very far in today's economy. Bloody Boomers and their inflation," he muttered.

"The money won't stay there," Rochelle said firmly. "And it isn't going into our pockets either. Forty million will go a long way toward helping people the Demons have hurt. Katrina, do you have access to the account?"

It was Evan who answered. "I set her up this morning."

Rochelle pinned him with her schoolteacher stare. "And you're absolutely sure there's no way any donations made from that account can be traced back to us or the Demons?"

"She can throw it around like confetti." Evan sounded confident. "There won't be any blowback."

"Good." Rochelle nodded at Katrina. "Start giving it away."

"That's a lot of responsibility," Katrina said. "Are you sure you want only me to handle it? Aren't you worried I might just transfer it all to my account and disappear?"

Rochelle smiled reassuringly. "Pull in help if it makes you feel better, but I have no problem trusting you to distribute the money." She cast a glance around the room, her eyes sparkling. "Couldn't say the same for the rest of you."

"Wise woman." Abasi grinned at her.

"Does the money have to be donated in America?" Katrina traced a pattern on the desk in front of her with her fingertip. "There's a small group in Invertary, Scotland that works with abused women; they could use some help too."

"Like I said, whatever you think fits. Just do good with it." Rochelle turned back to the rest of the team and was about to say something more when the office door burst open.

"What the hell have you done now?" Detective Johnson stalked into the room, his partner in tow.

"And are there more donuts?" McMillan glanced around, looking hopeful.

Noah had grabbed his gun at their unannounced entrance, and from the way his team was discreetly re-holstering their weapons, he wasn't the only one.

Rochelle gave the detectives a weary look before addressing Violet, who stood behind them. "I thought we talked about not letting anyone into the building without telling me first."

Violet shrugged. "I figured the Keystone Cops were exempt. Just be grateful I escorted them up here and didn't let them wander around on their own." With that, she turned on her heel and left.

"It's nothing personal," Rochelle told the detectives as they helped themselves to coffee. "It's about security."

"Forget it. We have bigger problems." Johnson pulled out a chair. "Somebody tried to take out Eddie Hanson about an hour ago. Please tell me it wasn't you."

Noah sat forward in his seat. "It wasn't us. Seriously, the whole team has been here and accounted for all morning."

"And I suppose the only corroboration you have for these *alibis* is from each other?" McMillan drawled, frowning at the lack of snacks to go with his coffee.

"You want to tell us what happened?" Noah asked, ignoring the sugar-deprived detective.

It was his younger partner who replied. "Somebody drove by Eddie's place and emptied an automatic weapon into his living room. Unfortunately for them, but not for

Eddie, he wasn't home at the time." Johnson shared a worried glance with his partner. "We're not exactly sure where he was... or where he is now."

That got everyone's attention.

Rochelle glared at the detectives. Who, to their credit, looked ashamed. "You've lost the head of the Demon Brothers? How's that even possible? I thought you were monitoring his every move?"

Johnson pinched the bridge of his nose. His suit wasn't as pristinely pressed as usual, and he had dark circles under his eyes. "We're still trying to figure out what happened. There was a mix-up over whose shift it was, and during the surveillance gap, he disappeared."

"Your mole," Noah said. "That's what happened. Somebody was behind the shift mix-up, and it bought Eddie just enough time to take off. Do you have any idea who the mole is yet?"

McMillan shifted in his seat, his crinkled shirt straining over his ample belly. Unlike his partner's, McMillan's shirt had probably never been pressed. "You know, we do have more than one case to deal with at a time. Oh yeah, and our area of responsibility doesn't end at the warehouse door. We have a whole city to police. So, no, we haven't found the mole yet."

Noah held up his hands, palms out. "No criticism. Just wondering. Sounds like your mole's been disrupting things again. Got any ideas where Eddie might be?"

"All we know is that he's still in Texas." Johnson swallowed a mouthful of the coffee and grimaced. "What the hell is this?"

"*That* is what you get when you let Scottish people make coffee." Rochelle frowned. "It's an abomination to your taste buds."

She pursed her lips, her eyes fixed on his coffee mug as though something might emerge from it any second and bite her.

Johnson apparently shared her sentiment, as he set the mug on the desk in front of him as if it were an unexploded bomb.

McMillan happily continued to drink his. "Are you sure you didn't get fed up waiting for Hanson to strike and decide to get rid of the problem? I mean, we wouldn't blame you if you did. It would just be good to know so we don't spend a whole day chasing a fictional gunman all over Houston."

Nobody bought his "we're all friends here together" act. McMillan couldn't pull off understanding if his life depended on it.

"If we wanted to eliminate Hanson," Abasi drawled, "you'd have found his body. But we don't do that sort of thing. We're the good guys now. Ain't that right, Boss?"

"I think that's stretching it a tad," Rochelle said drolly.

As Abasi flashed her a grin, Johnson's phone rang, followed quickly by McMillan's. The detectives answered, listened for a few seconds, and then got to their feet. The door opened while they were ending their calls, and the ADA poked her head in.

"My boss just rang," she said. "What's this about Eddie Hanson going missing? He wants me back at the office ASAP to devise a crisis plan in case the trial doesn't go ahead. My technician's packing everything up with Annabelle's help, and then we're leaving straight away."

"We have bigger problems than Eddie's absence," McMillan said, tugging his waistband back up onto his belly. "Somebody's attacking the Demon Brothers, and the boss wants everyone on the streets."

"Attacking?" Rochelle asked, her gaze laser focused on the cops.

McMillan looked weary. "We've got two gangbangers down and fights breaking out all over the city. Don't know what the hell's going on, but if we don't get it stopped, we're looking at full-blown gang warfare."

Violet's angry voice drifted in through the open door. "Carry your own damn equipment down the stairs. Do I look like a bloody porter?"

Margaret Grant glanced over her shoulder and winced. "I'd better go before Violet shoots my technician. Keep me posted," she ordered the detectives.

"We live to serve," McMillan muttered.

"We need to get a move on, Mac." Johnson followed her out the door.

"That's my cue to go," the older detective said.

Outside in the corridor, Johnson could be heard saying, "Here, I'll help with that. I'm heading down anyway."

"Looks like the tech found a porter after all." Rodrigo grinned at them.

"There goes my chance at hacking a state-of-the-art secure communications setup." Evan looked close to tears.

"I'm sure you'll get another chance." Harris patted his brother on the head like a dog.

"Not today, though," the depressed little puppy said.

"You got any more information you can share?" Noah asked McMillan as he lumbered toward the door.

McMillan sighed heavily as he attempted to brush a stain from his shirt as if it were lint. Funnily enough, it didn't work. "Sounds like the Demons have pissed off a South American cartel. That's all I know."

"Did they say which one?"

"Alvarez," McMillan said. "They're one of the smaller

operations, but we've been seeing a lot of their product in the city over the past couple of years." As he reached the door, Johnson shouted from downstairs for him to hurry. "Don't shoot anybody while we're gone."

Once he'd left, Noah turned to face his team. "Alvarez."

"Guess they realized their money was gone and they don't have any women to show for it." Rochelle stood and pulled on her gray suit jacket.

As she did so, the ADA walked back into the room. "Just wanted to let you know that Eddie's been spotted in Houston Heights. Looks like he hasn't skipped town after all. Unfortunately, my boss still needs to see me, so I'm going into the office." She shrugged. "My tech's left with the equipment we need, anyway. Guess we're trying that out another day. The sooner this trial is over the better."

"Amen to that," Noah agreed.

As the ADA left, Rochelle turned to Evan. "Are we absolutely sure Eddie Hanson can't trace his missing money back to us?"

"Absolutely," he said solemnly.

Abasi nodded in agreement. "It's hidden the same way my money's hidden. And I'm confident nobody's ever gonna find that."

"Remind me again," Logan said, trying to sound nonchalant. "Exactly how much money are we talking here?"

Abasi just stared at him in silence.

Rodrigo held up his phone. "Got a message from a friend saying the Alvarez cartel's out for blood. The drug house we busted, the women we intercepted, and the money we took are just the icing on the cake. They're more worried about Hanson's upcoming trial."

"There really is a war coming," Harris said, looking worried.

"Maybe we should hand the money over to the police," Katrina said. "If there's a gang war, a lot of innocent people will get caught in the crossfire. I'd hate for law enforcement officers to be hurt because of what we started."

"Won't make any difference." Rodrigo tipped his chair back to a precarious angle and balanced on its two back legs while talking. "This isn't about the money. It's about Eddie's failures. I'm betting he promised the cartel he'd take care of the witness and the trial wouldn't go ahead, but every attempt he's made to do that has been botched. Time's running out, and the Alvarez cartel can't risk having someone like Eddie turn on them. He knows too much. Add to that the national attention he's drawn over the past few months, and the cartel will be getting antsy. The Demons have become a weak link in the Alvarez business empire. They have no choice but to bring down the motorcycle gang. All taking the money did was move the deadline forward a few days."

"Are you saying Hanson has to get rid of Annabelle or the Alvarez cartel will kill him?" Noah's blood chilled.

Rodrigo nodded. "There's a chance he could turn state's evidence to avoid the death penalty. But even if he does keep his mouth shut, with him in jail, there's nothing to stop law enforcement from putting pressure on the weak links in the Demon Brothers gang. Somebody would eventually crack and sell everything they know about the Alvarez cartel."

"So even though the cartel's starting a war with his gang, Eddie's priority will still be to eliminate the witness," Noah said, an instinctive dread pooling in the pit of his stomach.

Abasi and Rodrigo shared a heavy look.

"Yeah," Rodrigo said.

"I need to get Annabelle into the panic room." Noah strode from the office. "She can stay there until the trial starts."

Whether she wanted to or not.

Chapter Thirty-Two

Noah strode down the corridor and opened the door to the small office the ADA planned to use as a virtual witness stand. Violet stood at the bottom of the stairs, staring out through the main entrance to the street beyond. She didn't glance up, even though she must have heard him. When she was in on-duty mode, nothing distracted her.

Without bothering to knock, he pushed the office door open and strode inside. "Annabelle—"

The room was empty, apart from a bunch of tech equipment scattered on top of the desk and credenza.

She must have gone back to the loft. Noah jogged up the stairs, taking them two at a time, and let himself into the apartment.

"Annabelle," he called as he entered the vast space.

There was no reply.

Harry and Logan followed him in. "Rochelle sent us to secure the windows," Harris said.

Logan nodded. "We're locking everything down for the duration."

"Should have got in snacks first," Harris complained.

"Annabelle?" Noah called as he hurried to the panic room.

There was no one inside. His heart racing, he walked straight through to check the guest rooms and bathroom. She wasn't there either. He rushed back into the loft.

"Have either of you seen Annabelle?"

"Wasn't she in the office downstairs?" Harris locked one of the window's shutters.

"No." An icy chill crept up Noah's spine.

Without another word, he ran back downstairs and into the open-plan office space. No Annabelle. His stomach performed somersaults as his mind raced over possibilities. He didn't like any of them.

"Has anybody seen Annabelle?" he asked Katrina, Evan, and Rochelle.

"She hasn't been in here." Rochelle frowned. "Did you check upstairs?"

"She isn't there, and Harris and Logan haven't seen her either." Sharp talons of panic pierced his mind. "I don't know where she is."

"I'll check the bathrooms." Katrina hurried from the room.

Evan turned to his beloved computer. "I'll go over the camera feeds for the last few minutes and see if we can find her that way."

"I'll get the rest of the team, and we'll comb the building." Rochelle strode out the door.

A second later, she shouted Annabelle's name in the stairwell.

There was no reply.

Noah tuned out the rushing footsteps and raised voices in the corridor and crossed the room to look over Evan's shoulder. There were no cameras inside the small office the ADA had been using, but there was one in the hallway right outside it, pointing down the stairs.

"That's her going in and you shutting the door behind her," Evan narrated unnecessarily. "Then we've got a whole lot of Violet standing guard. There's the ADA coming in here for a couple of mugs of coffee, leaving Annabelle in the room with the tech. Nice guy. Knows his stuff." He was rambling, worried.

"Did we run a background on the tech guy?"

"Aye. He's clean. No connections to Hanson or his gang." Evan pointed at the screen. "That's the detectives arriving and the ADA stepping into the hallway to take a phone call before briefly going back into the room and then coming in here. There's the tech guy moving the secure equipment back out of the room and Violet telling him he can carry it downstairs on his own. The detective helping because you can't thump thousands of dollars' worth of equipment down a flight of stairs." He ran a hand through his hair, making it stand on end. "The ADA goes back into the small office, gets her stuff, then stops in here again before going downstairs and straight into her car, which is parked right out front. Then the other detective leaves." He cast Noah a fearful glance. "No sign of Annabelle. I'll check a different angle."

He tapped the keyboard to zoom in on the footage from the camera covering the front door and the street beyond it. They watched, in silence this time, as Johnson helped the technician load his large black wheeled case into his van before going back to shout through the door for his partner. Ms. Grant dashed past Johnson and into her own car. The tech and the ADA drove away at the same time, heading in different directions before the detectives got into their vehicle.

No Annabelle.

Rochelle stalked back into the office. One glance at her expression, and Noah knew what she was going to say.

She said it anyway. "She isn't in the building, Noah."

It was as though all the air had been sucked from the room. The walls tilted, and the floor rolled beneath his feet. He staggered backward until a chair hit the back of his knees, and he sat with a thud. For a second, it was impossible to breathe. He bent over, closed his eyes and focused on getting control of himself. Annabelle needed him. He'd panic later.

A moment later, he looked up at his boss. "How?"

Her expression flitted between worry and fury. "I don't know. Evan, you got anything?"

"There's nothing on the cameras. She didn't leave the building." He was scared. It was in his voice. "She has to be here somewhere. Has anyone checked the roof? She went up there that night. She might have gone again."

"The roof's clear." Abasi strode in to join them. "I just came from there."

"What about the cameras covering other exits and the area around the warehouse?" Rochelle asked. "Have you been through those yet?"

Evan flushed. "No, just the front door and the corridor. I'll check the rest now." He hesitated. "But she wouldn't go outside, would she?"

"Not willingly." Noah got to his feet while fighting to keep his heart rate under control. "The mole," he muttered, trying to think when his head was filled with screaming. "Somebody in the building this morning has to be the mole. Maybe they sneaked someone in—"

"Not possible." Violet folded her arms. "I was on guard duty."

"There are other entrances, Violet," Rochelle pointed out.

"Annabelle didn't leave that room." Violet was adamant. "I would have noticed."

"She's right!" Noah was already running, very much afraid that he knew exactly what had happened.

Everyone followed close behind him, filling the corridor as he threw open the door to the small office near the stairwell.

He pointed at the equipment spread over the desk and credenza. "Evan, is this the high-tech security stuff you were supposed to hack?"

Evan looked bewildered. "Some of it."

Noah locked his knees to keep from falling. "The cases. There was a big black plastic case on wheels. They brought in the equipment using it, and Johnson helped carry it back down the stairs. But if the equipment's still here, why did the tech need help to carry the case?" He focused on Evan. "Was that case big enough to stash Annabelle?"

He paled. "I think so. She's kinda small."

Noah clenched his hands into fists, desperately wanting to punch a hole through the nearest wall. He faced his team. "The tech was in on it. Maybe Johnson too. We need to get that case before he takes her to Hanson."

Nobody argued with him or told him he'd lost his mind. There just wasn't another logical explanation.

"Evan," Rochelle snapped. "Go over all the camera footage, see if you can get a license plate for the tech's vehicle and a direction for us to head in."

"I could, um, access the local traffic cameras if need be,"

he offered. "But, em, I'm already on probation for hacking. I'm not supposed to..."

"Do it," Rochelle ordered without hesitation. "If there's fallout, I'll deal with it. You won't get into trouble for this. I promise. The rest of us will follow the tech van. We'll pair up—Abasi and Harris, Logan and Rodrigo, Katrina and Violet. Noah comes with me. When you have a specific location, Evan, notify the team. In the meantime, what are we looking for?"

It was Noah who replied. "A small white van. It has discreet signage on the side, identifying it as the property of the DA's office. That's about it. The guy driving it's in his twenties, medium everything, and wearing black." He wouldn't forget the sight of that van and its driver as long as he lived.

"I'll send a number plate as soon as I get it," Evan said. "Everybody, remember radios and earpieces. It makes it easier to talk to all of you at the same time."

"We've got them here," Harris said from the corridor. "Pick them up as you pass."

Rodrigo and Abasi came to stand with Rochelle and Noah as the others equipped themselves with comms and weapons.

"Why take her?" Noah asked, a massive weight pressing against his chest. "Why not kill her here?"

"My guess," Rochelle said, "is that leaving a dead body in the office would narrow the mole suspect list right down. Our traitor's hoping to escape unscathed."

Noah's hands shook. Adrenaline. Fear. Take your pick. Harris came over and handed them their comms gear.

"We'll get her." He patted Noah on the shoulder. "We've got your back, Noah."

Violet called from the doorway, "Boss, what do you want us to do if we see the vehicle? Or Hanson? Detain, disable, death?"

For a second, Rochelle appeared shocked that Violet had even asked. "No killing unless Annabelle's life is on the line. Everything else is on the table. Let's get our client back."

With a somber murmur of agreement, they hurried downstairs. As Noah climbed into Rochelle's large black SUV, his radio crackled.

"I have a direction," Evan said. "The van's heading northeast. I'll access the traffic cams and be in touch when I know something more."

They screeched away from the curb, Rochelle behind the wheel. The other team vehicles slid into place behind them.

"They must have sedated her," Noah said, more to himself than his partner. "Wouldn't have been able to get her out of the building if they hadn't. She'd have screamed the place down."

"Sedation would be the most efficient way of dealing with the situation, yes." Rochelle sped through traffic like a Formula One driver taking curves.

Noah remembered, yet again, that she'd once been in medicine. "What are we talking here? An injection? A pill?"

"Could be as simple as something slipped into her coffee."

He swallowed hard. "Is it possible they could have accidentally given her too much?"

She glanced his way before concentrating on the road again. "You mean an accidental overdose?"

"Yeah." It was stupid and irrational, but part of him just

wanted Rochelle to reassure him that Annabelle was indeed alive and well.

"Unlikely," Rochelle said. "Think about all the people dosed with date rape drugs every year. One pill is all it takes. Same with most sedatives. A hefty sleeping pill could knock her out in a minute or two. All you'd have to do is grind one up and slip it into her food or drink."

"Wouldn't she taste it?"

"Not if it was in that crap coffee the boys make."

Noah could barely see the road in front of them past the images in his head—Annabelle drugged and bound, or squashed into that small, dark space, or worse still, her coming round to find she was no longer in the warehouse. That her worst fear had come into being. That she'd been kidnapped—again—and taken away from the safety she so desperately needed.

"She's still alive, Noah," Rochelle said quietly. "If he'd wanted her dead straight away, we'd have found a body. No matter how eager the mole is to stay undiscovered, I can't imagine they'd have said no to Eddie Hanson if he'd ordered them to kill."

"Yeah, but how long will she stay alive once he gets his hands on her?" His stomach knotted until all he could taste was fear. "You heard Rodrigo and Abasi—they're the gang experts. Eddie can't afford for his case to go to trial. He *needs* to eliminate the witness."

"There's a lot going on for him," Rochelle said as she gripped the wheel tightly. "He may not be thinking straight. We have no idea what his priorities are or what he'll do next. Right now, Annabelle is alive, and we're not that far behind her. That's all that matters. Concentrate on that."

He nodded, once. But the dark thoughts filling his head wouldn't go away.

"I've only just found her," he whispered. He couldn't lose another woman he loved... he just couldn't.

He wouldn't.

Noah lifted his chin, staring out at the road. "We *will* get her back," he vowed.

"Hell yes, we will," Rochelle agreed.

Chapter Thirty-Three

Annabelle's head was filled with syrup, her thoughts sticky and hard to grasp in the thick, gloopy mess that coated her mind. But her instincts were working slightly better. And they were screaming that something was wrong.

Her limbs felt encased in lead, her body contorted into an almost fetal position. All she wanted was to sleep, to sink into that glorious marshmallow place where everything was fuzzy and soft and safe.

But that wasn't right.

Now wasn't the time to sleep. And this need to succumb wasn't natural. In fact, it was frightening. And familiar. She'd felt this way before. She scrunched up her eyes and tried to recall when she'd felt like this. The medicine! She'd been sick. That had made her feel dopey, she remembered, but as soon as the thought rose to the foreground, it sank back beneath the syrupy thickness in her mind. Below that thought swam another. One buried far deeper. Of a time, long ago, when she'd been forced to sleep...

It was so hot.

The air was dense and hard to breathe. Annabelle wrestled for control of her body, trying to find a position that made breathing easier. But her limbs refused to move. All communication between her addled brain and the rest of her had been cut.

With Herculean effort, she managed to crack open her eyes. All she could see was darkness. Thick, inky, black darkness.

It made no sense.

A spike of panic assailed her before, just as quickly, she succumbed to the syrupy miasma that dulled her senses.

There were voices. Far, far away, in the back of her foggy mind, she heard voices.

"Noah?" She struggled, fought, *clawed* to get the word out of her mouth.

It barely made a sound.

Sleep was pulling her under again, and no matter how hard she fought, she knew it would win. The thick, dusty air made breathing laborious. Was she suffocating?

The thought disappeared again, drowning in syrup.

"Noah?" Her call was but a breath.

The voices grew more distant now. Swallowed by the darkness and smothered by the thick, hot air.

"Noah!" she mouthed, making no sound at all.

Then, the syrup swept upward in a wave and dragged her down into its depths.

Chapter Thirty-Four

"Got it!" Evan's voice exploded into the SUV's interior. "Got eyes on the audiovisual van. It's just turned into Providence Street. Looks like it's heading for the I-10 West on-ramp. You're not far behind him. I'll keep watching."

Rochelle took a sharp turn, wheels screeching as she adjusted their direction to follow the DA's tech van. Up ahead, Abasi's vehicle skidded onto the road in front of them. The other two team vehicles appeared in their rearview mirror. It felt good—no, it felt *right*—to have his team close by.

"You pulled the plug too soon," Noah said as Rochelle veered onto the I-10, slicing through three lanes of busy traffic as though all other cars were invisible. "On the team. We just needed time."

"How about we find Annabelle, and then we discuss that?" she said as she cut off a large pickup truck. They hit their horn in protest.

The road was packed for rush hour. Cars sat bumper to bumper in the lanes opposite them, heading east. Up ahead, the same congested situation awaited them. At least if they were stuck in traffic, the tech van would be too.

The relentless Texan sun beat down on the motorway and bounced off the cars. It glinted off their windshield, blinding Noah for a second. He reached into the pocket of his battered leather jacket for his shades and slipped them on. It made little difference.

Inside their SUV, the air conditioning pumped out ice-cold air in an attempt to combat the stifling Houston heat.

There was no air conditioning in the case they'd stuffed Annabelle inside.

No. He couldn't think about that.

He had to focus on getting to her. Everything else could be fixed once she was safe in his arms.

"It has to be here somewhere," Rochelle muttered. "Anybody got eyes on the van?"

The team replied with a chorus of negatives.

"Evan," Noah snapped. "You're sure it was the I-10? And are you sure he was heading west?"

* * *

"Of course I'm sure." Evan fought to keep the irritation out of his voice because he knew Noah had to be barely holding on, terrified of what might happen to Annabelle.

He was pretty damn shaken himself. Despite her being older than him, he thought of her as the little sister they'd never had. She was... special. Even while dealing with all her setbacks and problems, she still managed to laugh and joke and create worlds that made others smile.

He growled at his screen. They had to get her back. They'd had one damn job—keep her safe—and they'd stuffed it up.

As he watched the video feed from the traffic system, his mind battled to figure out how the tech had pulled off Annabelle's abduction. Sure, the guy had been obsessively geeky about his audiovisual prowess, but he hadn't exactly come across as a criminal mastermind. Had he drugged Annabelle when the ADA left the room? And why hadn't the ADA been mad at him for leaving all that expensive equipment behind? Perhaps she told him they were coming back later.

Still...

"I've got him." Abasi's voice came over the comms system. "He's heading toward the Katy Freeway. Do we cut him off or wait until he exits?"

"We wait," Noah said. "We can't get to him on here anyway, not in this traffic. And not without causing a ton of damage."

"We can't risk an accident on the interstate," Rochelle agreed. "Anybody got any idea where he's heading?"

"Eddie has a property in Houston Heights," Rodrigo said.

"Isn't that where the ADA said they'd spotted him earlier?" Katrina asked.

"Yeah." Noah sounded deadly.

Evan brought up the records. "He's got an old Victorian in what looks like an exclusive gated community. Lots of space around it."

"I don't know," Rodrigo said. "If he was spotted there, the cops know where he is. So why risk having Annabelle taken straight to him?"

"Arrogance?" Harris suggested.

"It looks pretty isolated." Evan stared at the Google Earth images. "It's got a massive garden, lots of old trees, and looks like there's a couple of outbuildings too. From the fences and cameras, I doubt the cops could get close enough to see what's going on in there unless they walked up to the front door and knocked."

"I think the cops are more interested in the fighting that's breaking out all over the city," Rochelle said. "The situation's a powder keg. If it were me, and I knew where Eddie was located, I'd put checking on him on the back burner until I'd dealt with everything else."

"He's changing lanes," Abasi said, "taking an outer lane, maybe getting ready to exit."

As the radio went silent, Evan pictured their vehicles negotiating the traffic to stay with the van. On one of his screens, he could see the crammed traffic on the I-10. Nothing was moving very fast at all. Another screen displayed the past few hours' video surveillance, which he kept glancing at to see if he'd missed anything.

But Evan kept returning to what happened to Annabelle in that small office. How had the tech drugged her? Why hadn't the ADA noticed? If only they'd had a camera in there.

Then it hit him.

There *had* been a camera in there.

For a brief time, the secure audiovisual equipment had been up and running. Maybe long enough to capture some imagery that might help the team. All he had to do was hack into the video feed's cloud storage—the unhackable cloud storage owned by the district attorney's office. And he had to do it within the next couple of minutes. Hell, it was worth a try. And Rochelle had already told him that their situation merited all the hacking he could do—or something like that...

Evan cracked his knuckles and spun his chair to face the separate computer set up beside his. He could try to hack the DA's secure server while watching the traffic camera footage and glancing at the surveillance video. He was a multitasker. It's what his generation was born to do.

As he reached for the keyboard, something struck his arm with such force that it sent him flying from his chair. His head connected with the corner of his desk as he fell.

For one awful second, he thought he saw someone standing over him with a gun.

And then he saw nothing at all.

* * *

The Benson Security vehicles followed the DA's audiovisual van at a reasonable distance, waiting for it to signal which exit it planned to take.

It was all happening too damn slowly. But they couldn't rush it. They couldn't risk spooking the driver or running the vehicle off the road. Annabelle's life depended on it.

"Something isn't right," Rochelle said. "I keep coming back to the timing of things, and something isn't adding up. It's sitting there, niggling at the back of my brain, but I can't quite grasp what's annoying me."

Noah struggled to concentrate, but he knew from her tone that this was important. "What do you mean?"

"The detectives both received calls telling them that violence was breaking out all over the place, and they were worried the city was on the verge of full-blown gang warfare."

"Yeah," Noah said while inside, he screamed for her to hurry up.

"Then, Margaret Grant comes in to say that Annabelle was helping them pack up because the DA's called them back to the office." She frowned. "Next thing, Violet's shouting about not being the tech guy's porter. Why didn't Annabelle help carry the case down the stairs?"

Noah clenched his jaw before replying. "Because she was in the case."

"So, in the minute or two that the ADA was out of the room, the tech managed to drug Annabelle and stuff her into the case? It doesn't seem like enough time to do all that."

He stilled, staring at her with every ounce of focus he possessed.

"He's taking exit 767B toward Watson." Abasi's voice came over the radio.

Rochelle slid across the lanes to follow.

"Go on," Noah prompted.

She glanced at him warily. "I can't think of a drug that would've worked that fast. Something must have been slipped into her coffee earlier. And, if that was the case, wouldn't the ADA have noticed that Annabelle was behaving as though she was sedated?"

It felt like a bucket of ice water had been emptied over Noah's head.

"Evan," Rodrigo said over the radio. "You got an address for Hanson's property in the Heights?"

Sparks flew in Noah's brain as they waited for a reply. Connections formed where none had existed before.

"The ADA would've noticed the equipment all over the office," he said. "She was the one who ordered the tech to pack up. Why wasn't she annoyed he left it there?"

"Evan, I need that address," Rodrigo repeated.

Noah pulled out his phone and dialed the ADA. There was no reply. He dialed the DA's office, and the receptionist answered.

"I need to speak to ADA Grant," he said without preamble.

"Evan," Rodrigo snapped. "Are you there, damn it? We need that info."

"I'm calling him," one of the other triplets said. "He's probably on a bathroom break."

"I'm sorry," the receptionist said in Noah's ear. "ADA Grant called in sick this afternoon."

"This is Noah Merchant. ADA Grant was just with us at the warehouse. She said she was coming into the office for a meeting with the DA. Could you check again, please?"

"I'm afraid you must have misheard," the woman said. "DA Carpenter had a series of meetings in San Antonio today. He won't be back in Houston until tomorrow."

Noah hung up as the world tilted yet again. "Margaret Grant isn't at the office, and the DA's in San Antonio. Has been all day."

"He isn't picking up," one of the triplets said about Evan, sounding worried.

Rochelle cast him a worried look before speaking to the team. "Evan," she raised her voice. "Evan, come in."

There was no reply. Noah felt sick. Evan wasn't answering, the ADA had gone missing after lying to them, and there were serious questions over just how involved the tech guy had been in Annabelle's disappearance.

"Harris," Noah barked into their comms. "You can check your brother's location on your phone, right?"

"Doing it now," came the reply. "He's in the office. Why isn't he picking up?"

Because he couldn't. Noah had made a terrible mistake. He'd misread the situation, missed all the red flags, and had gone running in the wrong direction.

"Turn the car around," Noah ordered. "We need to get back to the warehouse now."

"We're on the interstate," Rochelle said. "I can't turn around."

"Then speed up and get to the next exit as fast as you can. We need to get back there."

"What about the van?" Abasi asked.

"I'm calling the DA's office for the driver's number. Just get off the interstate."

Noah rang the receptionist again and explained that he needed the tech's number. He hung up and immediately called the man.

He answered on the first ring. "Hello?" he said, sounding unstressed.

"This is Noah Merchant from Benson Security."

Rochelle cut off another driver as she slid across lanes to the nearest exit. Horns blared all around them.

"Oh, hi, Mr. Merchant," the tech said cheerily.

"I just wanted to ask why you left your equipment at the warehouse."

"Oh yeah, ADA Grant said she wanted Evan to check it out. Apparently, he's some hotshot hacker, and she's real worried about security for the trial. We were supposed to go over the system today, but she got a call telling her she was needed back at the office."

Fury coursed through Noah. "Why did you take the cases if you were leaving the tech?"

"I didn't get that either, but Ms. Grant said the DA needed them for something, so I brought them with me."

"Was Annabelle still in the room when you left?"

"Yeah, she was kinda wiped out though and kept yawning. Ms. Grant thought she was still fighting off the flu and said it was probably a good thing to give the prep a rest for the day. I hope she feels better soon." He sounded genuinely concerned and definitely not like a man who was lying to cover his ass.

"The DA's office isn't far from the warehouse. Why are you heading to Houston Heights?"

"Oh, Ms. Grant asked me to drop off a package for her first. Said it was something important to do with the case. Wait! How do you know I'm going to Houston Heights?"

Noah ignored the question. "What address did she give you?"

He rattled it off, and Noah hung up, uncaring that he'd cut the man off.

"How much do you bet that this is the address Rodrigo was after?" he said to Rochelle.

"She wanted the tech to lead us to Eddie's house," Rochelle said as she performed another illegal turn, cutting through traffic, to get them on the right road back to the warehouse.

"Which means he probably isn't there." Noah felt sick to his stomach. He lifted the radio. "Everybody, back to the warehouse as fast as you can. I don't give a crap what you do to get there. Just make it quick. The van's a decoy. Annabelle's still at the warehouse, and Eddie Hanson's still unaccounted for. ADA Grant has gone missing, and it looks like she set this whole thing up."

"What about Evan?" one of his brothers asked, a tremor in his voice. "Is he okay?"

"I don't know," Noah said, the weight of those words laying heavily on his soul. It was his fault Evan was in trouble. If he hadn't jumped to conclusions, the geeky tech would never have been left alone in the warehouse.

Now, Evan and Annabelle were vulnerable. And Eddie Hanson knew exactly where to find them.

Chapter Thirty-Five

A loud bang and a blinding light woke Annabelle. Her eyelids were too heavy to open all the way, which was fine because the light was far too bright anyway. She tried to lift her hand to shield her eyes, but her arm was just too weighty to move.

"About fucking time," a voice said as a viselike grip wrapped around her upper arm and dragged her into the harsh light before releasing her just as quickly.

Annabelle sprawled on the floor, its wood rough against her cheek. She blinked, working to clear her head, but every thought felt like it took a million years to form, and then, when it did, it evaporated in less than a second.

Limbs shaking, she tried to push up from the old floorboards as a sense of familiarity about the unfinished floor began to register. She needed to sit. To stand. To get some perspective on her situation and surroundings. Her muscles had been replaced with wet noodles, and coordination was a word that had lost all of its meaning.

A rough hand grasped the hair at the back of her head and yanked upward, forcing her to face the man crouched beside her. His smile was empty, his eyes dark with hatred.

"I can't believe something as fucking useless as you managed to bring me down." He shoved her head back toward the floor.

Unable to stop the momentum, Annabelle's face hit the hard wood, and she tasted blood.

Adrenaline coursed through her, counteracting the drug in her system, bringing strength to her muscles and clarity to her mind—if only a little. Awkward and ungainly, she crawled to the nearby table and used it to pull herself up onto her knees.

The room tilted, drifting in and out of focus as she watched the stranger pace in front of her. His movements jerky and tense, filled with rage.

Only, he wasn't a stranger.

Not really.

She'd seen his image far too many times not to recognize him now that her brain was less foggy. Annabelle sucked in a breath, fighting the urge to curl into a ball and cry.

"Eddie Hanson," she breathed.

Pure, visceral terror swept through her, bringing much-needed energy to her mind and body. But even though she felt more able to move, she was frozen in place by the sight of the man in front of her. His presence filled the tiny room they'd been using to go over her testimony, as though black tendrils of evil emanated from his very pores.

But... it didn't make any sense.

She'd been talking to the ADA, and then... nothing. Annabelle glanced behind him at the old wooden credenza, which now stood wide open. Had she been in there? Uncontrollable shivers racked her body as her eyes darted back to the killer in front of her.

Eddie stepped close, growing in size until he took up her whole world. He aimed his gun at her head.

"I should put a bullet in you right now," he said, as if making small talk. "But see, here's the thing, somebody cleaned out my accounts, and now I need a way to make some fast cash."

He crouched back down in front of her, making her recoil. He ran the tip of the gun down her cheek, like a deranged caress. "Did you take my money, Annabelle?"

"N-no. I-I didn't take your money." She started to shake her head, but it made the room spin.

Where was Noah? The team? The ADA? Why wasn't the building alarm screaming that someone had broken in? Why wasn't someone rushing into the room to save her?

Her heart jumped to her throat, making her gag—were they all dead?

Dear God, please don't let them be dead!

Eddie trailed the gun down her neck to the V of her plaid shirt. The barrel dug into the bone between her breasts. His attention seemed riveted to the mark it made in her flesh.

"You have any idea how much you'll make me at auction?" His gaze snapped up to meet hers. "Never sold an agoraphobe before," he whispered as he leaned in closer, his breath hot and rancid against her cheek. Annabelle tried to back away from him, but the table leg stopped her. "They say you'll crack if you go outside. One of my buyers wants to test that theory." There was a smug smile in his voice. "He plans to take you outside, Annabelle, and fuck you underneath the wide-open sky."

Her stomach spasmed, and there was no stopping it. Annabelle vomited all over the Demon Brother's leader.

He jerked back and leaped to his feet before

backhanding her across the cheek. The blow sent her under the desk, where she cowered, her stomach reeling and her head spinning wildly.

"Fucking bitch." He stormed from the room, and she heard doors open and close.

It was the only chance she'd get to make a run for the panic room.

With every ounce of energy she possessed, she hauled herself to her feet, using the desk as support, and launched herself at the open doorway. Momentum took her as far as the bottom of the stairs, where she grasped the banister and held on tight.

A sob escaped her, and she bit her lip to remain silent as she dragged herself up the stairs. She felt like a rag doll, boneless and awkward as she took each step. Below her, she heard running water and cursing. Eddie was cleaning himself up. She had to hurry.

But knowing that and doing it were two different things. Each step was a mountain. Her breathing was labored, and the syrup in her head still clung to the corners and dark places. She missed a step and crashed to one knee, making her cry out in pain.

Annabelle snapped her mouth shut, but it was too late.

"What the hell?" Eddie bellowed.

She made it up another step. Almost at the top. So close. Her apartment door was right there, mere feet away.

"Bitch!" Eddie shouted.

She heard his footsteps as they hurried after her.

And then she heard something else. There was a popping sound, then a strangled grunt, and she turned to see Eddie, stiff as a board and shaking at the bottom of the stairs with wires trailing from his side.

Her gaze shot to the hallway behind him. Halfway out

of the doorway to the Benson Security office, Evan lay on the floor, a Taser in his hand.

There was blood smeared on his shirt and the floor beneath him.

His eyes met hers. "Run," he grunted.

She couldn't. Evan was hurt. He needed her.

"Run," he shouted, as though he could read her mind. "Hide," he whispered just before his body went limp.

As the electric charge cut off, Eddie Hanson fell to the landing. He wouldn't be out long. With a sob and one last look at Evan, Annabelle staggered toward the door to her apartment.

The building swayed, and it felt like some steps took her forward while others took her back. She pushed open the door, then toppled through it and grabbed the back of the sofa to keep herself on her feet.

She could see the panic room now. Its door was open, ready for her to go through. All she had to do was make it there. She took one step. Then another. Her stomach lurched, and she fought the urge to vomit. All the while, great hiccupping sobs escaped her. Evan lay downstairs on the floor, bleeding. She'd left him there. And she didn't even know if he was dead or alive.

There was a roar behind her.

Eddie was awake.

And the panic room was a million miles away.

* * *

The roads were wall to wall with cars. There was barely enough space to move, let alone speed toward the warehouse.

"Damn it to hell!" Noah slammed his hands on the dash in front of him. "It'd be faster if we just got out and ran."

"No. It wouldn't," Rochelle snapped as she illegally squeezed between two vehicles before taking their SUV up onto the sidewalk for a second or two.

Horns blared, and Noah spotted several people with their phones out, filming them. The cops would turn up soon. Maybe that was a good thing. They could use an escort with sirens.

"I'm calling Johnson." He pulled out his phone. "We need his help now we know he isn't the mole."

"We can't be sure of that," Rochelle said. "All we have is a skewed timeline and a missing ADA."

Noah pinned her with a dark, anger filled look. "We're sure, Rochelle."

He dialed the detective. It rang a few times before he answered.

"This better be good," Johnson said. "We're up to our ears in it over here."

"Margaret Grant's your mole. She fooled us into believing Eddie paid one of the DA's tech guys to smuggle Annabelle out of the warehouse. We now know that isn't true, but we've lost contact with our people back at the building, and we're stuck in rush-hour traffic trying to get to them." He took a deep breath. "You need to send people to the warehouse. I think Hanson is there, and he has Annabelle."

"Wait, what? You think Hanson's at the warehouse and he has Annabelle? Why the hell aren't you there protecting her?" It sounded like World War Three in the background.

"We were tricked into believing that the mole sneaked Annabelle out of the building in an equipment case. But she's still there, Johnson. We can't get our guy on the phone, and Eddie knows where she is."

"I'm trying to stop all-out war here," Johnson said. "I don't have time to chase a theory."

Noah's hand curled into a fist as Rochelle gave up on trying to get through the traffic and took the SUV onto the sidewalk. She lay on the horn as a warning for people to get out of her way. One glance in the mirror told him that his team had fallen into line behind their vehicle, rushing through in Rochelle's wake.

"He's going to kill Annabelle," Noah spat out. "Get people to the warehouse before it's too late."

"Hell." Johnson must have covered the receiver, as Noah could hear only muffled voices. "McMillan and I will go there. We're about ten minutes out, though."

"Yeah, but you have sirens. See if you can get someone closer."

"I don't take orders from you, Merchant," Johnson snapped. "But I'll see what I can do." The line went dead.

"Not sure that helped," he told Rochelle.

She swerved over a corner, through a red light, and back onto the road. All hell broke loose behind her. They were getting closer. Only a few minutes from the warehouse now.

All he could do was pray they'd get there in time.

* * *

The door slammed open behind Annabelle, and the leader of the Demon Brothers stormed into the loft. Annabelle grasped the glass block wall as she glanced over her shoulder. She was so close to the panic room. Just a few more feet. But Eddie was coming up fast.

"I should kill you," he roared. "But I need the money

you'll make me. And I want the money you have in your accounts. Yeah, I looked into you. Found out you were a rich bitch. That's why those guys snatched you last time, isn't it? Did they get what they were after? Did you give it up without a fight?"

A sob tore from her throat as she lurched for the panic room.

She wasn't going to make it.

Inside, a well of anger she didn't know she possessed ripped open. Fury surged through her like a geyser, erupting from every vein.

Not.

Again.

She wouldn't be taken again.

NEVER AGAIN.

The rage was a cocktail of adrenaline and caffeine all rolled into one. Suddenly, she could move her body. And she took full advantage of it by launching herself like a football player in a flying tackle, straight through the panic room door.

But she wasn't fast enough.

Eddie came with her.

Annabelle scrambled across the floor, desperate to get away from him. Flipping onto her back as she retreated, anxious to keep an eye on her pursuer. She instantly regretted it, because Eddie loomed over her like the monster in every worst nightmare. A furious, red-faced maniac with blood lust in his eyes and spittle in the corners of his mouth.

He let out a howl and kicked her in the ribs before standing over her, one foot on either side of her body. Annabelle gasped for air, clutching her ribs while trying to wriggle away.

Eddie bent over, madness staring her in the face. "You

took everything from me, so I'm going to take everything from you."

"No!" she shouted as she drew up her leg and kicked him as hard as she could, right in the balls.

He doubled over with a groan and staggered toward the sofa bed.

Annabelle clawed and scrambled her way to the door into the guest room. As Eddie clutched himself and cursed at her, she slammed the button that opened the door. But before launching herself through it, she punched the lockdown code into the panel above it. She threw herself through the door, just a hair's breadth away from being caught in it when it slammed shut, locking Eddie inside the panic room.

She wasn't stupid. It wouldn't take Eddie long to escape the room, even without the code. But it did buy her a little time to get away from him.

And there was only one place left for her to go.

Chapter Thirty-Six

There was no time to hunt down her phone and call for help. Annabelle wasn't even sure where she'd left it. All she could do was try to buy herself some time until help came. And it would come. She didn't know why Noah wasn't in the building, but she knew he'd return for her.

Limping and staggering, she made her way to the stairs leading up to the roof. Behind her were deep, resounding thuds as Eddie bombarded the panic room door. Eventually, he'd calm down enough to use his brain, rather than brawn, to get out.

With her eyes fixed on the heavy steel door at the top of the stairs, she dragged herself upward. Her plan was simple: get to the roof and shout for help. It was the busiest time of the day. Someone would be out on the street. Someone would hear her.

Please...

She inched her way up to the door, aching with every step she took. Hands shaking, she unlocked it, slipped the key into her pocket, and threw it open. The bright summer sun blinded her, rendering her useless while her eyes adjusted.

And then, when they did, she gazed out at the wide-open expanse of the roof.

Of the city.

The sky.

The world...

There were no walls out there to keep her safe. Then again, the walls behind her weren't doing a great job of that right now, either. Ice-cold fingers of panic clawed at her as her hands curled around the doorframe. There was too much space. Anything might happen out there, where there was nowhere to hide.

Annabelle jumped at the sound of gunfire from below. Eddie had figured out how to disable the panel. Her time had run out.

For one agonizing second, she couldn't decide between stepping out onto the roof or staying to face Eddie Hanson. Her hands tingled, and her throat tightened. She couldn't breathe. Air was sucked into her lungs in short, painful gasps. The door at the bottom of the stairwell to the roof slammed open. It was now or never. But her feet wouldn't move. Couldn't move.

She was literally paralyzed with fear.

What had Sammy said? All she needed to do was hold Noah's hand, and she'd be fine.

But Noah wasn't with her. And there was no hand to hold.

"Stupid bitch," came the taunt from the bottom of the stairs. "Where the fuck are you going to run to?"

But she didn't need to run.

Because she also remembered Jacob's advice: When the

world gets too big, focus on something small. Something close.

Annabelle dragged her eyes from the vast expanse of the sky and stared down at her feet on the roof's gray surface. There was a shallow, surface crack about three feet from her toes. All she had to do was step forward and stand on that small crack.

She could do that. She could stare at the crack until it was under her toes.

"You can't do it." Eddie laughed at her. "You're too fucking scared even to run for your life. I can't wait to see what my buyers do to you. Whoever wins your auction is gonna have a party driving you insane."

With every ounce of strength within her, Annabelle moved her foot.

* * *

Their SUV screeched to a halt in front of the warehouse. There was no sign that anything had been disturbed. Noah was out the door before the engine was off, running for the main entrance.

The building was eerily quiet.

His team came up behind him as he cautiously entered the warehouse, gun in hand.

"Taking the back," Abasi said through Noah's earpiece. "Rodrigo, you're with me."

"I'm going down the side," Violet said.

"I'll cover Violet," Katrina said.

Noah, Rochelle, Logan, and Harris spread out on the ground floor. They checked the burned-out shop and storage area at the rear but found nothing. Noah noted that the boys had somehow armed themselves despite Rochelle telling them to get licensed first. If she noticed, she said nothing.

"Upstairs," Noah whispered to the rest of his team, and the four of them made their way to the second floor.

Noah, who took lead, spotted Evan first.

"Evan's down," he told his team.

Logan and Harris rushed up the stairs to get to their brother, and Noah signaled them to keep silent. Without making a sound, they fell to Evan's side and checked for a pulse.

"He's alive." Logan was pale but relieved.

"Bullet wound to the shoulder," Harris said. "I'll call an ambulance." He dug out his phone and whispered into it.

Noah lifted his chin to Rochelle, and they separated, guns ready as they checked each room on the second floor. He found signs of a struggle in the small office Annabelle had used to go over her testimony. One glance at the old wooden credenza, and he knew where ADA Grant had stashed her drugged body.

He'd castigate himself later for not thinking to check the cupboard.

"Clear," Rochelle whispered.

"Clear this end," Noah added.

"No one on the fire escape," Violet reported.

"Back of the building clear," Rodrigo said.

"I've got an vehicle parked outside the building next door," Abasi said. "Looks like the wheels Eddie was sitting on the other day."

Noah's stomach clenched. So he *was* in the building.

As if to confirm it, a loud, angry roar echoed from the floor above.

"He's in the loft," Noah said, sprinting for the stairs.

"Going up the fire escape," Violet said.

"We're coming round to join you," Rodrigo said.

Noah ran for the loft, taking the stairs two at a time.

* * *

Annabelle had taken one tiny step toward the crack. Her hands shook desperately now, and she felt strangely light-headed. But she couldn't pass out. If she did, Eddie Hanson would drag her back into his clutches.

Another tiny, shuffling step. The crack was marginally closer. She felt the sun on her skin, ever so slightly soothed by a barely-there breeze. She was outside now. Still clutching the doorframe but standing on the roof.

Two more steps, tiny steps, and she'd be able to slam the door behind her. Shutting Eddie inside the building, buying her time until Noah came for her.

She took another agonizing step.

Eyes on the crack. Only on the crack. Nothing else existed right now but that small crack.

"I don't have time for this crap," Eddie said before footsteps ran up the stairs.

She took another step, reached back, and yanked the door shut behind her. The lock clicked into place. And she had the key. As her gaze remained fixed on that crack, it felt like the entire building shook with Eddie's rage-filled roar. There was a dull thump behind her, but the door held fast. He couldn't shoot it out. The bullets would just ricochet into the stairwell. If he wanted her, he'd have to find another way to get to her—more difficult now that they'd pulled the fire escape ladder onto the roof to stop the Demons from using it.

Shivering wildly in the summer heat, Annabelle stood still, staring at the crack in the roof. She hadn't quite made it far enough to stand on it, but she'd made it outside.

Her grand plan of shouting for help wasn't going to happen, though. She was rooted to the spot, her throat so tight that shouting for any reason at all would have been impossible. Slowly, careful never to take her eyes off the crack that had become her entire world, she lowered herself to the roof. Shade from the stairwell meant she was in one of the few spots that weren't blisteringly hot. So she sat, knees to her chest, eyes on the crack, and waited for Noah.

* * *

"We take him alive if possible," Rochelle ordered the team as they made their way to the loft.

With Noah taking the lead, they spread out around the apartment, signaling one another when each area was cleared. Noah opened the door to the panic room and stepped inside.

Someone had shot out the override panel, and the door to the guest room was wide open.

There was no sign of Annabelle.

A loud thud sounded from above, making Noah jog for the stairwell.

Eddie Hanson stood at the top of the stairs, kicking the door to the roof. The man had completely lost control, unaware of his surroundings, intent only on venting his fury on the door in front of him.

Which meant...

Was Annabelle on the roof?

Violet wouldn't be able to get up that far. The fire escape went only as high as the loft, as they'd pulled the ladder onto the roof for security reasons. What if she was injured or panicking?

"Logan," he said through the comms, "is Evan okay?"

"He's holding in there. Looks like the bullet's gone straight through. There's a paramedic two minutes out."

Noah let out a breath. "Can you leave him with Harris and climb up to the roof? I think Annabelle's out there alone."

"On it," he said, and Noah relaxed slightly.

As he watched, Eddie unhooked his gun from the back of his jeans and aimed at the door.

"I wouldn't do that if I were you," Noah called. "The bullet will just ricochet, and you'll end up dead."

Eddie spun toward him, firing as he did so. Noah and Rochelle ducked back through the stairwell door.

"Well, at least we don't have to worry about him getting hit by a ricochet," she said drolly.

"Give it up, Eddie," Noah shouted. "You've got nowhere to go, and you're outgunned."

"Fuck that," Eddie shouted back.

On the first floor of the building, a door slammed open.

"Cops are here," Katrina said.

Rochelle put a hand on his arm. "We let them deal with him."

"That could take forever."

"He's one guy with limited firepower, Noah."

"Yeah." He stared at her, willing her to understand. "Annabelle's outside, Rochelle."

"And Logan's on his way to help her."

"We don't know what state she's in."

"She'll be okay until we've dealt with this situation."

Noah swallowed hard and decided to lay it all on the line. "I love her, Rochelle. I can't lose her."

"You won't," she said firmly. "Leave Eddie to the cops. I don't want another member of my team getting shot."

"Your team?" Noah said.

"Shut up." She rolled her eyes. "We wait for the cops."

"I've got Annabelle," Logan said in Noah's ear. His knees almost gave way.

"Is she okay?" He barely managed to get the words out.

"Bit banged up and a little loopy," Logan said. "She says she's not leaving the crack until you get here."

Against the odds, Noah laughed. It was short and dry, but it still counted. Rochelle shook her head and smiled.

"Tell her I'm coming, and I love her," he said, not giving a damn who heard or knew how he felt.

"I'm not telling her that." Logan sounded outraged.

Abasi came up beside them, grinning. "I have another suggestion for dealing with Hanson." He held up one of the flash-bangs they'd used in the drug house.

"The police are literally on their way up," Rochelle said.

"Yeah." Abasi grinned. "But you heard the man—he's in love."

"Fine." Rochelle heaved an exasperated sigh. "Have at it." She holstered her gun. "I'm going to make coffee while you guys get all macho with one pathetic criminal."

Noah grinned at Abasi, who handed over the flash-bang.

* * *

"You're okay now," Logan said to Annabelle.

She recognized that tone. People used it when they thought she was especially crazy.

"E-Evan?" She could barely get out his name.

"There's a bullet hole in his shoulder, and it looks like he banged his head, but he'll be fine."

Tears trickled down her cheeks. "I'm so sorry I left him there."

"It was probably the best thing you could have done. You took Eddie's attention away from Evan. You might have saved his life."

"You don't believe that. But thanks." She bit her bottom lip as she recalled the sight of him lying there in his own blood. "He was the one who saved me. He tasered Hanson and bought me time."

"Aye, he's a hero alright. And we'll never hear the end of it. Don't cry, Annabelle; none of this is your fault."

She caught sight of his hand in her peripheral vision, reaching out to comfort her. "Don't touch me! You'll block the crack."

His hand retreated. "Okay," he said slowly. "We wouldn't want to do that now, would we? You're getting a wee bit burned, though. How about we move back into the shade?"

"No. I'm not leaving the crack." She kept her eyes on it, only daring to blink when absolutely necessary. The crack was her lifeline. It was literally, in that moment, her entire world.

"Is this, uh, crack like an interdimensional portal only you can see?"

"What?" Annabelle almost looked at the idiot. "It's a crack. It's right there. Anybody can see it."

"Whatever you say," he said soothingly.

Now he was just making her mad. "Where's Noah? I can't leave without Noah." She needed to hold his hand. That's what Sammy said worked, and he had to be right. Jacob had been right about focusing on the little things. Ten years of expensive psychotherapy, and it was Noah's boys who'd given her the tools she needed to survive.

Go figure.

"He's dealing with the problem in the stairwell."

As if on cue, there was a series of explosions behind the stairwell door.

"Flash-bang," Logan said. "Nothing to worry about."

Gunshots rang out.

"That was a gun," Logan said. "We might have to worry about that."

There was banging at the door, which made Annabelle jump and almost take her eyes off the crack.

"Gimme a sec," Logan said as he stood. "Noah says we need to unlock the door. Do you have the key?"

Slowly, keeping her gaze steady, Annabelle shifted enough to reach into her pocket. She handed the key to Logan without looking at him. A few seconds later, the door opened, and then Noah was at her side.

At last.

He fell to the roof beside her and wrapped her up in his strong, solid arms.

"Don't do that!" Logan shouted. "You're blocking the crack."

Annabelle buried her face in Noah's chest, closed her eyes, and sobbed. Everything was okay now. The crack had done its job. Noah was here.

Chapter Thirty-Seven

"He really should go to the hospital," Dr. Mallory said as she watched the paramedic patch up Evan's bullet wound. "He's had a nasty blow to the head."

Annabelle's doctor had arrived quickly after they'd called her. While waiting for a different paramedic to tend to Annabelle's cuts and bruises, she'd popped into the main office area to check on Evan, citing professional curiosity. Noah suspected the doc had developed a soft spot for their team.

"Hospitals are boring," Evan declared, his eyes glassy. "How about I just come home with you instead, Doc?" He waggled his eyebrows suggestively.

Dr. Mallory burst out laughing. "My dear boy, I'd eat you alive."

Harris cocked his head, considering her. "I call dibs," he declared.

"You can't call dibs," Evan complained. "She's *my* doctor."

"Technically," Dr. Mallory said, "I'm Annabelle's doctor."

In his doped-up state, Evan had already moved on from the topic of who owned the doctor. He gave his brothers a soppy grin. "I love you guys," he gushed. He didn't wait for a reply. Instead, he announced to the room, "I'm a bloody hero!" He beamed at them.

"Yes, you are," Noah said with a laugh.

From the small storage room in the corner of the large office space, a voice called out, "All done here, Dr. Mallory."

Noah and the doc crossed to windowless closet where he's spent his first night sleeping beside Annabelle. Now the room contained nothing but a couple of old wooden chairs. Annabelle sat in one of them. She smiled, and the tension inside him eased somewhat. That tension had been a constant companion since she'd gone missing, and it reared its head every time she was out of his sight. He suspected it would take a long time to convince himself Annabelle was okay when she wasn't with him.

Noah crouched in front of her and placed his hands on her knees. "How're you doing?"

She rested her hands on top of his. "I'm one big bruise. My knee, my cheek, my side—but at least there are no cracked ribs or broken bones."

The sight of her blossoming black eye made him want to shoot Hanson in the kneecap all over again. Noah mentally smiled at the memory. The shot wasn't *absolutely* necessary. Hanson had been shooting wildly after being disorientated by the flash-bang and would have eventually run out of bullets. But Noah decided winging him would speed things up a little. It had been one of his better decisions.

"Your head?" He reached up to tuck her tangled hair behind her ear.

"Clear now. Although I feel like I have a hangover. My head's throbbing."

Noah turned to the doctor. "Can she take something for that?"

"Of course."

While she spoke with the paramedic, Noah focused on Annabelle. His gut clenched at the thought of almost losing her. And even though, logically, he knew she was safe now, he couldn't seem to convince his emotions. Deep down inside, he was waiting for something else to go wrong. But worst of all was the overwhelming guilt. There was no denying he was to blame for every bruise that marred her skin. If he'd just been there...

"I should have checked the office more thoroughly," he told her. "I should have looked inside the credenza. I shouldn't have jumped to the conclusion that you'd been taken from the building."

"You're right." She nodded solemnly. "And you *should* be in all places at all times, seeing all things at once, and never, ever making a mistake. Oh wait, that would make you God." She leaned in and pressed a gentle kiss to his lips. "Shoulda, coulda, woulda. The three pillars of undeserved guilt. Everybody believed I was in that case; it wasn't only you. But you came back for me as soon as you knew different. You didn't do anything wrong."

"But if I'd taken just a few minutes longer to lo—"

She pressed a finger to his mouth to silence him. "And *if* the ADA hadn't been in the Demons' pocket, and *if* the police had realized she was the mole sooner, and *if* Eddie hadn't been granted bail in the first place... There are so many ifs to fret over. But if you're intent on practicing some self-flagellation, I'm sure one of the triplets could make you a nice little flogger to use. Logan seems quite handy."

"Smart-ass," Noah grumbled.

The doc approached them with a smile. "Take these." She handed a couple of pills and a glass of water to Annabelle, who did as she was told.

Once finished, she set the glass on the floor beside her and spoke to her doctor. "Are we going to talk?"

"Do you want to?"

She glanced at Noah and shook her head. "Another day," she said. "I need time for things to settle before I can find the right words."

Dr. Mallory nodded. "What you really need is some care." She focused on Noah. "A shower, clean clothes, a decent meal, and sleep. Lots of sleep. That's my prescription."

"Yes, ma'am."

The doctor moved closer to Annabelle and gently brushed a hand over her hair. "Your aunt would have been proud of you today. I know I am."

"It's hard to believe that I went outside. It was only a couple of steps, but I did it."

"Not only that." Dr. Mallory's voice was thick with emotion. "You fought back. You defended yourself and had the courage to do what was needed to save yourself. I'm so incredibly proud of you, Annabelle." She blinked several times before straightening her shoulders and smiling at Noah. "I once told you that you were good for her, but I was wrong. You're good for *each other*." With that, she turned on her heel and strode toward the door. "Call if you need me, but I think you're in fine hands tonight." And then, she was gone.

Annabelle watched her leave with tears in her eyes. She visibly swallowed before facing Noah. "She's right, you know. I am *soooo* good for you."

"I couldn't agree more. Come on." He stood and gently tugged her to her feet. "Let's get you upstairs to shower and change."

"I don't think I can face going upstairs yet," she said. "I'll shower down here. Could you get me some clean clothes?"

"Absolutely."

As they made their way through the office, Evan, still delirious thanks to whatever they'd given him for the pain, grinned widely. "Anna-belly, I fried that guy for you!"

"Yes, you did," she said with a chuckle.

"I'm a hero," he announced again, making everyone laugh.

"Don't worry," Harris told them. "I'm videoing all of this for posterity."

"And our mother," Logan added.

Holding Annabelle's hand, Noah escorted her to the bathroom. He couldn't stop himself from checking it was clear before she entered. It would be a long time before he felt they were completely safe in the warehouse.

"The police will be here tomorrow to take statements," he said. "They have their hands full tonight with gang violence. Which means we can follow the doctor's orders and take care of you."

Wide, dark eyes met his. "Did we take Hanson's money? He asked if we did. I know we were trying to take it, but did we manage it?"

Noah winced internally, wondering which bruises were associated with that line of questioning. In hindsight, perhaps it hadn't been the best idea to go after the gang leader's money. "Yes, we did."

"I'm glad. What are we doing with it?"

"We're giving it away."

Her smile was pure satisfaction. "He'd hate that."

She wasn't wrong.

"I'm not sure I can sleep in the loft tonight, Noah. Do you think we could move a bed into the storeroom down here?"

He completely understood. The apartment still showed damage from the latest Demons attack. "I'll get the boys onto it. What about food? Katrina's ordering in. What do you feel like eating?"

Annabelle thought about it for a second. "Everything. I want all the food. And don't forget dessert."

Noah chuckled as he leaned in to kiss her. "Go shower. I'll make sure there's enough food here to feed an army when you get out."

"You know, that's exactly what we are," she said as she walked into the bathroom. "An army."

The door closed behind her, and Noah pressed his palm flat against it. Safe. She was safe. Eddie Hanson was in jail, and no matter what happened at his upcoming trial, he'd spend the rest of his life in prison. Today's events ensured that.

Noah closed his eyes and took the first easy breath he'd taken all day.

* * *

The "everything" Annabelle wanted to eat turned out to be copious amounts of pizza chased down with pints of ice cream. They ate in the second-floor office because Annabelle wasn't ready to face her loft just yet. Smiles had replaced tension, and the ragtag team laughed easily with each other as they ate.

Halfway through the pizza part of their meal, Evan laid

his head on the desk in front of him and fell asleep. There was no waking him. The self-declared hero had finally run out of steam. His brothers carried him to his bed in the room they shared at the back of the building and took turns checking on him throughout the evening.

As though scenting food, the detectives dropped by to update them on the Demons situation. MacMillan fell on the pizza with obvious delight. Johnson was more interested in a cold bottle of beer. He sipped it after loosening his tie.

"Long, long day," he told them as he relaxed into a chair. "We're on top of the fighting now and the city's cells are full of gangbangers. Should be a quiet night tonight."

Noah lifted his own beer in a toast. "To the cops," he said.

The team drank heartily.

"Any word on *former* ADA Grant?" Rochelle asked, her eyes narrowing.

MacMillan wiped his mouth on a napkin. "Got on a flight to Ecuador. They don't extradite to the US, so she's out of our reach for the time being. But I read up on Ecuador, not sure she'll want to hang out there forever. Doesn't look like it's as much fun as say Argentina."

Johnson grinned at his partner. "Mac's always fancied himself a great tango dancer."

"Don't be fooled by my curves." MacMillan patted his belly. "This boy is light on his feet."

As the team laughed, Noah caught Rodrigo's eye. "You know anyone in Ecuador?"

Rodrigo's smile was slow. "I believe I might know one or two people there."

"Handy." Noah sipped his beer.

After the team caught up on the details of the Demon Brothers' fight against the Alvarez cartel, and Mac finished the pizza, the detectives said their goodbyes. Promising to return early the next morning for their statements.

Meanwhile, Annabelle took her iPad to a corner and, much to Noah's delight, called his sons. He went over to say hello before leaving her to it.

"It worked," she told the boys with an ecstatic grin.

"What worked?" Jacob said.

"Your advice, Jake, your advice!" She peered into the camera excitedly. "I went out onto the roof, and I did what you said your aunt does; I focused on one tiny thing. And it worked! I mean, I didn't get far, but I was outside. I felt the sun on my face, and it's all because of you!"

Jacob looked like he'd burst from pride and, at the same time, die of embarrassment.

Sammy pushed to the foreground. "Did you do my thing too?" he asked eagerly. "Did you hold Dad's hand?"

"I did when he got there," Annabelle said seriously. "And that worked too. You guys are geniuses. I went outside, and it's all thanks to you!" She sobered somewhat. "I mean, it was just a little bit outside. A few steps onto the roof, but it still counts."

"Heck yeah, it counts," Jacob shouted. "That's awesome, Annabelle. Hey, Gran, Annabelle went outside, and she used our advice to do it!"

To Noah's surprise, Therese's mother appeared behind the boys. It always made his heart ache to see her, as he imagined that's exactly how his wife would have looked if she'd made it to the same age.

"That's wonderful, dear," Bernadette said. "I'm so proud of you." She put her arms around the boys. "And I'm so very proud of my wonderful grandsons too."

"Dad helped," Sammy piped up. "He held Annabelle's hand."

"Did he now?" Bernadette's eyes twinkled. "Well, next time we talk, I'll tell him he did a good job too."

"It was only onto the roof," Annabelle clarified.

"Nonsense." Bernadette waved a dismissive hand. "Only nothing. The roof today; tomorrow, you'll be visiting us in Atlantic City."

Annabelle looked awestruck at the thought. "That would be amazing."

Meanwhile, Noah wondered when she'd become such good friends with his in-laws. He shook his head in bewilderment. She was just that kind of person. If she hadn't been housebound for so long, he imagined she'd have adopted everyone she met and filled the warehouse with waifs and strays.

"I knew you could do it," Jacob said with confidence. "I told Sammy you could."

"He did." Sammy nodded vigorously.

"When we come back to Houston, we'll help you some more," Jacob vowed.

"I'd love that," Annabelle said sincerely. "Now, show me how your comic's progressing."

As the boys rushed away to get their artwork, Violet called out, "Noah, get over here and back me up."

After one last reassuring glance at Annabelle, he rejoined the group.

"What have you done now?" he asked Violet.

"Nothing." But Violet couldn't pull off innocent if she tried. She just wasn't in the mood to confess to whatever it was. "I'm trying to get Rochelle to see that I've been working hard at this team thing. Tell her what I was like in London." It was an order.

"A pain in the ass." Noah pulled up a chair at the table

and helped himself to some ice-cream. "That about sums it up."

"See?" Violet said as though he'd made her point.

From the look on Rochelle's face, it was clear he hadn't. He decided to elaborate.

"She barely spoke, considered orders optional, took out her frustrations on any offender that crossed her path, and refused to participate in group events." He frowned at Violet, realizing something. "She sure as hell never ate with any of us."

"See?" Violet said again, waving her pizza slice. "I deserve credit for trying this hard."

"Fine." Rochelle seemed more confused than convinced. "I award you credit for trying."

"Thank you." Violet sat back in her seat, satisfied.

It was late, and she'd changed out of her usual severe black attire. It took Noah a second to realize she was wearing a Hello Kitty T-shirt instead. The color wasn't fluorescent—it was a muddy green—but a complete change from her usual look.

"Gotta say," he said, "I think she's mellowing."

Violet glared at him. "I wouldn't go that far."

The team laughed.

Team...

Noah rested his elbows on the desk in front of him as he caught Rochelle's eye. "You were too hasty," he repeated his comment from earlier that day.

"No." She leaned back in her chair. Her suit jacket was off, her shirt sleeves rolled up, and she'd tied her hair in a topknot. She looked relaxed. "I was cautious. You know full well this office is a lawsuit waiting to happen."

"Wait," Harris said around a mouthful of ice-cream. "Is

that a bad thing? I thought Americans liked suing each other. Isn't it the national hobby or something?"

"Yes, it's a bad thing," Rochelle told him. "No insurance company on the planet would take a risk on this office."

"Bull." Abasi reached for his wallet and pulled out a card. He tossed it to Rochelle. "Call that number and tell them I referred you. They'll insure the office."

"Or what?" Rochelle said. "You'll *take them out?*"

"My aunt would be unhappy if I did that. Her son runs the New York office."

"You have family?" Harris' jaw dropped. "Family that aren't criminals?" It was clearly an alien concept.

"What can I say?" Abasi shrugged. "The English side of the family's filled with black sheep."

Harris gaped at Abasi as though he'd just realized the man didn't hatch in a lab and walk out a fully formed mobster.

Noah turned to Rochelle. "Lack of insurance isn't your only reason for disbanding the office, is it?"

She shrugged. "I'm just not sure we can work together."

"What if we made a blood oath?" Violet asked, making everyone stare at her.

"I'd rather make a pinky promise," Logan said.

"We worked as a team today," Rodrigo pointed out. "No subordination, no rogue behavior—unless you count Noah shooting Hanson in the knee."

"I'd have aimed slightly higher," Katrina said evenly.

"In fact," Rodrigo said, "I thought we made an excellent team."

"We're totally a team." The two remaining triplets high-fived each other, grinning.

"I was team-like," Violet declared, as though that were a thing.

"Hey"—Abasi held up his hands—"even I behaved."

"Face it," Noah said to Rochelle, "you have a fully formed *team*, whether you like it or not. Seems to me that all we need right now is a boss. So, what do you say, *Boss*? Want to get the band back together?"

"Damn," Rochelle said, sitting up straight. "If we do this, there's gonna be a few rules."

The team shared an anxious look.

"We can do rules," Logan said, although a tad unconvincingly.

"One"—Rochelle counted them off on her fingers—"no keeping the boss in the dark about anything."

"Seems reasonable," Rodrigo said.

"Two." Rochelle pointed to another finger. "Everybody undertakes firearms training, and you all volunteer for two hours a week each at a center for victims of violent crime."

"Come on!" Harris complained. "That's not fair; I've never shot anybody. Can't Violet do my hours?"

"And mine," Logan said.

"No." Rochelle narrowed her eyes. "You're all a little too gun-happy for my liking. You do the community time, or you aren't on the team."

There was much grumbling, but also agreement.

"Three," she said. "No dishonest, lawbreaking behavior."

"Abasi doesn't know how to behave any other way," Rodrigo said with a grin.

Abasi just grinned back.

"This is nonnegotiable. We obey the law." Rochelle was adamant.

"Unless you give the okay to do otherwise," Noah clarified. "Sometimes, laws just need to be bent—a little."

"Fine. My permission for any questionable behavior is essential."

There were mutters of reluctant agreement.

"And finally"—she looked at Noah—"no sleeping with the clients."

"Deal's off," Noah said as his team whooped and laughed.

Annabelle came up behind him and wrapped her arms around his neck. "How about I sweeten the pot in this negotiation?" she said to Rochelle. "Noah can definitely keep sleeping with me, and Benson Security can lease the lower two floors of this building at a cut-price rate."

"Sounds suspiciously like we're pimping out Noah," Abasi said, amused.

"Okay." Annabelle was undeterred. "On top of that, you all have to do your volunteer time with my charity instead of finding another victim center."

"You have a charity?" Noah twisted to look up at her.

"Yep. After my parents died and I inherited everything, I put it all into a charitable trust that works with victims of violence." She shrugged. "I didn't want it hanging over my head as a reason for people to kidnap me again, so I gave it away."

"That would have made it hard for Hanson to empty your bank accounts," Rochelle said with admiration.

"Yeah, there isn't a whole lot in there right now because my new book's been on hold." Annabelle hesitated. "Actually, as part of that cut-price deal, you could waive the fees for this case." She batted her eyelashes innocently.

"She looks so sweet," Harris said. "But really, she's a shark."

"Lemme get this straight," Abasi drawled. "For an old office in the middle of nowhere and a burned-out shop, you get to sleep with Noah, plus a free ride on your Benson Security bill and hours of volunteer work from the rest of us? Damn, girl, if you ever want to start a criminal empire, let me know."

"Too much?" Annabelle asked Noah, laughter in her eyes.

"You're worth it," he assured her.

"So, what do you say, Rochelle?" Annabelle asked.

As one, the team turned to their reluctant leader. Rochelle sighed and rose to her feet, a mug of coffee in her hand. It seemed as though the room itself held a breath, waiting for her verdict. At last, she raised her mug.

"Here's to the Benson Security Houston office," she said. "The biggest group of misfits this side of the Atlantic."

"I'll drink to that," Noah said with a grin.

Down the corridor, a voice rang out: "I'm a bloody hero!"

Harris turned to Logan. "It's your turn."

"I went last time," Logan complained.

As they argued, Noah met Rochelle's resigned gaze, and they smiled at each other.

Chapter Thirty-Eight

It was the early hours of the morning before everyone finally staggered off to bed. Noah was last to retire for the night—he wanted to do one final security sweep of the warehouse before joining Annabelle in the storage room. Eddie might be locked up tight, but the gang leader still had influence, and a few Demons still wandered the city.

Satisfied that the place was secure and the alarms all set, he walked through the quiet open-plan office to their makeshift bedroom. There'd never been any question as to where Noah would sleep. From now on, he planned to stick to Annabelle like glue.

The guys had helped him move the bed from the guest room upstairs into the storage room, and Annabelle was already in it when he arrived. The small, windowless room looked cozy, with a tiny lamp glowing and most of the space taken up by the bed.

"About time," Annabelle said with a smile. "I thought I'd have to sleep alone."

"Not tonight, Bella." Or any other night, either, if he had his way.

He started to undress, her eyes darkening as she watched.

"Don't bother with pj's," she said suggestively. "I didn't."

"Bella," he groaned, kicking off his jeans. "I don't think—"

She held up a hand. "Good. Don't think. Just get your cute backside into bed."

There was no dealing with her. All Noah could do was comply. Her gaze turned appreciative once he'd stepped out of his underwear, and there was no denying his ego liked that look on her face.

"You've been through a lot today," he said, trying a different tack. "You're bruised and sore. And the doctor said you need sleep."

"Don't worry." She smiled. "I'll sleep after."

Noah didn't have the fight in him to protest any further. Like he'd said, it'd been a tough day, and he wanted to reassure himself that Annabelle was alive and well and was going to be okay.

Carefully, so as not to jostle her injuries, he pulled back the covers and slipped in beside her. "I need to hold you," he confessed.

She willingly went into his embrace, pressing herself against his side as he slid an arm around her shoulders. There was something deeply reassuring about skin against skin. She hooked a leg over his as her hand splayed across his stomach. Noah held her tight, clasping her head as her cheek pressed against his chest.

Her fingertips traced the planes and indentations of his abdomen while he softly teased his fingers through her hair.

They lay like that, entwined together in the faint lamplight, breathing each other in and remembering they were still alive. Although the thought of what might have been still haunted him. He could have lost her. It'd all come far too close for comfort.

A shudder passed through him at the thought.

"Don't," Annabelle whispered before pressing a kiss to his chest. "We're here, we're alive, we won."

He stared up at the ceiling without really seeing it. "I feel like I'm back in that SUV, knowing you're still at the warehouse and I'm not there to help you."

"Dr. Mallory says that the best way to deal with feelings like that is to remind yourself you're in the present by being consciously aware of where you are now." She ran a hand over his stomach. "We're here together. Feel my touch. It's real. It's now. It's all that matters."

Noah shivered as she caressed him. "You are so much stronger than I am," he told her, meaning every word. He was in awe of her.

"True," she teased, and he felt her smile against his skin. "I'm also a delayed reactor. You can help calm me down when I freak out later this week."

"It's a deal," he promised.

Her hand slid lower, and he sucked in a breath as she wrapped her fist around his hard, ready length. Unlike his brain, other parts of his body had no problem with staying in the present.

"Bella," he whispered as his own hand found its way to the heavy weight of her breast.

She stroked him slowly. "Today, when everything was happening, I told myself all I had to do was wait for you." She angled her face to look up at him. "I never once doubted that you'd come for me."

Noah reluctantly moved his hand from her breast to clasp her wrist. "If you keep stroking me like that, I'll come for you right now too." Carefully, gently, he removed her hold and rolled her onto her back.

He leaned up over her, tracing the bruise around her eye. Hating that it was there.

Annabelle reached up to cup his cheek. "Stay in the present, remember?"

"It'll take some practice," he murmured, drinking her in with his eyes before closing the gap between them to sip at her lips. "Lots and lots of practice."

Their kiss was slow, each taste an act of adoration, of caring. She was precious to him. Inside and out. And Noah was in no hurry to end the sweet tangle of lips and tongue. Eventually, he pulled away. When he gazed down at her, he saw flushed cheeks and kiss-swollen lips. He felt her hands clasping his back, keeping him close. As if he'd ever want to be anywhere else.

"I love you," she whispered.

"Damn, I was going to say that first." In true Merchant fashion, he'd told everyone on his team that he loved her but hadn't gotten around to telling Annabelle. He *definitely* had a gift for romance.

"I know," she said with a wide, slow smile. "Nothing stopping you from saying it now, is there?"

Noah kissed the tip of her nose, then those laughing eyes, then the corner of her smiling lips before whispering the words against her mouth. "I love you." He kissed her chin. "I love you." He returned to her mouth. "I love you." The words tasted like ambrosia.

Her arms wrapped around his neck, pulling him closer as their kiss deepened into a tangle of tongues and gasps for air. Hands took on a life of their own, roaming, exploring, caressing. They were on a slow road to their destination, neither in any hurry to reach the end.

Mindful of her bruises, Noah supported most of his weight as he kissed his way down her throat to those luscious breasts. He twirled his tongue around one pert nipple, making her gasp and arch up into him. Her fingers twisted into his hair, holding his head against her. Needing him there. Needing his kiss. His touch. Noah recognized the need because he felt it too, burning inside him like a void, desperate to be filled. His hand slid down to her warm, wet heat, testing her readiness for him.

"Please," she said, "I don't want to go over without you."

He understood and grasped her hip to gently move her beneath him as he made space for himself between her legs. With his arms bearing his weight, he rose above her. She looked decadent—her dark, wild hair strewn across the pillow as she stared up at him with nothing but trust in her eyes.

They were beyond communicating with words now, in that place where only lovers could expound with touch and adoration. She drew her knees up alongside his thighs as she held on to his waist, and they gazed into each other's eyes as he slowly entered her.

This wasn't about sex. About climax. Or release. This was a joining. A promise. A shared need to love and know one another. He felt it in her touch, her look, her smile.

Slowly, reverently, he moved inside her.

His Bella.

Her Noah.

Together.

* * *

Annabelle sank back onto the bed, gasping as Noah collapsed beside her. A faint sheen of sweat covered both of them, glistening in the dim lamplight. The dull ache of her bruises mingled with the much more delicious ache of a body well loved. And that's what she felt—loved.

Her aunt often quoted an old Chinese proverb that said if you sat in one place long enough, the whole world would pass by. Or something like that. Well, Annabelle had sat in her warehouse for ten long years, and eventually, it had paid off because her world had come to her in the form of Noah. Her lips curved into a smile as she realized how soppy her thoughts were, yet they still felt true.

"What are you grinning about?" Noah asked breathlessly.

"I've just realized that I connived to have your business in the building so I can keep seeing you. It'll be kinda awkward if we ever go our separate ways."

He propped himself up on one elbow, looking intensely serious. "Is that what you think will happen?"

"No." She ran her fingertips down his brutish face. "But we're still so new. Only crazy people make plans to spend forever together after just a few weeks. Right?"

"I'm okay with being crazy," Noah said. "The building, the office, has nothing to do with us."

"But, Noah, I'm not normal. If you weren't around here all the time, I'd never see you. It's not like we can go on dates." She scoffed at herself. "Unless you want to hang out on the roof, near the door. I can just about manage that."

"Bella"—his expression softened—"I thought we were way past dating."

"Then what? I can't move in with you."

He ran a fingertip from the hollow in her throat, right down the center of her body to circle her belly button, and she shivered with an overwhelming awareness of all that was him.

"We could move in with you," he said evenly.

A surge of hope crashed through her like a tsunami. "But the boys hardly know me."

"Then we let them get to know you." He moved closer. "Before or after we move in is totally up to you."

She reached for him. "Are we insane? I mean, normal people don't move this fast, do they?"

"Bella." His smile was filled with humor. "You can't leave this building, and I spent years talking to my dead wife. There's nothing normal about either of us. And if we can't follow the normal pattern of things, then I say we make up our own." He leaned over and pressed his lips to the spot above her heart. "We do things our way. To hell with how the rest of the world does it."

"You say the most romantic things," she said, pulling him close.

"I'm much more of a doer than a talker," Noah said.

And then, he proved his point.

Epilogue

It'd been four months since Noah and the boys moved into Annabelle's loft. And she'd loved every single minute of it. They'd had the back of the apartment renovated, turning the guest bedrooms and shared bathroom over to Jacob and Sammy and building a new bedroom—with walls—where her old one used to be. The panic room had been converted into a closet, and a new panic room built on the second floor for everyone to use. All the new walls were now soundproofed, at Noah's insistence, and a small guest bathroom had been installed in the area where the gym equipment used to be.

It surprised Annabelle how easily they'd all adapted to living together. The boys loved the warehouse and hanging out with their dad's security team, and Annabelle loved having a huge extended family close by. No matter the time, there was always someone around to talk to, although everyone had moved out into other accommodation now, except for her and her boys. But there was always someone on duty, day or night, and even when Noah was out of town for work, the building was never empty.

The Benson Security team had renovated the first floor, turning the shop into their street-front office and the back area into a gym, training space, and storage. They were still renovating the second floor, but there were plans for a proper open-plan office space and a couple of small breakout rooms.

The triplets, meanwhile, had talked her into adding a climbing wall in the alleyway between the buildings, and that was next on the list for the builders. Rochelle had put her foot down about the inter-floor slide idea, saying it was a security risk. However, Annabelle suspected Rochelle just didn't want the triplets playing all day long. Not a good look for security officers.

"I'm getting fed up waiting," Annabelle called from where she sat at the kitchen island as she'd been ordered by Jacob and Sammy.

They'd run off, saying there was a surprise, but they needed to do some last-minute prep. She wondered if they'd finished the comic book they'd been working on.

"Right." Sammy ran back into the room and screeched to a halt beside her. "You can come with me now. I wanted to put a blindfold on you, but Dad said that would freak you out."

"I said"—Noah appeared in the doorway between the kitchen area and the boys' bedrooms—"that it might not be the best idea."

"Whatever." Sammy grabbed Annabelle's hand. "You need to come see."

"Yeah," Jacob called from beside Noah. "Hurry up."

"Hurry up," Annabelle grumbled. "I've been waiting here for half an hour, and now you want me to hurry up?"

Noah and Jacob shared a look of amusement.

"This way," Sammy said, pulling her along.

They walked into the back corridor and turned to the stairs up to the roof. Okay, she hadn't expected that. Annabelle still had a *developing* relationship with her roof. She'd been out on it several times since the incident with Hanson, trying to put the memory of hiding from him behind her. It helped that her friends and family went with her, and it also helped that Hanson was no longer a concern. He'd lasted only a few days in prison before a member of the Alvarez cartel had taken him out. That part of her life was well and truly behind her. Which just left getting used to the roof. But no matter how much the boys encouraged her to go up there more often, at the end of the day, it was just a plain old roof.

Or was it?

She cast a sidelong glance at Noah. "What have you done to the roof?"

"I told you she'd guess." Jacob grinned.

"Shh!" Sammy hissed. "You'll ruin the surprise."

With a sigh but secretly delighted, Annabelle let the boys hustle her up the stairs and out onto her roof. Where she came to a complete halt. Unable to do anything but stare in awe. The roof was no longer plain. She gasped and looked around, trying to take it all in. There was a grassy area, raised flower and vegetable beds, a basketball court, a fountain, and benches and seating everywhere. There were even trees! It was beautiful.

She took a shaky step away from the door and closer to the Benson Security team, who stood grinning at her in the bright afternoon sun. Noah took her hand and held it tight, giving her the courage she needed to take another step. Sammy and Jacob crowded in around her, protecting her— just like their father.

"We're here," Noah whispered to her. "We've got you. You're safe to explore. I promise."

She squeezed his hand hard.

"Look," Sammy said excitedly, although he didn't run off to show her what he meant; he stayed beside her, giving her support. "We've put a fence around the edge so you can't fall off."

"So *I* can't fall off?" She cocked an eyebrow at Noah.

Sammy leaned in to whisper loudly, "Really, it's for the triplets."

There was muffled laughter from Noah's team.

Jacob nudged her shoulder. At fourteen, he was already a head taller than her and growing every day. "We made trellis corridors that will be covered in plants by spring. That way, if looking up at the sky gets too much, you can stay on the paths and have a kind of roof over your head."

Tears stung her eyes as she bumped back into him. "Thank you," she whispered.

"Show her the best bit, Dad," Sammy demanded, bouncing on the spot.

"You mean the barbeque?" Noah asked innocently.

"No," Sammy wailed. "The gazebo!"

Noah gently turned Annabelle toward the corner of the roof above the living room area, facing Houston's skyline, where a beautiful wooden gazebo sat tucked into a space filled with plants.

She gasped at the sight.

"Do you think you can make it over there?" Noah asked.

The team moved toward her.

"Maybe if we all go?" Katrina said with understanding.

Annabelle nodded, her throat suddenly tight. "I can try."

Together, they made their way to the structure in the

corner, Annabelle keeping a death grip on Noah's hand as her makeshift family jostled around her. If anyone thought she was taking too long to get there, they kept it to themself. Mostly, there were observations about the roof and exclamations of delight when someone noticed something new.

"I got a call from detective Johnson this morning," Rochelle said as she came alongside them.

"Been a while since we heard from him," Noah said.

"Yeah, he wanted to tell me about something weird that'd happened." Her eyes sparkled as she cast a knowing glance in Rodrigo's direction. "Seems they got a call in the middle of the night that there were problems on a private airstrip on the edge of town. Rumor was that drugs were involved."

"And that's weird how?" Noah asked innocently.

Far too innocently. Annabelle glanced up at him to see him fighting a smile. When she looked around the rest of the team, only Rodrigo and Abasi seemed to be amused. Those three. Always up to mischief together. They were worse than the triplets.

"The weird part," Rochelle said, "is that there weren't any drugs on the plane. When they got on board, they found a sleeping woman and not much else." She eyed him knowingly. "You'll never guess who the woman was."

"Then don't make me try," Noah said with a grin.

"It was former ADA Grant. Apparently, she'd gone to sleep in her bed in Ecuador and was very confused about waking up in Houston." She eyed Rodrigo, Abasi and Noah. "I don't suppose you know anything about how that might have happened?"

Noah shook his head slowly. "I got nothing."

"Mystery to me," Rodrigo said.

"If I'd been involved, her sleep would have been of a more permanent kind," Abasi said solemnly.

"Yeah, right." Rochelle rolled her eyes. "You three are totally clueless."

The men shared a smile.

At last, they reached the gazebo. It had six sides and wooden benches around the inside walls, providing plenty of space for everyone to sit. They crowded in, Annabelle in the middle, and sat looking out over the array of flowers to the view beyond.

"I can't believe you did this," Annabelle said, sniffing.

"Everybody helped," Jacob said proudly.

"We put the basketball court as far away from the gazebo as possible so we wouldn't annoy you when we played," Sammy said. "Unless you play with us. Can you play basketball?"

"I've never tried," she said. There were so many things she'd never tried until she met Noah. So many experiences she'd missed out on. And he was making up for every last one. "I can learn, though."

Sammy nodded wisely. "We're teaching the triplets. You can join them. They don't know what they're doing either."

"Hey, I resent that," Evan said. "I googled it."

The scent of flowers wafted around Annabelle as she sat in her secret garden, surrounded by her friends. Her heart was full to bursting. This was a life she never thought she'd have.

"So." Noah bumped her shoulder with his. "What do you think? Could you get married up here?"

Annabelle gasped as he reached into his pocket and pulled out a ring box. She held her breath as he flipped it open with one hand because she still had a death grip on the other. An exquisite diamond glinted in its pale blue interior.

"Marry me," he whispered.

"No, Dad," Jacob said. "Marry *us*. We're a package deal."

"You heard the boy," Noah said with a smile. "What will it be?"

There was nothing Annabelle could do but bury her face in Noah's chest and sob her heart out, clinging to him and vowing she'd never let go.

He wrapped an arm around her. "I think that's a yes," he told the group, who cheered and laughed.

"I don't understand girls," Sammy said beside her.

About the Author

Although born and raised in Scotland, Janet now calls New Zealand home, where she lives with her two teenage daughters and three feral cats.

Janet loves to hang out with her readers. You can chat with her in her Facebook group, or join her subscriber group —Invertary Insiders—for lots of exclusive content.

And don't forget to sign up for her newsletter too!

Acknowledgments

A huge thank you to Debra Benedict, who shared her Houston knowledge with me and introduced me to Captain Michael McCoy. And another thank you to Captain McCoy for answering my questions about Houston and Harris County police procedure. There isn't much of police procedure in this book, but what little there is makes a lot more sense because of you two. Any mistakes are totally mine. Thank you so much for your time and wisdom.

An a shout out to Janice Mason who won a walk-on part in this book. Thank you for being part of my Insiders subscription book. I hope you like your small role in Who's Afraid of the Big, Bad World?

www.ingramcontent.com/pod-product-compliance
Lightning Source LLC
Chambersburg PA
CBHW051601100726
47898CB00001B/178